For Jane —

Congratulations on
your 25th —

and with thanks
for your
attention —

John B Boresh
87

THE SUBSTANCE
OF THINGS HOPED FOR

The Substance of

SELECTED WITH AN INTRODUCTION

Doubleday & Company, Inc.

Things Hoped For

Short Fiction by Modern Catholic Authors

BY John B. Breslin, S.J.

Garden City, New York *1987*

Library of Congress Cataloging-in-Publication Data

The Substance of things hoped for.

1. Short stories—Catholic authors. I. Breslin,
John B.
PN6120.92.C38S8 1987 808.83'1 86–16656
ISBN 0-385-23428-7

ACKNOWLEDGMENTS

"The Beginnings of a Sin" by Bernard MacLaverty, from *A Time to Dance,* Copyright ©
Bernard MacLaverty 1982, published by Jonathan Cape, Ltd., London and George
Braziller, Inc., New York. Reprinted by permission; "Delia" by Mary Gordon, Copyright
© 1978 by Mary Gordon. Reprinted by permission of Literistic, Ltd.; "A Christmas
Tale" ("Conte de Noël") from *Plongées* by François Mauriac published by Éditions Bernard Grasset, Paris, Copyright © 1938 by Éditions Bernard Grasset. Reprinted by permission of the publisher; "Alice Long's Dachshunds" by Muriel Spark, first published in
The New Yorker, Copyright © 1967 by Copyright Administration Limited. Reprinted by
permission of Harold Ober Associates Incorporated; "The Liar" from *In the Garden of
the North American Martyrs* by Tobias Wolff, Copyright © 1976, 1978, 1980, 1981 by
Tobias Wolff. Published by The Ecco Press in 1981. Reprinted by permission; "The Enduring Chill" from *The Complete Stories* by Flannery O'Connor, Copyright © 1958, 1965
by the Estate of Flannery O'Connor. Reprinted by permission of Farrar, Straus & Giroux,
Inc.; "Hot Ice," first published in *Antaeus,* appeared in *Prize Stories: The O. Henry
Awards 1985.* Reprinted by permission of the author, Stuart Dybek; "Life After Death"
from *Yellow Roses* by Elizabeth Cullinan, Copyright © 1976 by Elizabeth Cullinan. Origi-
nally published in *The New Yorker.* Reprinted by permission of Viking Penguin, Inc.;
"Polikushka" from *Emergency Exit* by Ignazio Silone, translated from the Italian by
Harvey Fergusson II, Volume 39 in World Perspectives planned and edited by Ruth
Nanda Anshen. Italian Copyright © 1968 by Ignazio Silone. Copyright © 1968 by
Harper & Row in the English translation. Reprinted by permission of Harper & Row,
Publishers, Inc. and Russell & Volkening, Inc. as agents for the author; "The Salvation of
Me" from *The Stories of Breece D'J Pancake* by Breece D'J Pancake, Copyright © 1983
by Helen Pancake. Reprinted by permission of Little, Brown & Company, in association
with The Atlantic Monthly Press; "A Father's Story" from *The Times Are Never So Bad*
by Andre Dubus, Copyright © 1982 by Andre Dubus. Reprinted by permission of David
R. Godine, Publisher, Boston; "Mothers" from *Stained Glass Elegies* by Shusaku Endo,
translated by Van C. Gessel and published by Peter Owen, Ltd., London, Copyright ©
1984 by Shusaku Endo and Van C. Gessel. Reprinted by permission of Peter Owen, Ltd.,
and Dodd, Mead & Company, Inc., New York; "Candles for the Madonna" from *Children Are Civilians Too* by Heinrich Böll, Copyright © 1970. Reprinted by permission of
McGraw-Hill Book Company; "The Warm Sand" by J. F. Powers from *The New Yorker,*
March 26, 1979. Copyright © 1979 by The New Yorker Magazine, Inc. Reprinted by
permission; "The Recruiting Officer" from *Nightlines* by John McGahern. Reprinted by
permission of Faber & Faber, Ltd.; "The Promiscuous Self" from *Lost in the Cosmos* by
Walker Percy, Copyright © 1983 by Walker Percy. Reprinted by permission of Farrar,
Straus & Giroux, Inc. and Arrow/Arena Books, Ltd.; "Crucifixus Etiam" by Walter M.
Miller, Jr., published in *Astounding Science Fiction,* February 1953, by Street & Smith
Publications. Reprinted by permission of Don Congdon Associates, Inc. Copyright ©
1953 by Walter M. Miller, Jr., renewed 1981 by Walter M. Miller, Jr.; "The Comedian"

by John L'Heureux from *The Atlantic,* November 1984, Copyright © John L'Heureux 1984. Reprinted by permission of the author; "A Visit to Morin" by Graham Greene from *Collected Stories* published by William Heinemann, Ltd. & The Bodley Head, Ltd. and *A Sense of Reality* Copyright © 1956 by The Hearst Corporation, Copyright renewed © 1984 by Graham Greene. Reprinted by permission of Laurence Pollinger, Ltd. and Viking Penguin, Inc. "Absolution" by Morley Callaghan first appeared in *The New Yorker,* December 5, 1931, Copyright © 1931 by Morley Callaghan, renewed 1959 by Morley Callaghan. Reprinted by permission of Don Congdon Associates, Inc.; "Jack Frost" by Josephine Jacobsen (first published in *Epoch)* appeared in *A Walk with Raschid and Other Stories,* Copyright © 1978 by The Jackpine Press, Winston-Salem, N.C. Reprinted by permission of the publisher.

Parentibus meis
in Christo quiescentibus

Contents

Introduction   *xi*

INITIATION

BERNARD MACLAVERTY
   The Beginnings of a Sin   *3*

MARY GORDON
   Delia   *13*

FRANÇOIS MAURIAC
   A Christmas Tale   *20*

MURIEL SPARK
   Alice Long's Dachshunds   *30*

TOBIAS WOLFF
   The Liar   *41*

EXPLORATION

FLANNERY O'CONNOR
   The Enduring Chill   *61*

STUART DYBEK
   Hot Ice   *85*

ELIZABETH CULLINAN
   Life After Death   *112*

IGNAZIO SILONE
   Polikushka   *126*

BREECE D'J PANCAKE
   The Salvation of Me   *135*

RESPONSIBILITY

ANDRE DUBUS
A Father's Story   *147*

SHUSAKU ENDO
Mothers   *168*

HEINRICH BÖLL
Candles for the Madonna   *197*

J. F. POWERS
The Warm Sand   *208*

JOHN MCGAHERN
The Recruiting Officer   *219*

WALKER PERCY
The Promiscuous Self   *231*

WALTER M. MILLER, JR.
Crucifixus Etiam   *244*

JOHN L'HEUREUX
The Comedian   *263*

RESIGNATION

GRAHAM GREENE
A Visit to Morin   *279*

MORLEY CALLAGHAN
Absolution   *293*

JOSEPHINE JACOBSEN
Jack Frost   *298*

Profiles of the Authors   *309*

Introduction

> "The bond between them, actually, was a belief in the physical,
> a conviction of the open-ended mystery of matter."
>
> Josephine Jacobsen, "Jack Frost"

In a self-consciously ecumenical era, it may seem invidious to publish a "Catholic" anthology of short fiction. Surely, a Christian collection would be more in keeping with efforts to break down ghetto walls and remove the scandal of division that has undercut the credibility of Christ's followers for the past four and a half centuries—and more. Twenty years ago, as the effects of the Second Vatican Council began to seep down into the lives and imaginations of Catholics, such considerations would have made this anthology an instant anachronism, perhaps even an embarrassment to the *bien pensants* of the day. And publishers being in this case the shrewd entrepreneurs they are (often wrongly) thought to be, no such book appeared. Besides, for those who still hankered after the old ways, Brunini and Connolly's *Stories of Our Century by Catholic Authors,* published twenty years earlier, remained in print as an Image Book and was still doing quite nicely, thank you.

The ground shift in Catholic sensibility between 1947 and 1967 has left clear markers: in theological terms, the dogmatic narrowness of Pius XII's *Humani generis* (1950) versus the world-affirming openness of Vatican II's *Gaudium et spes* (1965), for example; iconically, the contrasting images of Pius XII, the last of the papal recluses, blessing the crowds from his balcony, and of Paul VI, the first of the peripatetic popes, addressing the General Assembly of the United Nations. But what of the past twenty years? Again, on the most public of stages, a pontifical figure has captured both the imagination of the world and the paradoxes of contemporary Catholicism. John Paul II's unwearying capacity for travel has made even the innovative Paul VI seem like a papal day-tripper. He incarnates the universal dynamism of the Catholic Church in a way that has made him a world figure better known in Africa, Asia, and Latin America than either of the two reputedly most powerful men of the age, the President of the United States and the General Secretary of the Soviet Communist Party. At the same time, this pope has clearly and frequently indicated his intention of maintaining stricter discipline within his own camp, of curbing what he and several of his closest advisers see as dangerously centrifugal forces released in the wake of Vatican II. The tension between contraction and expansion, between insisting on internal cohesiveness (the spirit of orthodoxy) and exhibiting a sweeping universalism (the pastoral journeys), has been the hallmark of John Paul's papacy. And its effects are being felt.

Within the past year at the Catholic university where I teach, two separate grass-roots movements have sprung up spontaneously, both concerned with establishing a distinctly Catholic identity on campus. At the inaugural meeting of one group, after listening to several of the conveners speak passionately and eloquently about a desire for such an identity, I ventured the half-serious, half-joking comment that twenty years ago their counterparts, my contemporaries, were bewailing the parochialism of their fellow Catholics and insisting on being known as Christians first and foremost. Had I reflected a moment, I might have saved my breath, for they had as much interest in hearing about the ecumenism of the 1960s as we had then in hearing from a previous generation about the religious factionalism of the 1940s.

Does time march, then, only to the swing of the pendulum? Are we Catholics (and our anthologies) doomed to repetition? I think not, and I take some measure of the confirmation and comfort from the Extraordinary Synod of December 1985, scheduled to coincide with the twentieth anniversary of the close of the Second Vatican Council. For all the dire predictions that the Synod would be used to roll back the progressive work of the Council and for all the toing-and-froing between "liberals" and "conservatives" evident in the Synod's documents, one fact became clear: the bishops consider the fundamental direction of Vatican II to be irreversible. Instead of the fatalistic pendulum, they have, in effect, adopted the evolutionary spiral of Teilhard de Chardin as their image of the church's progress through time. Circularity, yes, but not simple repetition. With each turn of the spiral we move upward even as we swing back over our past, for the Resurrection of Jesus sprang us out of our two-dimensional prison into a universe with a divinely stamped future.

So, too, in a less cosmic way, the university students who want to make explicit for themselves their Catholic heritage have no real intention of overturning two decades of ecclesiology and ecumenism inspired by the Council. How could they? Their characters as Catholics have been molded by its liturgy, instructed (albeit at second hand) by its theology, and encouraged in their social concern by its commitment to human development. What they lack for the most part is any sense of where the Council came from, of Catholic life and traditions before the middle sixties. More than Catholic trivia games and books—however much fun they may be—will be needed to fill this gap.

Which brings us to this anthology and the connection between fiction and religious experience. Let me say at the outset that I do not believe that fiction—or art of any sort, for that matter—will serve as a substitute for authentic religious experience. The Romantic belief in salvation through art has long since proved bankrupt, inflating the aesthetic currency beyond our means. The burden of having to reinvent Sacred Writ in each generation has done writers no favor; it has only created a proliferating tribe of ever more ingenious scribes to interpret, or deconstruct, their texts. But a literal-minded Christian attitude that denies any connection between literature and the Bible, between metaphor and revelation has been no more helpful. It distorts the very message it claims to serve by severing the divine and the human, pretending that God's Word could come to us in any way other than through human words.

Insofar as it is possible to speak of a "Catholic sensibility," it means an attitude that avoids both of these extremes, instinctively preferring the conjunctive "and" to the disjunctive "or." Josephine Jacobsen captures well one dimension of the sensibility when she reflects in her story "Jack Frost" on the unspoken bond that unites Fr. O'Rourke and the main character, Mrs. Travis—"a belief in the physical, a conviction of the open-ended mystery of matter." The fact that the old woman "had never been a Catholic" stymies his desire to express that shared belief in a way that would make sense to her, but it also reveals, as does the story's minor apocalypse at the end, that a Catholic sensibility is no prerogative of card-carrying Romans.

Similarly, the title character of Andre Dubus's "A Father's Story" has this to say about his twenty-year-old daughter's religious stance:

> Jennifer is an agnostic, though I doubt she would call herself that, any more than she would call herself any other name that implied she had made a decision, a choice, about existence, death, and God. In truth she tends to pantheism, a good sign, I think; but not wanting to be a father who tells his children what they ought to believe, I do not say to her that Catholicism includes pantheism, like onions in a stew. Besides, I have no missionary instincts and do not believe everyone should or even could live with the Catholic faith.

I once had a Jesuit classics professor who claimed that unless you felt tempted toward pantheism at some point, you would never really understand Catholicism. Dubus reverses the point here but to the same effect and with an aptly earthy image that conveys the flavor of the idea as well as its content. Inclusivity—catholicity in that sense—is of the essence, but that humbly honest final sentence recognizes and rejects the easy temptation to make Catholicism an amorphous category of thought rather than a discipline of life with rituals and restraints.

That tension between celebrating the "open-ended mystery of matter" and confronting the limitations of human weakness and sinfulness runs through this whole collection of stories, whose diversity of style and subject matter rings its own changes on the idea of Catholicism. From one end of the world Shusaku Endo's novelist-narrator in "Mothers" finds his fascination with a group of schismatic Japanese Christians *(kakure),* descendants of seventeenth-century apostates, curiously intersecting with his unresolved guilt feelings toward his own devoutly Catholic mother. When he is finally allowed to visit a *kakure* shrine, the sight of the crude painting of the Madonna and Child strangely moves him: "These people had joined their gnarled hands together and offered up supplications for forgiveness to this portrait of a mother. Within me there welled up the feeling that their intent had been identical to mine." Thus does a traditional characteristic of Catholic experience, devotion to the Mother of God, take on a sharper edge, honed by both personal and cultural grief. The narrator's pathos and that of the isolated *kakure* fuse in a single image, and he leaves the shrine humming the melody of their endless prayer for mercy, to the consternation of his orthodox companions.

In other stories, set thousands of miles from Japan, in traditionally Catholic countries, we hear similar echoes of guilt and loss as characters face the narrowness of their own hearts and the distorted features of a cultural Catholicism. Graham Greene's Morin, the failed French Catholic novelist, inhabits the lonely no-man's-land between unbelief and faith. Like many of Greene's anti-heroes, Morin's faith exhibits a peculiarly Catholic intellectual and paradoxical flavor: having stopped practicing, he stopped believing, thus confirming his faith in the truth of the Church's doctrine. But he fears the risk of going back to the sacraments and not recovering his belief—thus destroying the last faint vestige of his faith. But Greene pushes the paradox one step further, for Morin remains an unwitting and unwilling carrier of the germ of belief for the story's agnostic narrator: "I had felt little curiosity since that moment of the war when I had spoken to the chaplain, but now I began to wonder again."

John McGahern's failed Irish Christian Brother mixes contempt and despair with his whiskey as he watches the spiral of his own life wind down into a daily circle of paralysis, "a feeling that any one thing in life is almost as worth doing as any other." He has escaped the Brothers but not the narrow world of the parochial school where he must silently condone the brutalizing of his pupils and observe the same recruiting process that lured him into the brotherhood. ("Do you think your parents would have any objection?" "It'd be an honour to have a Christian Brother in the family.") His only happiness is further escape, but even here his Irish Catholic sensibility asserts itself in a slightly blasphemous, Joycean pun as he heads from his schoolhouse prison to his favorite pub along the Shannon:

> I feel born again as I start to pedal towards the town. How, how, though, can a man be born again when he is old? Can he enter a second time his mother's bag of tricks? I laugh at last.
>   Was it not said by *Water* and the *Holy Spirit?*

Ignazio Silone's idealistic young narrator awakes to the beauty and power of literature when he reads Tolstoy's tale of the hapless Polikushka:

> The sad, slow pace of the story revealed a compassion beyond the usual pity of the man who is moved by his neighbor's troubles and averts his glance so that he will not suffer too. Divine compassion

must be like this, I thought, the compassion which does not relieve a creature of his pain, yet on the other hand does not abandon him but helps him to the end, without ever revealing itself.

But when he tries to convey its message to the illiterate members of the Farmers' League in his small Italian village—men whose social and economic plight mirrors Polikushka's—he meets resistance and incomprehension: " 'In other words, he was a real crook,' one of the old men interrupted, 'someone to lock up in jail and forget about.' " Fellow suffering is not always coincident with compassion, the student learns, nor does socialist ideology, any more than religious orthodoxy, guarantee human sympathy.

No one could accuse these authors of confusing the virtue of hope with "happy talk" theology. If the "mystery of matter" is indeed open-ended, then failure, entropy, and even despair have their own claims on the Catholic imagination. Another way of handling these troubling matters, a way that reflects the dual focus of the Catholic sensibility (spirit *and* matter, grace *and* sin, divine *and* human), is through a generous use of irony. Two American writers, both from the South, have specialized in revealing just how complex our motives and actions are; their stories represent, from one point of view, a set of intricate variations on the words of the prophet Jeremiah (17:9): "The heart is deceitful above all things, and desperately wicked: who can know it?"

Flannery O'Connor's Asbury Porter Fox lives in a world of aesthetic illusions, a latter-day Romantic who, having failed Art, yearns for Death and the final comfort of an intellectual conversation with a priest-of-the-world who is certainly not the coin-collecting retired Methodist minister his no-nonsense mother suggests. He dreams of just such a figure in his funeral procession:

A lean dark figure in a Roman collar followed [the bier]. He had a mysteriously saturnine face in which there was a subtle blend of asceticism and corruption . . . The Jesuit retired to a spot beneath a dead tree to smoke and meditate.

What he gets instead is "Father Finn—from Purrgatory" who admonishes him to say his morning and night prayers and learn his catechism. And that comic irony is hardly the last in this relentless, and relentlessly funny, depiction of languorous self-deception and chilling self-awakening.

Walker Percy's ironic strokes are more broadly laid on in the satiric sketch I have excerpted from *Lost in the Cosmos*. His send-up of the Phil Donahue show is merciless, but no more so than the whole book's witty dissection of much that passes for contemporary wisdom. Phil's announced guests for the occasion include a homosexual cruiser from San Francisco, a married heterosexual "connoisseur of the lunch-hour liaison," a pregnant fourteen-year-old, and "Dr. Joyce Friday, a well-known talk-show sex therapist, or in media jargon: a psych jockey," who alludes to abortions at one point as "viable options." But the star of the show turns out to be a surprise guest from outer space with a peremptory message of final judgment: "Within the next twenty-four hours, your last war will begin"; and an unlikely escape route: Lost Cove, Tennessee. Percy ends the sketch, as he does other "thought experiments" in the book, with a question for the reader: "If you heard this Donahue Show, would you head for Lost Cove, Tennessee? *(a)* Yes; *(b)* No." Thus, a 1980s version of the four last things set amid our culture's answer to the medieval disputation: Phil Donahue and friends on sexology.

This handful of examples provides, I hope, an enticing sampler of what this anthology offers, both in themes and techniques. The "Catholic thing," in Rosemary Haughton's generic phrase, describes not so much a separate world but a certain way of viewing the whole world— an attitude, a point of view that invests both outer and inner realities with fresh significance. It celebrates alike the perfume of flowers (Jacobsen) and the smell of horses (Dubus). It mourns the slow death of hope (McGahern) and the loss of faith (Endo and Greene). It can also laugh at the self-delusions of Romanticism (O'Connor) and the pride of knowingness (Percy).

Other authors push both themes and techniques even further. Stuart Dybek fuses the raw edges of urban decay with folk mysticism and conventional piety to give his ethnic street characters a heightened reality. John L'Heureux introduces surrealism to capture the transformation of a stand-up comedian pregnant with an abnormal child. Walter Miller pushes us forward in time for his sci-fi version of the Passion set in an Earth colony on Mars. The list could go on, but I think these examples are sufficient to indicate how Catholic in theme and catholic in approach these stories are. Reading them (and many others in the process of selection) reminded me of how generous the Catholic tradition has been in its scope without surrendering a certain common perspective. Or, put another way, how elastic it remains without losing its shape. The poet Gerard Manley Hopkins caught this tension most tellingly in his celebratory sonnet, "As kingfishers catch fire." First, the exuberant individuality of creation:

> Each mortal thing does one thing and the same:
> Deals out that being indoors each one dwells;
> Selves—goes itself; *myself* it speaks and spells,
> Crying, *What I do is me: for that I came.*

And then the incarnational theology that undergirds and gives unity, but not uniformity, to the staggering variety of all this catholic riot:

> . . . for Christ plays in ten thousand places,
> Lovely in limbs, and lovely in eyes not his
> To the Father through the features of men's faces.

Finally, I should say a few words about the principles of selection and arrangement in the anthology. I intended from the start to make the collection as "contemporary" as possible, with a good proportion of the stories representing the work of the two decades since the Council. At least ten of the twenty-one fit that description and, indeed, a number of those date from the current decade. I had thought at one point of further limiting the selections to living authors, but that is a capricious criterion at best (for example, Heinrich Böll died while the selecting was going on), and would have meant leaving out not only Flannery O'Connor, arguably the best American Catholic writer of this half century, but also the youngest writer included, Breece D'J Pancake, a convert to Catholicism who mysteriously ended his life in 1979 at age twenty-six. Of the senior writers represented, I have tried to pick later rather than earlier stories—for example, Graham Greene's dates from 1956, Ignazio Silone's from 1965, and J. F. Powers's from 1979.

Most of the selections are by North American, English, and Irish writers, since the anthology is primarily intended for an English-speaking audience and there is much to be said for getting your fiction at firsthand. But not everything, especially in a *Catholic* anthology, and so I've included several representations from other languages and traditions as well—French, German, Italian, and Japanese.

As for the stories themselves, the choice was ultimately and inevitably personal, for which I assume full responsibility, taking the blame for omitting a reader's favorite story while hoping to get occasional credit for introducing the same reader to a new author or a hitherto unknown tale.

As for the arrangement of the anthology, several schemes suggested themselves: most arbitrary of all, an alphabetical listing by author; slightly less so, a chronological order—but on what principle? by date of author's birth or date of composition? Given the thematic emphasis indicated earlier in this introduction, a thematic arrangement with a Catholic focus seemed the most natural. It is roughly chronological, but the time line follows not authors' careers but the development of the human life cycle, just as Catholic sacramental practice does with its seven privileged moments, beginning with baptism and ending with the sacrament of the sick, which is still closely linked in the popular imagination with dying. For the purposes of arrangement, I have settled on four stages, each with a dominant theme: childhood (Initiation), adolescence (Exploration), adulthood (Responsibility), and old age (Resignation). Like all sets of categories, this schema is somewhat arbitrary and will apply better to certain stories than to others, but it does provide a framework for the collection that corresponds to the Catholic commitment to time and growth as integral parts of the incarnational experience. The ratios, though fortuitous, are also intriguing: roughly two to one between adulthood and childhood, and between adolescence and old age. Lastly, it allows the reader to indulge personal intimations of mortality in choosing where to begin.

Acknowledgments

No book, certainly not this one, is ever a one-man show. Thanks go first to my former colleague, now my editor, Patricia Kossmann, who made me the delightful offer I couldn't refuse to put this book together. Equal thanks to another colleague, once and present in her case, Deborah McCann, who cheerfully and patiently, but also relentlessly, tracked down the myriad agents, subsidiary rights managers, and other intermediaries who seek to protect authors from their would-be anthologizers. Thanks also to my friend Evelyn Bence, yet another former colleague, who generously shared in both my fictional enthusiasms and my editorial setbacks.

I dedicated my doctoral dissertation to the memory of my parents, who taught me how to read and what to love, but since that work may never see the light of day beyond its microfilm container, I repeat the dedication here.

Part I

INITIATION

BERNARD MacLAVERTY

The Beginnings of a Sin

I believe he's late again thought Colum. He took a clean white surplice from his bag and slipped it over his head, steadying his glasses as he did so. It was five to eight. He sat on the bench and changed his shoes for a black pair of gutties. Father Lynch said that all his altar-boys must move as quietly as shadows. When he was late he was usually in his worst mood. Sometimes he did not turn up at all and Miss Grant, the housekeeper, would come over and announce from the back of the church that Father Lynch was ill and that there would be no Mass that day.

At two minutes to eight Colum heard his footstep at the vestry door. Father Lynch came in and nodded to the boy. Colum had never seen anyone with such a sleep-crumpled face in the mornings. It reminded him of a bloodhound, there was such a floppiness about his deeply wrinkled skin. His whole face sagged and sloped into lines of sadness. His black hair was parted low to the side and combed flat with Brylcreem. Colum thought his neat hair looked out of place on top of the disorder of his features.

"Is everything ready?" Father Lynch asked him.

"Yes, Father."

Colum watched him as he prepared to say Mass. He began by putting on the amice, like a handkerchief with strings, at the back of his neck. Next a white alb like a shroud, reaching to the floor. The polished toe-caps of his everyday shoes peeped out from underneath. He put the cincture about his waist and knotted it quickly. He kissed the embroidered cross on his emerald stole and hung it round his neck. Lastly he put on the chasuble, very carefully inserting his head through the neck-hole. Colum couldn't make up his mind whether he did not want to stain the vestments with hair-oil or wreck his hair. The chasuble was emerald green with yellow lines. Colum liked the feasts of the martyrs best, with their bright blood colour. Father Lynch turned to him.

"What are you staring at?"

"Nothing, Father."

"You look like a wee owl."

"Sorry."

"Let's get this show on the road," Father Lynch said, his face still like a sad bloodhound. "We're late already."

None of the other altar-boys liked Father Lynch. When they did something wrong, he never scolded them with words but instead would nip them on the upper arm. They said he was too quiet and you could never trust anybody like that. Colum found that he was not so quiet if you asked him questions. He seemed to like Colum better than the others, at least Colum thought so. One day he had asked him why a priest wore so much to say Mass and Father Lynch had spoken to him for about ten minutes, keeping him late for school.

"Normally when people wear beautiful things it is to make their personality stand out. With a priest it is the opposite. He wears so much to hide himself. And the higher up the Church you go, the more you have to wear. Think of the poor Pope with all that trumpery on him."

After Mass Father Lynch asked him how the ballot tickets were going.

"Great. I've sold—"

"Don't tell me. Keep it as a surprise."

In the darkness Colum stood at the door waiting. He had rolled up a white ballot ticket and was smoking it, watching his breath cloud the icy air. He pulled his socks up as high as he could to try and keep his legs warm. There was a funny smell from the house, like sour food. The woman came back out with her purse. She was still chewing something.

"What's it in aid of?"

"St. Kieran's Church Building Fund."

"How much are they?"

"Threepence each."

The woman hesitated, poking about in her purse with her index finger. He told her that the big prize was a Christmas hamper. There was a second prize of whiskey and sherry. She took four tickets, finishing his last book.

"Father Lynch'll not be wanting to win it outright, then."

He was writing her name on the stubs with his fountain pen.

"Pardon?"

"You're a neat wee writer," she said. He tore the tickets down the perforations and gave them to her. She handed him a shilling, which he dropped into his jacket pocket. It was swinging heavy with coins.

"There's the snow coming on now," said the woman, waiting to close the front door. He ran the whole way home holding on to the outside of his pocket. In the house he dried his hair and wiped the speckles of melted snow from his glasses. Two of his older brothers, Rory and Dermot, were sitting on the sofa doing homework balanced on their knees and when he told them it was snowing they ran out to see if it was lying.

He took down his tin and spilled it and the money from his pocket onto the table. He added it all together and counted the number of books of stubs. For each book sold the seller was allowed to keep six-pence for himself. Over the past weeks Colum had sold forty-two books around the doors. He took a pound note and a shilling and slipped them into his pocket. He had never had so much money in his life and there was still a full week to sell tickets before the ballot was drawn.

His mother stood at the range making soda farls on a griddle. When they were cooked they filled the house with their smell and made a dry scuffling noise as she handled them. He heard the front door close and Michael shout "Hello." At eighteen he was the eldest and the only wage earner in the house.

"Come on, Colum," said his mother. "Clear that table. The hungry working man is in."

After tea they always said the Family Rosary. Colum would half kneel, half crouch at the armchair with his face almost touching the seat. The cushion smelt of cloth and human. He tried to say the Rosary as best he could, thinking of the Sacred Mysteries while his mouth said the words. He was disturbed one night to see Michael kneeling at the sofa saying the prayers with the Sunday paper between his elbows. Colum counted off the Hail Marys, feeding his shiny lilac rosary beads between his finger and thumb. They were really more suitable for a woman but they had come all the way from Lourdes. Where the loop of the beads joined was a little silver heart with a bubble of Lourdes water in it—like the spirit level in his brother's tool kit.

When it came to his turn to give out the prayer Colum always waited until the response was finished—not like his brothers who charged on, overlapping the prayer and the response, slurring their words to get it finished as quickly as possible. They became annoyed with him and afterwards, in whispers, accused him of being "a creeping Jesus."

At the end of each Rosary their mother said a special prayer "for the Happy Repose of the Soul of Daddy." Although he had been dead two years, it still brought a lump to Colum's throat. It wouldn't have been so bad if she had said father or something but the word Daddy made him want to cry. Sometimes he had to go on kneeling when the others had risen to their feet in case they should see his eyes.

It was Colum's turn to do the dishes. They had their turns written up on a piece of paper so that there would be no argument. He poured some hot water into the basin from the kettle on the range. It had gone slightly brown from heating. He didn't like the look of it as much as the cold water from the pump. In the white enamel bucket under the scullery bench it looked pure and cool and still. Where the enamel had chipped off, the bucket was blue-black. If you put your hand in the water the fingers seemed to go flat.

He dipped a cup into the basin, rinsed it out and set it on the table. Father Lynch had funny fingers. He had tiny tufts of black hair on the back of each of them. They made Colum feel strange as he poured water from a cruet onto them. The priest would join his trembling index fingers and thumbs and hold them over the glass bowl, then he would take the linen cloth ironed into its folds and wipe them dry. He would put it back in its creases and lay it on Colum's arm. He had some whispered prayers to say when he was doing that. Colum always wondered why Father Lynch was so nervous saying his morning Mass. He had served for others and they didn't tremble like that. Perhaps it was because he was holier than them, that they weren't as much in awe of the Blessed Sacrament as he was. What a frightening thing it must be, to hold Christ's actual flesh—to have the responsibility to change the bread and wine into the body and blood of Jesus.

He dried the dishes and set them in neat piles before putting them back on the shelf. Above the bench Michael had fixed a small mirror for shaving. Colum had to stand on tiptoe to see himself. He was the only one of the family who had to wear glasses. He took after his father. For a long time he had to wear National Health round ones with the springy legs that hooked behind his ears, but after months of pleading and crying his mother had given in and bought him a good pair with real frames.

He went to the back door and threw out a basinful of water with a slap onto the icy ground. It steamed in the light from the scullery window. It was a still night and he could hear the children's voices yelling from the next street.

The kitchen was warm when he came back in again. Radio Luxembourg was on the wireless. Colum took all his money in his pocket and put the stubs in a brown paper bag.

"I'm away, Mammy," he said.

She was having a cigarette, sitting with her feet up on a stool.

"Don't be late," was all she said.

He walked a lamppost, ran a lamppost through the town until he reached the hill which led to the Parochial House. It was a large building made of the same red brick as the church. He could see lights on in the house so he climbed the hill. It was still bitterly cold and he was aware of his jaw shivering. He kept both hands in his pockets, holding the brown bag in the crook of his arm. He knocked at the door of the house. It was the priest's housekeeper who opened it a fraction. When she saw Colum she opened it wide.

"Hello, Miss Grant. Is Father Lynch in?"

"He is busy, Colum. What was it you wanted?"

"Ballot tickets, Miss. And to give in money."

She looked over her shoulder down the hallway, then turned and put out her hand for the money.

"It's all loose, Miss," said Colum, digging into his pocket to let her hear it.

"Oh, you'd best come in then—for a moment."

Miss Grant brought him down the carpeted hallway to her quarters —she had a flat of her own at the back of the house. She closed the door and smiled a jumpy kind of smile—a smile that stopped in the middle. Colum emptied the bag of stubs on the table.

"There's forty-two books . . ." he said.

"Goodness, someone has been busy."

". . . and here is five pounds, five shillings." He set two pound notes and a ten shilling note on the table and handfulled the rest of the coins out of his pocket. They rang and clattered on the whitewood surface. She began to check it, scraping the coins towards her quickly and building them into piles.

"All present and correct," she said.

Colum looked at the sideboard. There was a bottle of orange juice and a big box of biscuits which he knew was for the ticket sellers. She saw him looking.

"All right, all right," she said.

She poured a glass of juice and allowed him to choose two biscuits. His fingers hovered over the selection.

"Oh come on, Colum, don't take all night."

He took a chocolate one and a wafer and sat down. He had never seen Miss Grant so snappy before. Usually she was easygoing. She was very fat, with a chest like stuffed pillows under her apron. He had heard the grown-ups in the town say that if anybody had earned heaven it was her. They spoke of her goodness and kindness. "There's one saint in that Parochial House," they would say. For a long time Colum thought they were talking about Father Lynch.

In the silence he heard his teeth crunching the biscuit. Miss Grant did not sit down but stood by the table waiting for him to finish. He swallowed and said,

"Could I have ten more books, please?"

"Yes, dear." She put her hands in her apron pocket and looked all around her, then left the room.

Colum had never been in this part of the house before. He had always gone into Father Lynch's room or waited in the hallway. Although it was a modern house, it was full of old things. A picture of the Assumption of Our Lady in a frame of gold leaves hung by the front door. The furniture in Father Lynch's room was black and heavy. The dining room chairs had twisted legs like barley sugar sticks. Everything had a rich feel to it, especially the thick patterned carpet. Miss Grant's quarters were not carpeted but had some rugs laid on the red tiled floor. It was the kind of floor they had at home, except that the corners of their tiles were chipped off and they had become uneven enough to trip people.

"Vera!" he heard a voice shout. It was Father Lynch.

Vera's voice answered from somewhere. Colum looked up and Father Lynch was standing in the doorway with his arm propped against the jamb.

"Hello, Father."

"Well, if it isn't the owl," said Father Lynch.

He wasn't dressed like a priest but was wearing an ordinary man's collarless shirt, open at the neck.

"What brings you up here, Colum?"

He moved from the door and reached out to put his hand on a chair back. Two strands of his oiled hair had come loose and fallen over his forehead. He sat down very slowly on the chair.

"Ballot tickets, Father. I've sold all you gave me."

Father Lynch gave a loud whoop and slapped the table loudly with the flat of his hand. His eyes looked very heavy and he was blinking a lot.

"That's the way to do it. Lord, how the money rolls in."

He was slurring his words as if he was saying the Rosary. Miss Grant came into the room holding a wad of white ballot tickets.

"Here you are now, Colum. You'd best be off."

Colum finished his juice and stood up.

"Is that the strongest you can find for the boy to drink, Vera?" He laughed loudly. Colum had never heard him laugh before. He slapped the table again.

"Father—if you'll excuse us, I'll just show Colum out now."

"No. No. He came to see me—didn't you?"

Colum nodded.

"He's the only one that would. Let him stay for a bit."

"His mother will worry about him."

"No she won't," said Colum.

"Of course she won't," said Father Lynch. He ignored Miss Grant. "How many books did you sell?"

"Forty-two, Father."

The priest raised his eyes to heaven and blew out his cheeks. Colum smelt a smell like altar wine.

"Holy Saint Christopher. Forty-two?"

"Yes."

Miss Grant moved behind Colum and began to guide him with pressure away from the table.

"That calls for a celebration." Father Lynch stood up unsteadily. "Forty-two!"

He reached out to give Colum a friendly cuff on the back of the head but he missed and instead his hand struck the side of the boy's face, scattering his glasses on the tiled floor.

"Aw Jesus," said the priest. "I'm sorry." Father Lynch hunkered down to pick them up but lurched forward onto his knees. One lens was starred with white and the arc of the frame was broken. He hoisted himself to his feet and held the glasses close to his sagging face, looking at them.

"Jesus, I'm so sorry," he said again. He bent down, looking for the missing piece of frame, and the weight of his head seemed to topple him. He cracked his skull with a sickening thump off the sharp edge of a radiator. One of his legs was still up in the air trying to right his balance. He put his hand to the top of his head and Colum saw that the hand was slippery with blood. Red blood was smeared from his Brylcreemed hair onto the radiator panel as the priest slid lower. His eyes were open but not seeing.

"Are you all right, Father?" Miss Grant's voice was shaking. She produced a white handkerchief from her apron pocket. The priest shouted, his voice suppressed and hissing and angry. He cursed his housekeeper and the polish on her floor. Then he raised his eyes to her without moving his head and said in an ordinary voice,

"What a mess for the boy."

Miss Grant took the glasses which he was still clutching and put them in Colum's hand. Father Lynch began to cry with his mouth half open. Miss Grant turned the boy away and pushed him towards the door. Both she and Colum had to step over the priest to get out. She led him by the elbow down the hallway.

"That's the boy. Here's your ballot tickets."

She opened the front door.

"Say a wee prayer for him, Colum. He's in bad need of it."

"All right, but—"

"I'd better go back to him now."

The door closed with a slam. Colum put his glasses on but could only see through his left eye. His knees were like water and his stomach was full of wind. He tried to get some of it up but he couldn't. He started to run. He ran all the way home. He sat panting on the cold doorstep and only went in when he got his breath back. His mother was alone.

"What happened to you? You're as white as a sheet," she said, looking up at him. She was knitting a grey sock on three needles shaped into a triangle. Colum produced his glasses from his pocket. Within the safety of the house he began to cry.

"I bust them."

"How, might I ask?" His mother's voice was angry.

"I was running and they just fell off. I slipped on the ice."

"Good God, Colum, do you know how much those things cost? You'll have to get a new pair for school. Where do you think the money is going to come from? Who do you think I am, Carnegie? Eh?"

Her knitting needles were flashing and clacking. Colum continued to cry, tears rather than noise.

"Sheer carelessness. I've a good mind to give you a thumping."

Colum, keeping out of range of her hand, sat at the table and put the glasses on. He could only half see. He put his hand in his pocket and took out his pound note.

"Here," he said, offering it to his mother. She took it and put it beneath the jug on the shelf.

"That'll not be enough," she said, then after a while, "Will you stop that sobbing? It's not the end of the world."

The next morning Colum was surprised to see Father Lynch in the vestry before him. He was robed and reading his breviary, pacing the strip of carpet in the centre of the room. They said nothing to each other.

At the Consecration Colum looked up and saw the black congealed wound on the thinning crown of Father Lynch's head, as he lifted the tail of the chasuble. He saw him elevate the white disc of the host and heard him mutter the words,

"Hoc est enim corpus meum."

Colum jangled the cluster of bells with angry twists of his wrist. A moment later when the priest raised the chalice full of wine he rang the bell again, louder if possible.

In the vestry afterwards he changed as quickly as he could and was about to dash out when Father Lynch called him. He had taken off his chasuble and was folding it away.

"Colum."

"What?"

"Sit down a moment."

He removed the cincture and put it like a coiled snake in the drawer.

The boy remained standing. The priest sat down in his alb and beckoned him over.

"I'm sorry about your glasses."

Colum stayed at the door and Father Lynch went over to him. Colum thought his face no longer sad, simply ugly.

"Your lace is loosed." He was about to genuflect to tie it for him but Colum crouched and tied it himself. Their heads almost collided.

"It's hard for me to explain," said Father Lynch, "but . . . to a boy of your age sin is a very simple thing. It's not."

Colum smelt the priest's breath sour and sick.

"Yes, Father."

"That's because you have never committed a sin. You don't know about it."

He removed his alb and hung it in the wardrobe.

"Trying to find the beginnings of a sin is like . . ." He looked at the boy's face and stopped. "Sin is a deliberate turning away from God. That is an extremely difficult thing to do. To close Him out from your love . . ."

"I'll be late for school, Father."

"I suppose you need new glasses?"

"Yes."

Father Lynch put his hand in his pocket and gave him some folded pound notes.

"Did you mention it to your mother?"

"What?"

"How they were broken?"

"No."

"Are you sure? To anyone?"

Colum nodded that he hadn't. He was turning to get out the door. The priest raised his voice, trying to keep him there.

"I knew your father well, Colum," he shouted. "You remind me of him a lot."

The altar-boy ran, slamming the door after him. He heard an empty wooden coat-hanger rattle on the hardboard panel of the door and it rattled in his mind until he reached the bottom of the hill. There he stopped running. He unfolded the wad of pound notes still in his hand and counted one—two—three—four of them with growing disbelief.

MARY GORDON

Delia

People talked about how difficult it was to say which of the O'Reilley girls was the best-looking. Kathleen had the green eyes. She came over by herself at seventeen. She worked as a seamstress and married an Italian. The money that she earned, even with all the babies, one a year until she was thirty-five, was enough to bring over the three other girls. Bridget had black hair and a wicked tongue. She married a man who was only five feet tall. She had no children for seven years; then she had a red-haired boy. Some believed he was the child of the policeman. Nettie was small; her feet and her ankles were as perfect as dolls'. She married Mr. O'Toole, who sang in the choir and drank to excess. She had only daughters. Some thought Delia the most beautiful, but then she was the youngest. She married a Protestant and moved away.

In defense of her sister, Kathleen pointed out that John Taylor looked like an Irishman.

"He has the eyes," Kathleen said to Nettie and to Bridget. "I never saw a Protestant with eyes like that."

"Part of the trouble with Delia all along is you babied her, Kathleen," Bridget said. "You made her believe she could do no wrong. What about the children? Is it Protestant nephews and nieces you want?"

"He signed the form to have them baptized," said Nettie.

"And what does that mean to a Protestant?" Bridget said. "They'll sign anything."

"He's good to the children. My children are mad for him," said Kathleen.

"Your children are mad entirely. Hot-blooded," said Bridget. "It's you have fallen for the blue eyes yourself. You're no better than your sister."

"He's kind to my Nora," said Kathleen.

Then even Bridget had to be quiet. Nora was Kathleen's child born with one leg shorter than the other.

"There was never any trouble like that in our family," Bridget had said when she first saw Nora. "It's what comes of marrying outsiders."

John Taylor would sit Nora on his lap. He told her stories about the West.

"Did you see cowboys?" she would ask him, taking his watch out of the leather case he kept it in. The leather case smelled like soap; it looked like a doll's pocketbook. When Nora said that it looked like a doll's pocketbook, John Taylor let her keep it for her doll.

"Cowboys are not gentlemen," said John Taylor.

"Is Mr. du Pont a gentleman?" asked Nora.

"A perfect gentleman. A perfect employer."

John Taylor was the chauffeur for Mr. du Pont. He lived in Delaware. He told Nora about the extraordinary gardens on the estate of Mr. du Pont.

"He began a poor boy," said John Taylor.

"Go on about the gardens. Go on about the silver horse on the hood of the car."

Delia came over and put her hands on top of her husband's. Her hands were cool-looking and blue-white, the color of milk in a bowl. She was expecting her first baby.

"Some day you must come and visit us in Delaware, when the baby's born," she said to Nora. She looked at her husband. Nora knew that the way they looked at each other had something to do with the baby. When her mother was going to have a baby, she got shorter; she grew lower to the ground. But Delia seemed to get taller; she seemed lighter and higher, as though she were filled, not with a solid child like one of Nora's brothers or sisters, but with air. With bluish air.

Delia and John Taylor would let her walk with them. She would walk between them and hold both their hands. Their hands were very different. Delia's was narrow and slightly damp; John Taylor's was dry and broad. It reminded Nora of his shoes, which always looked as if he were wearing them for the first time. They knew how to walk with her: most people did not know how to walk with her. Most people walked too slowly. She wanted to tell them they did not have to walk so slowly for her. But she did not want to hurt their feelings. John Taylor and Delia knew just how to walk, she thought.

After only two weeks, they went back to Delaware.

"She's too thin entirely," said Bridget.

"She's beautiful," said Nora. Her mother clapped her hand over Nora's mouth for contradicting her aunt.

Delia never wrote. Nora sent her a present on her birthday, near Christmas. She had made her a rose sachet: blue satin in the shape of a heart, filled with petals she had saved in a jar since the summer. She had worked with her mother to do the things her mother had told her would keep the smell.

Delia sent Nora a postcard. "Thank you for your lovely gift. I keep it in the drawer with my linen."

Linen. Nora's mother read the card to her when the aunts were to tea at their house.

"Fancy saying 'linen' to a child," said Bridget. "In a postcard."

"She has lovely underthings," said Nettie.

"Go upstairs. See to your little brother, Nora," said her mother.

"When they came back to New York, he gave her twenty-five dollars, just to buy underthings. Hand-hemmed, all of them. Silk ribbons. Ivory-colored," said Nettie.

"Hand-done by some greenhorn who got nothing for it," said Bridget.

Now Nora knew what Delia meant by linen. She had thought before it was tablecloths she meant, and that seemed queer. Why would she put her good sachet in with the tablecloths? Now she imagined Delia's underclothes, white as angels, smelling of roses. Did John Taylor see her in her underclothing? Yes. No. He was her husband. What did people's husbands see?

She was glad the aunts had talked about it. Now she could see the underclothes more clearly. Ivory ribbons, Nettie had said. Delia's stomach swelled in front of her, but not as much as Nora's mother's. And Nora's mother was going to have a baby in May, which meant Delia would have hers first. March, they had said. But Delia's stomach was light/hard, like a balloon. Nora's mother's was heavy/hard, like a turnip. Why was that, Nora wondered. Perhaps it was because her mother had had five babies, and this was Delia's first.

When her mother wrote to Delia, Nora dictated a note to her too. She asked when John Taylor's birthday was. She thought it was in the summer. She would make him a pillow filled with pine needles if it was in the summer. In July, the family went to the country for a week and her mother would give her an envelope so she could fill it with pine needles for her Christmas gifts.

March came and went and no one heard anything of Delia's baby. Nora's mother wrote, Nettie wrote, even Bridget wrote, but no one heard anything.

"She's cut herself off," said Bridget. "She hasn't had the baby baptized and she's afraid to face us."

"First babies are always late," said Kathleen. "I was four weeks overdue with Nora."

"Perhaps something's happened to the baby. Perhaps it's ill and she doesn't want to worry us," said Nettie.

"Nothing like that used to happen in our family," said Bridget, sniffing. "Or anyone we knew in the old country."

"What about Tom Hogan? He had three daft children. And Mrs. Kelly had a blind boy," said Nettie.

"If you'd say a prayer for your sister instead of finding fault with her, you might do some good with your tongue, Bridget O'Reilley, for once in your life," said Kathleen.

"If she'd of listened to me, she wouldn't be needing so many prayers," said Bridget.

"God forgive you, we all need prayers," said Kathleen, crossing herself.

"What's the weather in Delaware?" said Nettie.

"Damp," said Bridget. "Rainy."

"They live right on the estate," said Kathleen. "They eat the same food as Mr. du Pont himself."

"Yes, only not at the same table," said Bridget. "Downstairs is where the servants eat. I'd rather eat plain food at my own table than rich food at a servant's board."

"Will we not write to her, then?" said Nettie, to Kathleen, mainly.

"Not if she's not written first. There must be some reason," said Kathleen.

"It's her made the first move away," said Bridget.

"If something was wrong, we'd hear. You always hear the bad. She must be all wrapped up. Probably the du Ponts have made a pet of her," said Kathleen.

Nora remembered that John Taylor had said that on Mrs. du Pont's birthday there was a cake in the shape of a swan. And ices with real strawberries in them, although it was the middle of November. And the ladies wore feathers and looked like peacocks, Delia had said. They're beautiful, the ladies, John Taylor had said. You should know, tucking the lap robes under them, Delia had said, standing on one foot like a bird. God knows where you'd of been if I hadn't come along to rescue you in good time. You've saved me from ruin, John Taylor had said, twirling an imaginary moustache.

Nora remembered how they had laughed together. John and Delia were the only ones she knew who laughed like that and were married.

"Do you think we'll never see Delia and John again?" said Nora to her mother.

"Never say never, it's bad luck," her mother said. She put her hand to her back. The baby made her back ache, she said. Soon, she told Nora, she would have to go to bed for the baby.

"And then you must mind your Aunt Bridget and keep your tongue in your head."

"Yes, ma'am," said Nora. But her mother knew she always minded; she never answered back. Only that once, about Delia, had she answered back.

When Nora's mother went to bed to have the baby, the younger children went to Nettie's, but Nora stayed home. "Keep your father company," her mother had said. "At least if he sees you it'll keep him from feeling in a house full of strangers entirely."

But even with her there, Nora's father walked in the house shyly, silently, as if he was afraid of disturbing something. He took her every evening, since it was warm, to the corner for an ice cream. She saw him so rarely that they had little to say to one another. She knew him in his tempers and in his fatigue. He would walk her home with a gallantry that puzzled her, and he went to sleep while it was still light. He woke in the morning before her, and he went away before she rose.

Bridget made Nora stay outside all day when her mother went into labor. She sat on the front steps, afraid to leave the area of the house, afraid to miss the first cry or the news of an emergency. Children would come past her, but she hushed them until they grew tired of trying to entice her away. She looked at her hands; she looked down at her white shoes, one of which was bigger than the other, her mother had said, because God had something special in mind for her. What could He have in mind? Did God change His mind? Did He realize He had been mistaken? She counted the small pink pebbles in the concrete banister. She could hear her mother crying out. Everyone on the block could, she thought, with the windows open. She swept the sand on the middle step with the outside of her hand.

Then in front of her were a man's brown shoes. First she was frightened, but a second later, she recognized them. She did not have to look up at the face. They were John Taylor's shoes; they were the most beautiful shoes she had ever seen.

"Hello, Nora," he said, as if she should not be surprised to see him.

"Hello," she said, trying not to sound surprised, since she knew he did not want her to.

"Is your mother in?"

"She's upstairs in bed."

"Not sick, I hope."

"No. She's having another baby."

John Taylor sucked breath, as if he had changed his mind about something. The air around him was brilliant as glass. He looked around him, wanting to get away.

"How is Delia?" said Nora, thinking that was what her mother would have said.

"She died," said John, looking over his shoulder.

"And the baby? Is it a boy or a girl?"

"Dead. Born dead."

"Do you still drive a car for that man?" she said, trying to understand what he had told her. Born dead. It did not sound possible. And Delia dead. She heard her mother's voice from the window.

"I'm on holiday," said John, reaching into his pocket.

She was trying to think of a way to make him stay. If she could think of the right thing, he would take her for a walk, he would tell her about the cars and the gardens.

"How've you been, then?" she said.

"Fine," said John Taylor.

But he did not say it as he would have to an adult, she knew. He did not say it as if he were going to stay.

"Nora," he said, bending down to her, "can we have a little secret? Can I give you a little present?"

"Yes," she said. He was going away. She could not keep him. She wanted something from him. She would keep his secret; he would give her a gift.

He reached into his pocket and took out a silver dollar. He put it in her hand and he closed her hand around it.

"Don't tell anyone I was here. Or what I said. About Delia, or about the baby."

It was very queer. He had come to tell them, and now she must not tell anyone, she thought. Perhaps he had come this way only to tell her. That was it: he had come from Delaware to tell her a secret, to give her a gift.

"I won't say anything," she said. She looked into his eyes; she had never looked into the eyes of an adult before. She felt an itching on the soles of her feet from the excitement of it.

"I'll count on you, then," he said, and walked quickly down the street, looking over his shoulder.

She went into the house. Upstairs, she could hear Bridget's voice, and her mother's voice in pain, but not yet the voice of the baby. She lifted her skirt. She put the silver dollar behind the elastic of her drawers. First it was cold against her stomach, but then it became warm from the heat of her body.

FRANÇOIS MAURIAC

A Christmas Tale

A scraggy plane tree, seemingly reaching up for air, stretched over the high walls of the courtyard into which we had just been released. But on that day we had not exploded with our usual shouts at the sound of Monsieur Garouste's whistle. It was the day before Christmas. We had been sentenced to a hike in the suburbs, through the fog and the mud, and we now felt as weary as only seven-year-old boys can feel whose young legs have trudged some fifteen kilometers.

The boarding students were putting on their house slippers. The flock of day students stood facing the gate, waiting for those who would come to deliver them from their daily captivity. I was munching absently and without appetite on a piece of bread, my mind already preoccupied with the mystique of that special evening which would soon excite me, and whose ritual never changed. They would have us wait behind the closed door of the guest room as the candles of the crèche were being lit. Then we would hear Mother call out, "You may come in." We would hurry eagerly into the room, which for us came to life only on that night. The tiny flames would draw us toward the little world of shepherds and beasts crowded around the Child. A night light illumining the interior of King Herod's crenelated castle, atop a mountain made of crumpled wrapping paper, would give us the illusion that we were present at secret and forbidden festivities. We would kneel and sing the carol of adoration:

> A stable was his lodging,
> A pile of hay his crib,

A stable was his lodging,
How humble for a God!

The humility of God would touch our hearts . . . Behind the crèche there would be a gift for each one of us, together with a letter in which God himself had written down our most grievous sin. As I stood in the courtyard facing the gate, I already felt the surrounding shadows of that unused room; no imaginary thief was now there, holding his breath behind the heavy, dark-flowered drapes drawn across the alcoves and windows. On the walls of the room, portraits of the dead listened from the depths of eternity to our feeble voices. Then, when the night would begin, before falling off to sleep, each child would take a last peek at his hobnailed shoes—the largest pair he possessed—which he had chosen to play a role in the miracle which every Christmas I tried in vain to surprise; but sleep is a chasm that no child can evade.

Thus I lived through in advance that blessed evening, as I stood facing the gate through which my nurse would soon appear. The light was already fading. Although it was not yet four o'clock, I waited impatiently, hoping that she would arrive early. All of a sudden a racket arose in a corner of the schoolyard. Many of the children rushed in that direction, yelling, "Look at the girl! Look at the girl!" The long curls of little Jean de Blaye doomed him to this persecution. His locks seemed hideous to us, with our shaved skulls. I was the only one who admired them, but secretly, mainly because they reminded me of the curls of little Lord Fauntleroy, whose story I had loved ever since it appeared in the *Saint-Nicolas* magazine of 1887. Whenever I was in the mood to pity myself or to cry, it was enough for me to look at the picture of the little lord in his mother's arms and to read the legend underneath: "Yes, she had always been his best, his most tender friend . . ." But the other children didn't have that issue of *Saint-Nicolas;* they didn't know that Jean de Blaye had a resemblance to Fauntleroy, so they tormented him; and I, a coward because I felt myself to be so weak against so many, kept my distance.

On that day, however, I was astonished because the pack didn't stop with "Look at the girl!" but used other taunting words as well, words that at first I didn't understand. I went closer, hugging the wall, afraid to attract the attention of the leader, the persecutor and sworn enemy of Jean de Blaye. His name was Campagne. He had been left back twice and was a head taller than any of us, a veritable giant in our eyes, endowed with almost supernatural physical strength. The children encircled Jean de Blaye, shouting:

"He believes it! He believes it! He believes it!"

"What does he believe?" I asked one of them.

"He believes that it is little Jesus who comes down the chimney . . ."

I didn't understand, and asked, "What of it?" But the other boy had again begun to howl with the wolves. I moved closer. Campagne had grabbed little de Blaye by the wrists and had pushed him against the wall.

"Do you believe it, yes or no?"

"Stop! You're hurting me!"

"Admit it and I'll let you go."

Then little de Blaye proclaimed in a loud, firm voice, like a martyr confessing his faith:

"Mama told me, and Mama never lies."

"Did you hear that!" howled Campagne. "Missy's mother never lies."

Through our servile laughter, Jean de Blaye repeated, "Mama does not lie! Mama would not fool me . . ." At that moment he saw me and appealed to me:

"Tell them, Frontenac—you know it's true. We were talking about it just a while ago, on the hike."

Campagne turned his cruel cat's eyes on me and I stammered, "I was only fooling him . . ." Seven years old—an age of weakness, of cowardice. Monsieur Garouste came up at that moment and the gang melted away. We went to get our raincoats and schoolbags.

When we got to the street, Jean de Blaye caught up to me. The manservant who had come for him was glad to walk with my nurse.

"You know very well it's true . . . but you were scared of Campagne . . . Wasn't that it? Wasn't it because you were scared?"

I was badly confused. I denied being afraid of Campagne. I said no, I didn't know whether or not it was true. After all, it didn't much matter as long as we got the toy we had asked for. But how did little Jesus know that Jean wanted some lead soldiers, a box of tools, and I a stable and a farm? . . . Why did the toys come from the Universal Department Store?

"Who told you that?"

"Last year I saw the labels . . ."

Jean de Blaye kept repeating, "Just the same, since Mama said so . . ." and I could see that he was upset.

"Listen," I said, "if we really want absolutely not to fall asleep, all we have to do is relight the candle, take a book, get settled in an armchair by the fireplace, and we will be sure to be awake when He comes . . ."

"Mama says that if you don't go to sleep, you keep Him from coming."

The lights of the store windows glittered on the sidewalks which were wet with the evening mist. Temporary booths lined the Concourse des Fossés. The acetylene lamps in the confectionary shop were shining on the pink candies which we longed for, but which were of such poor quality that we were not allowed to buy them.

"We could pretend to be asleep," I said.

"He'd know perfectly well that we were pretending, because He knows everything . . ."

"But if it is Mother who leaves the gifts and not He, she'll make believe she doesn't notice."

Jean de Blaye insisted, "It'll not be Mama!" We had reached the street corner where we were going to part until the end of the holidays, for Jean was leaving the next day for the country. I begged him to try not to fall asleep; as for myself, I was determined to stay awake. We'd tell each other what we saw. He promised that he'd try. I watched him go. For a few seconds I saw his long girlish curls bobbing on his shoulders; then his little figure vanished in the evening mist.

Our house was near the cathedral. On Christmas Eve the big bell in the Pey-Berland tower would fill the darkness with a thunderous booming. My bed would then become a ship's berth and the sound would hold me, rocking me in its tempest. The flickering night candle peopled the room with familiar phantoms. The curtain windows, the table, my clothes lying in disorder on the armchair no longer surrounded my bed menacingly—I had tamed these beasts. They would guard my sleep like the jungle beasts who watched over the boy Mowgli.

I wasn't going to take a chance of falling asleep that evening. The ringing of the cathedral bell helped keep me awake. My fingers grabbed the bars of the bedstead, so real seemed the feeling of being delivered up, body and soul, to a beneficent storm. Then Mother opened the door. My eyelids were closed but I recognized the silken sound of her dress. If it was she who placed the toys at my shoes, this would be the moment, I told myself, now, before she left for midnight Mass. I made an effort to breathe like a sleeping child. Mother bent over me and I felt her breath. This proved stronger than all my resolutions. I threw my arms around her neck and pressed against her with a kind of frenzy.

"Oh, you little madman! Oh, you little madman! How do you expect Him to come if you don't go to sleep? Go to sleep, Yves my darling, go to sleep my child . . ."

"Mother, I want to see Him!"

"He wants to be loved without being seen . . . You know, don't you, that in the Mass, the moment when He descends to the altar all heads are lowered . . ."

"Mother, don't be angry, but once I didn't lower my head—I kept looking—I saw Him . . ."

"What? You saw Him?"

"Yes . . . at least . . . the tip of a white wing . . ."

"Anyway, this isn't the night to keep your eyes open. You'll see Him best if you are asleep. You'd better not be awake by the time we get back from church!"

She closed the door after her, and I could hear her departing footsteps. I lit the candle and turned toward the fireplace; the last embers were dying. My shoes stood there, between the andirons and at the outside edge of the sooty square covered with cinders and ashes. It was down the chimney and through the trapdoor that the thunderous sound of the big bell flowed into my room. It filled it with an awesome song which, before reaching me, had rolled above the rooftops and up to the Milky Way where on Christmas Eve thousands of angels and stars mingled. What would have surprised me now would not have been the appearance of the Child in the dark recess of the hearth, but, on the contrary, if nothing had happened. Besides, something was already happening: my two shoes, the space around them still empty, those poor old heavy shoes which were so much a part of my daily life, suddenly took on a strange and unreal aspect, as if they had been placed there almost at a time beyond time, as if a little boy's shoes could suddenly be touched by an illumination cast from an invisible world. So close was the miracle that I blew out the candle in order not to startle the invisible ones on this night of nights.

If time seemed to pass quickly it was no doubt because I was suspended in timelessness. Someone pushed open the door and I closed my eyes. Hearing the silken whisper of the dress, the rustle of paper, I told myself it must be Mother. It was she and it wasn't she; it appeared to me rather that someone else had been transmuted into the form of my mother. During that midnight Mass, which I had not attended and which was beyond my imagination, I knew that Mother and my brothers must have received the little Host and that they had returned to their seats, as I had seen them do so often, with their hands folded in prayer and their eyelids closed so tight that I wondered how they were able to find their way. To be sure, it was Mother. After having lingered at the fireplace, she approached my bed. But He lived in her. I could not think of them separately. The breath which I felt on my hair came from her in whom the spirit of God still dwelt. It was at that moment that I sank into my mother's arms and into sleep.

The first morning back at school I wore the shoes that had been part of the miracle and which were now only a pair of ordinary, hobnailed, schoolboy's shoes, splashing like an ass's hoofs in the schoolyard puddles around the plane tree, as I waited for the eight o'clock bell. I looked in vain for the girlish locks of Jean de Blaye among the mob of children shouting and chasing each other. I couldn't wait to tell him the secret I had discovered . . . But, exactly what was the secret? I tried to imagine the words I would have to use to make him understand me.

Jean de Blaye's curls were still nowhere to be seen. Was he home, sick? Maybe it would be a long time before I found out what he had seen during his night of watching. After entering the classroom my eyes remained fixed on the seat he usually occupied. A different child was sitting there, a child without curls. At first I didn't realize that it was he. I would never have recognized him except by the blue eyes that turned toward me; and what astonished me the most was his air of casualness, of ease. He was shorn somewhat less than his schoolmates. The barber had left his hair long enough, so that he could part it on the left side.

At the ten o'clock recess, as soon as we were set loose in the courtyard, I went looking for him and saw him, erect as a little David in front of big Campagne, as if it had been his weakness and not his strength that he had lost with his hair. Campagne was so put off by what had just transpired between them that he left the field to Jean de Blaye, who coolly sat down on the steps to put on his roller skates. I watched him from a distance, undecided, thinking with a certain amount of sadness that I would never again see the curls of little Lord Fauntleroy gleam in the sunlight or dance on the shoulders of Jean de Blaye. I finally made up my mind to walk over to him.

"Well? Did you keep your promise?" I said. "Did you stay awake?"

He muttered, without raising his head, "Go on, did you really think I believed all that . . . that I could be so stupid?" And as I continued, "But, remember? . . . it was only two weeks ago," he bent a little lower over his skates and assured me that he had been pretending, that he had been making a fool of me, adding, "After all, at our age, when we are eight, we are no longer children."

He kept talking without looking at me; I could not see the expression in his eyes, and could no longer hold back the burning question:

"So, tell me—did your mother deceive you?"

He had put one knee on the ground in order to tighten the strap of his skate. Blood rushed to his ears, naked now as the wings of Zephyr. I kept mercilessly insisting:

"Come on, de Blaye, tell me: your mother—did she fool you?"

He straightened up suddenly and looked me in the eye. I can still see that young face, sullen and flushed, his lips tight. He brushed his hand over his head as if he sought the absent curls, and shrugged.

"She'll never fool me again."

I replied almost in spite of myself that our mothers had not lied to us, that it was all true, that I had seen . . . He interrupted me:

"You saw? . . . Is that true? You saw? . . . Well, I saw something too!"

With that he skated away, and to the end of the recess he never stopped skating around the plane tree. I understood that he was avoiding me. From that day we were no longer friends. The next year his family left Bordeaux, and I didn't know what became of him.

It happened only once during my youth in Paris that I didn't spend Christmas Eve in the provinces, with my people. That one time must have been only a few years before the war. I made the rounds of the nightclubs. I have since forgotten their names, but I still remember the consuming homesickness. In the atmosphere of those "dives," the big bell of the Pey-Berland tower of our cathedral must have resounded within me with a greater force than it did, that childhood evening, over the roofs of my native town. Its overpowering voice now drowned out the gypsies' violins. It is at such evocative moments in life that a person feels certain of having betrayed his ideals. My companions for the evening were not such traitors to themselves. They had no choice to make. Perhaps some of them had had a childhood like mine, but they had very likely forgotten it. I believe I was the only one in that room filled with food odors and the din of insipid melodies to recapture in my imagination the shadows of that guest room, the magic of the little island of the crèche. I must have been the only one there who recalled the ancient carol about the humility of God. Although I was only in the prime of my youth, those flickering candles in the past were now so remote that I seemed to be a thousand years old. I could feel their glow nevertheless, for I was a poet and in a poet's heart nothing is ever extinguished. How could I, then, have brought there, how had I dared to drag there that night the childhood which had never left me?"

I drank in order to lose awareness of my offense. The more I drank, the more distant did I feel from my companions. How their silly merriment annoyed me! I left the table and walked over to the bar, where the lights were more subdued. I leaned against it and ordered a whisky. And at the very moment when I was thinking about a little boy named Jean de Blaye, whom should I see but Jean de Blaye himself. He was perched on a stool next to me. I was certain it was he. The same gleaming periwinkle-blue eyes were lighting up the tired lines of this young man's face. His face was close enough for me to touch it. I said to him:

"They shouldn't have cut off your curls."

He didn't seem to be surprised, but he asked in a rather thick voice, "What curls?"

"The ones that were cut off during the Christmas holiday—when we were seven."

"You're taking me for someone else, of course, but that doesn't matter . . . I happen not to feel much like myself this evening."

"I know you're de Blaye."

"How do you know my name?"

I let out a sigh—it was he! It was, indeed, he! I reached for his hand, to shake it.

"Jean, do you remember that plane tree?"

He laughed. "The plane tree . . . which plane tree? By the way, my name isn't Jean but Philippe. My older brother's name was Jean. Perhaps you're mistaking me for him?"

"What a pity. You must be the younger brother about whom Jean used to speak." How could I have made such a mistake? Philippe's face lacked Jean's vivacity. He said suddenly:

"Those curls . . . yes, those curls of Jean's . . . that reminds me of an incident . . ."

He told me about it. In his mother's room there had been a chest on which she kept a locked silver casket. Jean had assured Philippe that it contained a treasure. They kept wondering about it, but their mother refused to show them what was in the casket, and she forbade them ever to open it. She and Jean were always bickering, always at odds. "She loved him more than me," said Philippe, "and in the end I became convinced that she had loved no one but him . . . Nevertheless, something set them against each other—I don't know what . . . One day Jean forced the lock on the casket . . . the first lock that he had forced, but, alas! not the last! The treasure . . . it was, would you believe it, his infant curls. One would have thought they were the hair of a corpse! Jean threw one of his tantrums . . . You know how he would carry on at such times. He stopped fuming only when he saw his old curls burning in the fireplace. That evening my mother . . . But I don't know why I'm telling you all this . . ." He returned to his drink. I thought to myself: "He speaks of his brother in the past." Somehow I knew in advance the answer to the question that I now asked him, "Is he dead?"

"Last year . . . in a hospital in Saigon. There was a notice in the paper but they didn't notify us . . . Who could blame them, after all those episodes, after the life he had led . . ."

I could have asked, "What kind of a life?" I preferred to say, "Yes, yes . . . I understand . . ." and I knew that Jean had perished as a depraved youth, a lost soul.

I remember returning later to my student lodgings on foot. Lean plane trees hung over the fences, over the muddy sidewalks, their branches bathed in the dawn mist. There were still many revelers in the streets. I saw my evening's companions hoist a drunken woman into a red cab. Far from the disorders of the evening's festivities, my eyes sought over the roofs, up in the frozen heights, the angels now wakened by the big bell of the Pey-Berland tower. There is such a thing as a lucid state of drunkenness. At the same time that I felt uplifted, not only by the reminiscences of my childhood but by my childhood itself, alive and vivid within me, I reconstructed with amazing ease Jean de Blaye's story. I may have been born a poet, but that night I became a novelist, at least I became aware of that gift, of that power. I walked rapidly, lightly, carried away by the force of creativity. I conceived the two poles of his fate: a small boy with girl's hair, whose soul was ruled by a wild compulsiveness and a powerful passion totally centered on his mother, and then the man, still almost a child, who suffered his last agony on a hospital bed, in Saigon.

I re-created the schoolboy for whom his mother's word was sacred. I saw his horror at the moment when he discovered that she was capable of lying; I saw a special meaning in his shorn curls: their demise marked the end of his filial love . . . Here ended the prologue to my novel and I launched into the heart of the theme: that young male and that mother in confrontation; the scene with the casket became the core of it. Jean de Blaye hated in her who had brought him into the world the determination to perpetuate the infant that he no longer was, to keep him prisoner of his childhood, in order to hold him more relentlessly under her domination. Barely had manhood begun to rise in him than the struggle against her resolve turned into a tragedy—his first friendship, his first love, the first night when he didn't come home, the demands for money, the clandestine companions, the first serious crime . . .

I arrived at my door. The day had dawned. The bells were announcing the sunrise Mass. Despite my need for sleep, I sat down at my desk at once, in my evening clothes and my boutonniere still in my lapel, and took up a pen and a blank sheet of paper, so anxious was I not to forget the ideas that had come to me! A novelist had just been born, opening his eyes on this sad world.

MURIEL SPARK

Alice Long's Dachshunds

The guns clank on the stone, one after the other, echoing against the walls outside the chapel, as the men come in for Mass before the shoot. Mamie, whose age is eight years and two months, kneels in the second row from the back, on the right-hand side, near the Virgin, where a warm candle is lit. There is no other warmth. Alice Long is kneeling on a front hassock. Her two brothers from London have come in—tall men in knickerbockers and green wool stockings that stride past Mamie's eyes as she kneels in her place.

Other big men have put their guns against the wall outside the chapel door. The Catholics from the cottages have come in. Everyone except the strangers is praying for more snow and a road blockage to the town, so that poor Alice Long can decently serve roe deer, roe deer, roe deer for all the meals that the London people are going to eat. The woods are cracking alive with roe deer, but meat from the town has got to be paid for with money.

Alice Long is round-shouldered and worried; she is the only daughter of old Sir Martin, and is always addressed, to her face, as Miss Long. Her money is her own, but it goes into the keeping of the House.

Alice Long's two brothers' wives have come into the chapel now. They are the last, because they have to look after their own babies when they get up. Before Mamie's birth, all the babies in the House had nurses. The two wives were differently made from the start, before they became Alice Long's sisters-in-law, and still look so, although their tweed coats were made more alike. One is called Lady Caroline and the other, Mrs. Martin Long, will be Lady Long when old Sir Martin dies and Martin Long comes into the title.

Mamie is watching Lady Caroline through her fingers. Lady Caroline is big and broad, with bobbed black hair under her black lace veil; she doesn't like Alice Long's dogs, and dogs are the only things Alice Long has for herself. Alice Long was made to be kept down by upkeep.

The big clock upstairs chimes seven. The priest comes in and the feet shuffle. Mamie cannot see the altar when everyone is standing. She stares at the candle. The service begins. Will the friends who have come from warm London catch their death of colds?

Mamie stops in the snow. The ends of the dogs' leashes are wound round her hands in their woollen gloves, three round the right hand and two round the left. She unwinds the leads to give her arms scope, and the dogs take advantage of the few extra inches of freedom, snuffling and wriggling away from Mamie until the leads pull taut. But she works them back, lifting her elbows to cup her hands to her mouth.

"Come out. I can see you."

No reply.

She repeats the words and drops her arms, aching from the weight of straining dogs.

There is a thud of snowfall from the clump of trees. The noise would have been only a little plop had there been any more sound besides that of the snuffling dogs.

She is taking Alice Long's dogs for a walk.

"She'll be glad to, Miss Long," said her mother. "Tomorrow after school. It's a half day."

This morning, her mother said, "Come straight home at two for Alice Long's dogs."

To do so, Mamie has missed her dancing lesson at the convent. She is learning the sword-dance. Alice Long had got her into the convent at reduced fees, and even those reduced fees Alice Long pays herself. She likes to keep the Catholic tenants Catholic.

Mamie walks on, satisfied there are no boys behind the trees. She is afraid the boys will find her and tease the dogs, laugh at her, laugh at the little padding, waddling dogs, do them harm before they can be returned to the House.

The snow in the wood is too deep for low-made dogs. Mamie wanders around the edge of the wood, on the crunchy path, with little running steps every now and then as the dogs get the better of her.

"My dachshunds," said Alice Long lovingly.

The country people said to each other, when she was out of sight, "Alice Long has only got her dogs. And all that upkeep."

"Lady Caroline hates dogs."

"No, she only hates dachshunds. German sausages. She likes big dogs for the country."

Alice Long is sitting with her teacup in Mamie's house, which has five rooms plus k.p.b.—standing for kitchen, pantry, and bathroom—and is semidetached. Next door are Alice Long's Couple. Mamie's father no longer works on the estate but is a foreman in the town at Heppleford and Styles' Linoleum.

"Lady Caroline can't bear them. They've been locked in the north wing since Friday. I have to keep a fire going . . ."

"That wing's not heated, of course."

"No. They are freezing and lonely. I keep putting logs on. I get up in the middle of the night to see to the fire."

"They'll be all right, Miss Long."

"They need a good run, that's all. I won't have time for the dogs today. But the family goes home tomorrow or Wednesday . . ."

Mamie has taken the dogs out for a run before. She is not allowed to go near the wood but must keep to the inhabited paths that pass the groups of houses on the estate and lead to the shop. Near the shop are usually the children from the village school, throwing snowballs in winter, wheeling bicycles in summer. Mamie has money for toffee and an orange drink. She wanders by the wood.

Her father has been at home for three working days. There is a strike. Alice Long sits downstairs. The father has gone to wait upstairs until she leaves. Then he opens the cupboard door where the television set is placed in a recess formed by the removal of one of the shelves. Alice Long has not seen this television set. The people next door, her Couple, took on a television many years ago, and keep it out in the living room.

Mitzi, Fritzi, Blitzi, Ritzi, and Kitzy.

"Alice Long's dogs are all she's got to herself."

The dogs go about together and sometimes all answer at once when Alice Long calls one of their names. Mamie does not know them apart. They vary slightly in size, fatness, and in the black scars on their brown coats.

The path has become a ridge of frozen earth where the field has been ploughed right up to the verge of the wood. The daylight is turning blue with cold while Mamie struggles with the leads. One gumboot digs deep in a furrow and the other stabs to keep its hold on the ridge. The dogs snuffle each other and snort steam. They strain toward the wood, and Hamilton is suddenly there—Alice Long's gamekeeper—coming out of the trees, tall and broad, with his grey moustache and deep-pink face. He looks at Mamie as if to say, "Come here." The dogs fuss round him, cutting into her gloves.

Mamie says, "I've got to go that way," pointing down towards her home across the field.

"I'll see you back at the House," he says, and stoops back into the wood, examining the undergrown branches.

Hamilton looks after old Sir Martin when he becomes beyond a woman's strength.

"I'm afraid my father is not very well anymore."

"I don't know how you do it, Miss Long."

Mamie's mother says that anybody else but Alice Long would have put the old man away.

Hamilton sees to the boilers that heat the heated wing. He has too much to do to air the dogs regularly.

"Without Hamilton, I don't know what we should do. Before your husband left us, we had it easier."

Mamie has turned away from the wood. She has taken the path to the houses, looking back all the time to see whether Hamilton is following her with his eyes, those eyes that are two poached eggs grown old, looking at her every time he sees her.

She takes the footpath on the main road. The dogs are trotting now. A car passes, and a delivery van from the grocer's shop in the town. She clutches the leads.

"Don't let one of them get run over. Alice Long would be up to ninety-nine."

She presses, at the sharp bend, into the high white bank which touches again on the wood, while a very big lorry, carrying sacks of coal, creeps fearfully around as if bewaring of the dogs.

Bump on her shoulder, then bump on her cap come the snowballs. The boys are up there on the bank. She turns and looks quickly and sees parts of children ducking out of sight with short, laughing squeals. There are two girls with the boys; she has seen their hair. One of the girls wears the dark-blue convent cap.

"Connie, come down!"

"It isn't Connie," Gwen's voice answers.

Gwen should be at the dancing class. She is learning to do the sword-dance with Mamie.

A snowball falls on the road and bursts open. There is no stone inside it. The dogs are yelping now, pelted with snowballs. They are up to ninety-nine, not used to this.

Mamie drags them round the corner and starts to run. The children scramble down after her and catch up. She recognises them all. She tries to gather up some snow, but it is impossible to make and throw a ball with the leads around her gloves.

"Where are you going with those dogs?" says a boy.

"To the shop, then up to the House."

"They look dirty."

Gwen says, "Do you like those dogs?"

"Not all of them together."

"Let them run loose," says the other girl. "It's good for them."

"No."

"Come on and play."

She is scrambling up the bank, while everyone is trying to pull the dogs up by their leads or push them up by their bottoms.

"Lift them up. You'll throttle them!"

"Let go the leads. We'll take one each."

"No."

Up on the bank, Mamie says, "I'll tie them to that tree." She refuses to let the leads out of her own hands, but she permits two of the boys to make the knots secure, as they have learned to do in the Scout Cubs.

Then it is boys against girls in a snow fight, with such fast pelting and splutters from drenched faces, such loud shrieks that the dogs' coughing and whining can scarcely be heard. When it is time to go, Mamie counts the dogs. Then she starts to untie them. The knots are difficult. She calls after one of the boys to come and untie the knots, but he does not look around. Gwen returns; she stands and looks. Mamie is kneeling in the slush, trying.

"How do you untie these knots?" All the leads are mixed up in a knotted muddle.

"I don't know. What's their names?"

"Mitzi, Fritzi, Blitzi, Ritzi, and Kitzy."

"Do you know one from the other?"

"No."

Mamie bends down with her strong teeth in the leather. She has loosened the first knot. All the knots are coming loose. She gets her woollen gloves on again and starts to wind the leads around her hands. One of them springs from her grasp, and the little dog scuttles away into the wood among the old wet leaves, so that it seems to slither like a snake on its belly with its cord bouncing behind it.

"Mitzi! Kitzy! Blitzi!"

The dog disappears and the four in hand are excited, anxious to be free and warmed up too.

"Catch him, Gwen! Can you see him? Where is it? Mitzi-mitzi-mitzi! Blitzi-blitzi!"

"I've got to go home," Gwen says. "You shouldn't have stopped to play."

Gwen is Sister Monica's model pupil for punctuality, neatness, and truthfulness. Mamie has no ground to answer Gwen's reproach as the girl starts to clamber down the bank.

The wood is dark and there is no sound of the dog. Mamie squelches with the four dogs among the leaves and snow lumps. "Fritzi-fritzi-fritzi mitzi!" A bark, a yap, behind her. Again a yap-yap. She turns and finds the dog tied once more to a tree. Hamilton? She peers all around her and sees nobody.

She should be hurrying toward the drive, but she is too tired to hurry. The Lodge gates are still open, although the sky looks late. The lights are on in the Lodge, which has been let to new people from Liverpool for their week-ends. They are having a long week-end this time. A young woman comes out to her car as Mamie comes in the gateway with the five dogs.

"Goodness, you're wet through!"

"I got in a snow-drift."

"Hurry home then, dear, and get changed."

Mamie cannot hurry. She is not very well anymore, like old Sir Martin. She is not very real anymore. The colour of the afternoon seems strange and the sky is banked with snow-drifts. She runs in little spurts only in obedience to the pull of the dogs. But she draws them as tight as she can and plods in the direction of the House. She turns to the right when she reaches the wide steps and the big front doors. Around to the right and into the yard, where Hamilton's door is. She tries to open his door. It is locked. To pull the bell would require raising her arm, and she is too tired to do so. She tries to knock. The dogs are full of noise and anxiety, are scratching the door to get inside. She looks at them and with difficulty switches those leads in her right hand to her left, winding them round her wrist, since the hand is already full. While she knocks with her free hand at the door, she realises that she has noticed something. There are only four dogs now. She counts—one, two, three, four. She counts the leads—one, two, three, four. She looks away again and knocks. It has not happened. Nothing has happened. It is not real. She knocks again. Hamilton is coming.

"Their food's in there," Hamilton says, not looking at the dogs but opening the door that leads from his room to another, more cluttered room. He lets the dogs scuttle in to their food without counting them. He does not remove their leads but throws them onto the floor to trail behind them. Finally, he shuts the inner door on them. He sits down in his chair and looks at Mamie as if to say, "Come here."

"I've got to go home."

"You're wet through. Get dry by the fire a minute. I'll get you a lift home."

"No, I'm late."

He pats his knee. "Sit here, dearie, lass." He has a glass and a bottle by him. "I want to give you a drop. Come on. I don't want sex."

She perches on his lap. He has not counted the dogs. Alice Long will be up to ninety-nine, but it's Hamilton's fault from now. Hamilton has taken the dogs.

"Now sip."

She recognises whisky.

"Take a good swallow."

He gives her a lemon drop to hide her breath, then gives her a kiss on her mouth while she is still sucking the sweet.

"I'm going now. I hope the dogs are all right."

"Oh, the dogs, they're all right."

He takes her hand and goes to find one of the workmen who are mending the House. Alice Long is not home yet from her meeting, and she will not miss the workman for a few minutes.

Mamie climbs into the foreman's car beside the workman. The seat is covered with white dust, but she does not brush it off the seat before sliding onto it. Her clothes will be spoiled. She feels safe beside the driver. The whisky has given her back a real afternoon.

"What's the time, please?" she asks.

"About twenty past four."

The man backs and turns. Hamilton has gone into his quarters. The car skirts the House, turning by the large new clearing where, in the summer, the tourists' coaches come.

"You can't get many up here in Northumberland. They all swarm to the old houses in the South. Here, it's out of the way . . ."

"Well, it's an experience for those who do come, Miss Long. Especially the Catholics."

The House was once turned into a hospital for the wounded English soldiers after the Battle of Flodden, which the English won.

The House was a Mass centre at the times of the Catholic Persecution. Outside the armoury, there is a chalice in a glass case dating from Elizabethan times. It has been sold to a museum, but the museum allows the family to keep it at the House during Sir Martin's lifetime. Mamie has been inside the priest hole, where the priests were hidden when the House was searched for priests; they would sometimes stay there several days. The hole is a large space behind a panel that comes out of the wall, up among the attics. You can stand in the priest hole and look up at the beams, where, in those days, food was always stored in case of emergency.

The workmen are mending the roof.

"Did you see the priest hole?" Mamie feels talkative.

"What's that?"

"A place where the priests used to hide, up in the roof. It's historic. Haven't you seen it?"

"No, but I seen plenty dry rot up there in that roof."

The gates are closed. The man gets out to open them; then he drives off again.

Is it possible that one of the dogs is lost? Mamie is confused. There must have been five. I found the lost one, tied to the tree. But then she sees herself again counting them outside Hamilton's door. One, two, three, four. Only four. No, no, no, it's not real. Hamilton has taken the dogs. It's for him to count.

The workman says, "Do you like the Beatles?"

"Oh, yes, they're great. Do you like them?"

"So-so. I'd like just one day's earnings that the Beatles get. Just one day. I could retire on it."

Sister Monica has said that there is no harm in the Beatles, and then Mamie felt indignant because it showed Sister Monica did not properly appreciate them. She ought to lump them together with things like whisky, smoking, and sex; the Beatles are quite good enough to be forbidden.

"I like dancing," Mamie says.

"Rock-'n'-roll stuff?"

"Yes, but at school we only get folk-dancing. I'm learning the sword-dance. It's historic in the Border country."

All the rest of the week, she hurries home from school to see if Alice Long has been to see her mother about the missing dog.

I counted. One, two, three, four. But I had five when I left the wood. I brought five out of the wood, and up the hill. I had five at the Lodge. I must have had . . .

Alice Long will be up to ninety-nine. She will come to Mamie's house to make enquiries:

"Hamilton says she only brought four . . .

"Hamilton says he didn't count them, he just took the leads from her hand . . .

"Hamilton must have been drinking and let one of them slip out of the door . . .

"I've only just counted them. One must have been missing since Monday. When Mamie . . ."

By Friday, Alice Long has not come. Mamie's mother says, "Alice Long hasn't dropped in. I must take a pie up to the House on Monday and see what's doing."

On Sunday afternoon, Alice Long's car stops at the door. "Come in, Miss Long, come in. Have you no family down this week-end?"

Mamie's father shuts away the television, puts on his coat, says good afternoon, and goes upstairs.

Alice Long sits trembling on the sofa beside Mamie while her mother puts on the tea.

She says, "It's Hamilton."

"The same thing again?"

"No, worse. A tragedy." Alice Long shuts her lips tight and pats Mamie's hair. Her hand is shaking.

"Mamie, go out and play," says her mother.

When Alice Long has driven her car away, Mamie comes in with the ends of her skipping-rope twined around her gloves. Her father comes down, takes off his coat, and opens up the television. "Oh, don't turn it on," says her mother, in anguish.

Mamie eats some of the remnants of cake and sandwiches while she listens.

"Hanging in the priest hole—all of them. She looked for them all night. Hamilton's gone, cleared off. It's the drink. The police have got a warrant out. They were found hanged on the beams after Mass this morning. Didn't I say poor Alice Long was looking bad at Mass? I thought it must be her father again. But she'd been up all night looking for the dogs, and at Mass she still didn't know where they were. It was after Mass they found them, herself and Mrs. Huddlestone. Think of the sight! Five of them hanging in a row. Poor little beasts. Hamilton disappeared yesterday. They'll get him, though, just wait."

"He's a bit of a lunatic," Mamie's father says.

"Lunatic! He's vicious. He ought to be hung himself. They were all Alice Long had. But he'll be caught!"

Her father says, "I doubt it. Not Hamilton. Even the roebuck called him Pussyfoot." He laughs at his own joke. The mother turns away her head.

Mamie says, "How many were hanging in the priest hole?"

"All of them in a row."

"How many?"

"Five. You know she had five. You took them out, didn't you?"

Mamie says, "I was only wondering if there was *room* for five in the priest hole. Did she really say there were five? It wasn't four?"

"She said all five of them. What are you talking about, no room in the priest hole? There's plenty room. He'd have killed six if she'd had six. She was so good to him."

"A shocking affair," says her father.

Mamie feels weightless as daylight. She waves her arms as if they are freed of a huge harness.

"Five of them." I counted wrong. I didn't lose one. There were five.

She skips over to fetch the shining brass pokers from the fender and places them criss-cross on the linoleum to practise her sword-dance. Then she starts to dance, heel-and-toe, heel-and-toe, over-and-across, one-two-three, one-two-three. Her mother stands amazed and is about to say stop it at once, this is no time to practise, children have no heart, Alice Long pays your school fees and I thought you loved animals. But her father is clapping his hands in time to her dancing—one-two-three, heel-and-toe, hand-on-hip, right-hand, left-hand, cross-and-back. Then her father starts to sing as well, loudly, tara rum-tum-tum, tara rum-tum-tum, clapping his hands while she dances the jig, and there isn't a thing anyone can do about it.

TOBIAS WOLFF

The Liar

My mother read everything except books. Advertisements on buses, entire menus as we ate, billboards; if it had no cover it interested her. So when she found a letter in my drawer that was not addressed to her she read it. "What difference does it make if James has nothing to hide?"— that was her thought. She stuffed the letter in the drawer when she finished it and walked from room to room in the big empty house, talking to herself. She took the letter out and read it again to get the facts straight. Then, without putting on her coat or locking the door, she went down the steps and headed for the church at the end of the street. No matter how angry and confused she might be, she always went to four o'clock Mass and now it was four o'clock.

It was a fine day, blue and cold and still, but Mother walked as though into a strong wind, bent forward at the waist with her feet hurrying behind in short, busy steps. My brother and sisters and I considered this walk of hers funny and we smirked at one another when she crossed in front of us to stir the fire or water a plant. We didn't let her catch us at it. It would have puzzled her to think that there might be anything amusing about her. Her one concession to the fact of humor was an insincere, startling laugh. Strangers often stared at her.

While Mother waited for the priest, who was late, she prayed. She prayed in a familiar, orderly, firm way: first for her late husband, my father, then for her parents—also dead. She said a quick prayer for my father's parents (just touching base; she had disliked them) and finally for her children in order of their ages, ending with me. Mother did not

consider originality a virtue and until my name came up her prayers
were exactly the same as on any other day.

But when she came to me she spoke up boldly. "I thought he wasn't
going to do it anymore. Murphy said he was cured. What am I supposed to do now?" There was reproach in her tone. Mother put great
hope in her notion that I was cured. She regarded my cure as an answer
to her prayers and by way of thanksgiving sent a lot of money to the
Thomasite Indian Mission, money she had been saving for a trip to
Rome. She felt cheated and she let her feelings be known. When the
priest came in Mother slid back on the seat and followed the Mass with
concentration. After communion she began to worry again and went
straight home without stopping to talk to Frances, the woman who
always cornered Mother after Mass to tell about the awful things done
to her by Communists, devil-worshipers, and Rosicrucians. Frances
watched her go with narrowed eyes.

Once in the house, Mother took the letter from my drawer and
brought it into the kitchen. She held it over the stove with her fingernails, looking away so that she would not be drawn into it again, and set
it on fire. When it began to burn her fingers she dropped it in the sink
and watched it blacken and flutter and close upon itself like a fist. Then
she washed it down the drain and called Dr. Murphy.

The letter was to my friend Ralphy in Arizona. He used to live across
the street from us but he had moved. Most of the letter was about a tour
we, the junior class, had taken of Alcatraz. That was all right. What got
Mother was the last paragraph where I said that she had been coughing
up blood and the doctors weren't sure what was wrong with her, but
that we were hoping for the best.

This wasn't true. Mother took pride in her physical condition, considered herself a horse: "I'm a regular horse," she would reply when
people asked about her health. For several years now I had been saying
unpleasant things that weren't true and this habit of mine irked Mother
greatly, enough to persuade her to send me to Dr. Murphy, in whose
office I was sitting when she burned the letter. Dr. Murphy was our
family physician and had no training in psychoanalysis but he took an
interest in "things of the mind," as he put it. He had treated me for
appendicitis and tonsillitis and Mother thought that he could put the
truth into me as easily as he took things out of me, a hope Dr. Murphy
did not share. He was basically interested in getting me to understand

what I did, and lately he had been moving toward the conclusion that I understood what I did as well as I ever would.

Dr. Murphy listened to Mother's account of the letter, and what she had done with it. He was curious about the wording I had used and became irritated when Mother told him she had burned it. "The point is," she said, "he was supposed to be cured and he's not."

"Margaret, I never said he was cured."

"You certainly did. Why else would I have sent over a thousand dollars to the Thomasite Mission?"

"I said that he was responsible. That means that James knows what he's doing, not that he's going to stop doing it."

"I'm sure you said he was cured."

"Never. To say that someone is cured you have to know what health is. With this kind of thing that's impossible. What do you mean by curing James, anyway?"

"You know."

"Tell me anyway."

"Getting him back to reality, what else?"

"Whose reality? Mine or yours?"

"Murphy, what are you talking about? James isn't crazy, he's a liar."

"Well, you have a point there."

"What am I going to do with him?"

"I don't think there's much you can do. Be patient."

"I've been patient."

"If I were you, Margaret, I wouldn't make too much of this. James doesn't steal, does he?"

"Of course not."

"Or beat people up or talk back."

"No."

"Then you have a lot to be thankful for."

"I don't think I can take any more of it. That business about leukemia last summer. And now this."

"Eventually he'll outgrow it, I think."

"Murphy, he's sixteen years old. What if he doesn't outgrow it? What if he just gets better at it?"

Finally Mother saw that she wasn't going to get any satisfaction from Dr. Murphy, who kept reminding her of her blessings. She said something cutting to him and he said something pompous back and she hung up. Dr. Murphy stared at the receiver. "Hello," he said, then replaced it on the cradle. He ran his hand over his head, a habit remaining from a time when he had hair. To show that he was a good sport he often joked about his baldness, but I had the feeling that he regretted it deeply. Looking at me across the desk, he must have wished that he hadn't taken me on. Treating a friend's child was like investing a friend's money.

"I don't have to tell you who that was."

I nodded.

Dr. Murphy pushed his chair back and swiveled it around so he could look out the window behind him, which took up most of the wall. There were still a few sailboats out on the Bay, but they were all making for shore. A woolly gray fog had covered the bridge and was moving in fast. The water seemed calm from this far up, but when I looked closely I could see white flecks everywhere, so it must have been pretty choppy.

"I'm surprised at you," he said. "Leaving something like that lying around for her to find. If you really have to do these things you could at least be kind and do them discreetly. It's not easy for your mother, what with your father dead and all the others somewhere else."

"I know. I didn't mean for her to find it."

"Well." He tapped his pencil against his teeth. He was not convinced professionally, but personally he may have been. "I think you ought to go home now and straighten things out."

"I guess I'd better."

"Tell your mother I might stop by, either tonight or tomorrow. And, James—don't underestimate her."

While my father was alive we usually went to Yosemite for three or four days during the summer. My mother would drive and Father would point out places of interest, meadows where boom towns once stood, hanging trees, rivers that were said to flow upstream at certain times. Or he read to us; he had that grown-ups' idea that children love Dickens and Sir Walter Scott. The four of us sat in the back seat with our faces composed, attentive, while our hands and feet pushed, pinched, stomped, goosed, prodded, dug, and kicked.

One night a bear came into our camp just after dinner. Mother had made a tuna casserole and it must have smelled to him like something worth dying for. He came into the camp while we were sitting around the fire and stood swaying back and forth. My brother Michael saw him first and elbowed me, then my sisters saw him and screamed. Mother and Father had their backs to him but Mother must have guessed what it was because she immediately said, "Don't scream like that. You might frighten him and there's no telling what he'll do. We'll just sing and he'll go away."

We sang "Row Row Row Your Boat" but the bear stayed. He circled us several times, rearing up now and then on his hind legs to stick his nose into the air. By the light of the fire I could see his doglike face and watch the muscles roll under his loose skin like rocks in a sack. We sang harder as he circled us, coming closer and closer. "All right," Mother said, "enough's enough." She stood abruptly. The bear stopped moving and watched her. "Beat it," Mother said. The bear sat down and looked from side to side. "Beat it," she said again, and leaned over and picked up a rock.

"Margaret, don't," my father said.

She threw the rock hard and hit the bear in the stomach. Even in the dim light I could see the dust rising from his fur. He grunted and stood to his full height. "See that?" Mother shouted: "He's filthy. Filthy!" One of my sisters giggled. Mother picked up another rock. "Please, Margaret," my father said. Just then the bear turned and shambled away. Mother pitched the rock after him. For the rest of the night he loitered around the camp until he found the tree where we had hung our food. He ate it all. The next day we drove back to the city. We could have bought more supplies in the valley, but Father wanted to go and would not give in to any argument. On the way home he tried to jolly everyone up by making jokes, but Michael and my sisters ignored him and looked stonily out the windows.

Things were never easy between my mother and me, but I didn't underestimate her. She underestimated me. When I was little she suspected me of delicacy, because I didn't like being thrown into the air, and because when I saw her and the others working themselves up for a roughhouse I found somewhere else to be. When they did drag me in I got hurt, a knee in the lip, a bent finger, a bloody nose, and this too Mother seemed to hold against me, as if I arranged my hurts to get out of playing.

Even things I did well got on her nerves. We all loved puns except Mother, who didn't get them, and next to my father I was the best in the family. My specialty was the Swifty—" 'You can bring the prisoner down,' said Tom condescendingly." Father encouraged me to perform at dinner, which must have been a trial for outsiders. Mother wasn't sure what was going on, but she didn't like it.

She suspected me in other ways. I couldn't go to the movies without her examining my pockets to make sure I had enough money to pay for the ticket. When I went away to camp she tore my pack apart in front of all the boys who were waiting in the bus outside the house. I would rather have gone without my sleeping bag and a few changes of underwear, which I had forgotten, than be made such a fool of. Her distrust was the thing that made me forgetful.

And she thought I was cold-hearted because of what happened the day my father died and later at his funeral. I didn't cry at my father's funeral, and showed signs of boredom during the eulogy, fiddling around with the hymnals. Mother put my hands into my lap and I left them there without moving them as though they were things I was holding for someone else. The effect was ironical and she resented it. We had a sort of reconciliation a few days later after I closed my eyes at school and refused to open them. When several teachers and then the principal failed to persuade me to look at them, or at some reward they claimed to be holding, I was handed over to the school nurse, who tried to pry the lids open and scratched one of them badly. My eye swelled up and I went rigid. The principal panicked and called Mother, who fetched me home. I wouldn't talk to her, or open my eyes, or bend, and they had to lay me on the back seat and when we reached the house Mother had to lift me up the steps one at a time. Then she put me on the couch and played the piano to me all afternoon. Finally I opened my eyes. We hugged each other and I wept. Mother did not really believe my tears, but she was willing to accept them because I had staged them for her benefit.

My lying separated us, too, and the fact that my promises not to lie anymore seemed to mean nothing to me. Often my lies came back to her in embarrassing ways, people stopping her in the street and saying how sorry they were to hear that . . . No one in the neighborhood enjoyed embarrassing Mother, and these situations stopped occurring once everybody got wise to me. There was no saving her from strangers, though. The summer after Father died I visited my uncle in Redding and when I got back I found to my surprise that Mother had come to meet my bus. I tried to slip away from the gentleman who had sat next to me but I couldn't shake him. When he saw Mother embrace me he came up and presented her with a card and told her to get in touch with him if things got any worse. She gave him his card back and told him to mind his own business. Later, on the way home, she made me repeat what I had said to the man. She shook her head. "It's not fair to people," she said, "telling them things like that. It confuses them." It seemed to me that Mother had confused the man, not I, but I didn't say so. I agreed with her that I shouldn't say such things and promised not to do it again, a promise I broke three hours later in conversation with a woman in the park.

It wasn't only the lies that disturbed Mother; it was their morbidity. This was the real issue between us, as it had been between her and my father. Mother did volunteer work at Children's Hospital and St. Anthony's Dining Hall, collected things for the St. Vincent de Paul Society. She was a lighter of candles. My brother and sisters took after her in this way. My father was a curser of the dark. And he loved to curse the dark. He was never more alive than when he was indignant about something. For this reason the most important act of the day for him was the reading of the evening paper.

Ours was a terrible paper, indifferent to the city that bought it, indifferent to medical discoveries—except for new kinds of gases that made your hands fall off when you sneezed—and indifferent to politics and art. Its business was outrage, horror, gruesome coincidence. When my father sat down in the living room with the paper Mother stayed in the kitchen and kept the children busy, all except me, because I was quiet and could be trusted to amuse myself. I amused myself by watching my father.

He sat with his knees spread, leaning forward, his eyes only inches from the print. As he read he nodded to himself. Sometimes he swore and threw the paper down and paced the room, then picked it up and began again. Over a period of time he developed the habit of reading aloud to me. He always started with the society section, which he called the parasite page. This column began to take on the character of a comic strip or a serial, with the same people showing up from one day to the next, blinking in chiffon, awkwardly holding their drinks for the sake of Peninsula orphans, grinning under sunglasses on the deck of a ski hut in the Sierras. The skiers really got his goat, probably because he couldn't understand them. The activity itself was inconceivable to him. When my sisters went to Lake Tahoe one winter weekend with some friends and came back excited about the beauty of the place, Father calmed them right down. "Snow," he said, "is overrated."

Then the news, or what passed in the paper for news: bodies un-
earthed in Scotland, former Nazis winning elections, rare animals
slaughtered, misers expiring naked in freezing houses upon mattresses
stuffed with thousands, millions; marrying priests, divorcing actresses,
high-rolling oilmen building fantastic mausoleums in honor of a favorite
horse, cannibalism. Through all this my father waded with a fixed and
weary smile.

Mother encouraged him to take up causes, to join groups, but he
would not. He was uncomfortable with people outside the family. He
and my mother rarely went out, and rarely had people in, except on
feast days and national holidays. Their guests were always the same,
Dr. Murphy and his wife and several others whom they had known
since childhood. Most of these people never saw each other outside our
house and they didn't have much fun together. Father discharged his
obligations as host by teasing everyone about stupid things they had
said or done in the past and forcing them to laugh at themselves.

Though Father did not drink, he insisted on mixing cocktails for the
guests. He would not serve straight drinks like rum-and-Coke or even
Scotch-on-the-rocks, only drinks of his own devising. He gave them
lawyerly names like "The Advocate," "The Hanging Judge," "The Ambulance Chaser," "The Mouthpiece," and described their concoction in
detail. He told long, complicated stories in a near-whisper, making everyone lean in his direction, and repeated important lines; he also repeated the important lines in the stories my mother told, and corrected
her when she got something wrong. When the guests came to the ends
of their own stories he would point out the morals.

Dr. Murphy had several theories about Father, which he used to test
on me in the course of our meetings. Dr. Murphy had by this time given
up his glasses for contact lenses, and lost weight in the course of fasts
which he undertook regularly. Even with his baldness he looked years
younger than when he had come to the parties at our house. Certainly
he did not look like my father's contemporary, which he was.

One of Dr. Murphy's theories was that Father had exhibited a classic
trait of people who had been gifted children by taking an undemanding
position in an uninteresting firm. "He was afraid of finding his limits,"
Dr. Murphy told me: "As long as he kept stamping papers and making
out wills he could go on believing that he didn't *have* limits." Dr.
Murphy's fascination with Father made me uneasy, and I felt traitorous
listening to him. While he lived, my father would never have submitted

himself for analysis; it seemed a betrayal to put him on the couch now that he was dead.

I did enjoy Dr. Murphy's recollections of Father as a child. He told me about something that happened when they were in the Boy Scouts. Their troop had been on a long hike and Father had fallen behind. Dr. Murphy and the others decided to ambush him as he came down the trail. They hid in the woods on each side and waited. But when Father walked into the trap none of them moved or made a sound and he strolled on without even knowing they were there. "He had the sweetest look on his face," Dr. Murphy said, "listening to the birds, smelling the flowers, just like Ferdinand the Bull." He also told me that my father's drinks tasted like medicine.

While I rode my bicycle home from Dr. Murphy's office Mother fretted. She felt terribly alone but she didn't call anyone because she also felt like a failure. My lying had that effect on her. She took it personally. At such times she did not think of my sisters, one happily married, the other doing brilliantly at Fordham. She did not think of my brother Michael, who had given up college to work with runaway children in Los Angeles. She thought of me. She thought that she had made a mess of her family.

Actually she managed the family well. While my father was dying upstairs she pulled us together. She made lists of chores and gave each of us a fair allowance. Bedtimes were adjusted and she stuck by them. She set regular hours for homework. Each child was made responsible for the next eldest, and I was given a dog. She told us frequently, predictably, that she loved us. At dinner we were each expected to contribute something, and after dinner she played the piano and tried to teach us to sing in harmony, which I could not do. Mother, who was an admirer of the Trapp family, considered this a character defect.

Our life together was more orderly, healthy, while Father was dying than it had been before. He had set us rules to follow, not much different really than the ones Mother gave us after he got sick, but he had administered them in a fickle way. Though we were supposed to get an allowance we always had to ask him for it and then he would give us too much because he enjoyed seeming magnanimous. Sometimes he punished us for no reason, because he was in a bad mood. He was apt to decide, as one of my sisters was going out to a dance, that she had better stay home and do something to improve herself. Or he would sweep us all up on a Wednesday night and take us ice-skating.

He changed after he learned about the cancer, and became more calm as the disease spread. He relaxed his teasing way with us, and from time to time it was possible to have a conversation with him which was not about the last thing that had made him angry. He stopped reading the paper and spent time at the window.

He and I became close. He taught me to play poker and sometimes helped me with my homework. But it wasn't his illness that drew us together. The reserve between us had begun to break down after the incident with the bear, during the drive home. Michael and my sisters were furious with him for making us leave early and wouldn't talk to him or look at him. He joked: though it had been a grisly experience we should grin and bear it—and so on. His joking seemed perverse to the others, but not to me. I had seen how terrified he was when the bear came into the camp. He had held himself so still that he had begun to tremble. When Mother started pitching rocks I thought he was going to bolt, really. I understood—I had been frightened too. The others took it as a lark after they got used to having the bear around, but for Father and me it got worse through the night. I was glad to be out of there, grateful to Father for getting me out. I saw that his jokes were how he held himself together. So I reached out to him with a joke: " 'There's a bear outside,' said Tom intently." The others turned cold looks on me. They thought I was sucking up. But Father smiled.

When I thought of other boys being close to their fathers I thought of them hunting together, tossing a ball back and forth, making birdhouses in the basement, and having long talks about girls, war, careers. Maybe the reason it took us so long to get close was that I had this idea. It kept getting in the way of what we really had, which was a shared fear.

Toward the end Father slept most of the time and I watched him. From below, sometimes, faintly, I heard Mother playing the piano. Occasionally he nodded off in his chair while I was reading to him; his bathrobe would fall open then, and I would see the long new scar on his stomach, red as blood against his white skin. His ribs all showed and his legs were like cables.

I once read in a biography of a great man that he "died well." I assume the writer meant that he kept his pain to himself, did not set off false alarms, and did not too much inconvenience those who were to stay behind. My father died well. His irritability gave way to something else, something like serenity. In the last days he became tender. It was as though he had been rehearsing the scene, that the anger of his life had been a kind of stage fright. He managed his audience—us—with an old trouper's sense of when to clown and when to stand on his dignity. We were all moved, and admired his courage, as he intended we should. He died downstairs in a shaft of late afternoon sunlight on New Year's Day, while I was reading to him. I was alone in the house and didn't know what to do. His body did not frighten me but immediately and sharply I missed my father. It seemed wrong to leave him sitting up and I tried to carry him upstairs to the bedroom but it was too hard, alone. So I called up my friend Ralphy across the street. When he came over and saw what I wanted him for he started crying but I made him help me anyway. A couple of hours later Mother got home and when I told her that Father was dead she ran upstairs, calling his name. A few minutes later she came back down. "Thank God," she said, "at least he died in bed." This seemed important to her and I didn't tell her otherwise. But that night Ralphy's parents called. They were, they said, shocked at what I had done and so was Mother when she heard the story, shocked and furious. Why? Because I had not told her the truth? Or because she had learned the truth, and could not go on believing that Father had died in bed? I really don't know.

"Mother," I said, coming into the living room, "I'm sorry about the letter. I really am."

She was arranging wood in the fireplace and did not look at me or speak for a moment. Finally she finished and straightened up and brushed her hands. She stepped back and looked at the fire she had laid. "That's all right," she said. "Not bad for a consumptive."

"Mother, I'm sorry."

"Sorry? Sorry you wrote it or sorry I found it?"

"I wasn't going to mail it. It was a sort of joke."

"Ha ha." She took up the whisk broom and swept bits of bark into the fireplace, then closed the drapes and settled on the couch. "Sit down," she said. She crossed her legs. "Listen, do I give you advice all the time?"

"Yes."

"I do?"

I nodded.

"Well, that doesn't make any difference. I'm supposed to. I'm your mother. I'm going to give you some more advice, for your own good. You don't have to make all these things up, James. They'll happen anyway." She picked at the hem of her skirt. "Do you understand what I'm saying?"

"I think so."

"You're cheating yourself, that's what I'm trying to tell you. When you get to be my age you won't know anything at all about life. All you'll know is what you've made up."

I thought about that. It seemed logical.

She went on. "I think maybe you need to get out of yourself more. Think more about other people."

The doorbell rang.

"Go see who it is," Mother said. "We'll talk about this later."

It was Dr. Murphy. He and Mother made their apologies and she insisted that he stay for dinner. I went to the kitchen to fetch ice for their drinks, and when I returned they were talking about me. I sat on the sofa and listened. Dr. Murphy was telling Mother not to worry. "James is a good boy," he said. "I've been thinking about my oldest, Terry. He's not really dishonest, you know, but he's not really honest either. I can't seem to reach him. At least James isn't furtive."

"No," Mother said, "he's never been furtive."

Dr. Murphy clasped his hands between his knees and stared at them. "Well, that's Terry. Furtive."

Before we sat down to dinner Mother said grace; Dr. Murphy bowed his head and closed his eyes and crossed himself at the end, though he had lost his faith in college. When he told me that, during one of our meetings, in just those words, I had the picture of a raincoat hanging by itself outside a dining hall. He drank a good deal of wine and persistently turned the conversation to the subject of his relationship with Terry. He admitted that he had come to dislike the boy. Then he mentioned several patients of his by name, some of them known to Mother and me, and said that he disliked them too. He used the word "dislike" with relish, like someone on a diet permitting himself a single potato chip. "I don't know what I've done wrong," he said abruptly, and with reference to no particular thing. "Then again maybe I haven't done anything wrong. I don't know what to think anymore. Nobody does."

"I know what to think," Mother said.

"So does the solipsist. How can you prove to a solipsist that he's not creating the rest of us?"

This was one of Dr. Murphy's favorite riddles, and almost any pretext was sufficient for him to trot it out. He was a child with a card trick.

"Send him to bed without dinner," Mother said. "Let him create that."

Dr. Murphy suddenly turned to me. "Why do you do it?" he asked. It was a pure question, it had no object beyond the satisfaction of his curiosity. Mother looked at me and there was the same curiosity in her face.

"I don't know," I said, and that was the truth.

Dr. Murphy nodded, not because he had anticipated my answer but because he accepted it. "Is it fun?"

"No, it's not fun. I can't explain."

"Why is it all so sad?" Mother asked. "Why all the diseases?"

"Maybe," Dr. Murphy said, "sad things are more interesting."

"Not to me," Mother said.

"Not to me, either," I said. "It just comes out that way."

After dinner Dr. Murphy asked Mother to play the piano. He particularly wanted to sing "Come Home, Abbie, the Light's on the Stair."

"That old thing," Mother said. She stood and folded her napkin deliberately and we followed her into the living room. Dr. Murphy stood behind her as she warmed up. Then they sang "Come Home, Abbie, the Light's on the Stair," and I watched him stare down at Mother intently, as if he were trying to remember something. Her own eyes were closed. After that they sang "O Magnum Mysterium." They sang it in parts and I regretted that I had no voice, it sounded so good.

"Come on, James," Dr. Murphy said as Mother played the last chords. "These old tunes not good enough for you?"

"He just can't sing," Mother said.

When Dr. Murphy left, Mother lit the fire and made more coffee. She slouched down in the big chair, sticking her legs straight out and moving her feet back and forth. "That was fun," she said.

"Did you and Father ever do things like that?"

"A few times, when we were first going out. I don't think he really enjoyed it. He was like you."

I wondered if Mother and Father had had a good marriage. He admired her and liked to look at her; every night at dinner he had us move the candlesticks slightly to right and left of center so he could see her down the length of the table. And every evening when she set the table she put them in the center again. She didn't seem to miss him very much. But I wouldn't really have known if she did, and anyway I didn't miss him all that much myself, not the way I had. Most of the time I thought about other things.

"James?"

I waited.

"I've been thinking that you might like to go down and stay with Michael for a couple of weeks or so."

"What about school?"

"I'll talk to Father McSorley. He won't mind. Maybe this problem will take care of itself if you start thinking about other people."

"I do."

"I mean helping them, like Michael does. You don't have to go if you don't want to."

"It's fine with me. Really. I'd like to see Michael."

"I'm not trying to get rid of you."

"I know."

Mother stretched, then tucked her feet under her. She sipped noisily at her coffee. "What did that word mean that Murphy used? You know the one?"

"Paranoid? That's where somebody thinks everyone is out to get him. Like that woman who always grabs you after Mass—Frances."

"Not paranoid. Everyone knows what that means. Sol-something."

"Oh. Solipsist. A solipsist is someone who thinks he creates everything around him."

Mother nodded and blew on her coffee, then put it down without drinking from it. "I'd rather be paranoid. Do you really think Frances is?"

"Of course. No question about it."

"I mean really *sick?*"

"That's what paranoid *is,* is being sick. What do you think, Mother?"

"What are you so angry about?"

"I'm not angry." I lowered my voice. "I'm not angry. But you don't believe those stories of hers, do you?"

"Well, no, not exactly. I don't think she knows what she's saying, she just wants someone to listen. She probably lives all by herself in some little room. So she's paranoid. Think of that. And I had no idea. James, we should pray for her. Will you remember to do that?"

I nodded. I thought of Mother singing "O Magnum Mysterium," saying grace, praying with easy confidence, and it came to me that her imagination was superior to mine. She could imagine things as coming together, not falling apart. She looked at me and I shrank; I knew exactly what she was going to say. "Son," she said, "do you know how much I love you?"

The next afternoon I took the bus to Los Angeles. I looked forward to the trip, to the monotony of the road and the empty fields by the roadside. Mother walked with me down the long concourse. The station was crowded and oppressive. "Are you sure this is the right bus?" she asked at the loading platform.

"Yes."

"It looks so old."

"Mother—"

"All right." She pulled me against her and kissed me, then held me an extra second to show that her embrace was sincere, not just like everyone else's, never having realized that everyone else does the same thing. I boarded the bus and we waved at each other until it became embarrassing. Then Mother began checking through her handbag for something. When she had finished I stood and adjusted the luggage over my seat. I sat and we smiled at each other, waved when the driver gunned the engine, shrugged when he got up suddenly to count the passengers, waved again when he resumed his seat. As the bus pulled out my mother and I were looking at each other with plain relief.

I had boarded the wrong bus. This one was bound for Los Angeles but not by the express route. We stopped in San Mateo, Palo Alto, San Jose, Castroville. When we left Castroville it began to rain, hard; my window would not close all the way, and a thin stream of water ran down the wall onto my seat. To keep dry I had to stay away from the wall and lean forward. The rain fell harder. The engine of the bus sounded as though it were coming apart.

In Salinas the man sleeping beside me jumped up, but before I had a chance to change seats his place was taken by an enormous woman in a print dress, carrying a shopping bag. She took possession of her seat and spilled over onto half of mine, backing me up to the wall. "That's a storm," she said loudly, then turned and looked at me. "Hungry?"

Without waiting for an answer she dipped into her bag and pulled out a piece of chicken and thrust it at me. "Hey, by God," she hooted, "look at him go to town on that drumstick!" A few people turned and smiled. I smiled back around the bone and kept at it. I finished that piece and she handed me another, and then another. Then she started handing out chicken to the people in the seats near us.

Outside of San Luis Obispo the noise from the engine grew suddenly louder and just as suddenly there was no noise at all. The driver pulled off to the side of the road and got out, then got on again dripping wet. A few moments later he announced that the bus had broken down and they were sending another bus to pick us up. Someone asked how long that might take and the driver said he had no idea. "Keep your pants on!" shouted the woman next to me. "Anybody in a hurry to get to L.A. ought to have his head examined."

The wind was blowing hard around the bus, driving sheets of rain against the windows on both sides. The bus swayed gently. Outside the light was brown and thick. The woman next to me pumped all the people around us for their itineraries and said whether or not she had ever been where they were from or where they were going. "How about you?" She slapped my knee. "Parents own a chicken ranch? I hope so!" She laughed. I told her I was from San Francisco. "San Francisco, that's where my husband was stationed." She asked me what I did there and I told her I worked with refugees from Tibet.

"Is that right? What do you do with a bunch of Tibetans?"

"Seems like there's plenty of other places they could've gone," said a man in front of us. "Coming across the border like that. We don't go there."

"What do you do with a bunch of Tibetans?" the woman repeated.

"Try to find them jobs, locate housing, listen to their problems."

"You understand that kind of talk?"

"Yes."

"Speak it?"

"Pretty well. I was born and raised in Tibet. My parents were missionaries over there."

Everyone waited.

"They were killed when the Communists took over."

The big woman patted my arm.

"It's all right," I said.

"Why don't you say some of that Tibetan?"

"What would you like to hear?"

"Say 'The cow jumped over the moon.' " She watched me, smiling, and when I finished she looked at the others and shook her head. "That was pretty. Like music. Say some more."

"What?"

"Anything."

They bent toward me. The windows suddenly went blind with rain. The driver had fallen asleep and was snoring gently to the swaying of the bus. Outside the muddy light flickered to pale yellow, and far off there was thunder. The woman next to me leaned back and closed her eyes and then so did all the others as I sang to them in what was surely an ancient and holy tongue.

Part II
EXPLORATION

FLANNERY O'CONNOR

The Enduring Chill

Asbury's train stopped so that he would get off exactly where his mother was standing waiting to meet him. Her thin spectacled face below him was bright with a wide smile that disappeared as she caught sight of him bracing himself behind the conductor. The smile vanished so suddenly, the shocked look that replaced it was so complete, that he realized for the first time that he must look as ill as he was. The sky was a chill gray and a startling white-gold sun, like some strange potentate from the east, was rising beyond the black woods that surrounded Timberboro. It cast a strange light over the single block of one-story brick and wooden shacks. Asbury felt that he was about to witness a majestic transformation, that the flat of roofs might at any moment turn into the mounting turrets of some exotic temple for a god he didn't know. The illusion lasted only a moment before his attention was drawn back to his mother.

She had given a little cry; she looked aghast. He was pleased that she should see death in his face at once. His mother, at the age of sixty, was going to be introduced to reality and he supposed that if the experience didn't kill her, it would assist her in the process of growing up. He stepped down and greeted her.

"You don't look very well," she said and gave him a long clinical stare.

"I don't feel like talking," he said at once. "I've had a bad trip."

Mrs. Fox observed that his left eye was bloodshot. He was puffy and pale and his hair had receded tragically for a boy of twenty-five. The thin reddish wedge of it left on top bore down in a point that seemed to lengthen his nose and give him an irritable expression that matched his tone of voice when he spoke to her. "It must have been cold up there," she said. "Why don't you take off your coat? It's not cold down here."

"You don't have to tell me what the temperature is!" he said in a high voice. "I'm old enough to know when I want to take my coat off!" The train glided silently away behind him, leaving a view of the twin blocks of dilapidated stores. He gazed after the aluminum speck disappearing into the woods. It seemed to him that his last connection with a larger world were vanishing forever. Then he turned and faced his mother grimly, irked that he had allowed himself, even for an instant, to see an imaginary temple in this collapsing country junction. He had become entirely accustomed to the thought of death, but he had not become accustomed to the thought of death *here*.

He had felt the end coming on for nearly four months. Alone in his freezing flat, huddled under his two blankets and his overcoat and with three thicknesses of the New York *Times* between, he had had a chill one night, followed by a violent sweat that left the sheets soaking and removed all doubt from his mind about his true condition. Before this there had been a gradual slackening of his energy and vague inconsistent aches and headaches. He had been absent so many days from his part-time job in the bookstore that he had lost it. Since then he had been living, or just barely so, on his savings and these, diminishing day by day, had been all he had between him and home. Now there was nothing. He was here.

"Where's the car?" he muttered.

"It's over yonder," his mother said. "And your sister is asleep in the back because I don't like to come out this early by myself. There's no need to wake her up."

"No," he said, "let sleeping dogs lie," and he picked up his two bulging suitcases and started across the road with them.

They were too heavy for him and by the time he reached the car, his mother saw that he was exhausted. He had never come home with two suitcases before. Ever since he had first gone away to college, he had come back every time with nothing but the necessities for a two-week stay and with a wooden resigned expression that said he was prepared to endure the visit for exactly fourteen days. "You've brought more than usual," she observed, but he did not answer.

He opened the car door and hoisted the two bags in beside his sister's upturned feet, giving first the feet—in Girl Scout shoes—and then the rest of her a revolted look of recognition. She was packed into a black suit and had a white rag around her head with metal curlers sticking out from under the edges. Her eyes were closed and her mouth open. He and she had the same features except that hers were bigger. She was eight years older than he was and was principal of the county elementary school. He shut the door softly so she wouldn't wake up and then went around and got in the front seat and closed his eyes. His mother backed the car into the road and in a few minutes he felt it swerve into the highway. Then he opened his eyes. The road stretched between two open fields of yellow bitterweed.

"Do you think Timberboro has improved?" his mother asked. This was her standard question, meant to be taken literally.

"It's still there, isn't it?" he said in an ugly voice.

"Two of the stores have new fronts," she said. Then with a sudden ferocity, she said, "You did well to come home where you can get a good doctor! I'll take you to Doctor Block this afternoon."

"I am not," he said, trying to keep his voice from shaking, "going to Doctor Block. This afternoon or ever. Don't you think if I'd wanted to go to a doctor I'd have gone up there where they have some good ones? Don't you know they have better doctors in New York?"

"He would take a personal interest in you," she said. "None of those doctors up there would take a personal interest in you."

"I don't want him taking a personal interest in me." Then after a minute, staring out across a blurred purple-looking field, he said, "What's wrong with me is way beyond Block," and his voice trailed off into a frayed sound, almost a sob.

He could not, as his friend Goetz had recommended, prepare to see it all as illusion, either what had gone before or the few weeks that were left to him. Goetz was certain that death was nothing at all. Goetz, whose whole face had always been purple-splotched with a million indignations, had returned from six months in Japan as dirty as ever but as bland as the Buddha himself. Goetz took the news of Asbury's approaching end with a calm indifference. Quoting something or other he said, "Although the Bodhisattva leads an infinite number of creatures into nirvana, in reality there are neither any Bodhisattvas to do the leading nor any creatures to be led." However, out of some feeling for his welfare, Goetz had put forth $4.50 to take him to a lecture on Vedanta. It had been a waste of his money. While Goetz had listened enthralled to the dark little man on the platform, Asbury's bored gaze had roved among the audience. It had passed over the heads of several girls in saris, past a Japanese youth, a blue-black man with a fez, and several girls who looked like secretaries. Finally, at end of the row, it had rested on a lean spectacled figure in black, a priest. The priest's expression was of a polite but strictly reserved interest. Asbury identified his own feelings immediately in the taciturn superior expression. When the lecture was over a few students met in Goetz's flat, the priest among them, but he was equally reserved. He listened with a marked politeness to the discussion of Asbury's approaching death, but he said little. A girl in a sari remarked that self-fulfillment was out of the question since it meant salvation and the word was meaningless. "Salvation," quoted Goetz, "is the destruction of a simple prejudice, and no one is saved."

"And what do you say to that?" Asbury asked the priest and returned his reserved smile over the heads of the others. The borders of this smile seemed to touch on some icy clarity.

"There is," the priest said, "a real probability of the New Man, assisted, of course," he added brittlely, "by the Third Person of the Trinity."

"Ridiculous!" the girl in the sari said, but the priest only brushed her with his smile, which was slightly amused now.

When he got up to leave, he silently handed Asbury a small card on which he had written his name, Ignatius Vogle, S.J., and an address. Perhaps, Asbury thought now, he should have used it for the priest appealed to him as a man of the world, someone who would have understood the unique tragedy of his death, a death whose meaning had been far beyond the twittering group around them. And how much more beyond Block. "What's wrong with me," he repeated, "is way beyond Block."

His mother knew at once what he meant: he meant he was going to have a nervous breakdown. She did not say a word. She did not say that this was precisely what she could have told him would happen. When people think they are smart—even when they are smart—there is nothing anybody else can say to make them see things straight, and with Asbury, the trouble was that in addition to being smart, he had an artistic temperament. She did not know where he had got it from because his father, who was a lawyer and businessman and farmer and politician all rolled into one, had certainly had his feet on the ground; and she had certainly always had hers on it. She had managed after he died to get the two of them through college and beyond; but she had observed that the more education they got, the less they could do. Their father had gone to a one-room schoolhouse through the eighth grade and he could do anything.

She could have told Asbury what would help him. She could have said, "If you would get out in the sunshine, or if you would work for a month in the dairy, you'd be a different person!" but she knew exactly how that suggestion would be received. He would be a nuisance in the dairy but she would let him work in there if he wanted to. She had let him work in there last year when he had come home and was writing the play. He had been writing a play about Negroes (why anybody would want to write a play about Negroes was beyond her) and he had said he wanted to work in the dairy with them and find out what their interests were. Their interests were in doing as little as they could get by with, as she could have told him if anybody could have told him anything. The Negroes had put up with him and he had learned to put the milkers on and once he had washed all the cans and she thought that once he had mixed feed. Then a cow had kicked him and he had not gone back to the barn again. She knew that if he would get in there now, or get out and fix fences, or do any kind of work—real work, not writing—that he might avoid this nervous breakdown. "Whatever happened to that play you were writing about the Negroes?" she asked.

"I am not writing plays," he said. "And get this through your head: I am not working in any dairy. I am not getting out in the sunshine. I'm ill. I have fever and chills and I'm dizzy and all I want you to do is to leave me alone."

"Then if you are really ill, you should see Doctor Block."

"And I am not seeing Block," he finished and ground himself down in the seat and stared intensely in front of him.

She turned into their driveway, a red road that ran for a quarter of a mile through the two front pastures. The dry cows were on one side and the milk herd on the other. She slowed the car and then stopped altogether, her attention caught by a cow with a bad quarter. "They haven't been attending to her," she said. "Look at that bag!"

Asbury turned his head abruptly in the opposite direction, but there a small, walleyed Guernsey was watching him steadily as if she sensed some bond between them. "Good God!" he cried in an agonized voice, "can't we go on? It's six o'clock in the morning!"

"Yes yes," his mother said and started the car quickly.

"What's that cry of deadly pain?" his sister drawled from the back seat. "Oh it's you," she said. "Well well, we have the artist with us again. How utterly utterly." She had a decidedly nasal voice.

He didn't answer her or turn his head. He had learned that much. Never answer her.

"Mary George!" his mother said sharply. "Asbury is sick. Leave him alone."

"What's wrong with him?" Mary George asked.

"There's the house!" his mother said as if they were all blind but her. It rose on the crest of the hill—a white two-story farmhouse with a wide porch and pleasant columns. She always approached it with a feeling of pride and she had said more than once to Asbury, "You have a home here that half those people up there would give their eyeteeth for!"

She had been once to the terrible place he lived in New York. They had gone up five flights of dark stone steps, past open garbage cans on every landing, to arrive finally at two damp rooms and a closet with a toilet in it. "You wouldn't live like this at home," she had muttered.

"No!" he'd said with an ecstatic look, "it wouldn't be possible!"

She supposed the truth was that she simply didn't understand how it felt to be sensitive or how peculiar you were when you were an artist. His sister said he was not an artist and that he had no talent and that that was the trouble with him; but Mary George was not a happy girl herself. Asbury said she posed as an intellectual but that her I.Q. couldn't be over seventy-five, that all she was really interested in was getting a man but that no sensible man would finish a first look at her. She had tried to tell him that Mary George could be very attractive when she put her mind to it and he had said that that much strain on her mind would break her down. If she were in any way attractive, he had said, she wouldn't now be principal of a county elementary school, and Mary George had said that if Asbury had had any talent, he would by now have published something. What had he ever published, she wanted to know, and for that matter, what had he ever written?

Mrs. Fox had pointed out that he was only twenty-five years old and Mary George had said that the age most people published something at was twenty-one, which made him exactly four years overdue. Mrs. Fox was not up on things like that but she suggested that he might be writing a very *long* book. Very long book, her eye, Mary George said, he would do well if he came up with so much as a poem. Mrs. Fox hoped it wasn't going to be just a poem.

She pulled the car into the side drive and a scattering of guineas exploded into the air and sailed screaming around the house. "Home again, home again jiggity jig!" she said.

"Oh God," Asbury groaned.

"The artist arrives at the gas chamber," Mary George said in her nasal voice.

He leaned on the door and got out, and forgetting his bags he moved toward the front of the house as if he were in a daze. His sister got out and stood by the car door, squinting at his bent unsteady figure. As she watched him go up the front steps, her mouth fell slack in her astonished face. "Why," she said, "there *is* something the matter with him. He looks a hundred years old."

"Didn't I tell you so?" her mother hissed. "Now you keep your mouth shut and let him alone."

He went into the house, pausing in the hall only long enough to see his pale broken face glare at him for an instant from the pier mirror. Holding onto the banister, he pulled himself up the steep stairs, across the landing and then up the shorter second flight and into his room, a large open airy room with a faded blue rug and white curtains freshly put up for his arrival. He looked at nothing, but fell face down on his own bed. It was a narrow antique bed with a high ornamental headboard on which was carved a garlanded basket overflowing with wooden fruit.

While he was still in New York, he had written a letter to his mother which filled two notebooks. He did not mean it to be read until after his death. It was such a letter as Kafka had addressed to his father. Asbury's father had died twenty years ago and Asbury considered this a great blessing. The old man, he felt sure, had been one of the courthouse gang, a rural worthy with a dirty finger in every pie and he knew he would not have been able to stomach him. He had read some of his correspondence and had been appalled by its stupidity.

He knew, of course, that his mother would not understand the letter at once. Her literal mind would require some time to discover the significance of it, but he thought she would be able to see that he forgave her for all she had done to him. For that matter, he supposed that she would realize what she had done to him only through the letter. He didn't think she was conscious of it at all. Her self-satisfaction itself was barely conscious, but because of the letter, she might experience a painful realization and this would be the only thing of value he had to leave her.

If reading it would be painful to her, writing it had sometimes been unbearable to him—for in order to face her, he had had to face himself. "I came here to escape the slave's atmosphere of home," he had written, "to find freedom, to liberate my imagination, to take it like a hawk from its cage and set it 'whirling off into the widening gyre' (Yeats) and what did I find? It was incapable of flight. It was some bird you had domesticated, sitting huffy in its pen, refusing to come out!" The next words were underscored twice. "I have no imagination. I have no talent. I can't create. I have nothing but the desire for these things. Why didn't you kill that too? Woman, why did you pinion me?"

Writing this, he had reached the pit of despair and he thought that reading it, she would at least begin to sense his tragedy and her part in it. It was not that she had ever forced her way on him. That had never been necessary. Her way had simply been the air he breathed and when at last he had found other air, he couldn't survive in it. He felt that even if she didn't understand at once, the letter would leave her with an enduring chill and perhaps in time lead her to see herself as she was.

He had destroyed everything else he had ever written—his two lifeless novels, his half-dozen stationary plays, his prosy poems, his sketchy short stories—and kept only the two notebooks that contained the letter. They were in the black suitcase that his sister, huffing and blowing, was now dragging up the second flight of stairs. His mother was carrying the smaller bag and came on ahead. He turned over as she entered the room.

"I'll open this and get out your things," she said, "and you can go right to bed and in a few minutes I'll bring your breakfast."

He sat up and said in a fretful voice, "I don't want any breakfast and I can open my own suitcase. Leave that alone."

His sister arrived in the door, her face full of curiosity, and let the black bag fall with a thud over the doorsill. Then she began to push it across the room with her foot until she was close enough to get a good look at him. "If I looked as bad as you do," she said, "I'd go to the hospital."

Her mother cut her eyes sharply at her and she left. Then Mrs. Fox closed the door and came to the bed and sat down on it beside him. "Now this time I want you to make a long visit and rest," she said.

"This visit," he said, "will be permanent."

"Wonderful!" she cried. "You can have a little studio in your room and in the mornings you can write plays and in the afternoons you can help in the dairy!"

He turned a white wooden face to her. "Close the blinds and let me sleep," he said.

When she was gone, he lay for some time staring at the water stains on the gray walls. Descending from the top molding, long icicle shapes had been etched by leaks and, directly over his bed on the ceiling, another leak had made a fierce bird with spread wings. It had an icicle crosswise in its beak and there were smaller icicles depending from its wings and tail. It had been there since his childhood and had always irritated him and sometimes had frightened him. He had often had the illusion that it was in motion and about to descend mysteriously and set the icicle on his head. He closed his eyes and thought: I won't have to look at it for many more days. And presently he went to sleep.

When he woke up in the afternoon, there was a pink openmouthed face hanging over him and from two large familiar ears on either side of it the black tubes of Block's stethoscope extended down to his exposed chest. The doctor, seeing he was awake, made a face like a Chinaman, rolled his eyes almost out of his head and cried, "Say AHHHH!"

Block was irresistible to children. For miles around they vomited and went into fevers to have a visit from him. Mrs. Fox was standing behind him, smiling radiantly. "Here's Doctor Block!" she said as if she had captured this angel on the rooftop and brought him in for her little boy.

"Get him out of here," Asbury muttered. He looked at the asinine face from what seemed the bottom of a black hole.

The doctor peered closer, wiggling his ears. Block was bald and had a round face as senseless as a baby's. Nothing about him indicated intelligence except two cold clinical nickel-colored eyes that hung with a motionless curiosity over whatever he looked at. "You sho do look bad, Azzberry," he murmured. He took the stethoscope off and dropped it in his bag. "I don't know when I've seen anybody your age look as sorry as you do. What you been doing to yourself?"

There was a continuous thud in the back of Asbury's head as if his heart had got trapped in it and was fighting to get out. "I didn't send for you," he said.

Block put his hand on the glaring face and pulled the eyelid down and peered into it. "You must have been on the bum up there," he said.

He began to press his hand in the small of Asbury's back. "I went up there once myself," he said, "and saw exactly how little they had and came straight on back home. Open your mouth."

Asbury opened it automatically and the drill-like gaze swung over it and bore down. He snapped it shut and in a wheezing breathless voice he said, "If I'd wanted a doctor, I'd have stayed up there where I could have got a good one!"

"Asbury!" his mother said.

"How long you been having the so' throat?" Block asked.

"She sent for you!" Asbury said. "She can answer the questions."

"Asbury!" his mother said.

Block leaned over his bag and pulled out a rubber tube. He pushed Asbury's sleeve up and tied the tube around his upper arm. Then he took out a syringe and prepared to find the vein, humming a hymn as he pressed the needle in. Asbury lay with a rigid outraged stare while the privacy of his blood was invaded by this idiot. "Slowly Lord but sure," Block sang in a murmuring voice, "Oh slowly Lord but sure." When the syringe was full, he withdrew the needle. "Blood don't lie," he said. He poured it in a bottle and stopped it up and put the bottle in his bag. "Azzbury," he started, "how long . . ."

Asbury sat up and thrust his thudding head forward and said, "I didn't send for you. I'm not answering any questions. You're not my doctor. What's wrong with me is way beyond you."

"Most things are beyond me," Block said. "I ain't found anything yet that I thoroughly understood," and he sighed and got up. His eyes seemed to glitter at Asbury as if from a great distance.

"He wouldn't act so ugly," Mrs. Fox explained, "if he weren't really sick. And *I* want you to come back every day until you get him well."

Asbury's eyes were a fierce glaring violet. "What's wrong with me is way beyond you," he repeated and lay back down and closed his eyes until Block and his mother were gone.

In the next few days, though he grew rapidly worse, his mind functioned with a terrible clarity. On the point of death, he found himself existing in a state of illumination that was totally out of keeping with the kind of talk he had to listen to from his mother. This was largely about cows with names like Daisy and Bessie Button and their intimate functions—their mastitis and their screwworms and their abortions. His mother insisted that in the middle of the day he get out and sit on the porch and "enjoy the view" and as resistance was too much of a struggle, he dragged himself out and sat there in a rigid slouch, his feet wrapped in an afghan and his hands gripped on the chair arms as if he were about to spring forward into the glaring china blue sky. The lawn extended for a quarter of an acre down to a barbed-wire fence that divided it from the front pasture. In the middle of the day the dry cows rested there under a line of sweetgum trees. On the other side of the road were two hills with a pond between and his mother could sit on the porch and watch the herd walk across the dam to the hill on the other side. The whole scene was rimmed by a wall of trees which, at the time of day he was forced to sit there, was a washed-out blue that reminded him sadly of the Negroes' faded overalls.

He listened irritably while his mother detailed the faults of the help. "Those two are not stupid," she said. "They know how to look out for themselves."

"They need to," he muttered, but there was no use to argue with her. Last year he had been writing a play about the Negro and he had wanted to be around them for a while to see how they really felt about their condition, but the two who worked for her had lost all their initiative over the years. They didn't talk. The one called Morgan was light brown, part Indian; the other, older one, Randall, was very black and fat. When they said anything to him, it was as if they were speaking to an invisible body located to the right or left of where he actually was, and after two days working side by side with them, he felt he had not established rapport. He decided to try something bolder than talk and one afternoon as he was standing near Randall, watching him adjust a milker, he had quietly taken out his cigarettes and lit one. The Negro had stopped what he was doing and watched him. He waited until Asbury had taken two draws and then he said, "She don't 'low no smoking in here."

The other one approached and stood there, grinning.

"I know it," Asbury said and after a deliberate pause, he shook the package and held it out, first to Randall, who took one, and then to Morgan, who took one. He had then lit the cigarettes for them himself and the three of them had stood there smoking. There were no sounds but the steady click of the two milking machines and the occasional slap of a cow's tail against her side. It was one of those moments of communion when the difference between black and white is absorbed into nothing.

The next day two cans of milk had been returned from the creamery because it had absorbed the odor of tobacco. He took the blame and told his mother that it was he and not the Negroes who had been smoking. "If you were doing it, they were doing it," she had said. "Don't you think I know those two?" She was incapable of thinking them innocent; but the experience had so exhilarated him that he had been determined to repeat it in some other way.

The next afternoon when he and Randall were in the milk house pouring the fresh milk into the cans, he had picked up the jelly glass the Negroes drank out of and, inspired, had poured himself a glassful of the warm milk and drained it down. Randall had stopped pouring and had remained, half-bent, over the can, watching him. "She don't 'low that," he said. "That *the* thing she don't 'low."

Asbury poured out another glassful and handed it to him.

"She don't 'low it," he repeated.

"Listen," Asbury said hoarsely, "the world is changing. There's no reason I shouldn't drink after you or you after me!"

"She don't 'low noner us to drink noner this here milk," Randall said.

Asbury continued to hold the glass out to him. "You took the cigarette," he said. "Take the milk. It's not going to hurt my mother to lose two or three glasses of milk a day. We've got to think free if we want to live free!"

The other one had come up and was standing in the door.

"Don't want noner that milk," Randall said.

Asbury swung around and held the glass out to Morgan. "Here, boy, have a drink of this," he said.

Morgan stared at him; then his face took on a decided look of cunning. "I ain't seen you drink none of it yourself," he said.

Asbury despised milk. The first warm glassful had turned his stomach. He drank half of what he was holding and handed the rest to the Negro, who took it and gazed down inside the glass as if it contained some great mystery; then he set it on the floor by the cooler.

"Don't you like milk?" Asbury asked.

"I likes it but I ain't drinking noner that."

"Why?"

"She don't 'low it," Morgan said.

"My God!" Asbury exploded, "she she she!" He had tried the same thing the next day and the next and the next but he could not get them to drink the milk. A few afternoons later when he was standing outside the milk house about to go in, he heard Morgan ask, "Howcome you let him drink that milk every day?"

"What he do is him," Randall said. "What I do is me."

"Howcome he talks so ugly about his ma?"

"She ain't whup him enough when he was little," Randall said.

The insufferableness of life at home had overcome him and he had returned to New York two days early. So far as he was concerned he had died there, and the question now was how long he could stand to linger here. He could have hastened his end but suicide would not have been a victory. Death was coming to him legitimately, as a justification, as a gift from life. That was his greatest triumph. Then too, to the fine minds of the neighborhood, a suicide son would indicate a mother who had been a failure, and while this was the case, he felt that it was a public embarrassment he could spare her. What she would learn from the letter would be a private revelation. He had sealed the notebooks in a manila envelope and had written on it: "To be opened only after the death of Asbury Porter Fox." He had put the envelope in the desk drawer in his room and locked it and the key was in his pajama pocket until he could decide on a place to leave it.

When they sat on the porch in the morning, his mother felt that some of the time she should talk about subjects that were of interest to him. The third morning she started in on his writing. "When you get well," she said, "I think it would be nice if you wrote a book about down here. We need another good book like *Gone With the Wind.*"

He could feel the muscles in his stomach begin to tighten.

"Put the war in it," she advised. "That always makes a long book."

He put his head back gently as if he were afraid it would crack. After a moment he said, "I am not going to write any book."

"Well," she said, "if you don't feel like writing a book, you could just write poems. They're nice." She realized that what he needed was someone intellectual to talk to, but Mary George was the only intellectual she knew and he would not talk to her. She had thought of Mr. Bush, the retired Methodist minister, but she had not brought this up. Now she decided to hazard it. "I think I'll ask Dr. Bush to come to see you," she said, raising Mr. Bush's rank. "You'd enjoy him. He collects rare coins."

She was not prepared for the reaction she got. He began to shake all over and give loud spasmodic laughs. He seemed about to choke. After a minute he subsided into a cough. "If you think I need spiritual aid to die," he said, "you're quite mistaken. And certainly not from that ass Bush. My God!"

"I didn't mean that at all," she said. "He has coins dating from the time of Cleopatra."

"Well if you ask him here, I'll tell him to go to hell," he said. "Bush! That beats all!"

"I'm glad something amuses you," she said acidly.

For a time they sat there in silence. Then his mother looked up. He was sitting forward again and smiling at her. His face was brightening more and more as if he had just had an idea that was brilliant. She stared at him. "I'll tell you who I want to come," he said. For the first time since he had come home, his expression was pleasant; though there was also, she thought, a kind of crafty look about him.

"Who do you want to come?" she asked suspiciously.

"I want a priest," he announced.

"A priest?" his mother said in an uncomprehending voice.

"Preferably a Jesuit," he said, brightening more and more. "Yes, by all means a Jesuit. They have them in the city. You can call up and get me one."

"What is the matter with you?" his mother asked.

"Most of them are very well-educated," he said, "but Jesuits are foolproof. A Jesuit would be able to discuss something besides the weather." Already, remembering Ignatius Vogle, S.J., he could picture the priest. This one would be a trifle more worldly perhaps, a trifle more cynical. Protected by their ancient institution, priests could afford to be cynical, to play both ends against the middle. He would talk to a man of culture before he died—even in this desert! Furthermore, nothing would irritate his mother so much. He could not understand why he had not thought of this sooner.

"You're not a member of that church," Mrs. Fox said shortly. "It's twenty miles away. They wouldn't send one." She hoped that this would end the matter.

He sat back absorbed in the idea, determined to force her to make the call since she always did what he wanted if he kept at her. "I'm dying," he said, "and I haven't asked you to do but one thing and you refuse me that."

"You are NOT dying."

"When you realize it," he said, "it'll be too late."

There was another unpleasant silence. Presently his mother said, "Nowadays doctors don't *let* young people die. They give them some of these new medicines." She began shaking her foot with a nerve-rattling assurance. "People just don't die like they used to," she said.

"Mother," he said, "you ought to be prepared. I think even Block knows and hasn't told you yet." Block, after the first visit, had come in grimly every time, without his jokes and funny faces, and had taken his blood in silence, his nickel-colored eyes unfriendly. He was, by definition, the enemy of death and he looked now as if he knew he was battling the real thing. He had said he wouldn't prescribe until he knew what was wrong and Asbury had laughed in his face. "Mother," he said, "I AM going to die," and he tried to make each word like a hammer blow on top of her head.

She paled slightly but she did not blink. "Do you think for one minute," she said angrily, "that I intend to sit here and let you die?" Her eyes were as hard as two old mountain ranges seen in the distance. He felt the first distinct stroke of doubt.

"Do you?" she asked fiercely.

"I don't think you have anything to do with it," he said in a shaken voice.

"Humph," she said and got up and left the porch as if she could not stand to be around such stupidity an instant longer.

Forgetting the Jesuit, he went rapidly over his symptoms: his fever had increased, interspersed by chills; he barely had the energy to drag himself out on the porch; food was abhorrent to him; and Block had not been able to give her the least satisfaction. Even as he sat there, he felt the beginning of a new chill, as if death were already playfully rattling his bones. He pulled the afghan off his feet and put it around his shoulders and made his way unsteadily up the stairs to bed.

He continued to grow worse. In the next few days he became so much weaker and badgered her so constantly about the Jesuit that finally in desperation she decided to humor his foolishness. She made the call, explaining in a chilly voice that her son was ill, perhaps a little out of his head, and wished to speak to a priest. While she made the call, Asbury hung over the banisters, barefooted, with the afghan around him, and listened. When she hung up he called down to know when the priest was coming.

"Tomorrow sometime," his mother said irritably.

He could tell by the fact that she made the call that her assurance was beginning to shatter. Whenever she let Block in or out, there was much whispering in the downstairs hall. That evening, he heard her and Mary George talking in low voices in the parlor. He thought he heard his name and he got up and tiptoed into the hall and down the first three steps until he could hear the voices distinctly.

"I had to call that priest," his mother was saying. "I'm afraid this is serious. I thought it was just a nervous breakdown but now I think it's something real. Doctor Block thinks it's something real too and whatever it is is worse because he's so run-down."

"Grow up, Mamma," Mary George said, "I've told you and I tell you again: what's wrong with him is purely psychosomatic." There was nothing she was not an expert on.

"No," his mother said, "it's a real disease. The doctor says so." He thought he detected a crack in her voice.

"Block is an idiot," Mary George said. "You've got to face the facts: Asbury can't write so he gets sick. He's going to be an invalid instead of an artist. Do you know what he needs?"

"No," his mother said.

"Two or three shock treatments," Mary George said. "Get that artist business out of his head once and for all."

His mother gave a little cry and he grasped the banister.

"Mark my words," his sister continued, "all he's going to be around here for the next fifty years is a decoration."

He went back to bed. In a sense she was right. He had failed his god, Art, but he had been a faithful servant and Art was sending him Death. He had seen this from the first with a kind of mystical clarity. He went to sleep thinking of the peaceful spot in the family burying ground where he would soon lie, and after a while he saw that his body was being borne slowly toward it while his mother and Mary George watched without interest from their chairs on the porch. As the bier was carried across the dam, they could look up and see the procession reflected upside down in the pond. A lean dark figure in a Roman collar followed it. He had a mysteriously saturnine face in which there was a subtle blend of asceticism and corruption. Asbury was laid in a shallow grave on the hillside and the indistinct mourners, after standing in silence for a while, spread out over the darkening green. The Jesuit retired to a spot beneath a dead tree to smoke and meditate. The moon came up and Asbury was aware of a presence bending over him and a gentle warmth on his cold face. He knew that this was Art come to wake him and he sat up and opened his eyes. Across the hill all the lights were on in his mother's house. The black pond was speckled with little nickel-colored stars. The Jesuit had disappeared. All around him the cows were spread out grazing in the moonlight and one large white one, violently spotted, was softly licking his head as if it were a block of salt. He awoke with a shudder and discovered that his bed was soaking from a night sweat and as he sat shivering in the dark, he realized that the end was not many days distant. He gazed down into the crater of death and fell back dizzy on his pillow.

The next day his mother noted something almost ethereal about his ravaged face. He looked like one of those dying children who must have Christmas early. He sat up in the bed and directed the rearrangement of several chairs and had her remove a picture of a maiden chained to a rock for he knew it would make the Jesuit smile. He had the comfortable rocker taken away and when he finished, the room with its severe wall stains had a certain cell-like quality. He felt it would be attractive to the visitor.

All morning he waited, looking irritably up at the ceiling where the bird with the icicle in its beak seemed poised and waiting too; but the priest did not arrive until late in the afternoon. As soon as his mother opened the door, a loud unintelligible voice began to boom in the downstairs hall. Asbury's heart beat wildly. In a second there was a heavy creaking on the stairs. Then almost at once his mother, her expression constrained, came in followed by a massive old man who plowed straight across the room, picked up a chair by the side of the bed and put it under himself.

"I'm Father Finn—from Purrgatory," he said in a hearty voice. He had a large red face, a stiff brush of gray hair and was blind in one eye, but the good eye, blue and clear, was focused sharply on Asbury. There was a grease spot on his vest. "So you want to talk to a priest?" he said. "Very wise. None of us knows the hour Our Blessed Lord may call us." Then he cocked his good eye up at Asbury's mother and said, "Thank you, you may leave us now."

Mrs. Fox stiffened and did not budge.

"I'd like to talk to Father Finn alone," Asbury said, feeling suddenly that here he had an ally, although he had not expected a priest like this one. His mother gave him a disgusted look and left the room. He knew she would go no farther than just outside the door.

"It's so nice to have you come," Asbury said. "This place is incredibly dreary. There's no one here an intelligent person can talk to. I wonder what you think of Joyce, Father?"

The priest lifted his chair and pushed closer. "You'll have to shout," he said. "Blind in one eye and deaf in one ear."

"What do you think of Joyce?" Asbury said louder.

"Joyce? Joyce who?" asked the priest.

"James Joyce," Asbury said and laughed.

The priest brushed his huge hand in the air as if he were bothered by gnats. "I haven't met him," he said. "Now. Do you say your morning and night prayers?"

Asbury appeared confused. "Joyce was a great writer," he murmured, forgetting to shout.

"You don't eh?" said the priest. "Well you will never learn to be good unless you pray regularly. You cannot love Jesus unless you speak to Him."

"The myth of the dying god has always fascinated me," Asbury shouted, but the priest did not appear to catch it.

"Do you have trouble with purity?" he demanded, and as Asbury paled, he went on without waiting for an answer. "We all do but you must pray to the Holy Ghost for it. Mind, heart and body. Nothing is overcome without prayer. Pray with your family. Do you pray with your family?"

"God forbid," Asbury murmured. "My mother doesn't have time to pray and my sister is an atheist," he shouted.

"A shame!" said the priest. "Then you must pray for them."

"The artist prays by creating," Asbury ventured.

"Not enough!" snapped the priest. "If you do not pray daily, you are neglecting your immortal soul. Do you know your catechism?"

"Certainly not," Asbury muttered.

"Who made you?" the priest asked in a martial tone.

"Different people believe different things about that," Asbury said.

"God made you," the priest said shortly. "Who is God?"

"God is an idea created by man," Asbury said, feeling that he was getting into stride, that two could play at this.

"God is a spirit infinitely perfect," the priest said. "You are a very ignorant boy. Why did God make you?"

"God didn't . . ."

"God made you to know Him, to love Him, to serve Him in this world and to be happy with Him in the next!" the old priest said in a battering voice. "If you don't apply yourself to the catechism how do you expect to know how to save your immortal soul?"

Asbury saw he had made a mistake and that it was time to get rid of the old fool. "Listen," he said, "I'm not a Roman."

"A poor excuse for not saying your prayers!" the old man snorted.

Asbury slumped slightly in the bed. "I'm dying," he shouted.

"But you're not dead yet!" said the priest, "and how do you expect to meet God face to face when you've never spoken to Him? How do you expect to get what you don't ask for? God does not send the Holy Ghost to those who don't ask for Him. Ask Him to send the Holy Ghost."

"The Holy Ghost?" Asbury said.

"Are you so ignorant you've never heard of the Holy Ghost?" the priest asked.

"Certainly I've heard of the Holy Ghost," Asbury said furiously, "and the Holy Ghost is the last thing I'm looking for!"

"And He may be the last thing you get," the priest said, his one fierce eye inflamed. "Do you want your soul to suffer eternal damnation? Do you want to be deprived of God for all eternity? Do you want to suffer the most terrible pain, greater than fire, the pain of loss? Do you want to suffer the pain of loss for all eternity?"

Asbury moved his arms and legs helplessly as if he were pinned to the bed by the terrible eye.

"How can the Holy Ghost fill your soul when it's full of trash?" the priest roared. "The Holy Ghost will not come until you see yourself as you are—a lazy ignorant conceited youth!" he said, pounding his fist on the little bedside table.

Mrs. Fox burst in. "Enough of this!" she cried. "How dare you talk that way to a poor sick boy? You're upsetting him. You'll have to go."

"The poor lad doesn't even know his catechism," the priest said, rising. "I should think you would have taught him to say his daily prayers. You have neglected your duty as his mother." He turned back to the bed and said affably, "I'll give you my blessing and after this you must say your daily prayers without fail," whereupon he put his hand on Asbury's head and rumbled something in Latin. "Call me any time," he said, "and we can have another little chat," and then he followed Mrs. Fox's rigid back out. The last thing Asbury heard him say was, "He's a good lad at heart but very ignorant."

When his mother had got rid of the priest she came rapidly up the steps again to say that she had told him so, but when she saw him, pale and drawn and ravaged, sitting up in his bed, staring in front of him with large childish shocked eyes, she did not have the heart and went rapidly out again.

The next morning he was so weak that she made up her mind he must go to the hospital. "I'm not going to any hospital," he kept repeating, turning his thudding head from side to side as if he wanted to work it loose from his body. "I'm not going to any hospital as long as I'm conscious." He was thinking bitterly that once he lost consciousness, she could drag him off to the hospital and fill him full of blood and prolong his misery for days. He was convinced that the end was approaching, that it would be today, and he was tormented now thinking of his useless life. He felt as if he were a shell that had to be filled with something but he did not know what. He began to take note of everything in the room as if for the last time—the ridiculous antique furniture, the pattern in the rug, the silly picture his mother had replaced. He even looked at the fierce bird with the icicle in its beak and felt that it was there for some purpose that he could not divine.

There was something he was searching for, something that he felt he must have, some last significant culminating experience that he must make for himself before he died—make for himself out of his own intelligence. He had always relied on himself and had never been a sniveler after the ineffable.

Once when Mary George was thirteen and he was five, she had lured him with the promise of an unnamed present into a large tent full of people and had dragged him backwards up to the front where a man in a blue suit and red and white tie was standing. "Here," she said in a loud voice. "I'm already saved but you can save him. He's a real stinker and too big for his britches." He had broken her grip and shot out of there like a small cur and later when he had asked for his present, she had said, "You would have got Salvation if you had waited for it but since you acted the way you did, you get nothing!"

As the day wore on, he grew more and more frantic for fear he would die without making some last meaningful experience for himself. His mother sat anxiously by the side of the bed. She had called Block twice and could not get him. He thought even now she had not realized that he was going to die, much less that the end was only hours off.

The light in the room was beginning to have an odd quality, almost as if it were taking on presence. In a darkened form it entered and seemed to wait. Outside it appeared to move no farther than the edge of the faded treeline, which he could see a few inches over the sill of his window. Suddenly he thought of that experience of communion that he had had in the dairy with the Negroes when they had smoked together, and at once he began to tremble with excitement. They would smoke together one last time.

After a moment, turning his head on the pillow, he said, "Mother, I want to tell the Negroes good-bye."

His mother paled. For an instant her face seemed about to fly apart. Then the line of her mouth hardened; her brows drew together. "Good-bye?" she said in a flat voice. "Where are you going?"

For a few seconds he only looked at her. Then he said, "I think you know. Get them. I don't have long."

"This is absurd," she muttered but she got up and hurried out. He heard her try to reach Block again before she went outside. He thought her clinging to Block at a time like this was touching and pathetic. He waited, preparing himself for the encounter as a religious man might prepare himself for the last sacrament. Presently he heard their steps on the stair.

"Here's Randall and Morgan," his mother said, ushering them in. "They've come to tell you hello."

The two of them came in grinning and shuffled to the side of the bed. They stood there, Randall in front and Morgan behind. "You sho do look well," Randall said. "You looks very well."

"You looks well," the other one said. "Yessuh, you looks fine."

"I ain't ever seen you looking so well before," Randall said.

"Yes, doesn't he look well?" his mother said. "I think he looks just fine."

"Yessuh," Randall said, "I speck you ain't even sick."

"Mother," Asbury said in a forced voice. "I'd like to talk to them alone."

His mother stiffened; then she marched out. She walked across the hall and into the room on the other side and sat down. Through the open doors he could see her begin to rock in little short jerks. The two Negroes looked as if their last protection had dropped away.

Asbury's head was so heavy he could not think what he had been going to do. "I'm dying," he said.

Both their grins became gelid. "You looks fine," Randall said.

"I'm going to die," Asbury repeated. Then with relief he remembered that they were going to smoke together. He reached for the package on the table and held it out to Randall, forgetting to shake out the cigarettes.

The Negro took the package and put it in his pocket. "I thank you," he said. "I certainly do prechate it."

Asbury stared as if he had forgotten again. After a second he became aware that the other Negro's face had turned infinitely sad; then he realized that it was not sad but sullen. He fumbled in the drawer of the table and pulled out an unopened package and thrust it at Morgan.

"I thanks you, Mist Asbury," Morgan said, brightening. "You certly does look well."

"I'm about to die," Asbury said irritably.

"You looks fine," Randall said.

"You be up and around in a few days," Morgan predicted. Neither of them seemed to find a suitable place to rest his gaze. Asbury looked wildly across the hall where his mother had her rocker turned so that her back faced him. It was apparent she had no intention of getting rid of them for him.

"I speck you might have a little cold," Randall said after a time.

"I takes a little turpentine and sugar when I has a cold," Morgan said.

"Shut your mouth," Randall said, turning on him.

"Shut your own mouth," Morgan said. "I know what I takes."

"He don't take what you take," Randall growled.

"Mother!" Asbury called in a shaking voice.

His mother stood up. "Mister Asbury has had company long enough now," she called. "You all can come back tomorrow."

"We be going," Randall said. "You sho do look well."

"You sho does," Morgan said.

They filed out agreeing with each other how well he looked but Asbury's vision became blurred before they reached the hall. For an instant he saw his mother's form as if it were a shadow in the door and then it disappeared after them down the stairs. He heard her call Block again but he heard it without interest. His head was spinning. He knew now there would be no significant experience before he died. There was nothing more to do but give her the key to the drawer where the letter was, and wait for the end.

He sank into a heavy sleep from which he awoke about five o'clock to see her white face, very small, at the end of a well of darkness. He took the key out of his pajama pocket and handed it to her and mumbled that there was a letter in the desk to be opened when he was gone, but she did not seem to understand. She put the key down on the bedside table and left it there and he returned to his dream in which two large boulders were circling each other inside his head.

He awoke a little after six to hear Block's car stop below in the driveway. The sound was like a summons, bringing him rapidly and with a clear head out of his sleep. He had a sudden terrible foreboding that the fate awaiting him was going to be more shattering than any he could have reckoned on. He lay absolutely motionless, as still as an animal the instant before an earthquake.

Block and his mother talked as they came up the stairs but he did not distinguish their words. The doctor came in making faces; his mother was smiling. "Guess what you've got, Sugarpie!" she cried. Her voice broke in on him with the force of a gunshot.

"Found theter ol' bug, did ol' Block," Block said, sinking down into the chair by the bed. He raised his hands over his head in the gesture of a victorious prizefighter and let them collapse in his lap as if the effort had exhausted him. Then he removed a red bandanna handkerchief that he carried to be funny with and wiped his face thoroughly, having a different expression on it every time it appeared from behind the rag.

"I think you're just as smart as you can be!" Mrs. Fox said. "Asbury," she said, "you have undulant fever. It'll keep coming back but it won't kill you!" Her smile was as bright and intense as a lightbulb without a shade. "I'm so relieved," she said.

Asbury sat up slowly, his face expressionless; then he fell back down again.

Block leaned over him and smiled. "You ain't going to die," he said, with deep satisfaction.

Nothing about Asbury stirred except his eyes. They did not appear to move on the surface but somewhere in their blurred depths there was an almost imperceptible motion as if something were struggling feebly. Block's gaze seemed to reach down like a steel pin and hold whatever it was until the life was out of it. "Undulant fever ain't so bad, Azzberry," he murmured. "It's the same as Bang's in a cow."

The boy gave a low moan and then was quiet.

"He must have drunk some unpasteurized milk up there," his mother said softly and then the two of them tiptoed out as if they thought he were about to go to sleep.

When the sound of their footsteps had faded on the stairs, Asbury sat up again. He turned his head, almost surreptitiously, to the side where the key he had given his mother was lying on the bedside table. His hand shot out and closed over it and returned it to his pocket. He glanced across the room into the small oval-framed dresser mirror. The eyes that stared back at him were the same that had returned his gaze every day from that mirror but it seemed to him that they were paler. They looked shocked clean as if they had been prepared for some awful vision about to come down on him. He shuddered and turned his head quickly the other way and stared out the window. A blinding red-gold sun moved serenely from under a purple cloud. Below it the treeline was black against the crimson sky. It formed a brittle wall, standing as if it were the frail defense he had set up in his mind to protect him from what was coming. The boy fell back on his pillow and stared at the ceiling. His limbs that had been racked for so many weeks by fever and chill were numb now. The old life in him was exhausted. He awaited the coming of new. It was then that he felt the beginning of a chill, a chill so peculiar, so light, that it was like a warm ripple across a deeper sea of cold. His breath came short. The fierce bird which through the years of his childhood and the days of his illness had been poised over his head, waiting mysteriously, appeared all at once to be in motion. Asbury blanched and the last film of illusion was torn as if by a whirlwind from his eyes. He saw that for the rest of his days, frail, racked, but enduring, he would live in the face of a purifying terror. A feeble cry, a last impossible protest escaped him. But the Holy Ghost, emblazoned in ice instead of fire, continued, implacable, to descend.

STUART DYBEK

Hot Ice

SAINTS

The saint, a virgin, was incorrupted. She had been frozen in a block of ice many years ago.

Her father had found her half-naked body floating face down among water lilies, her blond hair fanning at the marshy edge of the overgrown duck pond people still referred to as the Douglas Park Lagoon.

That's how Eddie Kapusta had heard it.

Douglas Park was a black park now, the lagoon curdled in milky green scum as if it had soured, and Kapusta didn't doubt that were he to go there they'd find his body floating in the lily pads too. But sometimes in winter, riding by on the California Avenue bus, the park flocked white, deserted, and the lagoon frozen over, Eddie could almost picture what it had been like back then: swans gliding around the small, wooded island at the center, and rowboats plying into sunlight from the gaping stone tunnels of the haunted-looking boathouse.

The girl had gone rowing with a couple of guys—some said they were sailors, neighborhood kids going off to the war—nobody ever said who exactly or why she went with them, as if it didn't matter. They rowed her around to the blind side of the little island. Nobody knew what happened there either. It was necessary for each person to imagine it for himself.

They were only joking at first was how Kapusta imagined it, laughing at her broken English, telling her be friendly or swim home. One of them stroked her hair, gently undid her bun, and as her hair fell cascad-

ing over her shoulders surprising them all, the other reached too suddenly for the buttons on her blouse; she tore away so hard the boat
rocked violently, her slip and bra split, breasts sprung loose, she dove.
Even the suddenness was slow motion the way Kapusta imagined it.
But once they were in the water the rest went through his mind in a
flash—the boat capsizing, the sailors thrashing for the little island, and
the girl struggling alone in that sepia water too warm from summer,
just barely deep enough for bullheads, with a mud bottom kids said was
quicksand exploding into darkness with each kick. He didn't want to
wonder what she remembered. His mind raced over that to her father
wading out into cattails, scooping her half-naked and still limp from the
resisting water lilies, and running with her in his arms across the park
crying in Polish or Slovak or Bohemian, whatever they were, and riding
with her on the streetcar he wouldn't let stop until it reached the ice
house he owned, where crazy with grief he sealed her in ice.

"I believe it up to the part about the streetcar," Manny Santora said
that summer when they told each other such stories, talking often about
things Manny called *weirdness,* while pitching quarters in front of Buddy's Bar. "I don't believe he hijacked no streetcar, man."

"What you think, man, he called a cab?" Pancho, Manny's older
brother asked, winking at Eddie like he'd scored.

Every time they talked like this Manny and Pancho argued. Pancho
believed in everything—ghosts, astrology, legends. His nickname was
Padrecito which went back to his days as an altar boy when he would
dress up as a priest and hold mass in the backyard with hosts punched
with bottle caps from stale tortillas and real wine he'd collected from
bottles the winos had left on doorstoops. Eddie's nickname was Edwardo, though the only person who called him that was Manny, who
had made it up. Manny wasn't the kind of guy to have a nickname—he
was Manny or Santora.

Pancho believed if you played certain rock songs backwards you'd
hear secret messages from the devil. He believed in devils and angels.
He still believed he had a guardian angel. It was something like being
lucky, like making the sign of the cross before you stepped in the bat-
ter's box. "It's why I don't get caught even when I'm caught," he'd say
when the cops would catch him dealing and not take him in. Pancho
believed in saints. For a while he had even belonged to a gang called the
Saints. They'd tried to recruit Manny too, who, though younger, was

tougher than Pancho, but Manny had no use for gangs. "I already belong to the Loners," he said.

Pancho believed in the girl in ice. In sixth grade, Sister Joachim, the ancient nun in charge of the altar boys, had told him the girl should be canonized and that she'd secretly written to the Pope informing him that already there had been miracles and cures. "All the martyrs didn't die in Rome," she'd told Pancho. "They're still suffering today in China and Russia and Korea and even here in your own neighborhood." Like all nuns she loved Pancho. Dressed in his surplice and cassock he looked as if he should be beatified himself, a young St. Sebastian or Juan de la Cruz, the only altar boy in the history of the parish to spend his money on different-colored gym shoes so they would match the priest's vestments—red for martyrs, white for Feast Days, black for requiems. The nuns knew he punished himself during Lent, offering up his pain for the Poor Souls in Purgatory.

Their love for Pancho had made things impossible for Manny in the Catholic school. He seemed Pancho's opposite in almost every way and dropped out after they'd held him back in sixth grade. He switched to public school, but mostly he hung out on the streets.

"I believe she worked miracles right in this neighborhood, man," Pancho said.

"Bullshit, man. Like what miracles?" Manny wanted to know.

"Okay, man, you know Big Antek," Pancho said.

"Big Antek the wino?"

They all knew Big Antek. He bought them beer. He'd been a butcher in every meat market in the neighborhood, but drunkenly kept hacking off pieces of his hands, and finally quit completely to become a full-time alky.

Big Antek had told Pancho about Kedzie Avenue when it was still mostly people from the Old Country and he had gotten a job at a Czech meat market with sawdust on the floor and skinned rabbits in the window. He wasn't there a week when he got so drunk he passed out in the freezer and when he woke the door was locked and everyone was gone. It was Saturday and he knew they wouldn't open again until Monday and by then he'd be stiff as a two-by-four. He was already shivering so bad he couldn't stand still or he'd fall over. He figured he'd be dead already except that his blood was half alcohol. Parts of him were going numb and he started staggering around, bumping past hanging sides of meat, singing, praying out loud, trying to let the fear out. He knew it was hopeless but he was looking anyway for some place to smash out, some plug to pull, something to stop the cold. At the back of the freezer, behind racks of meat, he found a cooler. It was an old one, the kind that used to stand packed with blocks of ice and bottles of beer in taverns during the war. And seeing it Big Antek suddenly remembered a moment from his first summer back from the Pacific, discharged from the hospital in Manila and back in Buddy's lounge on Twenty-fourth Street catty-corner from a victory garden where a plaque erroneously listed his name among the parish war dead. It was an ordinary moment, nothing dramatic like his life flashing before his eyes, but the memory filled him with such clarity that the freezer became dreamlike beside it. The ball game was on the radio over Buddy's bar, DiMaggio in center again, while Bing Crosby crooned for the jukebox which was playing at the same time. Antek was reaching into Buddy's cooler, up to his elbows in ice water feeling for a beer, while looking out through the open tavern door that framed Twenty-fourth Street as if it were a movie full of girls blurred in brightness, slightly overexposed blondes, a movie he could step into any time he chose now that he was home; but right at this moment he was taking his time, stretching it out until it encompassed his entire life, the cold bottles bobbing away from his fingertips, clunking against ice, until finally he grabbed one, hauled it up dripping, wondering what he'd grabbed—a Monarch or Yusay Pilsner or Foxhead 400—then popped the cork in the opener on the side of the cooler, the foam rising as he tilted his head back and let it pour down his throat, privately celebrating being alive. That moment was what drinking had once been about. It was a good thing to be remembering now when he was dying with nothing else to do for it. He had the funny idea of climbing inside the cooler and going to sleep to continue the memory like a dream. The cooler was thick with frost, so white it seemed to glow. Its lid had been replaced with a slab of dry ice that smoked even within the cold of the freezer, reminding Antek that as kids they'd always called it hot ice. He nudged it aside. Beneath it was a block of ice as clear as if the icemen had just delivered it. There was something frozen inside. He glanced away, but knew already, immediately, it was a body. He couldn't move away. He looked again. The longer he stared, the calmer he felt. It was a girl. He could make out her hair, not just blond, but radiating gold like a candleflame behind a window in winter. Her breasts were bare. The ice seemed even clearer. She was beautiful and dreamy looking, not dreamy like sleeping, but the dreamy look DPs sometimes get when they first come to the city. As long as he stayed beside her he didn't shiver. He could feel the blood return; he was warm as if the smoldering dry ice really was hot. He spent the weekend huddled against her, and early Monday morning when the Czech opened the freezer he said to Antek, "Get out . . . you're fired." That's all either one of them said.

"You know what I think," Pancho said. "They moved her body from the ice house to the butcher shop because the cops checked, man."

"You know what I think," Manny said, "I think you're doing so much shit that even the winos can bullshit you."

They looked hard at one another, Manny especially looking bad because of a beard he was trying to grow that was mostly stubble except for a black knot of hair frizzing from the cleft under his lower lip—a little lip beard like a jazz musician's—and Pancho covered in crosses, a wooden one dangling from a leather thong over his open shirt, and a small gold cross on a fine gold chain tight about his throat, and a tiny platinum cross in his right earlobe, and a faded India-ink cross tattooed on his wrist where one would feel for a pulse.

"He got a cross-shaped dick," Manny said.

"Only when I got a hard-on, man," Pancho said, grinning, and they busted up.

"Hey, Eddie, man," Pancho said, "what you think of all this, man?"

Kapusta just shrugged like he always did. Not that he didn't have any ideas exactly, or that he didn't care. That shrug *was* what Kapusta believed.

"Yeah. Well, man," Pancho said, "I believe there's saints, and miracles happening everywhere only everybody's afraid to admit it. I mean like Ralph's little brother, the blue baby who died when he was eight. He knew he was dying all his life, man, and never complained. He was a saint. Or Big Antek who everybody says is a wino, man. But he treats everybody as human beings. Who you think's more of a saint—him or the President, man? And Mrs. Corillo who everybody thought was crazy because she was praying loud all the time. Remember? She kneeled all day praying for Puerto Rico during that earthquake—the one Roberto Clemente crashed going to help. Remember that, man? Mrs. Corillo prayed all day and they thought she was still praying at night and she was kneeling there dead. She was a saint, man, and so's Roberto Clemente. There should be like a church, St. Roberto Clemente. Kids could pray to him at night. That would mean something to them."

"The earthquake wasn't in Puerto Rico, man," Manny told him, "and I don't believe no streetcar'd stop for somebody carrying a dead person."

AMNESIA

It was hard to believe there ever were streetcars. The city back then, the city of their fathers, which was as far back as family memory extended, even the city of their childhoods, seemed as remote to Eddie and Manny as the capital of some foreign country.

The past collapsed about them—decayed, bulldozed, obliterated. They walked past block-length gutted factories, past walls of peeling, multicolored doors hammered up around flooded excavation pits, hung out in half-boarded storefronts of groceries that had shut down when they were kids, dusty cans still stacked on the shelves. Broken glass collected everywhere mounding like sand in the little, sunken front yards and gutters. Even the church's stained-glass windows were patched with plywood.

They could vaguely remember something different before the cranes and wrecking balls gradually moved in, not order exactly, but rhythms: five-o'clock whistles, air-raid sirens on Tuesdays, Thursdays when the stockyards blew over like a brown wind of boiling hooves and bone, at least that's what people said, screwing up their faces, "Phew! they're making glue today!"

Streetcar tracks were long paved over; black webs of trolley wires vanished. So did the victory gardens that had become weed beds taking the corroded plaques with the names of the neighborhood dead with them.

Things were gone they couldn't remember, but missed; and things were gone they weren't sure ever were there—the pickle factory by the railroad tracks where a DP with a net worked scooping rats out of the open vats, troughs for ragmen's horses, ragmen and their wooden wagons, knife-sharpeners pushing screeching whetstones up alleys hollering "Scissors! Knives!" hermits living in cardboard shacks behind billboards.

At times, walking past the gaps, they felt as if they were no longer quite there themselves, half-lost despite familiar street signs, shadows of themselves superimposed on the present, except there was no present—everything either rubbled past or promised future—and they were walking as if floating, getting nowhere as if they'd smoked too much grass.

That's how it felt those windy nights that fall when Manny and Eddie circled the county jail. They'd float down California past the courthouse, Bridewell Correctional, the auto pound, Communicable Disease Hospital, and then follow the long, curving concrete wall of the prison back towards Twenty-sixth Street, sharing a joint, passing it with cupped hands, ready to flip it if a cop should cruise by, but one place you could count on not to see cops was outside the prison.

Nobody was there; just the wall, railroad tracks, the river and the factories that lined it—boundaries that remained intact while neighborhoods came and went.

Eddie had never noticed any trees, but swirls of leaves scuffed past their shoes. It was Kapusta's favorite weather, wild, blowing nights that made him feel free, flagpoles knocking in the wind, his clothes flapping like flags. He felt both tight and loose, and totally alive even walking down a street that always made him sad. It was the street that followed the curve of the prison wall, and it didn't have a name. It was hardly a street at all, more a shadow of the wall, potholed, puddled, half-paved, rutted with rusted railroad tracks.

"Trains used to go down this street," Manny said.

"I seen tanks going down this street."

"Tank cars?"

"No, Army tanks," Kapusta said.

"Battleships too, Edwardo?" Manny asked seriously. Then the wind ripped a laugh from his mouth loud enough to carry over the prison wall.

Kapusta laughed loud too. But he could remember tanks, camouflaged with netting, rumbling on flatcars, their cannons outlined by the red lanterns of the dinging crossing gates which were down all along Twenty-sixth Street. It was one of the first things he remembered. He must have been very small. The train seemed endless. He could see the guards in the turrets on the prison wall watching it, the only time he'd ever seen them facing the street. "Still sending them to Korea or someplace," his father had said, and for years after, Eddie believed you could get to Korea by train. For years after, he would wake in the middle of the night when it was quiet enough to hear the trains passing blocks away, and lie in bed listening, wondering if the tanks were rumbling past the prison, if not to Korea then to some other war that tanks went to at night; and he would think of the prisoners in their cells locked up for their violence with knives and clubs and cleavers and pistols, and wonder if they were lying awake, listening too as the netted cannons rolled by their barred windows. Even as a child Eddie knew the names of men inside there: Milo Hermanski, who had stabbed some guy in the eye in a fight at Andy's Tap; Billy Gomez, who set the housing project on fire every time his sister Nina got gang-banged; Ziggy's uncle, the war hero, who one day blew off the side of Ziggy's mother's face while she stood ironing in her slip during an argument over a will; and other names of people he didn't know, but had heard about—Benny Bedwell, with his "Elvis" sideburns, who may have killed the Grimes sisters, Mafia hitmen, bank robbers, junkies, perverts, murderers on death row —he could sense them lying awake listening, the tension of their sleep-lessness, and Pancho lay among them now as he and Manny walked outside the wall.

They stopped again as they'd been stopping and yelled together: "Pancho, Panchooooooo," dragging out the last vowel the way they had as kids standing on the sidewalk calling up at one another's win-dows as if knocking at the door were not allowed.

"Pancho, we're out here, brother, me and Eddie," Manny shouted. "Hang tough, man, we ain't forgetting you."

Nobody answered. They kept walking, stopping to shout at intervals the way they had been doing most every night.

"If only we knew what building he was in," Eddie said.

They could see the upper stories of the brick buildings rising over the wall, their grated windows low lit, never dark, floodlights on the roof glaring down.

"Looks like a factory, man," Eddie said. "Looks like the same guy who planned the Harvester foundry on Western did the jail."

"You rather be in the Army or in there?" Manny asked.

"No way they're getting me in there," Kapusta said.

That was when Eddie knew Pancho was crazy, when the judge had given Pancho a choice at the end of his trial.

"You're a nice-looking kid," the judge had said, "too nice for prison. What do you want to do with your life?"

"Pose for holy cards," Pancho said, "St. Joseph my specialty." Pancho was standing there wearing the tie they had brought him wound around his head like an Indian headband. He was wearing a black satin jacket with the signs of the zodiac on the back.

"I'm going to give you a chance to straighten out, to gain some self-respect. The court's attitude would be very sympathetic to any signs of self-direction and patriotism, joining the Army for instance."

"I'm a captain," Pancho told him.

"The Army or jail, which is it?"

"I'm a captain, man, *soy capitán, capitán,*" Pancho insisted, humming "La Bomba" under his breath.

"You're a misfit."

Manny was able to visit Pancho every three weeks. Each time it got worse. Sometimes Pancho seemed hardly to recognize him, looking away, refusing to meet Manny's eyes the whole visit. Sometimes he'd cry. For a while at first he wanted to know how things were in the neighborhood. Then he stopped asking, and when Manny tried to tell him the news Pancho would get jumpy, irritable, and lapse into total silence. "I don't wanna talk about out there, man," he told Manny. "I don't wanna remember that world until I'm ready to step into it again. You remember too much in here you go crazy, man. I wanna forget everything like I never existed."

"His fingernails are gone, man," Manny told Eddie, "he's gnawing on himself like a rat and when I ask him what's going down all he'll say is I'm locked in hell, my angel's gone, I've lost my luck—bullshit like that, you know? Last time I seen him he says I'm gonna kill myself, man, if they don't stop hitting on me."

"I can't fucking believe it. I can't fucking believe he's in there," Kapusta said. "He should be in a monastery somewhere; he should of been a priest. He had a vocation."

"He had a vocation to be an altar boy, man," Manny said, spitting it out like he was disgusted by what he was saying, talking down about his own brother. "It was that nuns and priests crap that messed up his head. He was happy being an altar boy, man, if they'd of let him be an altar boy all his life he'd still be happy."

By the time they were halfway down the nameless street it was drizzling a fine, misty spray, and Manny was yelling in Spanish, *"Estamos contigo, hermano! San Roberto Clemente te ayudará!"*

They broke into "La Bomba," Eddie singing in Spanish too, not sure exactly what he was singing, but it sounded good: *"Yo no soy marinero, soy capitán, capitán, ay, ay Bomba! ay, ay Bomba!"* He had lived beside

Spanish in the neighborhood all his life and every so often a word got through, like *juilota* which was what Manny called pigeons when they used to hunt them with slingshots under the railroad bridges. It seemed a perfect word to Eddie, in which he could hear both their cooing and the whistling rush of their wings. He didn't remember any words like that in Polish, which his grandma had spoken to him when he was little, and which, Eddie had been told, he could once speak too.

By midnight they were at the end of their circuit, emerging from the unlighted, nameless street, stepping over tracks that continued to curve past blinded switches. Under the streetlights on Twenty-sixth the prison wall appeared rust-stained, oozing at cracks. The wire spooled at the top of the wall looking rusty in the wet light as did the tracks as if the rain were rusting everything overnight.

They stopped on the corner of Twenty-sixth where the old ice house stood across the nameless street from the prison. One could still buy ice from a vending machine in front. Without realizing it, Eddie guarded his breathing as if still able to detect the faintest stab of ammonia, although it had been a dozen years since the louvered fans on the ice house roof had clacked through clouds of vapor.

"Padrecitooooo!" they both hollered.

Their voices bounced back off the wall.

They stood on the corner by the ice house as if waiting around for someone. From there they could stare down Twenty-sixth—five dark blocks, then an explosion of neon at Kedzie Avenue: taco places, bars, a street plugged in, winking festive as a pinball machine, traffic from it coming towards them in the rain.

The streetlights surged and flickered.

"You see that?" Eddie asked. "They used to say when the streetlights flickered it meant they just fried somebody in the electric chair."

"So much bullshit," Manny said. *"Compadre no te rajes!"* he yelled at the wall.

"Whatcha tell him?"

"It sounds different in English," Manny said. " *'Godfather, do not give up.'* It's words from an old song."

Kapusta stepped out into the middle of Twenty-sixth and stood in the misting drizzle squinting at Kedzie through cupped hands as if he had a spyglass. He could make out the traffic light way down there changing to green. He could almost hear the music from the bars that would serve them without asking for ID's so long as Manny was there. "You thirsty by any chance, man?" he asked.

"You buyin'?" Manny grinned.

"Buenas noches, Pancho," they hollered, "catch you tomorrow, man."

"Good night, guys," a falsetto voice echoed back from over the wall.

"That ain't Pancho," Manny said.

"Sounds like the singer on old Platters' records," Eddie said. "Ask him if he knows Pancho, man."

"Hey, you know a guy named Pancho Santora?" Manny called.

"Oh, Pancho?" the voice inquired.

"Yeah, Pancho."

"Oh, Cisco!" the voice shouted. They could hear him cackling. "Hey baby, I don't know no Pancho. Is that rain I smell?"

"It's raining," Eddie hollered.

"Hey baby, tell me something. What's it like out there tonight?"

Manny and Eddie looked at each other. "Beautiful!" they yelled together.

GRIEF

There was never a requiem, but by Lent everyone knew that one way or another Pancho was gone. No wreaths, but plenty of rumors: Pancho had hung himself in his cell; his throat had been slashed in the showers; he'd killed another inmate and was under heavy sedation in the psycho ward at Kankakee. And there was talk he'd made a deal and was in the Army, shipped off to a war he had sworn he'd never fight; that he had turned snitch and had been secretly relocated with a new identity; or that he had become a trustee, and had simply walked away while mowing the grass in front of the courthouse, escaped maybe to Mexico, or maybe just across town to the North Side around Diversey where, if one made the rounds of the leather bars, they might see someone with Pancho's altar-boy eyes staring out from the makeup of a girl.

Some saw him late at night like a ghost haunting the neighborhood, collar up, in the back of the church lighting a vigil candle; or veiled in a black mantilla, speeding past, face floating by on a greasy El window.

Rumors were becoming legends, but there was never a wake, never an obituary, and no one knew how to mourn a person who had just disappeared.

For a while Manny disappeared too. He wasn't talking and Kapusta didn't ask. They had quit walking around the prison wall months before, around Christmas when Pancho refused to let anyone, even Manny, visit. But their night walks had been tapering off before that.

Eddie remembered the very last time they had gone. It was in December and he was frozen from standing around a burning garbage can on Kedzie, selling Christmas trees. About ten, when the lot closed, Manny came by and they stopped to thaw out at the Carta Blanca. A guy named José kept buying them whiskeys and they staggered out after midnight into a blizzard.

"Look at this white bullshit," Manny said.

Walking down Twenty-sixth they stopped to fling snowballs over the wall. Then they decided to stand there singing Christmas carols. Snow was drifting against the wall, erasing the street that had hardly been there. Eddie could tell Manny was starting to go silent. He would get the first few words into a carol, singing at the top of his voice, then stop as if choked by the song. His eyes stayed angry when he laughed. Everything was bullshit to him and finally Eddie couldn't talk to him anymore. Stomping away from the prison through fresh snow, Eddie had said, "If this keeps up, man, I'll need boots."

"It don't *have* to *keep up,* man," Manny snapped. "Nobody's making you come, man. It ain't your brother."

"All I said is I'll need boots, man," Eddie said.

"You said it hopeless, man; things are always fucking hopeless to you."

"Hey, you're the big realist, man," Eddie told him.

"I never said I was no realist," Manny mumbled.

Kapusta hadn't had a lot of time since then. He had dropped out of school again and was loading trucks at night for UPS. One more semester didn't matter, he figured, and he needed some new clothes, cowboy boots, a green leather jacket. The weather had turned drizzly and mild, a late Easter, but an early spring. Eddie had heard Manny was hanging around by himself, still finding bullshit everywhere, only worse. Now he muttered as he walked like some crazy, bitter old man, or one of those black guys reciting the gospel to buildings, telling off posters and billboards, neon signs, stoplights, passing traffic—bullshit, all of it bullshit.

It was Tuesday in Holy Week, the statues inside the church shrouded in violet, when Eddie slipped on his green jacket and walked over to Manny's before going to work. He rang the doorbell, then stepped outside in the rain and stood on the sidewalk under Manny's windows, watching cars pass.

After a while Manny came down the stairs and slammed out the door.

"How you doin', man?" Eddie said like they'd just run into each other by accident.

Manny stared at him. "How far'd you have to chase him for that jacket, man?" he said.

"I knew you'd dig it." Eddie smiled.

They went out for a few beers later that night, after midnight, when Eddie was through working, but instead of going to a bar they ended up just walking. Manny had rolled a couple bombers and they walked down the boulevard along California watching the headlights flash by like a procession of candles. Manny still wasn't saying much, but they were passing the reefer like having a conversation. At Thirty-first, by the Communicable Disease Hospital, Eddie figured they would follow the curve of the boulevard towards the bridge on Western, but Manny turned as if out of habit towards the prison.

They were back walking along the wall. There was still old ice from winter at the base of it.

"The only street in Chicago where it's still winter," Kapusta mumbled.

"Remember yelling?" Manny said, almost in a whisper.

"Sure," Eddie nodded.

"Called, joked, prayed, sang Christmas songs, remember that night, how cold we were, man?"

"Yeah."

"What a bunch of stupid bullshit, huh?"

Eddie was afraid Manny was going to start the bullshit stuff again. Manny had stopped and stood looking at the wall.

Then he cupped his hands over his mouth and yelled, "Hey! you dumb fuckers in there! We're back! Can you hear me? Hey, wake up niggers, hey spics, hey honkies, you buncha fucken monkeys in cages, hey! we're out here *free!*"

"Hey, Manny, come on, man," Eddie said.

Manny uncupped his hands, shook his head and smiled. They took a few steps, then Manny whirled back again. "We're out here free, man! We're smokin' reefer, drinking cold beer while you're in there, you assholes! We're on our way to fuck your wives, man, your girlfriends are giving us blow jobs while you jack-offs flog it. Hey man, I'm pumping your old lady out here right now. She likes it in the ass like you!"

"What are you doing, man," Eddie was pleading. "Take it easy."

Manny was screaming his lungs out, almost incoherent, shouting every filthy thing he could think of, and voices, the voices they'd never heard before, had begun shouting back from the other side of the wall.

"Shadup! Shadup! Shadup out there you crazy fuck!" came the voices.

"She's out here licking my balls while you're punking each other through the bars of your cage!"

"Shadup!" they were yelling and then a voice howling over the others, "I'll kill you motherfucker! When I get out you're dead!"

"Come on out," Manny was yelling. "Come and get me you piece of shit, you sleazeballs, you scumbag cocksuckers, you creeps are missing it all, your lives are wasted garbage!"

Now there were too many voices to distinguish, whole tiers, whole buildings yelling and cursing and threatening, *shadup, shadup, shadup,* almost a chant, and then the searchlight from the guardhouse slowly turned and swept the street.

"We gotta get outa here," Eddie said, pulling Manny away. He dragged him to the wall, right up against it where the light couldn't follow, and they started to run, stumbling along the banked strip of filthy ice, dodging stunted trees that grew out at odd angles, running toward Twenty-sixth until Eddie heard the sirens.

"This way, man," he panted, yanking Manny back across the nameless street, jumping puddles and tracks, cutting down a narrow corridor between abandoned truck docks seconds before a squad car, blue dome light revolving, sped past.

They jogged behind the truck docks, not stopping until they came up behind the ice house. Manny's panting sounded almost like laughing, the way people laugh sometimes after they've hurt themselves.

"I hate those motherfuckers," Manny gasped, "all of them, the fucking cops and guards and fucking wall and the bastards behind it. All of them. That must be what makes me a realist, huh, Eddie? I fucking hate them all."

They went back the next night.

Sometimes a thing wasn't a sin—if there was such a thing as sin—Eddie thought, until it's done a second time. There were accidents, mistakes that could be forgiven once; it was repeating them that made them terribly wrong. That was how Eddie felt about going back the next night.

Manny said he was going whether Eddie came or not, so Eddie went, afraid to leave Manny on his own, even though he'd already had trouble trying to get some sleep before going to work. Eddie could still hear the voices yelling from behind the wall and dreamed they were all being electrocuted; electrocuted slowly, by degrees of their crimes, screaming with each surge of current and flicker of streetlights as if in a hell where electricity had replaced fire.

Standing on the dark street Wednesday night, outside the wall again, felt like an extension of his nightmare: Manny raging almost out of control, shouting curses and insults, baiting them over the wall the way a child tortures penned watchdogs, until he had what seemed like the entire west side of the prison howling back, the guards sweeping the street with searchlights, sirens wailing towards them from both Thirty-first and Twenty-sixth.

This time they raced down the tracks that curved towards the river, picking their way in the dark along the junkyard bank, flipping rusted cables of moored barges, running through the fire-truck graveyard, following the tracks across the blackened trestles where they'd once shot pigeons and from which they could gaze across the industrial prairie that stretched behind factories all the way to the skyline of downtown. The skyscrapers glowed like luminescent peaks in the misty spring night. Manny and Eddie stopped in the middle of the trestle and leaned over the railing catching their breaths.

"Downtown ain't as far away as I used to think when I was a kid," Manny panted.

"These tracks'll take you right there," Eddie said quietly, "to railroad yards under the street, right by the lake."

"How you know, man?"

"A bunch of us used to hitch rides on the boxcars in seventh grade." Eddie was talking very quietly, looking away.

"I usually take the bus, you know?" Manny tried joking.

"I ain't goin' back there with you tomorrow," Eddie said. "I ain't goin' back there with you ever."

Manny kept staring off towards the lights downtown as if he hadn't heard. "Okay," he finally said, more to himself as if surrendering. "Okay, how about tomorrow we do something else, man?"

NOSTALGIA

They didn't go back.

The next night, Thursday, Eddie overslept and called in sick for work. He tried to get back to sleep, but kept falling into half dreams in which he could hear the voices shouting behind the prison wall. Finally he got up and opened a window. It was dark out. A day had passed almost unnoticed, and now the night felt as if it were a part of the night before, and the night before a part of the night before that, all connected by his restless dreams, fragments of the same continuous night.

Eddie had said that at some point: "It's like one long night," and later Manny had said the same thing as if it had suddenly occurred to him.

They were strung out almost from the start, drifting stoned under the El tracks before Eddie even realized they weren't still sitting on the stairs in front of Manny's house. That was where Eddie had found him, sitting on the stairs out in front, and for a while they had sat together watching traffic, taking sips out of a bottle of Gallo into which Manny had dropped several hits of speed.

Cars gunned by with their windows rolled down and radios playing loud. It sounded like a summer night.

"Ain't you hot wearin' that jacket, man?" Manny asked him.

"Now that you mention it," Eddie said. He was sweating.

Eddie took his leather jacket off and they knotted a handkerchief around one of the cuffs, then slipped the Gallo bottle down the sleeve. They walked along under the El tracks passing a joint. A train, only two cars long, rattled overhead.

"So what we doing, Edwardo?" Manny kept repeating.

"Walking," Eddie said.

"I feel like doing *something*, you know?"

"We are doing something," Eddie insisted.

Eddie led them over to the Coconut Club on Twenty-second. They couldn't get in, but Eddie wanted to look at the window with its neon green palm tree and winking blue coconuts.

"That's maybe my favorite window."

"You drag me all the way here to see your favorite window, man!" Manny said.

"It's those blue coconuts," Eddie tried explaining. His mouth was dry, but he couldn't stop talking. He started telling Manny how he had collected windows from the time he was a little kid, even though talking about it made it sound more important to him than it was. Half the time he didn't even know he was doing it. He would see a window from a bus like the Greek butcher shop on Halsted with its pyramid of lamb skulls and make a mental photograph of it. He had special windows all over the city. It was how he held the city together in his mind.

"I'd see all these windows from the El," Eddie said, "when I'd visit my *busha,* my grandma. Like I remember we'd pass this one building where the curtains were all slips hanging by their straps—black ones, white ones, red ones. At night you could see the lightbulbs shining through the lace tops. My *busha* said gypsies lived there." Eddie was walking down the middle of the street, jacket flung over his shoulder, staring up at the windows as if looking for the gypsies as he talked.

"Someday they're gonna get you as a peeper, man," Manny laughed. "And when they do, don't try explaining to them about this thing of yours for windows, Edwardo."

They were walking down Spaulding back towards Twenty-sixth. The streetlights beamed brighter and brighter and Manny put his sunglasses on. A breeze was blowing that felt warmer than the air and they took their shirts off. They saw rats darting along the curb into the sewer on the other side of the street and put their shirts back on.

"The rats get crazy where they start wrecking these old buildings," Manny said.

The cranes and wrecking balls and urban renewal signs were back with the early spring. They walked around a barricaded site. Water trickled along the gutters from an open hydrant, washing brick dust and debris towards the sewers.

"Can you smell that, man?" Manny asked him, suddenly excited. "I can smell the lake through the hydrant."

"Smells like rust to me," Eddie said.

"I can smell fish! Smelt—the smelt are in! I can smell them right through the hydrant!"

"Smelt?" Eddie said.

"You ain't ever had smelt?" Manny asked. "Little silver fish!"

They caught the Twenty-sixth Street bus—the Polish Zephyr, people called it—going east, towards the lake. The back was empty. They sat in the swaying, long backseat, taking hits out of the bottle in Eddie's sleeve.

"It's usually too early for them yet, but they're out there, Edwardo," Manny kept reassuring him as if they were actually going fishing.

Eddie nodded. He didn't know anything about smelt. The only fish he ate was canned tuna, but it felt good to be riding somewhere with the windows open and Manny acting more like his old self—sure of himself, laughing easily. Eddie still felt like talking but his molars were grinding on speed.

The bus jolted down the dark blocks past Kedzie and was flying when it passed the narrow street between the ice house and the prison, but Eddie and Manny caught a glimpse out the back window of the railroad tracks that curved down the nameless street. The tracks were lined with fuming red flares that threw red reflections off the concrete walls. They were sure the flares had been set there for them.

Eddie closed his eyes and sank into the rocking of the bus. Even with his eyes closed he could see the reddish glare of the walls. The glare was ineradicable, at the back of his sockets. The wall had looked the same way it had looked in his dreams. They rode in silence.

"It's like one long night," Eddie said somewhere along the way.

His jaws were really grinding and his legs had forgotten gravity by the time they got to the lakefront. They didn't know the time, but it must have been around four and the smelt fishers were still out. The lights of their kerosene lanterns reflected along the breakwater over the glossy black lake. Eddie and Manny could hear the water lapping under the pier, and the fishermen talking in low voices in different languages.

"My Uncle Carlos would talk to the fish," Manny said. "No shit. He'd talk to them in Spanish. He didn't have no choice. Whole time here he couldn't speak English. Said it made his brain stuck. We used to come fishing here all the time—smelt, perch, everything. I'd come instead of going to school. If they weren't hitting he'd start talking to them, singing them songs."

"Like what?" Eddie said.

"He'd make them up. They were funny, man. It don't come across in English: '*Little silver ones fill up my shoes. My heart is lonesome for the fish of the sea.*' It was like very formal how he'd say it. He'd always call this the sea. I'd tell him it's a lake but he couldn't be talked out of it. He was very stubborn—too stubborn to learn English. I ain't been fishing since he went back to Mexico."

They walked to the end of the pier, then back past the fishermen. A lot of them were old men gently tugging lines between their fingers, lifting nets like flying underwater kites, plucking the wriggling silver fish from the netting, the yellow light of their lamps glinting off the bright scales.

"I told you they were out here," Manny said.

They killed the bottle sitting on a concrete ledge and dropped it into the lake. Then they rode the El back. It was getting lighter without a dawn. The El windows streaked with rain, the Douglas Avenue station smelled wet. It was a dark morning. They should have ended it then. Instead they sat at Manny's kitchen table drinking instant coffee with Pet milk. Eddie kept getting lost in the designs the milk would make, swirls and thunderclouds in his mug of coffee. He was numb and shaky. His jaw ached.

"I'm really crashin'," he told Manny.

"Here," Manny said. "Bring us down easier, man."

"I don't like doing downers, man," Eddie said.

"Ludes," Manny said, "from Pancho's stash."

They sat across the table from each other for a long time, talking, telling their memories and secrets, only Eddie was too numb to remember exactly what they said. Their voices—his own as well as Manny's—seemed *outside,* removed from the center of his mind.

At one point Manny looked out at the dark morning and said, "It still seems like last night."

"That's right," Eddie agreed. He wanted to say more, but couldn't express it. He didn't try. Eddie didn't believe it was what they said that was important. Manny could be talking Spanish; I could be talking Polish, Eddie thought. It didn't matter. What meant something was sitting at the table together, wrecked together, still awake watching the rainy light spatter the window, walking out again, to the Prague bakery for bismarcks, past people under dripping umbrellas on their way to church.

"Looks like Sunday," Manny said.

"Today's Friday," Eddie said. "It's Good Friday."

"I seen ladies with ashes on their heads waiting for the bus a couple days ago," Manny told him.

They stood in the doorway of the Prague, out of the rain, eating their bismarcks. Just down from the church, the bakery was a place people crowded into after mass. Its windows displayed colored eggs and little frosted Easter lambs.

"One time on Ash Wednesday I was eating a bismarck and Pancho made a cross on my forehead with the powdered sugar like it was ashes. When I went to church the priest wouldn't give me real ashes," Manny said with a grin.

It was one of the few times Eddie had heard Manny mention Pancho. Now that they were outside, Eddie's head felt clearer than it had in the kitchen.

"I used to try and keep my ashes on until Good Friday," he told Manny, "but they'd make me wash."

The church bells were ringing, echoes bouncing off the sidewalks as if deflected by the ceiling of clouds. The neighborhood felt narrower, compressed from above.

"I wonder if it still looks the same in there," Manny said as they passed the church.

They stepped in and stood in the vestibule. The saints of their childhood stood shrouded in purple. The altar was bare, stripped for Good Friday. Old ladies, ignoring the new liturgy, chanted a litany in Polish.

"Same as ever," Eddie whispered as they backed out.

The rain had almost let up. They could hear its accumulated weight in the wing-flaps of pigeons.

"Good Friday was Pancho's favorite holiday, man," Manny said. "Everybody else always picked Christmas or Thanksgiving or Fourth of July. He hada be different, man. I remember he used to drag me along visiting churches. You ever do that?"

"Hell yeah," Eddie said. "Every Good Friday we'd go on our bikes. You hada visit seven of them."

Without agreeing to it they walked from St. Roman's to St. Michael's, a little wooden Franciscan church in an Italian neighborhood; and from there to St. Casimir's, a towering, mournful church with twin copper-green towers. Then, as if following an invisible trail, they walked north up Twenty-second towards St. Anne's, St. Pius, St. Adalbert's. At first they merely entered and left immediately, as if touching base, but their familiarity with small rituals quickly returned: dipping their fingers in the holy-water font by the door, making the automatic sign of the cross as they passed the life-sized crucified Christs that hung in the vestibules where old women and school kids clustered to kiss the spikes in the bronze or bloody plaster feet. By St. Anne's, Manny removed his sunglasses, out of respect the way one removes a hat. Eddie put them on. His eyes felt hard-boiled. The surge of energy he had felt at the bakery had burned out fast. While Manny genuflected to the altar,

Eddie slumped in the back pew pretending to pray, drowsing off behind the dark glasses. It never occurred to Eddie to simply go home. His head ached, he could feel his heart racing, and would suddenly jolt awake wondering where Manny was. Manny would be off—jumpy, frazzled, still popping speed on the sly—exploring the church as if searching for something, standing among lines of parishioners waiting to kiss relics the priest wiped repeatedly clean with a rag of silk. Then Manny would be shaking Eddie awake. "How you holding up, man?"

"I'm cool," and they would be back on the streets heading for another parish under the overcast sky. Clouds, a shade between slate and lilac, smoked over the spires and roofs; lights flashed on in the bars and *taquerias*. On Eighteenth Street a great blue neon fish leapt in the storefront window of a tiny *ostenaria*. Eddie tried to remember exactly where it was. They headed to St. Procopius where, Manny said, he and Pancho had been baptized, along a wall of viaducts that schoolchildren had painted into a mural that seemed to go for miles.

"I don't think we're gonna make seven churches, man," Eddie said. He was walking without lifting his feet, his hair plastered with a sweatlike drizzle. It was around 3 P.M. It had been 3 P.M.—Christ's dark hour on the cross—inside the churches all day, but now it was turning 3 P.M. outside too. They could hear the ancient-sounding *Tantum Ergo* carrying from down the block.

Eddie sank into the last pew, kneeling in the red glow of vigil lights that brought back the red flicker of the flares they had seen from the window of the bus as it sped by the prison. Manny had already faded into the procession making the Stations of the Cross—a shuffling crowd circling the church, kneeling before each station while altar boys censed incense and the priest recited Christ's agony. Old women answered with prayers like moans.

Old women were walking on their knees up the marble aisle to kiss the relics. A few were crying, and Eddie remembered how back in grade school he had heard old women cry sometimes after confession, crying as if their hearts would break, and even as a child he had wondered how such old women could possibly have committed sins terrible enough to demand such bitter weeping. Most everything from that world had changed or disappeared, but the old women had endured—Polish, Bohemian, Spanish, he knew it didn't matter; they were the same, dressed in black coats and babushkas the way holy statues wore violet, in constant mourning. A common pain of loss seemed to burn at the core of their lives, though Eddie had never understood exactly what it was they mourned. Nor how day after day they had sustained the intensity of their grief. He would have given up long ago. In a way he had, and the ache left behind couldn't be called grief. He had no name for it. He had felt it before Pancho or anyone was lost, almost from the start of memory. If it was grief, it was grief for the living. The hymns, with their ancient, keening melodies and mysterious words, had brought the feeling back, but when he tried to discover the source, to give the feeling a name, it eluded him as always, leaving in its place nostalgia and triggered nerves.

Oh God, he prayed, I'm really crashing.

He was too shaky to kneel, so he stretched out on the pew, lying on his back, eyes shut behind sunglasses, until the church began to whirl. To control it he tried concentrating on the stained-glass window overhead. None of the windows that had ever been special for him were from a church. This one was an angel, its colors like jewels and coals. Afternoon seemed to be dying behind it, becoming part of the night, part of the private history that he and Manny continued between them like a pact. He could see night shining through, its neon and wet streetlights illuminating the angel on the window.

LEGENDS

It started with ice.

That's how Big Antek sometimes began the story.

At dusk a gang of little Mexican kids appeared with a few lumps of dry ice covered in a shoe box as if they had caught a bird. *Hot ice,* they called it, though the way they said it sounded to Antek like *hot eyes.* Kids always have a way of finding stuff like that. One boy touched his tongue to a piece and screamed *"Aye!"* when it stuck. They watched it boil and fume in a rain puddle along the curb, and finally they filled a bottle part way with water, inserted the fragments of ice they had left, capped the bottle and set it in the mouth of an alley waiting for an explosion. When it popped they scattered.

Manny Santora and Eddie Kapusta came walking up the alley, wanting Antek to buy them a bottle of rum at Buddy's. Rum instead of beer. They were celebrating, Kapusta said, but he didn't say what. Maybe one of them had found a job or had just been fired, or graduated, or joined the Army instead of waiting around to get drafted. It could be anything. They were always celebrating. Behind their sunglasses Antek could see they were high as usual, even before Manny offered him a drag off a reefer the size of a cigar.

Probably nobody was hired or fired or had joined anything; probably it was just so hot they had a good excuse to act crazy. They each had a bottle of Coke they were fizzing up, squirting. Eddie had limes stuffed in his pockets and was pretending they were his balls. Manny had a plastic bag of the little ice cubes they sell at gas stations. It was half-melted and they were scooping handfuls of cubes over each other's head, stuffing them down their jeans and yowling, rubbing ice on their chests and under their arms as if taking cold showers. They looked like wild men— shirts hanging from their back pockets, handkerchiefs knotted around their heads, wearing their sunglasses, their bodies slick with melted ice water and sweat; two guys in the prime of life going nowhere, both lean, Kapusta almost as tan as Santora—Santora with that frizzy beard under his lip, and Kapusta trying to juggle limes.

They were drinking rum using a method Antek had never seen before and he had seen his share of drinking—not just in the neighborhood— all over the world when he was in the Navy, and not the Bohemian Navy either like somebody would always say when he would start telling Navy stories.

They claimed they were drinking Cuba Libres, only they didn't have glasses so they were mixing the drinks in their mouths, starting with some little cubes, then pouring in rum, Coke, a squeeze of lime, and swallowing. Swallowing if one or the other didn't suddenly bust up over some private joke, spraying the whole mouthful out, and both of them choking and coughing and laughing.

"Hey Antek, lemme build you a drink," Manny kept saying, but Antek shook his head no thanks, and he wasn't known for passing up too many.

This was all going on in front of Buddy's, everyone catching a blast of music and air-conditioning whenever the door opened. It was hot. The moths sizzled as soon as they hit Buddy's buzzing orange sign. A steady beat of moths dropped like cinders on the blinking orange sidewalk where the little kids were pitching pennies. Manny passed around what was left in the plastic bag of ice, and the kids stood sucking and crunching the cubes between their teeth.

It reminded Antek of summers when the ice trucks still delivered to Buddy's—flatbeds covered with canvas, the icemen, mainly DPs, wearing leather aprons, with Popeye forearms that even in August looked ruddy with cold. They would slide the huge, clear blocks off the tailgate so the whump reverberated through the hollow under the sidewalks, and deep in the ice the clarity shattered. Then with their ice hooks they'd lug the blocks across the sidewalk trailing a slick, and boot them skidding down the chute into Buddy's beery-smelling cellar. And after the truck pulled away, kids would pick the splinters from the curb and suck them as if they were ice-flavored Popsicles.

Nobody seemed too interested when Antek tried to tell them about the ice trucks, or anything else about how the world had been, for that matter. Antek had been sick and had only recently returned from the VA hospital. He returned feeling old and as if the neighborhood had changed in the few weeks he had been gone. People had changed. He couldn't be sure, but they treated him differently, colder, as if he were becoming a stranger in the place he had grown up in, now, just when he needed the most to belong.

"Hey Antek," Manny said, "you know what you can tell me? That girl that saved your life in the meat freezer, did she have good tits?"

"I tell you about a miracle and you ask me about tits?" Antek said. "I don't talk about that anymore because now somebody always asks me did she have good tits. Go see."

Kids had been trying for years to sneak into the ice house to see her. It was what the neighborhood had instead of a haunted house. Each generation had grown up with the story of how her father had ridden with her half-naked body on the streetcar. Even the nuns had heard Antek's story about finding the girl still frozen in the meat freezer. The butcher shop on Kedzie had closed long ago and the legend was that after the cops had stopped checking, her body had been moved at night back into the ice house. But the ice house wasn't easy to break into. It had stood padlocked and heavily boarded for years.

"They're gonna wreck it," Eddie said. "I went by on the bus and they got the crane out in front."

"Oh-oh, last chance, Antek," Manny said. "If you're sure she's in there maybe we oughta go save her."

"She's in there," Antek said. He noticed the little kids had stopped pitching pennies and were listening.

"Well, you owe her something after what she done for you—don't he, Edwardo?"

The kids who were listening chuckled, then started to go back to their pennies.

"You wanna go, I'll go!" Antek said loudly.

"All right, let's go."

Antek got up unsteadily. He stared at Eddie and Manny. "You guys couldn't loan me enough for a taste of wine just until I get my disability check?"

The little kids tagged after them to the end of the block, then turned back bored. Manny and Eddie kept going, picking the pace up a step or two ahead of Antek, exchanging looks and grinning. But Antek knew that no matter how much they joked or what excuses they gave, they were going like him for one last look. They were just old enough to have seen the ice house before it shut down. It was a special building, the kind a child couldn't help but notice and remember—there, on the corner across the street from the prison, a factory that made ice, humming with fans, its louvered roof dripping and clacking, lost in acrid clouds of its own escaping vapor.

The automatic ice machine in front had already been carted away. The doors were still padlocked, but the way the crane was parked it was possible for Manny and Eddie to climb the boom onto the roof.

Antek waited below. He gazed up at the new Plexiglas guard turrets on the prison wall. From his angle all he could see was the bluish fluorescence of their lighting. He watched Manny and Eddie jump from the boom to the roof, high enough to stare across at the turrets like snipers, to draw a level bead on the backs of the guards, high enough to gaze over the wall at the dim, barred windows of the buildings that resembled foundries more than ever in the sweltering heat.

Below, Antek stood swallowing wine, expecting more from the night than a condemned building. He didn't know exactly what else he expected. Perhaps only a scent, like the stab of remembered ammonia he might have detected if he were still young enough to climb the boom. Perhaps the secret isolation he imagined Manny and Eddie feeling now, alone on the roof, as if lost in clouds of vapor. At street level, passing traffic droned out the tick of the single cricket keeping time on the roof —a cricket so loud and insistent that Manny didn't stop to worry about the noise when he kicked in the louvers. And Antek, though he had once awakened in a freezer, couldn't imagine the shock of cold that Manny and Eddie felt as they dropped out of the summer night to the floor below.

Earlier, on their way down Twenty-sixth, Manny had stopped to pick up an unused flare from along the tracks, and Antek pictured them inside now, Manny, his hand wrapped in a handkerchief, holding the flare away from him like a Roman candle, its red glare sputtering off the beams and walls.

There wasn't much to see—empty corners, insulated pipes. Their breaths steamed. They tugged on their shirts. Instinctively, they traced the cold down a metal staircase. Cold was rising from the ground floor through the soles of their gym shoes.

The ground floor was stacked to the ceiling with junked ice machines. A wind like from an enormous air-conditioner was blowing down a narrow aisle between the machines. At the end of the aisle a concrete ramp slanted down to the basement.

That was where Antek suspected they would end up, the basement, a cavernous space extending under the nameless street, slowly collapsing as if the thick, melting pillars of ice along its walls had served as its foundation. The floor was spongy with waterlogged sawdust. An echoing rain plipped from the ceiling. The air smelled thawed, and ached clammy in the lungs.

"It's fucken freezing," Eddie whispered.

Manny swung the flare in a slow arc, its reflections glancing as if they stood among cracked mirrors. Blocks of ice, framed in defrosted freezer coils, glowed back faintly like aquarium windows from niches along the walls. They were melting unevenly and leaned at precarious angles. Several had already tottered to the sawdust where they lay like quarry stones from a wrecked cathedral. Manny and Eddie picked their way among them, pausing to wipe the slick of water from their surfaces and peer into the ice, but deep networks of cracks refracted the light. They could see only frozen shadows and had to guess at the forms: fish, birds, shanks of meat, a dog, a cat, a chair, what appeared to be a bicycle.

But Antek knew they would recognize her when they found her. There would be no mistaking the light. In the smoky, phosphorous glare her hair would reflect gold like a candle behind a frosted pane. He was waiting for them to bring her out. He had finished the wine and flung the pint bottle onto the street so that it shattered. The streets were empty. He was waiting patiently and though he had nowhere else to be it was still a long wait. He could hear the cricket now, composing time instead of music, working its way headfirst from the roof down the brick wall. Listening to it, Antek became acutely aware of the silence of the prison across the street. He thought of all the men on the other side of the wall and wondered how many were still awake, listening to a cricket, waiting patiently as they sweated in the heavy night.

Manny and Eddie, shivering, their hands burning numb from grappling with ice, unbarred the rear door that opened onto the loading platform behind the ice house. They pushed out an old handcar and rolled it onto the tracks that came right up to the dock. They had already slid the block of ice onto the handcar and draped it with a canvas tarp. Even gently inching it on they had heard the ice cracking. The block had felt too light for its size, fragile, ready to break apart.

"It feels like we're kidnapping somebody," Eddie whispered.

"Just think of it as ice."

"I can't."

"We can't just leave her here, Edwardo."

"What'll we do with her?"

"We'll think of something."

"What about Antek?"

"Forget him."

They pushed off. Rust slowed them at first, but as the tracks inclined towards the river they gained momentum. It was like learning to row. By the trestle they hit their rhythm; speed became wind—hair blowing, shirts flapping open, the tarp billowing up off the ice. The skyline gleamed ahead, and though Manny couldn't see the lake, he could feel it stretching beyond the skyscrapers. The smelt would have disappeared to wherever they disappeared to, but the fishermen would still be sitting at the edge of the breakwater, their backs to the city, dreaming up fish. He knew now where they were taking her. They were rushing through waist-deep weeds crossing the vast tracts of prairie behind the factories, clattering over bridges and viaducts. Below, streetlights shimmered watery in the old industrial neighborhoods. Shiny with sweat, with the girl already melting free between them, they forced themselves faster, rowing like a couple of sailors.

ELIZABETH CULLINAN

Life After Death

Yesterday evening I passed one of President Kennedy's sisters in the street again. They must live in New York—and in this neighborhood— the sister I saw and one of the others. They're good-looking women with a subdued, possibly unconscious air of importance that catches your attention. Then you recognize them. I react to them in the flesh the way I've reacted over the years to their pictures in the papers. I feel called on to account for what they do with their time, as if it were my business as well as theirs. I find myself captioning these moments when our paths cross. *Sister of the late President looks in shop window. Sister of slain leader buys magazine. Kennedy kin hails taxi on Madison Avenue.* And yesterday: *Kennedy sister and friend wait for light to change at Sixty-eighth and Lexington.* That was the new picture I added to the spread that opens out in my mind under the headline "LIFE AFTER DEATH."

It was beautifully cold and clear yesterday, and sunny and windless, so you could enjoy the cold without having to fight it, but I was dressed for the worst, thanks to my mother. At three o'clock she called to tell me it was bitter out, and though her idea of bitter and mine aren't the same, when I went outside I wore boots and put on a heavy sweater under my coat. I used to be overwhelmed by my mother's love; now it fills me with admiration. I've learned what it means to keep on loving in the face of resistance, though the resistance my two sisters and I offered wasn't to the love itself but to its superabundance, too much for our reasonable natures to cope with. My mother should have had simple, good-hearted daughters, girls who'd tell her everything, seated at the kitchen table, walking arm in arm with her in and out of department stores. But Grace and Rosemary and I aren't like that, not simple at all, and what goodness of heart we possess is qualified by the disposition we inherited from our father. We have a sense of irony that my mother with the purity of instinct and the passion of innocence sees as a threat to our happiness and thus to hers. Not one of us is someone she has complete confidence in.

Grace, the oldest of us, is married and has six children and lives in another city. Grace is a vivid person—vivid-looking with her black hair and high color, vivid in her strong opinions, her definite tastes. And Grace is a perfectionist who day after day must face the facts—that her son, Jimmy, never opens a book unless he has to and not always then; that her daughter Carolyn has plenty of boyfriends but no close girl-friends; that just when she gets a new refrigerator the washing machine will break down, then the dryer, then the house will need to be painted. My mother tells Grace that what can't be cured must be endured, but any such attitude would be a betrayal of Grace's ideals.

My middle sister, Rosemary, is about to marry a man of another religion. Rosemary is forty and has lived in Brussels and Stuttgart and Rome and had a wonderful time everywhere. No one thought she'd ever settle down, and my mother is torn between relief at the coming marriage and a new anxiety—just as she's torn, when Rosemary cooks Christmas dinner, between pleasure and irritation. Rosemary rubs the turkey with butter, she whips the potatoes with heavy cream; before Rosemary is through, every pot in the kitchen will have been used. This is virtue carried to extremes and no virtue at all in the eyes of my mother, whose knowledge of life springs from the same homely frame of reference as my sister's but has led to a different sort of conclusion: Rubbed with margarine the turkey will brown perfectly well; to bring the unbeliever into the fold, you needn't go so far as to marry him.

Every so often I have a certain kind of dream about Mother—a dream that's like a work of art in the way it reveals character and throws light on situations. In one of these dreams she's just died— within minutes. We're in the house where I grew up, which was my grandmother's house. There are things to be done, and Grace and Rose-mary and I are doing them, but the scene is one of lethargy, of a reluctance to get moving that belongs to adolescence, though in the dream, as in reality, my sisters and I are grown women. Suddenly I realize that Mother, though still dead, has got up and taken charge.

There's immense weariness but no reproach in this act. It's simply that she's been through it all before, has helped bury her own mother and father and three of her brothers. She knows what has to be done but she's kept this grim knowledge from Grace and Rosemary and me. She's always tried to spare the three of us, with the result that we lack her sheer competence, her strength, her powers of endurance, her devotedness. In another dream Mother is being held captive in a house the rest of us have escaped from and can't get back into. We stand in the street, helpless, while inside she's being beaten for no reason. The anguish I feel, the tears that wake me are not so much for the pain she's suffering as for the fact that this should be happening to her of all people, someone so ill-equipped to make sense of it. Harshness of various kinds and degrees has been a continuing presence and yet a continuing mystery to her, the enemy she's fought blindly all her life. "I don't think that gray coat of yours is warm enough," she said to me yesterday.

"Sure it is," I said.

"It isn't roomy enough." As she spoke, she'd have been throwing her shoulders back in some great imaginary blanket of a coat she was picturing on me.

"It fits so close, the wind can't get in," I explained. "That's its great virtue."

"Let me give you a new coat," she said.

When I was four years old I had nephrosis, a kidney disease that was almost unheard of and nearly always fatal then. It singled me out. I became a drama, then a miracle, then my mother's special cause in life. From this it of course follows that I should be living the life she'd have liked for herself—a life of comfort—but desire has always struck me as closer to the truth of things than comfort could ever be. "I don't really want a new coat," I told her yesterday. "I like my gray one."

"Dress warmly when you go out," she said. "It's bitter cold."

As I was hanging up there was an explosion—down the street from me, half a block on either side of Lexington Avenue is being reconstructed. The School for the Deaf and the local Social Services Office were torn down, and now in place of those old, ugly buildings, battered into likenesses of the trouble they'd tried to mend, there are two huge pits where men drill and break rocks and drain water, yelling to each other like industrious children in some innovative playground. And all day long there are these explosions. There was another; then the phone rang again. It was Francis, for the second time that day. "Constance," he said, "what a halfwit I am."

I said, "You are?"

He gave the flat, quick, automatic laugh I hate, knowing it to be false. When Francis truly finds something funny, he silently shakes his head. "Yes, I am," he said. "I'm a halfwit. Here I made an appointment with you for tomorrow afternoon and I just turned the page of my calendar and found I've got some sort of affair to go to."

"What sort of affair?" I asked. It could have been anything from a school play to a war. Francis produces documentaries for television. He's also married and has four sons, two of them grown. He's a popular man, a man everyone loves, and when I think of why, I think of his face, his expression, which is of someone whose prevailing mood is both buoyant and sorrowful. He has bright brown eyes. His mouth is practically a straight line, bold and pessimistic. He has a long nose and a high forehead and these give his face severity, but his thick, curly, untidy gray-blond hair softens the effect.

"I'm down for some sort of cocktail party," he said. "This stupid, busy life of mine," he added.

This life of his, in which I figure only marginally, is an epic of obligation and entertainment. Work, eat, drink, and be merry is one way of putting it. It could also be put, as Francis might, this way: Talent, beauty, charm, taste, money, art, love—these are the real good in life, and each of these goods borrows from the others. Beauty is the talent of the body. Charm and taste must sooner or later come down to money. Art is an aspect of love, and love is a variable. And all this being, to Francis's way of thinking, so—our gifts being contingents—we can do nothing better than pool them. Use me, use each other, he all but demands. I say, no—we're none of us unique, but neither are we interchangeable. "Well, if you've got something else to do, Francis," I said to him yesterday, "I guess you'd better do it."

He said, "Why don't I come by the day after tomorrow instead?"

I said, "I'm not sure."

"Not sure you're free or not sure you want to?"

"Both." I wasn't exactly angry or hurt. I have no designs on Francis Hughes, no claim on him. It would be laughable if I thought I did.

"Ah," he said, "Inconstance."

I said, "No, indefinite."

He said, "Well, I'm going to put Thursday down on my calendar and I'll call you in the morning and see how you feel about it."

"All right," I said, but on Thursday morning I won't be here—if people aren't interchangeable, how much less so are people and events.

"Tell me you love me," said Francis.

I said, "I do."

He said, "I'll talk to you Thursday."

"Good-bye, Francis," I said, and I hung up and put on my boots and my heavy sweater and my gray coat and went out.

The college I went to is a few blocks from this brownstone where I have an apartment. It's a nice school, and I was happy there and I can feel that happiness still, as though these well-kept streets, these beautiful houses are an account that was held open for me here. But New York has closed out certain other accounts of mine, such as the one over in the West Fifties. Down one of those streets is the building where I used to work and where I first knew Francis. His office was across the hall from mine. His life was an open book, a big, busy novel in several different styles—part French romance, part character study, part stylish avant-garde, part nineteenth-century storytelling, all plot and manners, part Russian blockbuster, crammed with characters. His phone rang constantly. He had streams of visitors. People sent him presents—plants, books, cheeses, bottles of wine, boxes of English crackers. I was twenty-two or three at the time, but I saw quite clearly that the man didn't need more love, that he needed to spend some of what he'd accumulated, and being twenty-two or three I saw no reason why I shouldn't be the one to make that point. Or rather, what should have put me off struck me as reason for going ahead—for the truth is I'm not Francis's type. The girls who came to see him were more or less voluptuous, more or less blond, girls who looked as if they were ready to run any risk, whereas I'm thin, and my hair is brown, and the risks I run with Francis are calculated, based on the fact that the love of someone like me can matter to someone like him only by virtue of its being in doubt. And having, as I say, no designs, I find myself able to be as hard on him as if he meant very little to me when, in fact, he means the world. I try now to avoid the West Fifties. Whenever I'm in that part of the city, the present seems lifeless, drained of all intensity in relation to that lost time when my days were full of Francis, when for hours on end he was close by.

I also try to avoid Thirty-fourth Street, where my father's brother-in-law used to own a restaurant, over toward Third Avenue. Flynn's was the name of it, and when I was twelve my father left the insurance business to become manager of Flynn's. He's an intelligent man, a man who again and again redeems himself with a word, the right word he's hit on effortlessly. His new raincoat, he told me the other day, "creaks." I asked if there was much snow left after a recent storm, and he said only a "batch" here and there. Sometimes he hits on the wrong word and only partly accidentally. "Pompadour," he was always calling French Premier Pompidou. He also has a perfect ear and a loathing for the current cliché. He likes to speak, with cheery sarcasm, of his "life-style." He also likes to throw out the vapid "Have a good day!" "No way" is an expression that simply drives him crazy.

The other night I dreamed a work of art about my father. He was in prison, about to be executed for some crime having to do with money. Rosemary and my mother and I had tried everything, but we failed to save him. At the end we were allowed—or obliged—to sit with him in his cell, sharing his terror and his misery and his amazing pluck. For it turned out that he'd arranged to have his last meal not at night but in the morning—so he'd have it to look forward to, he said. I woke up in despair. My father's spirit is something I love, as I love his sense of language, but common sense is more to the point in fathers, and mine has hardly any. As for business sense—after eight months at Flynn's, it was found that he'd been tampering with the books; six thousand dollars was unaccounted for. No charges were pressed, but my father went back to the insurance business, and from then on we didn't meet his family at Christmas and Easter, they didn't come to any more graduations or to Grace's wedding, Rosemary no longer got a birthday check from Aunt Kay Flynn, her godmother. You could say those people disappeared from our lives except that they didn't, at least not from mine. Once, when I was shopping with some friends in a department store, I spotted my Aunt Dorothy, another of my father's sisters. She was looking at skirts with my cousins Joan and Patricia, who are Grace's age—I must have been about sixteen at the time. A couple of summers later I had a job at an advertising agency where my cousin Bobby Norris turned out to be a copywriter. He was a tall, skinny, good-natured fellow, and he used to come and talk to me, and once or twice he took me out to lunch. He never showed any hard feelings toward our family, and neither did he seem to suspect how ashamed of

us I was. Around this time I began running into my cousin Paul Hal-
loran, who was my own age. At school dances and at the Biltmore,
where everybody used to meet, he'd turn up with his friends and I with
mine. Then one Christmas I got a part-time job as a salesgirl at
Altman's. A boy I knew worked in the stockroom, and sometimes we
went for coffee after work, and once he asked me to have a drink. We
were walking down Thirty-fourth Street when he told me where we
were going—a bar that he passed every day and that he wanted me to
inspect with him. Too late to back out, I realized he was taking me to
Flynn's. As soon as I walked in, I saw my father's brother-in-law sitting
at a table, talking to one of the waiters. He didn't recognize me, but I
couldn't believe he wouldn't. I'm the image of my mother and I was
convinced this would have to dawn on him, and that he'd come over
and demand to know if I was who he thought I was, and so I drank my
whiskey sour sitting sideways in the booth, one hand shielding my face,
like a fugitive from justice. Or like the character in a movie who, when
shot, will keep on going, finish the business at hand, and then keel over,
dead.

It's three blocks north and three blocks east from the house where I
live to the building where I went to college. Sometimes, of an afternoon,
I work there now, in the Admissions Office, and yesterday I had to pick
up a check that was due me. The Admissions Office is in a brownstone.
The school has expanded. Times have changed. On the way in I met
Sister Catherine, who once taught me a little biology. "Is it going to
snow?" she asked.

I said, "It doesn't look like snow to me."

In the old days these nuns wore habits with diamond-shaped head-
pieces that made them resemble figures on playing cards, always looking askance. Yesterday Sister Catherine had on a pants suit and an
imitation-fur jacket with a matching hat on her short, curly gray hair,
and it was I who gave the sidelong glance, abashed in the face of this
flowering of self where self had for so long been denied.

"It's cold enough for snow," Sister Catherine said.

I said, "It certainly is," and fled inside.

The house was adapted rather than converted into offices, which is to
say the job was only half done. Outside Admissions there's a pullman
kitchen—stove, sink, cabinets, refrigerator, dishes draining on a rack.
Food plays an important part in the life of this office, probably because

the clerical staff is made up of students who, at any given moment, may get the urge for a carton of yogurt, or a cup of soup, or an apple, or a can of diet soda. I went and stood in the doorway of the room where they sit: Delia, Yeshi, Eileen, Maggie. They knew someone was there, but no one looked up. They always wait to make a move until they must, and then they wait to see who'll take the initiative. One reason they like it when I'm in the office is that I can be counted on to reach for the phone on the first ring, to ask at once if I can help the visitor. But the routine of Admissions is complicated; every applicant seems to be a special case, and I work there on such an irregular basis that I can also be counted on not to be able to answer the simplest questions, and this makes the students laugh, which is another reason they like having me around. That someone like me, someone who's past their own inherently subordinate phase of life, should come in and stuff promotional material into envelopes, take down telephone requests for information, type up lists and labels—and do none of this particularly well—cheers them. I stepped into the office and said, "Hello, everybody." They stopped everything. I said, "Guess what I want."

"You want your check," said Yeshi, who comes from Ethiopia—the cradle of mankind. Lately I've been studying history. A friend of mine who's an Egyptologist lent me the text of a survey course, and now there are these facts lodged in my mind among the heaps of miscellaneous information accumulating there. "Where is Constance's check?" asked Yeshi. She speaks with a quaver of a French accent. Her hands are tiny, her deft brown fingers as thin as pencils. She has enormous eyes. "Who made out Constance's time sheet?" she asked.

Maggie said, "I did." She wheeled her chair over to the file cabinet where the checks are kept. "It should be here. I'm sure I saw it this morning with the others." Maggie is Haitian. Her hair is cut close and to the shape of her head. She has a quick temper, a need to be listened to, and a need, every bit as great, to receive inspiration. "Uh-oh," she said.

"Not there?" I asked.

"It's got to be. I made out that time sheet myself," said Maggie. "I remember it was on Thursday—I'm not in on Wednesdays, and Friday would have been too late."

I said, "Well, I don't suppose anyone ran off with it. It was only for a few dollars."

"Money is money around here." This came from Delia, a pre-med student and the brightest of the girls. Her wavy light-brown hair hangs below her waist. She has prominent features—large hazel eyes, an almost exaggeratedly curved mouth, and a nose that manages to be both thin and full; but there's a black-haired, black-eyed sister, the beauty of the family, and so Delia must make fun of her own looks. She's Puerto Rican and must also make fun of that. She speaks in sagas of self-deprecation that now and again register, with perfect pitch, some truth of her existence. "There's no poor like the student poor," she said yesterday.

"That's a fact, Delia," I said. "But I don't plan on contributing my wages to the relief of the Student Poor."

Maggie began pounding the file cabinet. "I made out that time sheet *myself.* I brought it in *myself* and had Mrs. Keene sign it; then I took it right over to the business office and handed it to feebleminded Freddy. He gave me a hard time because it wasn't with the others. I hate that guy." She pounded the cabinet again.

Yeshi said, "Maybe Mrs. Keene has it."

"Is she in her office?" I could see for myself by stepping back; Olivia was at her desk.

"Come on in," she called.

I said to the students, "I'll be back," and I went to talk to my friend.

"You're just in time for tea and strumpets," she said.

Olivia was in school with me here, but her name then was McGrath. She's been married and divorced and has two sons, and I say to myself, almost seriously, that the troubled course of her life must be the right course since it's given her the name Keene, which describes her perfectly. She's clever, capable, resilient, dresses well, wears good jewelry, leads a busy life. Except for the divorce, Olivia is an example of what my mother would like me to be, though her own mother continually finds fault. "I wonder what it's like to be proud of your children," Mrs. McGrath will say.

Olivia reached for the teapot on her desk and said, "Have a cup."

"No, thanks," I said. "I only came by to pick up my check, but it doesn't seem to be outside."

She opened her desk drawer, fished around, and came up with a brown envelope. "Someone must have put it here for safest keeping." She handed me the envelope and said, "Come on, sit down for a minute. Hear the latest outrage."

I sat down in the blue canvas chair beside the desk. I love offices and in particular that office, where the person I am has very little fault to find with the person I was. I begin to wonder, when I'm there, whether the movement of all things isn't toward reconciliation, not division. I'm half convinced that time is on our side, that nothing is ever lost, that we need only have a little more faith, we need only believe a little more and the endings will be happy. Grace's children will be a credit to her. Rosemary will find herself living in a style in keeping with her generous nature. My mother will come to trust the three of us. Olivia's mother will learn to appreciate Olivia. Francis will see how truly I love him. I'll be able to walk down Thirty-fourth Street and not give it a thought. "All right," I said to Olivia, "let's hear the latest outrage."

"Yesterday was High School Day."

"How many came?" I asked.

"A record hundred and seventy, of whom one had her gloves stolen, five got stuck in the elevator, and twelve sat in on a psychology class where the visiting lecturer was a transsexual."

"Oh God," I said.

"Tomorrow I get twelve letters from twelve mothers and dads."

"Maybe they won't tell their parents." I never told mine about seeing Aunt Dorothy shopping for skirts, or about the time I went to Flynn's for a drink, or how my first boyfriend, Gene Kirk, tried to get me to go to bed with him. To this day, I tell people nothing. No one knows about Francis.

Olivia said, "Nowadays kids tell all. Last week Barney came home and announced that his teacher doesn't wear a bra."

I looked at the two little boys in the picture on Olivia's desk. "How old is Barney?" I asked.

"Ten."

He has blond hair that covers his ears, and light-brown eyes with a faraway look. He calls the office and says, "Can I speak to Mrs. Keene? It's me." His brother, Bartholomew, is a couple of years older. Like Olivia, Bart has small, neat features and an astute expression. He sometimes does the grocery shopping after school. He'll call the office and discuss steaks and lamb chops with his mother, and I remember how when I was a little older than he I used to have to cook supper most evenings. The job fell to me because Grace wasn't at home—she'd won a board-and-tuition scholarship to college—and Rosemary was studying piano, which kept her late most evenings, practicing or at her lessons. And after my father's trouble at Flynn's my mother had to go back to teaching music herself. She's a good—a born—musician, but the circumstances that made her take it up again also made her resent it. I resented it too, because of what it did to my life. After school, I'd hang around till the last minute at the coffee shop where everyone went; then I'd rush home and peel the potatoes, shove the leftover roast in the oven or make the ground beef into hamburgers, heat the gravy, set the table—all grudgingly. But Bartholomew Keene takes pride in his shopping and so does Olivia. In our time, people have made trouble manageable. I sat forward and said, "I'd better get going."

"Think of it," said Olivia. "A transsexual."

I said, "Put it out of your mind."

In the main office, the students were in a semi-demoralized state. Their feelings are in constant flux; anything can set them up or down, and though they work hard, they work in spurts. My turning up was an excuse to come to a halt. I showed them my pay envelope. Maggie pounded the desk and said, "I *knew* it had to be around here somewhere."

"And I believed in you, Maggie," I said.

" 'I be-lieve for ev-ry drop of rain that falls,' " sang Delia, " 'a flow-er grows.' " They love to sing—when they're tired, when they're fresh, when they're bored or happy or upset.

" 'I be-lieve in mu-sic!' " Maggie snapped her fingers, switching to the rock beat that comes naturally to them. Eileen got up and went into her dance—she's a thin, pretty blonde with a sweet disposition and the soul of a stripper.

" 'I be-lieve in mu-sic!' " they all yelled—all except Yeshi, who only smiled. Yeshi is as quiet as the others are noisy but she loves their noise. Noise gives me eyestrain. I began backing off.

"When are you coming in again?" asked Delia.

I said, "Next week, I think."

Yeshi laughed. Her full name is Yeshimebet. Her sisters are named Astair, Neghist, Azeb, Selamawit, and Etsegenet. Ethiopia lies between Somalia and the Sudan on the Red Sea, whose parting for Moses may have been the effect of winds on its shallow waters.

After I left the office yesterday, I went to evening Mass. I often do. I love that calm at the end of the day. I love the routine, the prayers, the ranks of monks in their white habits, who sit in choir stalls on the altar —I go to a Dominican church, all gray stone and vaulting and blue stained glass. Since it's a city parish, my companions at Mass are diverse—businessmen and students and women in beautiful fur coats side by side with nuns and pious old people, the backbone of congregations. I identify myself among them as someone who must be hard to place—sometimes properly dressed, sometimes in jeans, not so much devout as serious, good-looking but in some undefined way. It's a true picture of me but not, of course, the whole truth. There's no such thing as the whole truth with respect to the living, which is why history appeals to me. I like the finality. Whatever new finds the archeologists may make for scholars to dispute, the facts stand. Battles have been won or lost, civilizations born or laid waste, and the labor and sacrifice entailed are over, can perhaps even be viewed as necessary or at least inevitable. The reasons I love the Mass are somewhat the same. During those twenty or so minutes, I feel my own past to be not quite coherent but capable of eventually proving to be that. And if my life, like every other, contains elements of the outrageous, that ceremony of death and transfiguration is a means of reckoning with the outrageousness, as work and study are means of reckoning with time.

Yesterday Father Henshaw said the five-o'clock Mass. He doesn't linger over the prayers—out of consideration, you can tell, for these people who've come to church at the end of a day's work—but he's a conscientious priest and he places his voice firmly on each syllable of each word as he addresses God on behalf of us all, begging for pardon, mercy, pity, understanding, protection, love. By the time Mass was over yesterday, the sun had set, and as I stepped onto the sidewalk I had the feeling I was leaving one of the side chapels for the body of the church. The buildings were like huge, lighted altars. The sky was streaked with color—a magnificent fresco, too distant for the figures to be identified. The rush hour had started. The street was crowded with people—flesh-and-blood images, living tableaux representing virtue and temptation: greed on one face, faith on another, on another charity, or sloth, fortitude, or purity. And there, straight out of Ecclesiastes, I thought—vanity of vanities, all is vanity. Then I realized I was looking at President Kennedy's sister. She was with a dark-haired man in a navy-blue overcoat. I had the impression at first that he was one of the Irish cousins, but I changed my mind as she smiled at him. It was a full and formal smile, too full and formal for a cousin and for that drab stretch of Lexington Avenue. It was a smile better given at official receptions to heads of state, and I got a sense, as I walked behind the couple, of how events leave people stranded, how from a certain point in our lives on—a different point for each life—we seem only to be passing time. I thought of the Kennedys in Washington, the Kennedys in London, the Kennedys in Boston and Hyannis Port. Which were the important days? The days in the White House? The days at the Court of St. James's? Or had everything that mattered taken place long before, on the beaches of Cape Cod where we saw them sailing and swimming and playing games with one another?

We reached the corner of Sixty-eighth and had to wait for the light to change. It's a busy corner, with a subway station, a newsstand, a hot-dog stand, and a flower stand operated by a man and his wife. The flower sellers are relative newcomers to the corner. I began noticing them last summer, when they were there all day, but when winter came they took to setting up shop in late afternoon. For the cold they dress alike in parkas, and boots, and trousers, and gloves with the fingers cut out. They have the dark features of the Mediterranean countries and they speak to each other in a foreign language. They have a little boy who's almost always with them. I'd guess he's about five, though he's big for five, but at the same time he also seems young for whatever age he may be, possibly because he appears to be so contented on that street corner. A more sophisticated child might sulk or whine or get into trouble, but not that little boy. Sometimes he has a toy with him—a truck or an airplane or a jump rope. He also has a tricycle that he rides when the weather is good. If it's very cold he may shelter in the warmth of the garage a few doors down from the corner, or he'll sit in his parents' old car, surrounded by flowers that will replenish the stock as it runs out. In hot weather, he sometimes stretches out on the sidewalk, but that's the closest I've ever seen him come to being at loose ends. He's a resourceful little boy, and he's independent like his parents, who work hard and for the most part silently. I've never seen them talking with the owner of the hot-dog stand or the newsdealer. Business is business on that corner, and not much of it comes from me. I never buy hot dogs, flowers only once in a blue moon, and newspapers not as a rule but on impulse. Yesterday, I put my hand in my pocket and found a dollar bill there and I decided to get a paper. I picked up a *Post* and put my money in the dealer's hand. As he felt through his pockets full of coins, the flower sellers' little boy suddenly appeared, dashed over to his parents' cart, seized a daisy, and put his nose to the yellow center. The newsdealer gave me three quarters back. The traffic lights changed.

President Kennedy's sister started across the street. The flower seller's wife grabbed the daisy from her son, and he ran off. I put the quarters in my pocket and moved on.

Yesterday's headlines told of trouble in the Middle East—Israel of the two kingdoms, Israel and Judah; Iran that was Alexander's Persia; Egypt of the Pharaohs and the Ptolemies. I love those ancient peoples. I know them. They form a frieze, a band of images carved in thought across my mind—emperors, princesses, slaves, scribes, farmers, soldiers, musicians, priests. I see them hunting, harvesting, dancing, embracing, fighting, eating, praying. The attitudes are all familiar. The figures are noble and beautiful and still.

IGNAZIO SILONE

Polikushka

After the earthquake, the headquarters of the Farmers' League had been reestablished in a hut belonging to the county. But it was almost deserted because most of the active members had been drafted on account of the war. The hut was surrounded by donkey stables and pigsties, in the dirtiest part of the village. Three or four old farmers met there every Sunday night, mainly to give the impression, especially to themselves, that the Farmers' League was still in operation. Depending on the season, they would sit just outside or indoors around a table, exchanging a word or two, or smoking a pipe, in the dark because there were no lights. At that hour the other farmers were usually at the inns. The three or four League members, understandably, would rather have been at an inn with glasses of wine in their hands, but the authorities had already tried to take the hut away on the ground that it was not used, so they had to show that it was. "We need it for our meetings," they had declared.

To give up their "headquarters" would mean the end of the League. One day or another the war would have to end, and they could not let the young demobilized farmers find it gone just when they would need it most. One day or another, of course, was just a manner of speaking. The women went to church to pray for peace, but the men knew that impatience with fate never did any good.

Within the hut were some relics which had been found after the earthquake among the ruins of the old headquarters. Hanging on a wall was a picture representing Christ the Redeemer, wearing long red overalls with a banner above Him that read, "Blessed are they which do hunger and thirst after righteousness." Under the picture, hanging from a nail, was the trumpet that had once been used to call together the members, since many of them could not read and thus could not be summoned by posters. All in all, the use of the trumpet was an expeditious and pleasant way of getting people together. But with posters it would have been easy to explain in advance why the meeting was being called. With the trumpet this was impossible. And so it happened that every time its blast was heard echoing through the streets of the village, an understandable anxiety would arise. This happened at night, when the farmers were coming back from the fields, and it was understood that the meeting was to take place right away. In the families of the landowners and other rich, well-born people this uncertainty took the form of apprehension if not downright fear. What's happening? Another meeting? But what do they want? Are they mad? Then mothers would lean out of windows and balconies and call home their children in loud voices, as a brood hen calls her chicks, so they would not get involved in any trouble.

There was no one to call me anymore, and perhaps for that reason I felt strangely attracted to those poor people who, worn out by their day's labors, came at the summons of the trumpet. And so I became involved in their meetings, which were held in the courtyard of an old Franciscan convent which in its day had been founded by another poor man, St. Francis of Assisi. Even though they were the same people I saw on other occasions, in town, at church, or at the market, these sudden gatherings made a profound impression on me. My heart would beat violently. There was always some stranger at those meetings who would talk in a loud voice, but I could not understand much of what he was saying. All my attention was focused on the people, who seemed to me transfixed.

Usually no one paid any attention to me. But one night something unpleasant happened.

"What're you doing here?" a farmer asked me in a threatening voice. I looked at him without breathing, as if I had been caught doing something wrong. "Are you going to plow a furrow, too?" he insisted with growing anger.

"No," I answered, forcing a smile on my face to placate him. "Right now I'm in school." And I showed him some books I was carrying.

An older man I knew by sight came to my rescue and put his hand on my shoulder as a sign that I was under his protection. I stayed next to him until the end of the meeting, and then I walked with him to his home, which was in the new part of the village that had grown up among the vineyards.

"What's your name?" I asked him.

"Lazzaro," he answered. Then he added, "When I was a young man, I was very close to your father."

"Why did that man want to kick me out of the meeting?"

"Maybe on account of your books."

"What?" I exclaimed. "Is there anything wrong with studying?"

"No, there's nothing wrong with it, but there are some educated people who use their education to take advantage of the poor. Didn't you hear what was said at the meeting?"

I admitted that I had not. Then he tried to explain it to me. For several years, there had been a special law which exempted farmers in the southern part of Italy from certain petty taxes. The farmers in our region, however, did not know about this law and therefore continued to pay them. Why hadn't anyone told us? Without a doubt the clerks in the tax collector's office knew about it, as well as the town clerks, the lawyers, the schoolteachers and the priests—in short, all the educated people who read the papers. Why had they hidden it from us? This news seemed unbelievable to me.

"How can it be possible?" I asked. "Lazzaro, tell me what you think. Why hasn't anyone said anything about it?"

He hesitated to answer me, perhaps to avoid saying unpleasant things about people I knew. But I insisted.

"Lazzaro, why won't you tell me? Do you think the truth should be kept from boys, too?"

But some other people came up just then, and we could not continue our conversation.

From that meeting grew my friendship with Lazzaro. I liked him; he did not have much to say; he was rough, modest, and without a trace of obsequiousness or fear. He had not had much education and he could barely read and write, but he knew a side of life of which I was entirely ignorant. For example, on the origins of the war then going on, and of all wars, Lazzaro's knowledge was simple and sure. Wars, he explained, are a remedy governments use to keep down the ever-increasing number of farmers. And for the same purpose they send cholera and other epidemics to the poor people.

"But don't the rich die too?" I countered.

"Yes, they do, and that's God's vengeance," he explained. "Of course, governments have no interest in exterminating the people who work the earth. Otherwise who'd do that work? And what would the gentlemen eat? And that's why wars last only so long. During the fighting the Red Cross keeps a constant control of the number of victims. And at a certain point it says, 'O.K. That's enough for now.'"

Of course, these were paradoxical opinions which did not convince me in every detail, but that an honest and reasonable man like Lazzaro would give them out as his own was cause enough for bitter pain and torment for me.

My visits to the League to meet Lazzaro were not unobserved, and they soon became cause for scandal among those who knew me, since I was still a student, and because my family, without being rich, was considered above the farmer class. I did not do much in the League, except to write some protests to the authorities on its behalf; sometimes even to the government in Rome on problems which Lazzaro explained clearly to me, and which I had to rewrite several times before I arrived at something satisfactory.

One day one of my classmates took me aside to tell me, "Do you know that they've started saying that you're a Red?"

"Nonsense," I answered. "I've never been to the dye-works." But I told Lazzaro about it when I next saw him.

"There're people who say I'm a Red, too."

As often happened Lazzaro did not answer right away.

"I haven't the least feeling of having changed my skin," I added.

"As for color," Lazzaro finally answered, "it seems to me that a man's like water. If you take a glass of water, you see right away that it has no color. But a lot of water, a great river or the sea, easily takes on a coloration."

"Because of the sky?" I asked.

"Because of the sky," he confirmed. "In the same way each of us alone is like a glass of water. Where does the color come from?"

"From the mass?" I asked.

"Not from the mass," he explained. "A mass of sheep is still a mass of sheep. And there are hardly three or four of us."

"From what then?" I insisted.

"Whenever we get together, He promised to be with us," Lazzaro explained, pointing to the picture of Christ in the red overalls.

By the way he expressed himself, and everything else, Lazzaro was what is called a good Christian. For many years he had been a Prior of the Confraternity of Saint Francis. But he had not set foot in church since the priests had used the church bells to disrupt the farmers' meetings. The first time it happened, it was a great surprise for the people who filled the square. Given the hour, no one could explain the unexpected ringing. It was late for Vespers and early for the Ave Maria. Even less explicable was the fact that all the church bells were going full blast as if the Resurrection had come. The foreigner who was talking about the new agricultural contracts, standing on a table at one side of the square, was inundated by the wave of sound which came from the nearby church and paused, waiting for it to stop. It did stop, only to be unleashed again as soon as the man started talking once more. The murmuring in the square took on a threatening tone; but Lazzaro, by standing with open arms at the threshold of the church, prevented the crowd from invading it. From that day he had stayed away from church, particularly since the same thing happened again in the same circumstances.

"Why don't you go to church?" the parish priest asked Lazzaro one day. "Don't you hear the bells? You used to come regularly."

"Yes, I once thought those bells were the voice of God," Lazzaro answered him. "But now you've made them the voice of the landowners. May God forgive you."

Hearing these words, some other farmers who were about to enter the church withdrew and went away.

One evening, I made my usual appearance at the League. Seeing some schoolbooks under my arm, Lazzaro suggested, "Why don't you try to read us something from those printed pages?"

"Sure," I answered, "I'll pick out something good."

And since the next day was a holiday, we made a date for that evening. The idea of reading excited me a lot, and I was surprised that I had not thought of it on my own. But as soon as I started thinking of what text to choose, I was rather embarrassed. My education had been entirely scholastic, and we no longer lived in a period when Dante's *Divine Comedy* could be read in public in the squares of Tuscany. Even less suitable seemed the nonscholastic books I then had, most of them D'Annunzio. To take one of those in hand seemed far worse than reading in Latin, with which the farmers had some contact through the Liturgy. But I had to keep my word, and I had to push myself not to fail in the important undertaking.

At one point I remembered the words of a poor doctor who practiced in a village in our county. He was known as an anarchist; he led a very difficult life and was therefore treated with mistrust and contempt by the respectable families.

"I have a book I could lend you," he had once said to me.

The next day I went to his house to ask for his help and advice. In the summer sun, on a road covered with blinding dust, it was not a pleasant trip. I found the doctor in his squalid kitchen, fixing something to eat.

"Will you have a bite with me?" he asked.

I excused myself. "I have a date," I said.

While he talked, he broke up some bread, put it on a plate and poured bean soup over it from a pan. I explained my problem to him.

"Read to the peasants?" he asked. "I don't know what to tell you to read them."

"They're simple, but they're not stupid," I insisted.

"I know them and I know it's hard," he countered. "Come on," he said suddenly, going into the next room which served as his study.

The room did not show much respect for hygiene. Books, medicine samples, sanitary objects, and clothes were scattered everywhere in a state of confusion, even on the chairs and floor.

"Try this," he said, handing me a dog-eared little book. "If it's successful, I'll give you another one."

It was a collection of stories by Tolstoy.

On the way back I thought of resting awhile under a tree at the edge of a meadow, to get out of the great heat, and to have a look at those stories. I knew that Tolstoy was known as a great writer, but I had never read anything of his. When I began reading, I forgot about time and appetite. I was deeply affected. I was stirred most of all by the story of Polikushka, which describes the tragic end of a servant whom everyone had held in contempt because of his drinking and pilfering. Hoping to rehabilitate himself by doing an important job for his mistress, he lost the money entrusted to him and hanged himself in desperation. The writer who could portray a servant's suffering with such sincerity must have been a very good and brave man. The sad, slow pace of the story revealed a compassion beyond the usual pity of the man who is moved by his neighbor's troubles and averts his glance so that he will not suffer too. Divine compassion must be like this, I thought, the compassion which does not relieve a creature of his pain, yet on the other hand does not abandon him but helps him to the end, without ever revealing itself.

It was incomprehensible, even absurd, to me that I had come to know a story like that only by chance. Why didn't they read it in school?

I read the whole story over again that afternoon, finding new beauties which I had missed in the first reading. I was sure that my little audience would like it, in spite of some difficulties with the Russian names, especially the nicknames—and I thought of ways to get around them.

But when I arrived at the League building, I got the impression that the old men had forgotten all about our agreement. They were sitting on the doorstep, and one of them was reciting the long-drawn-out account of his encounter with a priest. I showed Lazzaro the book I had in my hand.

"Let's be quiet and listen to the book," he suggested.

"We're not kids anymore," grumbled one of them. "Fairy tales are for kids."

"But there are stories for grownups, too," I protested. "Just be patient and listen."

"What's it about?" one of them wanted to know. "Can't you tell us what happens?"

"It's a story about a man like you, who was born in Russia," I answered, losing patience. "I thought you'd like the story of a poor man."

It looked as if they were tolerating it more for my sake than out of real curiosity.

I began reading in a confident voice, but after the first few sentences I realized that the minute description of the overseer Igor Mikhailovich visiting his master, the notation of every detail of his behavior, and the examination of his most deeply hidden thoughts formed a skein whose thread my listeners had probably already lost. My voice faltered, and I raised my eyes from the page to look at Lazzaro.

"Do you follow?" I asked.

"Couldn't you tell us in two or three words what happens?" repeated one of the old men.

"If that were possible, the author would have written just two or three words and nothing else," I tried to explain.

"Read on," Lazzaro encouraged me.

Then it occurred to me that this was not a text to be read aloud. The doctor who had lent it to me was right. Give up? Impossible! But since I had already read it twice alone, I tried to proceed with my eyes skimming the text, summarizing or skipping whatever seemed like a digression.

I lingered a little over the description of the drawing of lots for military service in the little community of Pokrovskoye, and again over the portrait of Polikushka, a good man who after every drunken binge, and every time he was caught pilfering, promised to mend his ways, a man who had practiced a little of every trade in his life—stable boy, weaver, brick maker, and even veterinarian—though he knew next to nothing about any of them.

"In other words, he was a real crook," one of the old men interrupted, "someone to lock up in jail and forget about."

I felt my voice fading. If they had not the least sympathy for poor Polikushka, what good was it to read the story?

"Go on," Lazzaro told me.

I put the book aside and told them the end in a few words: about Polikushka's trip to the city on his mistress's confidential errand, the withdrawal of the money from the rich merchant, the loss of the precious hoard, finally his desperation, his vain search, and his suicide.

"They didn't find the money?" Lazzaro asked me.

"It was found and brought back to the lady to whom it belonged. But she was so shocked at seeing Polikushka hanged that she refused to accept it."

"How did the story end?" one of the old men asked me.

"What?"

"That money. You said there was a lot of it."

"The lady left it to the man who found it, named Dutlov."

"Didn't she give it to the servant's widow?"

"No. Not to the widow."

I said that I was tired and left them.

I didn't know what to think of what had happened, or rather I did not want to think about it. That evening while I was doing the homework that had piled up in the last few days, I was told that someone in the street wanted to see me. It was a farmer who belonged to the League but who was not very active.

"No one told me," he complained. "If I had known, I would have come. What's the story about the man who hangs himself and then they find the money he lost?"

"I'll tell you about it some other time," I promised him, "but I'm busy now."

In the years that followed I was too emotionally involved in other things to have much time to read literary works. The only books I used were histories and economic tracts, but not even these were for educational purposes; rather were they for immediate practical use, to write little newspaper articles, in which the rashness of my judgment was equaled only by my sincerity. I was reminded of Polikushka just once, during a visit to Moscow. One night, around the Pushkin Monument, when I was with some leaders of the Soviet Young Communist League, I saw two soldiers hauling a drunken farmer away by the scruff of the neck. I recognized him at once.

"Couldn't you get him released?" I asked my friends.

"Why?" one of them answered. "He's nothing but a parasitic insect!"

BREECE D'J PANCAKE

The Salvation of Me

Chester was smarter than any shithouse mouse because Chester got out before the shit began to fall. But Chester had two problems: number one, he became a success, and number two, he came back. These are not your average American problems like drinking, doping, fucking, or being fucked, because Rock Camp, West Virginia, is not your average American problem maker, nor is it your average hillbilly town.

You have never broken a mirror or walked under ladders or celebrated Saint Paddy's day if you have never heard of Rock Camp, but you might have lost a wheel, fallen off a biplane wing, or crossed yourself left-handedly if you have. The three latter methods are the best ways to get into Rock Camp, and any viable escape is unknown to anybody but Chester, and he is unavailable for comment.

It was while Archie Moore—the governor, not the fighter—was in his heyday that the sweet tit of the yellow rose of Texas ran dry, forcing millions of Americans down to the survival speed of 55 mph. I have heard it said that Georgians are unable to drive in snow, and that Arizonans go bonkers behind the wheel in the rain, but no true-blooded West Virginia boy would ever do less than 120 mph on a straight stretch, because those runs are hard won in a land where road maps resemble a barrel of worms with Saint Vitus's dance. It was during this time that Chester discovered people beating it through West Virginia via Interstate 64 on their way to more interesting places like Ohio and Iowa, and for the first time in his life Chester found fourth gear in his Chevy with the Pontiac engine. Don't ask me what the transmission was, because I was sick the day they put it in, and don't ask me where

Chester went, because I didn't see him again for four years, and then he wasn't talking.

All I know for sure is that Chester made it big, and came back to show it off, and that I never hated him more in the years he was gone than I did the two hours he was home. The fact that without Chester I had twice as many cars to fix, half as much gas to pump, and nobody to road-race or play chicken with on weekends made up for itself in giving me all my own cigarettes, since Chester was the only bum in the station. And his leaving warmed over an old dream.

Back in '61 when I was a school kid, everybody from one end of Rock Camp to the other switched over from radio to TV, and although I still believe that was a vote purchase on Kennedy's part, everyone swears it was a benefit of working in the pre-Great Society days. So the old Hallicrafters radio found its place next to my desk and bed, looking at me, as it later did through hours of biology homework, like any minute the Day of Infamy would come out of its speakers again.

What did come out, and only between the dusk and dawn, was WLS from Chicago. Chicago became a dream, then more of a habit than pubescent self-abuse, replaced beating off, then finally did what the health teacher said pounding the pud would do—made me crazy as a damn loon.

Chicago, Chicago, that toddlin' town . . .

Don't ask me to sing the rest, because I have forgotten it, and don't ask me what became of the dream, either, because I have a sneaking suspicion Chester did it in for me when he came back. But the dream was more beautiful than the one about Mrs. Dent, my sex-goddess math teacher, raping hell out of me during a tutoring session, and the dream was more fun because I believed it could happen. When I asked Mr. Dent, the gym teacher, if the angle of his dangle was equal to the heat of her meat, he rammed my head into a locker, and I swore forever to keep my hand out of my Fruit of the Looms. Besides, Chicago had it over Mrs. Dent by a mile, and Chicago had more Mrs. Dents than could rape me in a million years.

Dex Card, the then–night jock for 'LS, had a Batman fan club that even *I* could belong to, and the kids in Chicago all had cars, wore h.i.s. slacks—baked by the friendly h.i.s. baker in his own little oven so the crease would never wash out. They all chewed Wrigley gum, and all went to the Wrigley Building, which for some reason seems, even today, like a giant pack of Juicy Fruit on end. The kids in Chicago were so close to Motown they could drive up and *see* Gladys Knight or the Supremes walking on the goddamned street. And the kids in Chicago had three different temperatures: if it was cold at O'Hare Airport, it was colder in the Loop, and it was always below zero on the El. It took me ten years to get the joke. It took us two days to get the weather—if it rained in Chicago on Monday, I wore a raincoat on Wednesday, and thought of it as Chicago rain.

After the dream came the habit. I decided to run off to Chicago, but hadn't figured what I could do to stay alive, and I didn't know Soul One in the town. But the guys on 'LS radio sounded like decent sorts, and they had a real warmth you could just hear when they did those Save the Children ads. You knew those guys would be the kind to give a poor kid a break. And that is where the habit and the dream got all mixed up.

I would maybe take the train—since that was the only way I knew to get out, from my father's Depression stories—and I might even meet A-Number-One on some hard-luck flatcar, and him tracing old dreams on the car floor with a burned-out cigarette. Then me and old A-Number-One would take the Rock Island out of Kentucky, riding nonstop coal into the Chicago yards, and A-Number-One would tell about whole trains getting swallowed up, lost, bums and all, in the vastness of everything, never found. But I would make it off the car before she beat into the yards, skirt the stink on that side, and there I was at the Loop.

I would find WLS Studios and ask for a job application, and the receptionist, sexier than Mrs. Dent and a single to boot, would ask me what I could do. I would be dirty from the train, and my clothes would not be h.i.s., so what could I say but that I would like to sweep up. Bingo, and they hire me because nobody in Chicago ever wants to sweep up, and when I get down to scrape the Wrigley's off the floor, they think I'm the best worker in the world. I figure I'd better mop, and Dex Card says I'm too smart to mop and for me to take this sawbuck, go buy me some h.i.s. clothes and show up here tomorrow. He says he wants me to be the day jock, and he will teach me to run the board, make echoes, spin the hits, double-up the sound effects, and switch to the news-weather-and-sports. Hot damn.

So I sat at the desk every night, learning less biology, dreaming the dream over and over, until one night I looked at my respectable— nevertheless Woolworth—slacks, and realized that the freight trains no longer slowed down at Rock Camp. There was always the bus, but in all three times I collected enough pop bottles for a ticket to where the train slowed down, the pool balls would break in my ears, and quarters would slip away into slots of time and chance.

"You can't see the angles," Chester said to me one day after he ran the table in less than a minute.

I was in the tenth grade and didn't give two shits for his advice. All I knew was all my quarters were gone, there were no more pop bottles along the Pike, and Chicago was still a thousand miles away. I just leaned on my stick: I was sheared and I knew it.

"You know anything about cars?" I shook my head no. "Can you work a gas pump?" Again no. "You *can* wash a car." I sneered a who-the-hell-couldn't.

And from that day I went to work for E. B. "Pop" Sullivan in his American Oil station at seventy-five cents an hour, one third of which went to Chester for getting me the job. I told myself it didn't matter, I wasn't going to make a career of it, I was hitting it for Chicago as soon as I got the money—I'd ride the buses all the way, I'd drive. What the hell, I'd save up and buy a car to take me to Chicago in style.

When I told Chester I wanted to buy a car, he let me off the hook for his fee, even took me to look at the traps on the car lot. Then I told Chester I didn't want a trap, I wanted a real car.

"That's the way you get a real one," he said. "You make it to suit yourself—Motown just makes them to break down."

We looked at a Pontiac with only 38,000 and a 327. Somebody had lammed in the rear and pushed the trunk into the back seat. There was a clump of hair hanging from the chrome piece around the window. Chester crawled under this car and was gone for almost five minutes, while I was more attracted to a Chevy Impala with a new paint job and a backyard, install-it-yourself convertible top that came down of its own when you pressed a button. Chester came out from under the Pontiac like he had found a snake, then walked over to me grinning.

"She's totaled to hell and back, but the engine's perfect."

I told Chester I liked the Impala, but he just sucked his teeth like he knew what happened to tops that come down of their own. He walked all around the car, bent over to look under it, rubbed his fingers along the tread of the tires, and all the time I kept staring at the *$325* soaped on the windshield. Sure, the Pontiac was cheaper, but who wanted to pay $130 to walk around with an engine under his arm? Not me, I wanted to drive it away, make the top go up and down.

"Tell you what," he said. "I got me a nice Chevy for that Pontiac's motor. You buy the motor—I'll rent the body to you."

I wasn't about to bite, so I shook my head.

"We'll be partners, then. We'll each only sell out to the other, and we'll stick together on weekends. You know, double dates."

That made a little more sense, and the rest of that month the Chicago dream went humming away to hide someplace in my brain. I had nightmares about adapters being stretched out to fit an engine that shouldn't be in a Chevy. I worried about tapping too far from the solid part of the block, could just see cast steel splintering the first time we forced her up to 80. I went to drag races, asked anybody I saw if you could put a Pony engine in a Chevy, and most people laughed, but one smart-ass leaned back in his chair: "Son," says the smart-ass, "go play with yourself."

But the month went by, and the engine, for some reason I never understood, went in, but all the fire wall and all the fender wells came out. When Chester came down to the transmission problem, I came down with the flu, and for three days I neither dreamed of Chicago nor my car because I was too busy being sick. On returning to school, I saw her in the parking lot, the rear end jacked up with shackles, and when I looked in on the gearshift, Chester had a four-speed pattern knob screwed on it. I thought it was a joke, because I never saw the last gear used. She did 50 wound tight in third, and that was enough for the straight piece in the Pike.

That summer was just one big time. Chester and I spent every cent we earned on gas and every free minute on the back roads. We discovered a bridge with enough hump that hitting it at 45 would send us airborne every time and make the buggy rock like a chair until we could get new shocks on it. Unbeknownst to him, Pop Sullivan supplied shocks all summer. We found a curved section of one-lane that was almost always good for a near head-on with a Pepsi truck. A couple of times, Pop supplied red-lead to disguise the fact that we had gotten too close to the Pepsi truck. Pepsi, I take it, got the message and rerouted the driver. Chester told me, "They sent a boy to do a man's job."

But the best fun came when a Cabell County deputy was on his way to summons some ridge runner to court for not sharing his liquor revenues with the state. Deputy met us coming downhill and around a curve at top speed, and there was little else for Deputy to do but give us the right-of-way or kiss all our sweet asses good-bye. Deputy was a very wise man. Figuring that anybody coming from nowhere that fast had something to hide, Deputy then radioed ahead the liquor was in our car. They nabbed us at the foot of the hill, stone-cold sober, and found us holding no booze at all. What they did find were Deputy's two daughters—both out with their momma's permission. Chester got three days for driving away from a deputy, and neither of us was allowed to call the girls again. Don't ask me what their momma got, as I am not sure if Deputy was the wife-beating kind or not.

Chester served his three days in Sundays reading the paper at the county jail, and the first Sunday changed him considerably for the worse. At work the next day he wouldn't talk about who he wanted to go out with or where we were going to find money for the next tankful, but by the weekend he loosened up. "It's all a matter of chance," he said. I thought he was trying to explain his jail sentence. It took four years before I figured it out. After his second Sunday, he came back with a sneak in his eyes like he was just waiting for something to drop on his back out of thin air. "It's out there for sure, but it's just a matter of being in the right place when the shit falls." I agreed all the way. It was all in Chicago, and school was starting and I was still in Rock Camp.

The next morning, Chester went on the lam in a most interesting manner. It was his turn to cruise around town in the car during lunch, smooching his woman, and I would get snatch for my grab on the high-school steps. We had both been caught getting too fresh with our girls, and now there was not a decent girl in Rock Camp that wouldn't claim one of us raped her after her football boyfriend knocked her up. So it was that Chester's main squeeze was a girl from Little Tokyo Hollow, where twice-is-nice-but-incest-is-best and all the kids look like gooks. So it was I had no woman that day. And Chester was making the main circuit with regular rounds so that from where I sat, I could see every move this slant-eye made.

The first three go-arounds were pretty standard, and I could almost measure the distance her hand had moved on the way to Chester's crotch, but on the fourth trip she had him wide and was working the mojo. I knew Chester had done some slick bargaining to get that much action that soon, and I figured it was over from there, since I saw him turn around and head west back to the school. He was still only cruising, taking his time like he knew the bell would never ring unless he had gone to his locker. Then on the way by, I saw the slant-eye going down on him, her head bobbing like mad, Chester smiling, goosing the gas in short spurts. It wasn't until he stopped at the town limits and put the girl out that I figured Chester didn't care about coming back to class, but I went on anyway, sure as I could be that he'd be back tomorrow.

That afternoon the guidance counselor called me in and asked me what I was doing with the rest of my life. It seemed Chester's slant-eye had spilled the beans, and they were thinking there was something in me they could save. I told the guidance counselor I wanted to work for a radio station in Chicago—just as a joke.

"Well, you'll have to go to college for that, you know."

It was news to me, because Dex Card didn't sound like a teacher or a doctor, and I said no.

That evening, when Chester didn't show for work, I asked Pop Sullivan to sponsor me through college. I promised to stay at the station until I got my journalism degree, then send him the difference.

"I got all the difference I need" was all Pop would say. He kept looking out the window for Chester to come fix his share of cars. Chester never came, so I stayed until the next morning and figured out how to fix both our shares of cars with a book, and I thought maybe that was the way Chester had done it all along.

A week later, Pop hired another kid to pump gas and raised me to minimum wage, which by Archie's heyday was about a buck fifty. That was when I got a telegram from Cleveland saying: "Sorry Pard, I got it into fourth and couldn't get it out. I'll make it up sometime, C."—and I wondered why Chester bothered to waste four cents on the "Pard."

I left the radio off and my grades went up a little, but I didn't think I'd learned much worth knowing. The guidance counselor kept this shit-eating grin for when she passed me in the hall. Then weird stuff started happening—like my old man would come to bed sober at night and go to church twice on Sunday and drink orange juice at breakfast without pitching a bitch at me. And I got invited to parties the football players' parents threw for them and their girls, but I never went. Then a teacher told me if I made a B in World History before Christmas I would be a cinch for the Honor Society, but I told that teacher in no uncertain terms what the Honor Society could go do with themselves, and the teacher said I was a smart-ass. I agreed. I still got the B. I started dating Deputy's youngest daughter again, and he acted like I was a quarterback.

Then the real shit came down. It was snowing tons before Christmas, so I cut school to help Pop clear the passage around the pumps, and he called the principal to tell him what was up. I was salting the sidewalks when Pop yelled at me to come inside, then he loaded his pipe and sat down behind the desk.

"What'd I tell you about stealing?" he says, but I set him straight that I wasn't holding anything of his. "I don't mean you are, only I want to know if you remember." I told him that he had said once-a-thief-always-a-thief about a million times. "Do you think that's so?" I asked him if he'd stolen before. "Just once, but I put it back." I told him once-a-thief-always-a-thief, but he just laughed. "You need a college sponsor. I need another Catholic in this town." I assured Pop that my old man had suddenly seen the light, but I was in no way, shape, or form walking his path with him, and he was Methodist to boot. "You think about it." I said I would think about it and went in to grease a car. All I could think was, Dex Card doesn't sound like a Catholic name.

I walked home in the snow that night, and it did not seem like Chicago snow—it seemed like I was a kid before the radio moved into my room, and like when I got home from sledding and my old lady was still alive, still pumping coffee into me to cut the chill, and I missed her just a little.

I went inside hoping my old man would have a beer in his hand just so I could put things back to normal again, but he was sitting in the kitchen reading a newspaper, and he was stoned sober out of his mind.

I fixed us some supper, and while we ate he asked me if Pop had said anything to me about college. I said he would sponsor me if I turned mackerel-snapper. "Not a bad deal. You going to take it?" I assured him I was thinking on it. "There's mail for you," and he handed me an envelope postmarked Des Moines, Iowa. Inside was seventy-five bucks and a scrap of paper that said: "Less depreciation. *Adios,* C." I put the money in my wallet and balled up the note. "You can buy some clothes with that wad," he said. I assured my old man that I would need a car more if I was to drive to college every day, but he just laughed, gave me a dutch rub from across the table. He told me I was a good kid for a punk. Even the women in the school cafeteria sent me a card saying I was bound to become a man of letters—on the inside was a cartoon mailman. It took me awhile to get the joke.

And about that time the price of gas went up. I bought a '58 VW without a floor, drove it that way until it rained, then bought a floor for more than I paid for the whole car. Deputy's daughter missed a couple of months and decided it was me, and it probably was, so she joined me in catechism and classes at the community college in Huntington, and we lived in a three-room above Pop's station. The minute Deputy's daughter lost the kid, Deputy had the whole thing annulled, and Pop made me move back in with my old man. My old man started drinking again. I quit school, but stayed on at Pop Sullivan's garage to pay him back, and it was about then that I saw the time had gone by too soon. I had not turned the old radio on in all these years and I couldn't stand to now. I decided working for Pop wasn't too bad, and pretty soon my old man was going to have to be put away, and I'd need the money for that.

I drove home in the VW singing, *"Chicago, Chicago, that toddlin' town . . ."* and that was when I knew I had forgotten the rest of the words.

Then I saw it coming down the Pike, just a glimpse of metallic blue, a blur with yellow fog-lights that passed in the dusk, and the driver's face was Chester's. I wheeled the bug around, headed back into town, wound the gears tight to gain some speed, but he was too far gone to catch up with. I cruised town for an hour before I saw him barreling down the Pike again, and this time I saw the blonde in his car. When they pulled in on Front Street to get a bite at the café, I wheeled up beside the new Camaro. I had seen that girl of his lick her teeth in toothpaste ads on TV.

I asked Chester how it was going, but he forgot to know me: "Beg pardon?" I saw all his teeth were capped, but I told him who I was. "Oh, yes," he said. I asked him where he got the mean machine, and his girl looked at me funny, smiled to herself. "It's a rental." His girl broke out laughing, but I didn't get the joke. I told Chester he ought to go by and say hello to Pop on the way out. "Yes, yes, well, I will." I invited them out to eat with me and my old man, but Chester got a case of rabbit. "Perhaps another time. Nice to see you again." He slammed the car door, went into the café ahead of his girl.

I sat there in the VW, stared at the grease on my jeans, thought I ought to go in there and shove a couple of perhaps-another-times down Chester's shit-sucking face. Don't ask me why I didn't do it, because it was what I wanted most to do all my life, and don't ask me where the dream went, because it never hummed to me again.

When Chester left town, he left a germ. Not the kind of germ you think makes a plant grow, but a disease, a virus, a contagion. Chester sowed them in the café when Deputy recognized him, asked what he'd been doing with himself. Chester told Deputy he was on Broadway, and gave away free tickets to the show he was in, and a whole slough of people went up to New York. They all came back humming show songs. And the germ spread all over Rock Camp, made any kid on the high-school stage think he could be Chester. A couple of the first ones killed themselves, then the real hell was watching the ones who came back, when Pop told them there was no work at the station for faggots.

But one thing was for sure good to know, and that was when Chester was chewed up and spit out by New York because he thought his shit didn't stink, or at least that was what the folks said. I don't know what happened in New York, but I think I've got a hitch on what Chester did here. He was out to kill everybody's magic and make his own magic the only kind, and it worked on those who believed in Archie's heyday, or those who thought the sweet tit would never go dry, and it worked on Chester when he came back, started to believe it himself.

Standing in the station on a slow day, I sometimes think up things that might have happened to Chester, make up little plays for him to act out, wherever he is. When I do that, I very often lose track of when and where I am, and sometimes Pop has to yell at me to put gas in a car because I haven't heard the bell ring. Every time that sort of thing happens, I cross myself with my left hand and go out whistling a chorus of "Chicago."

Check the oil? Yessir.

Part III
RESPONSIBILITY

ANDRE DUBUS

A Father's Story

My name is Luke Ripley, and here is what I call my life: I own a stable of thirty horses, and I have young people who teach riding, and we board some horses, too. This is in northeastern Massachusetts. I have a barn with an indoor ring, and outside I've got two fenced-in rings and a pasture that ends at a woods with trails. I call it my life because it looks like it is, and people I know call it that, but it's a life I can get away from when I hunt and fish, and some nights after dinner when I sit in the dark in the front room and listen to opera. The room faces the lawn and the road, a two-lane country road. When cars come around the curve northwest of the house, they light up the lawn for an instant, the leaves of the maple out by the road and the hemlock closer to the window. Then I'm alone again, or I'd appear to be if someone crept up to the house and looked through a window: a big-gutted gray-haired guy, drinking tea and smoking cigarettes, staring out at the dark woods across the road, listening to a grieving soprano.

My real life is the one nobody talks about anymore, except Father Paul LeBoeuf, another old buck. He has a decade on me: he's sixty-four, a big man, bald on top with gray at the sides; when he had hair, it was black. His face is ruddy, and he jokes about being a whiskey priest, though he's not. He gets outdoors as much as he can, goes for a long walk every morning, and hunts and fishes with me. But I can't get him on a horse anymore. Ten years ago I could badger him into a trail ride; I had to give him a western saddle, and he'd hold the pommel and bounce through the woods with me, and be sore for days. He's looking at seventy with eyes that are younger than many I've seen in people in their twenties. I do not remember ever feeling the way they seem to; but I was lucky, because even as a child I knew that life would try me, and I must be strong to endure, though in those early days I expected to be tortured and killed for my faith, like the saints I learned about in school.

Father Paul's family came down from Canada, and he grew up speaking more French than English, so he is different from the Irish priests who abound up here. I do not like to make general statements, or even to hold general beliefs, about people's blood, but the Irish do seem happiest when they're dealing with misfortune or guilt, either their own or somebody else's, and if you think you're not a victim of either one, you can count on certain Irish priests to try to change your mind. On Wednesday nights Father Paul comes to dinner. Often he comes on other nights too, and once, in the old days when we couldn't eat meat on Fridays, we bagged our first ducks of the season on a Friday, and as we drove home from the marsh, he said: For the purposes of Holy Mother Church, I believe a duck is more a creature of water than land, and is not rightly meat. Sometimes he teases me about never putting anything in his Sunday collection, which he would not know about if I hadn't told him years ago. I would like to believe I told him so we could have philosophical talk at dinner, but probably the truth is I suspected he knew, and I did not want him to think I so loved money that I would not even give his church a coin on Sunday. Certainly the ushers who pass the baskets know me as a miser.

I don't feel right about giving money for buildings, places. This starts with the Pope, and I cannot respect one of them till he sells his house and everything in it, and that church too, and uses the money to feed the poor. I have rarely, and maybe never, come across saintliness, but I feel certain it cannot exist in such a place. But I admit, also, that I know very little, and maybe the popes live on a different plane and are tried in ways I don't know about. Father Paul says his own church, St. John's, is hardly the Vatican. I like his church: it is made of wood, and has a simple altar and crucifix, and no padding on the kneelers. He does not have to lock its doors at night. Still it is a place. He could say Mass in my barn. I know this is stubborn, but I can find no mention by Christ of maintaining buildings, much less erecting them of stone or brick, and decorating them with pieces of metal and mineral and elements that people still fight over like barbarians. We had a Maltese woman taking riding lessons, she came over on the boat when she was ten, and once she told me how the nuns in Malta used to tell the little girls that if they wore jewelry, rings and bracelets and necklaces, in purgatory snakes would coil around their fingers and wrists and throats. I do not believe in frightening children or telling them lies, but if those nuns saved a few girls from devotion to things, maybe they were right. That Maltese woman laughed about it, but I noticed she wore only a watch, and that with a leather strap.

The money I give to the church goes in people's stomachs, and on their backs, down in New York City. I have no delusions about the worth of what I do, but I feel it's better to feed somebody than not. There's a priest in Times Square giving shelter to runaway kids, and some Franciscans who run a bread line; actually it's a morning line for coffee and a roll, and Father Paul calls it the continental breakfast for winos and bag ladies. He is curious about how much I am sending, and I know why: he guesses I send a lot, he has said probably more than tithing, and he is right; he wants to know how much because he believes I'm generous and good, and he is wrong about that; he has never had much money and does not know how easy it is to write a check when you have every thing you will ever need, and the figures are mere numbers, and represent no sacrifice at all. Being a real Catholic is too hard; if I were one, I would do with my house and barn what I want the Pope to do with his. So I do not want to impress Father Paul, and when he asks me how much, I say I can't let my left hand know what my right is doing.

He came on Wednesday nights when Gloria and I were married, and the kids were young; Gloria was a very good cook (I assume she still is, but it is difficult to think of her in the present), and I liked sitting at the table with a friend who was also a priest. I was proud of my handsome and healthy children. This was long ago, and they were all very young and cheerful and often funny, and the three boys took care of their baby sister, and did not bully or tease her. Of course they did sometimes, with that excited cruelty children are prone to, but not enough so that it was part of her days. On the Wednesday after Gloria left with the kids and a U-Haul trailer, I was sitting on the front steps, it was summer, and I was watching cars go by on the road, when Father Paul drove around the curve and into the driveway. I was ashamed to see him because he is a priest and my family was gone, but I was relieved, too. I went to the car to greet him. He got out smiling, with a bottle of wine, and shook my hand, then pulled me to him, gave me a quick hug, and said: "It's Wednesday, isn't it? Let's open some cans."

With arms about each other we walked to the house, and it was good to know he was doing his work but coming as a friend, too, and I thought what good work he had. I have no calling. It is for me to keep horses.

In that other life, anyway. In my real one I go to bed early and sleep well and wake at four forty-five, for an hour of silence. I never want to get out of bed then, and every morning I know I can sleep for another four hours and still not fail at any of my duties. But I get up, so have come to believe my life can be seen in miniature in that struggle in the dark of morning. While making the bed and boiling water for coffee, I talk to God: I offer Him my day, every act of my body and spirit, my thoughts and moods, as a prayer of thanksgiving, and for Gloria and my children and my friends and two women I made love with after Gloria left. This morning offertory is a habit from my boyhood in a Catholic school; or then it was a habit, but as I kept it and grew older it became a ritual. Then I say the Lord's Prayer, trying not to recite it, and one morning it occurred to me that a prayer, whether recited or said with concentration, is always an act of faith.

I sit in the kitchen at the rear of the house and drink coffee and smoke and watch the sky growing light before sunrise, the trees of the woods near the barn taking shape, becoming single pines and elms and oaks and maples. Sometimes a rabbit comes out of the treeline, or is already sitting there, invisible till the light finds him. The birds are awake in the trees and feeding on the ground, and the little ones, the purple finches and titmice and chickadees, are at the feeder I rigged outside the kitchen window; it is too small for pigeons to get a purchase. I sit and give myself to coffee and tobacco, that get me brisk again, and I watch and listen. In the first year or so after I lost my family, I played the radio in the mornings. But I overcame that, and now I rarely play it at all. Once in the mail I received a questionnaire asking me to write down everything I watched on television during the week they had chosen. At the end of those seven days I wrote in *The Wizard of Oz* and returned it. That was in winter and was actually a busy week for my television, which normally sits out the cold months without once warming up. Had they sent the questionnaire during baseball season, they would have found me at my set. People at the stables talk about shows and performers I have never heard of, but I cannot get interested; when

I am in the mood to watch television, I go to a movie or read a detective novel. There are always good detective novels to be found, and I like remembering them next morning with my coffee.

I also think of baseball and hunting and fishing, and of my children. It is not painful to think about them anymore, because even if we had lived together, they would be gone now, grown into their own lives, except Jennifer. I think of death, too, not sadly, or with fear, though something like excitement does run through me, something more quickening than the coffee and tobacco. I suppose it is an intense interest, and an outright distrust: I never feel certain that I'll be here watching birds eating at tomorrow's daylight. Sometimes I try to think of other things, like the rabbit that is warm and breathing but not there till twilight. I feel on the brink of something about the life of the senses, but either am not equipped to go further or am not interested enough to concentrate. I have called all of this thinking, but it is not, because it is unintentional; what I'm really doing is feeling the day, in silence, and that is what Father Paul is doing too on his five-to-ten-mile walks.

When the hour ends I take an apple or carrot and I go to the stable and tack up a horse. We take good care of these horses, and no one rides them but students, instructors, and me, and nobody rides the horses we board unless an owner asks me to. The barn is dark and I turn on lights and take some deep breaths, smelling the hay and horses and their manure, both fresh and dried, a combined odor that you either like or you don't. I walk down the wide space of dirt between stalls, greeting the horses, joking with them about their quirks, and choose one for no reason at all other than the way it looks at me that morning. I get my old English saddle that has smoothed and darkened through the years, and go into the stall, talking to this beautiful creature who'll swerve out of a canter if a piece of paper blows in front of him, and if the barn catches fire and you manage to get him out he will, if he can get away from you, run back into the fire, to his stall. Like the smells that surround them, you either like them or you don't. I love them, so am spared having to try to explain why. I feed one the carrot or apple and tack up and lead him outside, where I mount, and we go down the driveway to the road and cross it and turn northwest and walk then trot then canter to St. John's.

A few cars are on the road, their drivers looking serious about going to work. It is always strange for me to see a woman dressed for work so early in the morning. You know how long it takes them, with the makeup and hair and clothes, and I think of them waking in the dark of winter or early light of other seasons, and dressing as they might for an evening's entertainment. Probably this strikes me because I grew up seeing my father put on those suits he never wore on weekends or his two weeks off, and so am accustomed to the men, but when I see these women I think something went wrong, to send all those dressed-up people out on the road when the dew hasn't dried yet. Maybe it's because I so dislike getting up early, but am also doing what I choose to do, while they have no choice. At heart I am lazy, yet I find such peace and delight in it that I believe it is a natural state, and in what looks like my laziest periods I am closest to my center. The ride to St. John's is fifteen minutes. The horses and I do it in all weather; the road is well plowed in winter, and there are only a few days a year when ice makes me drive the pickup. People always look at someone on horseback, and for a moment their faces change and many drivers and I wave to each other. Then at St. John's, Father Paul and five or six regulars and I celebrate the Mass.

Do not think of me as a spiritual man whose every thought during those twenty-five minutes is at one with the words of the Mass. Each morning I try, each morning I fail, and know that always I will be a creature who, looking at Father Paul and the altar, and uttering prayers, will be distracted by scrambled eggs, horses, the weather, and memories and daydreams that have nothing to do with the sacrament I am about to receive. I can receive, though: the Eucharist, and also, at Mass and at other times, moments and even minutes of contemplation. But I cannot achieve contemplation, as some can; and so, having to face and forgive my own failures, I have learned from them both the necessity and wonder of ritual. For ritual allows those who cannot will themselves out of the secular to perform the spiritual, as dancing allows the tongue-tied man a ceremony of love. And, while my mind dwells on breakfast, or Major or Duchess tethered under the church eave, there is, as I take the Host from Father Paul and place it on my tongue and return to the pew, a feeling that I am thankful I have not lost in the forty-eight years since my first Communion. At its center is excitement; spreading out from it is the peace of certainty. Or the certainty of peace. One night Father Paul and I talked about faith. It was long ago, and all I remember is him saying: Belief is believing in God; faith is believing that God believes in you. That is the excitement, and the peace; then the Mass is over, and I go into the sacristy and we have a cigarette and chat, the mystery ends, we are two men talking like any two men on a morning in America, about baseball, plane crashes, presidents, governors, murders, the sun, the clouds. Then I go to the horse and ride back to the life people see, the one in which I move and talk, and most days I enjoy it.

It is late summer now, the time between fishing and hunting, but a good time for baseball. It has been two weeks since Jennifer left, to drive home to Gloria's after her summer visit. She is the only one who still visits; the boys are married and have children, and sometimes fly up for a holiday, or I fly down or west to visit one of them. Jennifer is twenty, and I worry about her the way fathers worry about daughters but not sons. I want to know what she's up to, and at the same time I don't. She looks athletic, and she is: she swims and runs and of course rides. All my children do. When she comes for six weeks in summer, the house is loud with girls, friends of hers since childhood, and new ones. I am glad she kept the girl friends. They have been young company for me and, being with them, I have been able to gauge her growth between summers. On their riding days, I'd take them back to the house when their lessons were over and they had walked the horses and put them back in the stalls, and we'd have lemonade or Coke, and cookies if I had some, and talk until their parents came to drive them home. One year their breasts grew, so I wasn't startled when I saw Jennifer in July. Then they were driving cars to the stable, and beginning to look like young women, and I was passing out beer and ashtrays and they were talking about college.

When Jennifer was here in summer, they were at the house most days. I would say generally that as they got older they became quieter, and though I enjoyed both, I sometimes missed the giggles and shouts. The quiet voices, just low enough for me not to hear from wherever I was, rising and falling in proportion to my distance from them, frightened me. Not that I believed they were planning or recounting anything really wicked, but there was a female seriousness about them, and it was secretive, and of course I thought: love, sex. But it was more than that: it was womanhood they were entering, the deep forest of it, and no matter how many women and men too are saying these days that there is little difference between us, the truth is that men find their way into that forest only on clearly marked trails, while women move about in it like birds. So hearing Jennifer and her friends talking so quietly, yet intensely, I wanted very much to have a wife.

But not as much as in the old days, when Gloria had left but her presence was still in the house as strongly as if she had only gone to visit her folks for a week. There were no clothes or cosmetics, but potted plants endured my neglectful care as long as they could, and slowly died; I did not kill them on purpose, to exorcise the house of her, but I could not remember to water them. For weeks, because I did not use it much, the house was as neat as she had kept it, though dust layered the order she had made. The kitchen went first: I got the dishes in and out of the dishwasher and wiped the top of the stove, but did not return cooking spoons and pot holders to their hooks on the wall, and soon the burners and oven were caked with spillings, the refrigerator had more space and was spotted with juices. The living room and my bedroom went next; I did not go into the children's rooms except on bad nights when I went from room to room and looked and touched and smelled, so they did not lose their order until a year later when the kids came for six weeks. It was three months before I ate the last of the food Gloria had cooked and frozen: I remember it was a beef stew, and very good. By then I had four cookbooks, and was boasting a bit, and talking about recipes with the women at the stables, and looking forward to cooking for Father Paul. But I never looked forward to cooking at night only for myself, though I made myself do it; on some nights I gave in to my daily temptation, and took a newspaper or detective novel to a restaurant. By the end of the second year, though, I had stopped turning on the radio as soon as I woke in the morning, and was able to be silent and alone in the evening too, and then I enjoyed my dinners.

It is not hard to live through a day, if you can live through a moment. What creates despair is the imagination, which pretends there is a future, and insists on predicting millions of moments, thousands of days, and so drains you that you cannot live the moment at hand. That is what Father Paul told me in those first two years, on some of the bad nights when I believed I could not bear what I had to: the most painful loss was my children, then the loss of Gloria, whom I still loved despite or maybe because of our long periods of sadness that rendered us helpless, so neither of us could break out of it to give a hand to the other. Twelve years later I believe ritual would have healed us more quickly than the repetitious talks we had, perhaps even kept us healed. Marriages have lost that, and I wish I had known then what I know now, and we had performed certain acts together every day, no matter how we felt, and perhaps then we could have subordinated feeling to action, for surely that is the essence of love. I know this from my distractions during Mass, and during everything else I do, so that my actions and feelings are seldom one. It does happen every day, but in proportion to everything else in a day, it is rare, like joy. The third most painful loss, which became second and sometimes first as months passed, was the knowledge that I could never marry again, and so dared not even keep company with a woman.

On some of the bad nights I was bitter about this with Father Paul, and I so pitied myself that I cried, or nearly did, speaking with damp eyes and breaking voice. I believe that celibacy is for him the same trial it is for me, not of the flesh, but the spirit: the heart longing to love. But the difference is he chose it, and did not wake one day to a life with thirty horses. In my anger I said I had done my service to love and chastity, and I told him of the actual physical and spiritual pain of practicing rhythm: nights of striking the mattress with a fist, two young animals lying side by side in heat, leaving the bed to pace, to smoke, to curse, and too passionate to question, for we were so angered and oppressed by our passion that we could see no further than our loins. So now I understand how people can be enslaved for generations before they throw down their tools or use them as weapons, the form of their slavery—the cotton fields, the shacks and puny cupboards and untended illnesses—absorbing their emotions and thoughts until finally they have little or none at all to direct with clarity and energy at the owners and legislators. And I told him of the trick of passion and its slaking: how during what we had to believe were safe periods, though all four children were conceived at those times, we were able with some coherence to question the tradition and reason and justice of the law against birth control, but not with enough conviction to soberly act against it, as though regular satisfaction in bed tempered our revolutionary as well as our erotic desires. Only when abstinence drove us hotly away from each other did we receive an urge so strong it lasted all the way to the drugstore and back; but always, after release, we threw away the remaining condoms; and after going through this a few times, we knew what would happen, and from then on we submitted to the calendar she so precisely marked on the bedroom wall. I told him that living two lives each month, one as celibates, one as lovers, made us tense and short-tempered, so we snapped at each other like dogs.

To have endured that, to have reached a time when we burned slowly and could gain from bed the comfort of lying down at night with one who loves you and whom you love, could for weeks on end go to bed tired and peacefully sleep after a kiss, a touch of the hands, and then to be thrown out of the marriage like a bundle from a moving freight car, was unjust, was intolerable, and I could not or would not muster the strength to endure it. But I did, a moment at a time, a day, a night, except twice, each time with a different woman and more than a year apart, and this was so long ago that I clearly see their faces in my memory, can hear the pitch of their voices, and the way they pronounced words, one with a Massachusetts accent, one midwestern, but I feel as though I only heard about them from someone else. Each rode at the stables and was with me for part of an evening; one was badly married, one divorced, so none of us was free. They did not understand this Catholic view, but they were understanding about my having it, and I remained friends with both of them until the married one left her husband and went to Boston, and the divorced one moved to Maine. After both those evenings, those good women, I went to Mass early while Father Paul was still in the confessional, and received his absolution. I did not tell him who I was, but of course he knew, though I never saw it in his eyes. Now my longing for a wife comes only once in a while, like a cold: on some late afternoons when I am alone in the barn, then I lock up and walk to the house, daydreaming, then suddenly look at it and see it empty, as though for the first time, and all at once I'm weary and feel I do not have the energy to broil meat, and I think of driving to a restaurant, then shake my head and go on to the house, the refrigerator, the oven; and some mornings when I wake in the dark and listen to the silence and run my hand over the cold sheet beside me; and some days in summer when Jennifer is here.

Gloria left first me, then the Church, and that was the end of religion for the children though on visits they went to Sunday Mass with me, and still do, out of a respect for my life that they manage to keep free of patronage. Jennifer is an agnostic, though I doubt she would call herself that, any more than she would call herself any other name that implied she had made a decision, a choice, about existence, death, and God. In truth she tends to pantheism, a good sign, I think; but not wanting to be a father who tells his children what they ought to believe, I do not say to her that Catholicism includes pantheism, like onions in a stew. Besides, I have no missionary instincts and do not believe everyone should or even could live with the Catholic faith. It is Jennifer's womanhood that renders me awkward. And womanhood now is frank, not like when Gloria was twenty and there were symbols: high heels and cosmetics and dresses, a cigarette, a cocktail. I am glad that women are free now of false modesty and all its attention paid the flesh; but, still, it is difficult to see so much of your daughter, to hear her talk as only men and bawdy women used to, and most of all to see in her face the deep and unabashed sensuality of women, with no tricks of the eyes and mouth to hide the pleasure she feels at having a strong young body. I am certain, with the way things are now, that she has very happily not been a virgin for years. That does not bother me. What bothers me is my certainty about it, just from watching her walk across a room or light a cigarette or pour milk on cereal.

She told me all of it, waking me that night when I had gone to sleep listening to the wind in the trees and against the house, a wind so strong that I had to shut all but the lee windows, and still the house cooled; told it to me in such detail and so clearly that now, when she has driven the car to Florida, I remember it all as though I had been a passenger in the front seat, or even at the wheel. It started with a movie, then beer and driving to the sea to look at the waves in the night and the wind, Jennifer and Betsy and Liz. They drank a beer on the beach and wanted to go in naked but were afraid they would drown in the high surf. They bought another six-pack at a grocery store in New Hampshire, and drove home. I can see it now, feel it: the three girls and the beer and the ride on country roads where pines curved in the wind and the big deciduous trees swayed and shook as if they might leap from the earth. They would have some windows partly open so they could feel the wind; Jennifer would be playing a cassette, the music stirring them, as it does the young, to memories of another time, other people and places in what is for them the past.

She took Betsy home, then Liz, and sang with her cassette as she left the town west of us and started home, a twenty-minute drive on the road that passes my house. They had each had four beers, but now there were twelve empty bottles in the bag on the floor at the passenger seat, and I keep focusing on their sound against each other when the car shifted speeds or changed directions. For I want to understand that one moment out of all her heart's time on earth, and whether her history had any bearing on it, or whether her heart was then isolated from all it

had known, and the sound of those bottles urged it. She was just leaving
the town, accelerating past a night club on the right, gaining speed to
climb a long, gradual hill, then she went up it, singing, patting the beat
on the steering wheel, the wind loud through her few inches of open
window, blowing her hair as it did the high branches alongside the
road, and she looked up at them and watched the top of the hill for
someone drunk or heedless coming over it in part of her lane. She
crested to an open black road, and there he was: a bulk, a blur, a thing
running across her headlights, and she swerved left and her foot went
for the brake and was stomping air above its pedal when she hit him,
saw his legs and body in the air, flying out of her light, into the dark.
Her brakes were screaming into the wind, bottles clinking in the fallen
bag, and with the music and wind inside the car was his sound, already
a memory but as real as an echo, that car-shuddering thump as though
she had struck a tree. Her foot was back on the accelerator. Then she
shifted gears and pushed it. She ejected the cassette and closed the
window. She did not start to cry until she knocked on my bedroom
door, then called: "Dad?"

Her voice, her tears, broke through my dream and the wind I heard
in my sleep, and I stepped into jeans and hurried to the door, thinking
harm, rape, death. All were in her face, and I hugged her and pressed
her cheek to my chest and smoothed her blown hair, then led her,
weeping, to the kitchen and sat her at the table where still she could not
speak, nor look at me; when she raised her face it fell forward again, as
of its own weight, into her palms. I offered tea and she shook her head,
so I offered beer twice, then she shook her head, so I offered whiskey
and she nodded. I had some rye that Father Paul and I had not finished
last hunting season, and I poured some over ice and set it in front of her
and was putting away the ice but stopped and got another glass and
poured one for myself too, and brought the ice and bottle to the table
where she was trying to get one of her long menthols out of the pack,
but her fingers jerked like severed snakes, and I took the pack and lit
one for her and took one for myself. I watched her shudder with her
first swallow of rye, and push hair back from her face, it is auburn and
gleamed in the overhead light, and I remembered how beautiful she
looked riding a sorrel; she was smoking fast, then the sobs in her throat
stopped, and she looked at me and said it, the words coming out with
smoke: "I hit somebody. With the *car.*"

Then she was crying and I was on my feet, moving back and forth, looking down at her, asking *Who? Where? Where?* She was pointing at the wall over the stove, jabbing her fingers and cigarette at it, her other hand at her eyes, and twice in horror I actually looked at the wall. She finished the whiskey in a swallow and I stopped pacing and asking and poured another, and either the drink or the exhaustion of tears quieted her, even the dry sobs, and she told me; not as I tell it now, for that was later as again and again we relived it in the kitchen or living room, and, if in daylight, fled it on horseback out on the trails through the woods and, if at night, walked quietly around in the moonlit pasture, walked around and around it, sweating through our clothes. She told it in bursts, like she was a child again, running to me, injured from play. I put on boots and a shirt and left her with the bottle and her streaked face and a cigarette twitching between her fingers, pushed the door open against the wind, and eased it shut. The wind squinted and watered my eyes as I leaned into it and went to the pickup.

When I passed St. John's I looked at it, and Father Paul's little white rectory in the rear, and wanted to stop, wished I could as I could if he were simply a friend who sold hardware or something. I had forgotten my watch but I always know the time within minutes, even when a sound or dream or my bladder wakes me in the night. It was nearly two; we had been in the kitchen about twenty minutes; she had hit him around one-fifteen. Or her. The road was empty and I drove between blowing trees; caught for an instant in my lights, they seemed to be in panic. I smoked and let hope play its tricks on me: it was neither man nor woman but an animal, a goat or calf or deer on the road; it was a man who had jumped away in time, the collision of metal and body glancing not direct, and he had limped home to nurse bruises and cuts. Then I threw the cigarette and hope both out the window and prayed that he was alive, while beneath that prayer, a reserve deeper in my heart, another one stirred: that if he were dead, they would not get Jennifer.

From our direction, east and a bit south, the road to that hill and the night club beyond it and finally the town is, for its last four or five miles, straight through farming country. When I reached that stretch I slowed the truck and opened my window for the fierce air; on both sides were scattered farmhouses and barns and sometimes a silo, looking not like shelters but like unsheltered things the wind would flatten. Corn bent toward the road from a field on my right, and always something blew in front of me: paper, leaves, dried weeds, branches. I slowed approaching the hill, and went up it in second, staring through my open window at the ditch on the left side of the road, its weeds alive, whipping, a mad dance with the trees above them. I went over the hill and down and, opposite the club, turned right onto a side street of houses, and parked there, in the leaping shadows of trees. I walked back across the road to the club's parking lot, the wind behind me, lifting me as I strode, and I could not hear my boots on pavement. I walked up the hill, on the shoulder, watching the branches above me, hearing their leaves and the creaking trunks and the wind. Then I was at the top, looking down the road and at the farms and fields; the night was clear, and I could see a long way; clouds scudded past the half-moon and stars, blown out to sea.

I started down, watching the tall grass under the trees to my right, glancing into the dark of the ditch, listening for cars behind me; but as soon as I cleared one tree, its sound was gone, its flapping leaves and rattling branches far behind me, as though the greatest distance I had at my back was a matter of feet, while ahead of me I could see a barn two miles off. Then I saw her skid marks: short, and going left and downhill, into the other lane. I stood at the ditch, its weeds blowing; across it were trees and their moving shadows, like the clouds. I stepped onto its slope, and it took me sliding on my feet, then rump, to the bottom, where I sat still, my body gathered to itself, lest a part of me should touch him. But there was only tall grass, and I stood, my shoulders reaching the sides of the ditch, and I walked uphill, wishing for the flashlight in the pickup, walking slowly, and down in the ditch I could hear my feet in the grass and on the earth, and kicking cans and bottles. At the top of the hill I turned and went down, watching the ground above the ditch on my right, praying my prayer from the truck again, the first one, the one I would admit, that he was not dead, was in fact home, and began to hope again, memory telling me of lost pheasants and grouse I had shot, but they were small and the colors of their home, while a man was either there or not; and from that memory I left where I was and while walking in the ditch under the wind was in the deceit of imagination with Jennifer in the kitchen, telling her she had hit no one, or at least had not badly hurt anyone, when I realized he could be in the hospital now and I would have to think of a way to check there, something to say on the phone. I see now that, once hope returned, I should have been certain what it prepared me for: ahead of me, in high grass and the shadows of trees, I saw his shirt. Or that is all my mind would allow itself: a shirt, and I stood looking at it for the moments it took my mind to admit the arm and head and the dark length covered by pants. He lay face down, the arm I could see near his side, his head turned from me, on its cheek.

"Fella?" I said. I had meant to call, but it came out quiet and high, lost inches from my face in the wind. Then I said, "Oh God," and felt Him in the wind and the sky moving past the stars and moon and the fields around me, but only watching me as He might have watched Cain or Job, I did not know which, and I said it again, and wanted to sink to the earth and weep till I slept there in the weeds. I climbed, scrambling up the side of the ditch, pulling at clutched grass, gained the top on hands and knees, and went to him like that, panting, moving through the grass as high and higher than my face, crawling under that sky, making sounds, too, like some animal, there being no words to let him know I was here with him now. He was long; that is the word that came to me, not tall. I kneeled beside him, my hands on my legs. His right arm was by his side, his left arm straight out from the shoulder, but turned, so his palm was open to the tree above us. His left cheek was clean-shaven, his eye closed, and there was no blood. I leaned forward to look at his open mouth and saw the blood on it, going down into the grass. I straightened and looked ahead at the wind blowing past me through grass and trees to a distant light, and I stared at the light, imagining someone awake out there, wanting someone to be, a gathering of old friends, or someone alone listening to music or painting a picture, then I figured it was a night light at a farmyard whose house I couldn't see. *Going,* I thought. *Still going.* I leaned over again and looked at dripping blood.

So I had to touch his wrist, a thick one with a watch and expansion band that I pushed up his arm, thinking *he's left-handed,* my three fingers pressing his wrist, and all I felt was my tough fingertips on that smooth underside flesh and small bones, then relief, then certainty. But against my will, or only because of it, I still don't know, I touched his neck, ran my fingers down it as if petting, then pressed, and my hand sprang back as from fire. I lowered it again, held it there until it felt that faint beating that I could not believe. There was too much wind. Nothing could make a sound in it. A pulse could not be felt in it, nor could mere fingers in that wind feel the absolute silence of a dead man's artery. I was making sounds again; I grabbed his left arm and his waist, and pulled him toward me, and that side of him rose, turned, and I lowered him to his back, his face tilted up toward the tree that was groaning, the tree and I the only sounds in the wind. Turning my face from his, looking down the length of him at his sneakers, I placed my ear on his heart, and heard not that but something else, and I clamped a hand over my exposed ear, heard something liquid and alive, like when you pump a well and after a few strokes you hear air and water moving in the pipe, and I knew I must raise his legs and cover him and run to a phone, while still I listened to his chest, thinking *raise with what? cover with what?* and amid the liquid sound I heard the heart, then lost it, and pressed my ear against bone, but his chest was quiet, and I did not know when the liquid had stopped, and do not know now when I heard air, a faint rush of it, and whether under my ear or at his mouth or whether I heard it at all. I straightened and looked at the light, dim and yellow. Then I touched his throat, looking him full in the face. He was blond and young. He could have been sleeping in the shade of a tree, but for the smear of blood from his mouth to his hair, and the night sky, and the weeds blowing against his head, and the leaves shaking in the dark above us.

I stood. Then I kneeled again and prayed for his soul to join in peace and joy all the dead and living; and, doing so, confronted my first sin against him, not stopping for Father Paul, who could have given him the last rites, and immediately then my second one, or, I saw then, my first, not calling an ambulance to meet me there, and I stood and turned into the wind, slid down the ditch and crawled out of it, and went up the hill and down it, across the road to the street of houses whose people I had left behind forever, so that I moved with stealth in the shadows to my truck.

When I came around the bend near my house, I saw the kitchen light at the rear. She sat as I had left her, the ashtray filled, and I looked at the bottle, felt her eyes on me, felt what she was seeing too: the dirt from my crawling. She had not drunk much of the rye. I poured some in my glass, with the water from melted ice, and sat down and swallowed some and looked at her and swallowed some more, and said: "He's dead."

She rubbed her eyes with the heels of her hands, rubbed the cheeks under them, but she was dry now.

"He was probably dead when he hit the ground. I mean, that's probably what killed—"

"Where was he?"

"Across the ditch, under a tree."

"Was he—did you see his face?"

"No. Not really. I just felt. For life, pulse. I'm going out to the car."

"What for? Oh."

I finished the rye, and pushed back the chair, then she was standing too.

"I'll go with you."

"There's no need."

"I'll go."

I took a flashlight from a drawer and pushed open the door and held it while she went out. We turned our faces from the wind. It was like on the hill, when I was walking, and the wind closed the distance behind me: after three or four steps I felt there was no house back there. She took my hand, as I was reaching for hers. In the garage we let go, and squeezed between the pickup and her little car, to the front of it, where we had more room, and we stepped back from the grill and I shone the light on the fender, the smashed headlight turned into it, the concave chrome staring to the right, at the garage wall.

"We ought to get the bottles," I said.

She moved between the garage and the car, on the passenger side, and had room to open the door and lift the bag. I reached out, and she gave me the bag and backed up and shut the door and came around the car. We sidled to the doorway, and she put her arm around my waist and I hugged her shoulders.

"I thought you'd call the police," she said.

We crossed the yard, faces bowed from the wind, her hair blowing away from her neck, and in the kitchen I put the bag of bottles in the garbage basket. She was working at the table: capping the rye and putting it away, filling the ice tray, washing the glasses, emptying the ashtray, sponging the table.

"Try to sleep now," I said.

She nodded at the sponge circling under her hand, gathering ashes. Then she dropped it in the sink and, looking me full in the face, as I had never seen her look, as perhaps she never had, being for so long a daughter on visits (or so it seemed to me and still does: that until then our eyes had never seriously met), she crossed to me from the sink and kissed my lips, then held me so tightly I lost balance, and would have stumbled forward had she not held me so hard.

I sat in the living room, the house darkened, and watched the maple and the hemlock. When I believed she was asleep I put on *La Bohème,* and kept it at the same volume as the wind so it would not wake her. Then I listened to *Madama Butterfly,* and in the third act had to rise quickly to lower the sound: the wind was gone. I looked at the still maple near the window, and thought of the wind leaving farms and towns and the coast, going out over the sea to die on the waves. I smoked and gazed out the window. The sky was darker, and at daybreak the rain came. I listened to *Tosca,* and at six-fifteen went to the kitchen where Jennifer's purse lay on the table, a leather shoulder purse crammed with the things of an adult woman, things she had begun accumulating only a few years back, and I nearly wept, thinking of what sandy foundations they were: driver's license, credit card, disposable lighter, cigarettes, checkbook, ballpoint pen, cash, cosmetics, comb, brush, Kleenex, these the rite of passage from childhood, and I took one of them—her keys—and went out, remembering a jacket and hat when the rain struck me, but I kept going to the car, and squeezed and lowered myself into it, pulled the seat belt over my shoulder and fastened it and backed out, turning in the drive, going forward into the road, toward St. John's and Father Paul.

Cars were on the road, the workers, and I did not worry about any of them noticing the fender and light. Only a horse distracted them from what they drove to. In front of St. John's is a parking lot; at its far side, past the church and at the edge of the lawn, is an old pine, taller than the steeple now. I shifted to third, left the road, and, aiming the right headlight at the tree, accelerated past the white blur of church, into the black trunk growing bigger till it was all I could see, then I rocked in that resonant thump she had heard, had felt, and when I turned off the ignition it was still in my ears, my blood, and I saw the boy flying in the wind. I lowered my forehead to the wheel. Father Paul opened the door, his face white in the rain.

"I'm all right."

"What happened?"

"I don't know. I fainted."

I got out and went around to the front of the car, looked at the smashed light, the crumpled and torn fender.

"Come to the house and lie down."

"I'm all right."

"When was your last physical?"

"I'm due for one. Let's get out of this rain."

"You'd better lie down."

"No. I want to receive."

That was the time to say I want to confess, but I have not and will not. Though I could now, for Jennifer is in Florida, and weeks have passed, and perhaps now Father Paul would not feel that he must tell me to go to the police. And, for that very reason, to confess now would be unfair. It is a world of secrets, and now I have one from my best, in truth my only, friend. I have one from Jennifer too, but that is the nature of fatherhood.

Most of that day it rained, so it was only in early evening, when the sky cleared, with a setting sun, that two little boys, leaving their confinement for some play before dinner, found him. Jennifer and I got that on the local news, which we listened to every hour, meeting at the radio, standing with cigarettes, until the one at eight o'clock; when she stopped crying, we went out and walked on the wet grass, around the pasture, the last of sunlight still in the air and trees. His name was Patrick Mitchell, he was nineteen years old, was employed by CETA, lived at home with his parents and brother and sister. The paper next day said he had been at a friend's house and was walking home, and I thought of that light I had seen, then knew it was not for him; he lived on one of the streets behind the club. The paper did not say then, or in the next few days, anything to make Jennifer think he was alive while she was with me in the kitchen. Nor do I know if we—I—could have saved him.

In keeping her secret from her friends, Jennifer had to perform so often, as I did with Father Paul and at the stables, that I believe the acting, which took more of her than our daylight trail rides and our night walks in the pasture, was her healing. Her friends teased me about wrecking her car. When I carried her luggage out to the car on that last morning, we spoke only of the weather for her trip—the day was clear, with a dry cool breeze—and hugged and kissed, and I stood watching as she started the car and turned it around. But then she shifted to neutral and put on the parking brake and unclasped the belt, looking at me all the while, then she was coming to me, as she had that night in the kitchen, and I opened my arms.

I have said I talk with God in the mornings, as I start my day, and sometimes as I sit with coffee, looking at the birds, and the woods. Of course He has never spoken to me, but that is not something I require.

Nor does He need to. I know Him, as I know the part of myself that knows Him, that felt Him watching from the wind and the night as I kneeled over the dying boy. Lately I have taken to arguing with Him, as I can't with Father Paul, who, when he hears my monthly confession, has not heard and will not hear anything of failure to do all that one can to save an anonymous life, of injustice to a family in their grief, of deepening their pain at the chance and mystery of death by giving them nothing—no one—to hate. With Father Paul I feel lonely about this, but not with God. When I received the Eucharist while Jennifer's car sat twice-damaged, so redeemed, in the rain, I felt neither loneliness nor shame, but as though He were watching me, even from my tongue, intestines, blood, as I have watched my sons at times in their young lives when I was able to judge but without anger, and so keep silent while they, in the agony of their youth, decided how they must act; or found reasons, after their actions, for what they had done. Their reasons were never as good or as bad as their actions, but they needed to find them, to believe they were living by them, instead of the awful solitude of the heart.

I do not feel the peace I once did: not with God, nor the earth, or anyone on it. I have begun to prefer this state, to remember with fondness the other one as a period of peace I neither earned nor deserved. Now in the mornings while I watch purple finches driving larger titmice from the feeder, I say to Him: I would do it again. For when she knocked on my door, then called me, she woke what had flowed dormant in my blood since her birth, so that what rose from the bed was not a stable owner or a Catholic or any other Luke Ripley I had lived with for a long time, but the father of a girl.

And He says: I am a Father too.

Yes, I say, as You are a Son Whom this morning I will receive; unless You kill me on the way to church, then I trust You will receive me. And as a Son You made Your plea.

Yes, He says, but I would not lift the cup.

True, and I don't want You to lift it from me either. And if one of my sons had come to me that night, I would have phoned the police and told them to meet us with an ambulance at the top of the hill.

Why? Do you love them less?

I tell Him no, it is not that I love them less, but that I could bear the pain of watching and knowing my sons' pain, could bear it with pride as they took the whip and nails. But You never had a daughter and, if You had, You could not have borne her passion.

So, He says, you love her more than you love Me.

I love her more than I love truth.

Then you love in weakness, He says.

As You love me, I say, and I go with an apple or carrot out to the barn.

SHUSAKU ENDO

Mothers

I reached the dock at nightfall.

The ferry-boat had not yet arrived. I peered over the low wall of the quay. Small grey waves laden with refuse and leaves licked at the jetty like a puppy quietly lapping up water. A single truck was parked in the vacant lot by the dock; beyond the lot stood two warehouses. A man had lit a bonfire in front of one of the warehouses; the red flames flickered.

In the waiting-room, five or six local men wearing high boots sat patiently on benches, waiting for the ticket booth to open. At their feet were dilapidated trunks and boxes loaded with fish. I also noticed several cages packed full of chickens. The birds thrust their long necks through the wire mesh and writhed as though in pain. The men sat quietly on the benches, occasionally glancing in my direction.

I felt as though I had witnessed a scene like this in some Western painting. But I couldn't recall who had sketched it, or when I had seen it.

The lights on the broad grey shore of the island across the water twinkled faintly. Somewhere a dog was howling, but I couldn't tell whether it was over on the island or here on my side of the bay.

Gradually some of the lights which I had thought belonged to the island began to move. I finally realized that they belonged to the ferry-boat that was heading this way. At last the ticket booth opened, and the men got up from the benches and formed a queue. When I lined up behind them, the smell of fish was overpowering. I had heard that most of the people on the island mixed farming with fishing.

Their faces all looked the same. Their eyes seemed sunken, perhaps because of the protruding cheekbones; their faces were void of expression, as if they were afraid of something. In short, dishonesty and dread had joined together to mould the faces of these islanders. Perhaps I felt that way because of the preconceived notions I had about the island I was about to visit. Throughout the Edo period, the residents of the island had suffered through poverty, hard, grinding labour, and religious persecution.

After some time I boarded the ferry-boat, which soon pulled away from the harbour. Only three trips a day connected the island with the Kyushu mainland. Until just two years before, boats had made the crossing only twice a day, once in the morning and once in the evening.

It was in fact little more than a large motor launch and had no seats. The passengers stood between bicycles and fish crates and old trunks, exposed to the chilling sea winds that blew through the windows. Had this been Tokyo, some passengers would undoubtedly have complained at the conditions, but here no one said a word. The only sound was the grinding of the boat's engine; even the chickens in the cages at our feet did not utter a peep. I jabbed at some of the chickens with the tip of my shoe. A look of fear darted across their faces. They looked just like the men from the waiting-room, and I had to smile.

The wind whipped up; the sea was dark, and the waves black. I tried several times to light a cigarette, but the wind extinguished my match at every attempt. The unlit cigarette grew damp from my lips, and finally I hurled it overboard . . . though the winds may very well have blown it back onto the boat. The weariness of the twelve-hour bus-ride from Nagasaki overcame me. I was stiff from the small of my back to my shoulders. I closed my eyes and listened to the droning of the engine.

Several times, out on the pitch-black ocean, the pounding of the engine grew suddenly faint. In an instant it would surge up again, only to slacken once more. I listened to that process repeat itself several times before I opened my eyes again. The lights of the island were directly ahead.

"Hello!" a voice called. "Is Watanabe there? Throw the line!"

There was a dull, heavy thud as the line was thrown to the quay.

I got off after the locals had disembarked. The cold night wind bore the smells of fish and of the sea. Just beyond the dock gate stood five or six shops selling dried fish and local souvenirs. I had heard that the best-known local product was a dried flying-fish called *ago*. A man dressed in boots and wearing a jacket stood in front of the shops. He watched me closely as I stepped through the gate, then came up to me and said, "Sensei, thank you for coming all this way. The church sent me to meet you."

He bowed to me an embarrassing number of times, then tried to wrest my suitcase from my hands. No matter how often I refused, he would not let go of it. The palms that brushed against my hand were as solid and large as the root of a tree. They were not like the soft, damp hands of the Tokyo Christians that I knew so well.

I tried to walk beside him, but he stubbornly maintained a distance of one pace behind me. I remembered that he had called me "Sensei," and I felt bewildered. If the church people persisted in addressing me in terms of respect, the locals might be put on their guard against me.

The smell of fish that permeated the harbour trailed persistently after us. That odour seemed to have imbedded itself in the low-roofed houses and the narrow road over the course of many years. Off to my left, across the sea, the lights of Kyushu now shone faintly in the darkness.

"How is the Father?" I asked. "I came as soon as I got his letter . . ."

But there was no answer from behind. I tried to detect whether I had done something to offend him, but that did not appear to be the case. Perhaps he was just diffident and determined not to engage in idle chatter. Or possibly, after long years of experience, the people of this island had concluded that the best way to protect themselves was to avoid imprudent conversation.

I had met their priest in Tokyo. He had come up from Kyushu to attend a meeting just after I had published a novel about the Christian era in Japan. I went up and introduced myself to him. He too had the deep-set eyes and the prominent cheekbones of the island's fishermen. Bewildered perhaps to be in Tokyo among all the notable clerics and nuns, his face tightened and he said very little when I spoke to him. In that sense, he was very much like the man who was now carrying my suitcase.

"Do you know Father Fukabori?" I had asked the priest. A year earlier, I had taken a bus to a fishing village an hour from Nagasaki. There I met the village priest, Father Fukabori, who was from the Urakami district. Not only did he teach me how to deep-sea fish, he also provided me with considerable assistance in my research. The purpose of my visit had been to visit the *kakure,* descendants of some of the original Christian converts in the seventeenth century who had, over the space of many years, gradually corrupted the religious practices. Father Fukabori took me to the homes of several of the *kakure,* who still stubbornly refused to be reconverted to Catholicism. As I have said, the faith of the *kakure* Christians over the long years of national isolation had drifted far from true Christianity and had embraced elements of Shinto, Buddhism, and local superstition. Because of this, one of the missions of the Church in this region, ever since the arrival of Father Petitjean in the Meiji period, was the reconversion of the *kakure* who were scattered throughout the Gotō and Ikitsuki Islands.

"He let me stay at his church." I continued to grasp for threads of conversation, but the priest clutched his glass of juice tightly and muttered only monosyllabic responses.

"Are there any *kakure* in your parish?"

"Yes."

"They're starting to show up on television these days, and they look a little happier now that they're making some money out of it. The old man that Father Fukabori introduced me to was just like an announcer on a variety show. Is it easy to meet the *kakure* on your island?"

"No, it's very difficult."

Our conversation broke off there, and I moved on in search of more congenial company.

Yet, to my surprise, a month ago I received a letter from this artless country priest. It opened with the customary Catholic "Peace of the Lord" salutation and went on to say that he had persuaded some of the *kakure* who lived in his parish to show me their religious icons and copies of their prayers. His handwriting was surprisingly fluent.

I looked back at the man walking behind me and asked, "Are there any *kakure* around here?"

He shook his head. "No, they all live in the mountains."

Half an hour later we reached the church. A man dressed in a black cassock, his hands clasped behind him, stood at the doorway. Beside him was a young man with a bicycle.

Since I had already met the priest—though only once—I greeted him casually, but he looked somewhat perplexed and glanced at the other two men. I had been thoughtless. I had forgotten that, unlike Tokyo or Osaka, in this district the priest was like a village headman, or in some cases as highly respected as a feudal lord.

"Jirō, go and tell Mr. Nakamura that the Sensei has arrived," he ordered. With a deep bow the young man climbed on his bicycle and disappeared into the darkness.

"Which way is the *kakure* village?" I asked. The priest pointed in the opposite direction to that from which I had come. I couldn't see any lights, perhaps because the mountains obstructed my view. In the age of persecution, to escape the eyes of the officials, the *kakure* Christians had settled as much as possible in secluded mountain fastnesses or on inaccessible coastlines. Undoubtedly that was the case here. We'll have to walk quite a way tomorrow, I thought, surveying my own rather fragile body. Seven years before, I had undergone chest surgery, and though I had recovered, I still had little faith in my physical strength.

I dreamed of my mother. In my dream I had just been brought out of the operating theatre, and was sprawled out on my bed like a corpse. A rubber tube connected to an oxygen tank was thrust into my nostril, and intravenous needles pierced my right arm and leg, carrying blood from the transfusion bottles dangling over my bed.

Although I should have been half unconscious, through the languid weight of the anaesthetic I recognized the grey shadow that held my hand. It was my mother. Strangely, neither my wife nor any of the doctors was in the room.

I have had that dream many times. Frequently I wake up unable to distinguish dream from reality and lie in a daze on my bed, until I realize with a sigh that I am not in the hospital where I spent three years, but in my own home.

I have not told my wife about that dream. She was the one who watched over me through every night after each of my three operations, and I felt remorseful that my wife did not even seem to exist in my dreams. The main reason I said nothing to her, however, was my distasteful realization that the firm bonds between my mother and myself —stronger than even I had suspected—continued to link us some twenty years after her death, even in my dreams.

I know little about psychoanalysis, so I have no idea exactly what this dream means. In it, I cannot actually see my mother's face. Nor are her movements distinct. When I reflect back on the dream, the figure seems to be my mother, but I cannot positively say that it is. But it most definitely is not my wife or any kind of nurse or attendant, or even a doctor.

So far as my memory serves me, I can recollect no experience in my youth when I lay ill in bed with my mother holding my hand. Normally the image of my mother that pops into my mind is the figure of a woman who lived her life fervently.

When I was five years old, we were living in Dairen in Manchuria in connection with my father's work. I can still vividly recall the icicles that hung down past the windows of our tiny house like the teeth of a fish. The sky is overcast, and it looks as if it will begin to snow at any moment, but the snow never comes. In a nine-by-twelve room my mother is practising the violin. For hours on end she practises the same melody over and over again. With the violin wedged under her chin, her face is hard, stone-like, and her eyes are fixed on a single point in space as she seems to be trying to isolate that one true note somewhere in the void. Unable to find that elusive note, she heaves a sigh; her irritation mounts, and she continues to scrape the bow across the strings. The brownish callouses on her chin were familiar to me. They had formed when she was still a student at the music academy and had kept her violin tucked constantly under her chin. The tips of her fingers, too, were as hard to the touch as pebbles, the result of the many thousands of times she had pressed down on the strings in her quest for that one note.

The image of my mother in my school-days—that image within my heart was of a woman abandoned by her husband. She sits like a stone statue on the sofa in that dark room at nightfall in Dairen. As a child I could not bear to see her struggling so to endure her grief. I sat near her, pretending to do my homework but concentrating every nerve in my body on her. Because I could not fathom the complex situation, I was all the more affected by the picture of her suffering, her hand pressed against her forehead. I was in torment, not knowing what I should do.

Those dismal days stretched from autumn into winter. Determined not to see her sitting in that darkened room, I walked home from school as slowly as I could. I followed the old White Russian who sold Russian bread everywhere he went. Around sunset I finally turned towards home, kicking pebbles along the side of the road.

One day, when my father had taken me out on one of our rare walks together, he said suddenly, "Your mother . . . she's going back to Japan on an important errand . . . Would you like to go with her?"

Detecting a grown-up's lie, I grunted, "Uh-huh," and went on walking along behind him in silence, kicking at every rock I could find. The following month, with financial assistance from her older sister in Kobe, my mother took me back to Japan.

And then my mother during my middle-school days. Though I have various memories of her, they all congeal on one spot. Just as she had once played her violin in search of the one true note, she subsequently adopted a stern, solitary life in quest of the one true religion. On wintry mornings, at the frozen fissure of dawn, I often noticed a light in her room. I knew what she was doing in there. She was fingering the beads of her rosary and praying. Eventually she would take me with her on the first Hankyū-line train of the day and set out for Mass. On the deserted train I slouched back in my seat and pretended to be rowing a boat. But occasionally I would open my eyes and see my mother's fingers gliding along those rosary beads.

In the darkness, I opened my eyes to the sound of rain. I dressed hurriedly and ran from my bungalow to the brick chapel across the way.

The chapel was almost too ornate for this beggarly island village. The previous evening, the priest had told me that the village Christians had worked for two years to erect this chapel, hauling the stones and cutting the wood themselves. They say that three hundred years ago, the faithful also built churches with their own hands to please the foreign missionaries. That custom has been passed down undiluted on this remote island off Kyushu.

In the dimly lit chapel knelt three peasant women in their work attire, with white cloths covering their heads. There were also two men in working clothes. Since the nave was bereft of kneelers or benches, they each knelt on straw mats to offer up their prayers. One had the impression that, as soon as Mass was over, they would pick up their hoes and head straight for the fields or the sea. At the altar, the priest turned his sunken eyes towards the tiny congregation, lifted up the chalice with both hands and intoned the prayer of Consecration. The light from the candles illuminated the text of the large Latin missal. I thought of my mother. I couldn't help but feel that this chapel somehow resembled the church she and I had attended thirty years before.

When we stepped outside after Mass the rain had stopped, but a dense fog had settled in. The direction in which the *kakure* village lay was shrouded in a milky haze; the silhouettes of trees hovered like ghosts amid the fog.

"It doesn't look like you'll be able to set out in all this fog," the priest muttered from behind me, rubbing his hands together. "The mountain roads are very slippery. You'd better spend the day resting yourself. Why don't you go tomorrow?"

He proposed a tour of the Christian graves in his village for the afternoon. Since the *kakure* district lay deep in the mountains, it would be no easy matter for even a local resident to make the climb, and with only one lung I certainly did not have the strength to walk there in the dense, soaking mist.

Through breaks in the fog, the ocean appeared, black and cold. Not a single boat had ventured out. Even from where I stood, I could make out the frothy white fangs of the waves.

I had breakfast with the priest and went to lie down in the six-mat room that had been provided for me. In bed I reread a book about the history of this region. A thin rain began to fall; its sound, like shifting sands, deepened the solitude within my room, which was bare except for a bus timetable tacked to the wall. Suddenly I wanted to go back to Tokyo.

According to the historical documents, the persecution of Christians in this area commenced in 1607 and was at its fiercest between 1615 and 1617.

Father Pedro de San Dominico
Matthias
Francisco Gorosuke
Miguel Shin'emon
Dominico Kisuke

This list includes only the names of the priests and monks who were martyred in the village in 1615. No doubt there were many more nameless peasants and fisherwomen who gave up their lives for the faith. In the past, as I devoted my free time to reading the history of Christian martyrdoms in Japan, I formulated within my mind an audacious theory. My hypothesis is that these public executions might have been carried out as warnings to the leaders of each village rather than to each individual believer. This will, of course, never be anything more than my own private conjecture so long as the historical records offer no supportive evidence. But I can't help feeling that the faithful in those days, rather than deciding individually whether to die for the faith or to apostatize, were instead bowing to the will of the entire community.

It has been my long-held supposition that, because the sense of community, based on blood relationships, was so much stronger among villagers in those days, it was not left up to individuals to determine whether they would endure persecution or succumb. Instead this matter was decided by the village as a whole. In other words, the officials, knowing that they would be exterminating their labour force if they executed an entire community that stubbornly clung to its faith, would only kill selected representatives of the village. In cases where there was no choice but apostasy, the villagers would renounce their beliefs en masse to ensure the preservation of the community. That, I felt, was the fundamental distinction between Japanese Christian martyrdoms and the martyrs in foreign lands.

The historical documents clearly indicate that, in former times, nearly fifteen hundred Christians lived on this ten-by-three-and-a-half-kilometre island. The most active proselytizer on the island in those days was the Portuguese father Camillo Constanzo, who was burned at the stake on the beach of Tabira in 1622. They say that even after the fire was lit and his body was engulfed in black smoke, the crowd could hear him singing the *Laudate Dominum.* When he finished singing, he cried "Holy! Holy!" five times and breathed his last.

Peasants and fishermen found to be practising Christianity were executed on a craggy islet—appropriately named the Isle of Rocks—about a half hour from here by rowing-boat. They were bound hand and foot, taken to the top of the sheer precipice of the island, and hurled to their deaths. At the height of the persecutions, the number of believers killed on the Isle of Rocks never fell below ten per month, according to contemporary reports. To simplify matters, the officers would sometimes bind several prisoners together in a rush mat and toss them into the frigid seas. Virtually none of the bodies of these martyrs was ever recovered.

I read over the grisly history of the island's martyrs until past noon. The drizzling rain continued to fall.

At lunchtime the priest was nowhere to be seen. A sunburned, middle-aged woman with jutting cheekbones served my meal. I judged her to be the wife of some fisherman, but in the course of conversation I learned to my surprise that she was a nun who had devoted herself to a life of celibate service. The image I had always fostered of nuns was limited to those women I often saw in Tokyo with their peculiar black robes. This woman told me about the order of sisters in this area, known in the local jargon as "The Servants' Quarters." The order, to which she belonged, practised communal living, worked in the fields the same as the other farm women, looked after children at the nursery school, and tended the sick in the hospital.

"Father went on his motorcycle to Mount Fudō. He said he'd be back around three o'clock." Her eyes shifted towards the rain-splattered window. "With this awful weather, you must be terribly bored, Sensei. Jirō from the office said he'd be by soon to show you the Christian graves."

Jirō was the young man with the bicycle who had been standing beside the priest when I arrived the previous night.

Just as she predicted, Jirō appeared soon after I had finished lunch and invited me to accompany him. He even brought along a pair of boots for me to wear.

"I didn't think you'd want to get your shoes all muddy."

He apologized that the boots were so old, bowing his head so incessantly that I was embarrassed.

"I'm ashamed to make you ride in a truck like this," he added.

As we drove along the streets in his little van, I found that the mental picture I had drawn the previous night was accurate. All the houses were squat, and the village reeked of fish. At the dock, about ten small boats were preparing to go to sea. The only buildings made of reinforced concrete were the village office and the primary school. Even the "main street" gave way to thatched-roofed farmhouses after less than five minutes. The telephone poles were plastered with rain-soaked advertisements for a strip show. They featured a picture of a nude woman cupping her breasts; the show bore the dreadful title "The Sovereign of Sex."

"Father is heading a campaign to stop these shows in the village."

"But I'll bet the young men spend all their free time there. Even the young Christians . . ."

My attempt at humour fell on deaf ears as Jirō tightened his grip on the steering wheel. I quickly changed the subject.

"About how many Christians are there on the island now?"

"I think around a thousand."

In the seventeenth century the number had been calculated at fifteen hundred, meaning a loss of about one-third since that time.

"And how many *kakure*?"

"I'm really not sure. I imagine they get fewer in number every year. Only the old people stick to their practices. The young ones say the whole thing's ridiculous."

Jirō related an interesting story. In spite of frequent encouragement from the priests and believers, the *kakure* had refused to reconvert to Catholicism. They claimed that it was their brand of Christianity which had been handed down from their ancestors, making it the true original faith; they further insisted that the Catholicism brought back to Japan in the Meiji period was a reformed religion. Their suspicions were confirmed by the modern attire of the priests, which differed radically from that of the padres they had been told about over the generations.

"And so one French priest had a brilliant idea. He dressed up like one of the padres from those days and went to visit the *kakure.*"

"What happened?"

"The *kakure* admitted he looked a lot like the real thing, but something was wrong. They just couldn't believe him!"

I sensed a degree of contempt towards the *kakure* in Jirō's tale, but I laughed aloud anyway. Surely the French priest who went to all the trouble of dressing up like a friar from the seventeenth century had had a sense of humour about him. The story seemed somehow exhilaratingly typical of this island.

Once we left the village, the grey road extended out along the coast. Mountains pressed in from our left, the ocean to our right. The waters churned, a leaden colour, and when I rolled down the window an inch, a gust of rainy wind pelted my face.

Jirō stopped his truck in the shelter of a windbreak and held out an umbrella for me. The earth was sandy, dotted here and there with growths of tiny pine shrubs. The Christian graveyard lay at the crest of a sand-dune perched precariously over the ocean. It hardly deserved to be called a graveyard. The single stone marker was so tiny that even I could have lifted it with a little effort, and a good third of it was buried beneath the sand. The face of the stone was bleached grey by the wind and rain; all that I could make out was a cross that seemed to have been scratched into the rock with some object, and the Roman letters M and R. Those two characters suggested a name like "Maria," and I wondered if the Christian buried here might have been a woman.

I had no idea why this solitary grave had been dug in a spot so far removed from the village. Perhaps some relative had quietly moved it to this inconspicuous location after the exterminations. Or possibly, during the persecution, this woman had been executed on this very beach.

A choppy sea stretched out beyond this forsaken Christian grave. The gusts pounding the windbreak sounded like electric wires chafing together. In the offing I could see a tiny black island, the Isle of Rocks where Christians from this district had been strung together like beads and hurled into the waters below.

I learned how to lie to my mother.

As I think back on it now, I suppose my lies must have sprung from some sort of complex I had about her. This woman, who had been driven to seek consolation in religion after being abandoned by her husband, had redirected the fervour she had once expended in search of the one true violin note towards a quest for the one true God. I can comprehend that zeal now, but as a child it suffocated me. The more she compelled me to share her faith, the more I fought her oppressive power, the way a drowning child struggles against the pressure of the water.

One of my friends at school was a boy called Tamura. His father ran a brothel at Nishinomiya. He always had a filthy bandage wound about his neck and he was often absent from school; I suppose he must have had tuberculosis even then. He had very few friends and was constantly mocked by the conscientious students. Certainly part of the reason I latched onto him was a desire to get back at my strict mother.

The first time I smoked a cigarette under Tamura's tutelage, I felt as though I was committing a horrid sin. Behind the archery range at school, Tamura, sensitive to every noise around us, stealthily pulled a crumpled cigarette pack from the pocket of his school uniform.

"You can't inhale deeply right at first. Try just a little puff at a time."

I hacked, choked by the piercing smoke that filled my nose and throat. At that moment, my mother's face appeared before me. It was her face as she prayed with her rosary in the predawn darkness. I took a deeper drag on the cigarette to exorcize this vision.

Another thing I learned from Tamura was going to movies on my way home from school. I slipped into the darkened Niban Theatre near the Nishinomiya Hanshin Station, following Tamura like a criminal. The smell from the toilet filled the auditorium. Amid the sounds of crying babies and the coughs of old men, I listened to the monotonous gyrations of the movie projector. My whole mind was absorbed with thoughts of what my mother would be doing just then.

"Let's go home."

Over and over I pressed Tamura to leave, until finally he snarled angrily, "Stop pestering me! Go home by yourself, then!"

When we finally went outside, the Hanshin train that sped past us was carrying workers back to their homes.

"You've got to stop being so scared of your mother." Tamura shrugged his shoulders derisively. "Just make up a good excuse."

After we parted, I walked along the deserted road, trying to think up a convincing lie. I hadn't come up with one until I stepped through the doorway.

"We had some extra classes today," I caught my breath and blurted out. "They said we have to start preparing for entrance exams." When it was obvious that my mother had believed me, a pain clutched at my chest even as I experienced an inner feeling of satisfaction.

To be quite honest, I had no true religious faith whatsoever. Although I attended church at my mother's insistence, I merely cupped my hands together and made as if to pray, while inwardly my mind roamed over empty landscapes. I recalled scenes from the many movies I had seen with Tamura, and I even thought about the photographs of naked women he had shown me one day. Inside the chapel the faithful stood or knelt in response to the prayers of the priest reciting the Mass. The more I tried to restrain my fantasies, the more they flooded into my brain with mocking clarity.

I truly could not understand why my mother believed in such a religion. The words of the priest, the stories in the Bible, the crucifix— they all seemed like intangible happenings from a past that had nothing to do with us. I doubted the sincerity of the people who gathered there each Sunday to clasp their hands in prayer even as they scolded their children and cleared their throats. Sometimes I would regret such thoughts and feel apologetic towards my mother. And I prayed that, if there was a God, He would grant me a believing heart. But there was no reason to think that such a plea would change how I felt.

Finally I stopped going to morning Mass altogether. My excuse was that I had to study for my entrance exams. I felt not the slightest qualms when, after that, I lay in bed listening to my mother's footsteps as she set out alone for church each winter morning. By then she had already begun to complain of heart spasms. Eventually I stopped going to church even on Sundays, though out of consideration for my mother's feelings I left the house and then slipped away to pass my time wandering around the bustling shopping centre at Nishinomiya or staring at the advertisements in front of the movie theatres.

Around that time my mother often had trouble breathing. Sometimes, just walking down the street, she would stop suddenly and clutch her chest, her face twisted into an ugly grimace. I ignored her. A sixteen-year-old boy could not imagine what it was to fear death. The attacks passed quickly, and she was back to normal within five minutes, so I assumed it was nothing serious. In reality, her many years of torment and weariness had worn out her heart. Even so, she still got up at five o'clock every morning and, dragging her heavy legs, walked to the station down the deserted road. The church was two stops away on the train.

One Saturday, unable to resist the temptation, I decided to play truant from school and got off the train near an amusement district. I left my school bag at a coffee shop that Tamura and I had begun to frequent. I still had quite a bit of time before the film started. In my pocket I carried a one-yen note I had taken from my mother's purse several days earlier. Somewhere along the way I had picked up the habit of dipping into her wallet. I sat through several movies until sunset, then returned home with a look of innocence on my face.

When I opened the door, I was surprised to see my mother standing there. She stared at me without saying a word. Then slowly her face contorted, and tears trickled down her twisted cheeks. It seems she had found out everything through a phone call from my school. She wept softly in the room adjoining mine until late into the night. I stuck my fingers in my ears, trying to block out the sound, but somehow it insinuated itself into my eardrums. Thoughts of a convenient lie to get me out of this situation left me little room for remorse.

Afterwards Jirō took me to the village office. While I was examining some local artefacts, sunlight began to warm the windows. I glanced up and saw that the rain had finally stopped.

"You can see a few more of these if you go over to the school." Mr. Nakamura, a deputy official in the village, stood beside me with a worried expression on his face, as though it were his personal responsibility that there was nothing here worth looking at. The only displays at the village office and the elementary school were of some earthenware fragments from remote antiquity, dug up by the teachers at the school. They had none of the *kakure* relics that I was eager to examine.

"Don't you have any *kakure* rosaries or crosses?"

Mr. Nakamura shook his head with embarrassed regret. "Those people like to keep things to themselves. You'll just have to go there yourself. They're a bunch of eccentrics, if you ask me."

His words were filled with the same contempt for the *kakure* that I had detected in Jirō's remarks.

Jirō, having observed the weather conditions, returned to the village office and announced cheerfully, "It's cleared up. We'll be able to go tomorrow for sure. Would you like to go and see the Isle of Rocks now?"

When we had visited the Christian grave, I had especially asked to see the Isle of Rocks.

Mr. Nakamura made a quick phone call to the fishermen's union. Village offices can be useful at such times; the union was more than willing to provide us with a small motorboat.

I borrowed a mackintosh from Mr. Nakamura. He accompanied Jirō and me to the dock, where a fisherman had the boat waiting. A mat had been laid in the wet bilges for us to sit on. In the murky waters that slopped around our feet floated the tiny silver body of a dead fish.

With a buzz from the motor, the boat set out into the still-rough seas, vibrating ever more fiercely. It was invigorating to ride the crest of a wave, but each time we sank into a trough, I felt as though my stomach were cramping.

"The fishing's good at the Isle of Rocks," Nakamura commented. "We often go there on holidays. Do you fish, Sensei?"

When I shook my head, he gave me a disappointed look and began boasting to Jirō and the fisherman about the large silthead he had once caught.

The spray drenched my mackintosh. The chill of the sea winds rendered me speechless. The surface of the water, which had started out grey, was now a dark, cold-looking black. I thought of the Christians who had been hurled into these waters four centuries before. If I had been born in such a time, I would not have had the strength to endure such a punishment. Suddenly I thought of my mother. I saw myself strolling around the entertainment district at Nishinomiya, then telling lies to my mother.

The little island drew closer. True to its name, it was composed entirely of craggy rocks, the very crest of which was crowned with a scant growth of vegetation. In response to a question from me, Mr. Nakamura reported that, aside from occasional visits by officials of the Ministry of Postal Services, the island was used by the villagers only as a place from which to fish.

Ten or so crows squawked hoarsely as they hovered over the top of the islet. Their calls pierced the wet grey sky, giving the scene an eerie, desolate air. Now we had a clear view of the cracks and fissures in the rocks. The waves beat against the crags with a roar, spewing up white spray.

I asked to see the spot from which the Christians were cast into the sea, but neither Jirō nor Nakamura knew where it was. Most likely there had not been one particular location; the faithful had probably been thrown down from any convenient place.

"It's frightening even to think about it."

"It's impossible to imagine nowadays."

Evidently the thoughts that had been running through my head had not even occurred to my two Catholic companions.

"There's lots of bats in these caves. When you get up close, you can hear them shrieking."

"They're strange creatures. They fly so fast, and yet they never bump into anything. I hear they've got something like radar."

"Well, Sensei, shall we take a walk around and then go back?"

The island from which we had come was being pounded by white surf. The rainclouds split open, and we had a clear view of the mountain slopes in the distance.

Mr. Nakamura, pointing towards the mountains as the priest had done the previous evening, said, "That's where the *kakure* village is."

"Nowadays I suppose they don't keep to themselves like they used to, do they?"

"As a matter of fact, they do. We had one working as a janitor at the school. Shimomura was his name. He was from the *kakure* village. But I didn't much care for him. There wasn't anything to talk to him about."

The two men explained that the Catholics on the island were hesitant about associating with the *kakure* or intermarrying with them. Their reluctance seemed to have more to do with psychological conflicts than with religious differences. Even now the *kakure* married their own kind;

if they did otherwise, they would not be able to preserve their faith. This custom reinforced their conviction that they were a peculiar people.

On the breast of those mountains half concealed in mist, the *kakure* Christians had sustained their religious faith for three hundred years, guarding their secret institutions from outsiders, as was done in all the *kakure* villages, by appointing people to such special village posts as "Waterworks Official," "Watchman," "Greeter," and "Ombudsman." From grandfather to father, and from father to son, their formal prayers were passed through the generations, and their objects of worship were concealed behind the dark Buddhist altars. My eyes searched the mountain slope for that isolated village, as though I were gazing at some forsaken landscape. But of course it was impossible to spot it from there.

"Sensei, why are you interested in such a strange group of people?" Nakamura asked me in amazement. My reply was noncommittal.

One clear autumn day, I bought some chrysanthemums and set out for the cemetery. My mother's grave is in a Catholic cemetery in Fuchū. I can't begin to count the number of times I have made the journey to that graveyard since my school-days. In the past, the road was surrounded by groves of chestnut and buckeye trees and fields of wheat; in the spring it was a pleasant path for a leisurely stroll. But now it is a busy thoroughfare crowded with all manner of shops. Even the stone carver's little hut that once stood all by itself at the entrance to the cemetery has turned into a solid one-storey building.

Memories flood my mind each time I visit that place. I went to pay my respects the day I graduated from the university. The day before I was due to board a ship for France to continue my studies, I again made the journey there. It was the first spot I visited when I fell ill and had to return to Japan. I was careful to visit the grave on the day I was married, and on the day I went into the hospital. Sometimes I make the pilgrimage without telling anyone, not even my wife. It is the spot where I conduct private conversations with my mother. In the depths of my heart lurks a desire not to be disturbed even by those who are close to me. I make my way down the path. A statue of the Holy Mother stands in the centre of the graveyard, surrounded by a tidy row of stone markers belonging to the graves of foreign nuns who have been buried here in Japan. Branching out from this centre point are white crosses and gravestones. A bright sun and a peaceful silence hover over each of the graves.

Mother's grave is small. My heart constricts whenever I look at that tiny grave marker. I pluck the wild grasses that surround it. With buzzing wings, insects swarm around me as I work in solitude. There is no other sound.

As I pour a ladle of water into the flower vase, I think (as I always do) of the day my mother died. The memory is a painful one for me. I was not with her when she collapsed in the hallway from a heart attack, nor was I beside her when she died. I was at Tamura's house, doing something that would have made her weep had she seen it.

Tamura had pulled a sheaf of postcards wrapped in newspaper from his desk drawer. And he smiled that thin smile he always wore when he was about to teach me something.

"These aren't like the phoney ones they sell around here."

There were something like ten photographs inside the newspaper wrapping. Their edges were yellow and faded. The dark figure of a man was stretched out on top of the white body of a woman. She had a look as though of pain on her face. I caught my breath and flipped through the pictures one after another.

"Lecher! You've seen enough, haven't you?" Tamura cackled.

Their telephone rang, and after it was answered, we heard footsteps approaching. Hurriedly Tamura stuffed the photographs into his drawer. A woman's voice called my name.

"You must go home right away! Your mother's had an attack!"

"What's up?" Tamura asked.

"I don't know." I was still glancing at the drawer. "How did she know I was here?"

I was less concerned about her attack than the fact that she knew I was at Tamura's. She had forbidden me to go there after she found out that Tamura's father ran a whorehouse. It was not unusual for her to have to go to bed with heart palpitations, but if she took the white pills (I've forgotten the name) that the doctor gave her, the attack was always brought under control.

I made my way slowly along the back streets still warmed by the bright sun. Rusted scraps of metal were piled up in a field marked with a "For Sale" sign. Beside the field was a small factory. I didn't know what they manufactured there, but a dull, heavy, pounding noise was repeated regularly inside the building. A man came riding towards me on a bicycle, but he stopped beside the dusty, weed-covered field and began to urinate.

My house came into view. The window to my room was half open, the way it always was. Neighbourhood children were playing in front of the house. Everything was normal, and there was no sign that anything unusual had happened. The priest from our church was standing at the front door.

"Your mother . . . died just a few moments ago." He spoke each word softly and clearly. Even a mindless middle-school student like myself could tell that he was struggling to suppress the emotion in his voice. Even a mindless middle-school student like myself could sense the criticism in his voice.

In the back room, my mother's body was surrounded by neighbours and people from the church, sitting with stooped shoulders. No one turned to look at me; no one spoke a word to me. I knew from the stiffness of their backs that they all were condemning me.

Mother's face was white as milk. A shadow of pain still lingered between her brows. Her expression reminded me of the look on the face of the woman in the photographs I had just been examining. Only then did I realize what I had done, and I wept.

I finish pouring the water from the bucket and put the chrysanthemums into the vase that is part of the gravestone. The insects that have been buzzing about my face now cluster around the flowers. The earth beneath which my mother lies is the dark soil peculiar to the Musashi Plain. At some point I too will be buried here, and as in my youth, I will be living alone again with my mother.

I had not given Mr. Nakamura a satisfactory answer when he asked me why I was interested in the *kakure*.

Public curiosity about the *kakure* has increased recently. This "hidden" religion is an ideal subject for investigation by those doing research in comparative religion. NHK, the national educational channel, has done several features on the *kakure* of Gotō and Ikitsuki, and many of the foreign priests of my acquaintance come to visit the *kakure* whenever they are in Nagasaki. But I am interested in the *kakure* for only one reason—because they are the offspring of apostates. Like their ancestors, they cannot utterly abandon their faith; instead they live out their lives, consumed by remorse and dark guilt and shame.

I was first drawn to these descendants of apostates after I had written a novel set in the Christian era. Sometimes I catch a glimpse of myself in these *kakure,* people who have had to lead lives of duplicity, lying to the world and never revealing their true feelings to anyone. I too have a secret that I have never told anyone, and that I will carry within myself until the day I die.

That evening I drank *sake* with the Father, Jirō, and Mr. Nakamura. The nun who had served me lunch brought out a large tray stacked with raw sea urchins and abalone. The local *sake* was too sweet for someone like myself who drinks only the dry variety, but the sea urchins were so fresh they made the Nagasaki ones seem almost stale. The rain had let up earlier, but it began to pour again. Jirō got drunk and began to sing.

> Oh, let us go, let us go
> To the Temple of Paradise, let us go,
> Oh, oh.

> They call it the Temple of Paradise,
> They say it is spacious and grand.
> But whether it is large or small
> Is really up to my heart.

I knew the song. When I'd visited Hirado two years before, the Christians there had taught it to me. The melody was complicated and impossible to remember, but as I listened to Jirō's plaintive singing, I thought of the dark expressions on the faces of the *kakure.* Protruding cheekbones and sunken eyes that seemed to be fixed on a single point in space. Perhaps, as they waited through the long years of national isolation for the boats of the missionaries that might never return, they muttered this song to themselves.

"Mr. Takaishi on Mount Fudō—his cow died. It was a good old cow." The priest was unlike the man I had met at the party in Tokyo. With a cup or so of *sake* in him, he was flushed down to his neck as he spoke to Mr. Nakamura. Over the course of the day, he and Jirō had perhaps ceased to regard me as an outsider. Gradually I warmed to this countrified priest, so unlike the swaggering prelates of Tokyo.

"Are there any *kakure* on Mount Fudō?" I asked.

"None. Everyone there belongs to our parish." He thrust out his chest a bit as he spoke, and Jirō and Nakamura nodded solemnly. I had noticed that morning how these people seemed to look down upon the *kakure* and regard them with contempt.

"There's nothing we can do about them. They won't have anything to do with us. Those people behave like some kind of secret society."

The *kakure* of Gotō and Ikitsuki were no longer as withdrawn as those on this island. Here even the Catholics appeared to be wary of the secretiveness of the *kakure*. But Jirō and Mr. Nakamura had *kakure* among their ancestors. It was rather amusing that the two of them now seemed to be oblivious of that fact.

"What exactly do they worship?"

"What do they worship? Well, it's no longer true Christianity." The priest sighed in consternation. "It's a form of superstition."

They gave me another interesting piece of information. The Catholics on the island celebrate Christmas and Easter according to the Western calendar, but the *kakure* secretly continue to observe the same festivals according to the old lunar calendar.

"Once when I went up the mountain, I found them all gathered together on the sly. Later I asked around and discovered they were celebrating their Easter."

After Nakamura and Jirō left, I returned to my room. My head felt feverish, perhaps due to the *sake,* and I opened the window. The ocean was pounding like a drum. Darkness had spread thickly in all directions. It seemed to me that the drumming of the waves deepened the darkness and the silence. I have spent nights in many different places, but I have never known a night as fathomless as this.

I was moved beyond words as I reflected on the many long years that the *kakure* on this island would have listened to the sound of this ocean. They were the offspring of traitors who had abandoned their religious beliefs because of the fear of death and the infirmities of their flesh. Scorned by the officials and by the Buddhist laity, the *kakure* had moved to Gotō, to Ikitsuki, and here to this island. Nevertheless, they had been unable to cast off the teachings of their ancestors, nor did they have the courage to defend their faith boldly like the martyrs of old. They had lived amid their shame ever since.

Over the years, that shame had shaped the unique features of their faces. They were all the same—the four or five men who had ridden with me on the ferry-boat, Jirō, and Mr. Nakamura. Occasionally a look of duplicity mingled with cowardice would dart across their faces.

Although there were minor differences between the *kakure* village organizations on this island and those in the settlements on Gotō or Ikitsuki, in each village the role of the priest was filled either by the "Watchman" or the "Village Elder." The latter would teach the people the essential prayers and important festival days. Baptism was administered to newly born infants by the "Waterworks Official." In some villages the positions of "Village Elder" and "Waterworks Official" were assumed by the same individual. In many instances these offices had been passed down through the patriarchal line for many generations. On Ikitsuki I had observed a case where units of organization had been established for every five households.

In front of the officials, the *kakure* had of course pretended to be practising Buddhists. They belonged to their own parish temples and had their names recorded as Buddhist believers in the religious registry. Like their ancestors, at certain times they were forced to trample on the *fumie* in the presence of the authorities. On the days when they had trodden on the sacred image, they returned to their villages filled with remorse over their own cowardice and filthiness, and there they scourged themselves with ropes woven of fibres, which they called *"tempensha."* The word originally meant "whip," and was derived from their misinterpretation of the Portuguese word for "scourge." I have seen one of these *"tempensha"* at the home of a Tokyo scholar of the Christian era. It was made from forty-six strands of rope, woven together, and did in fact cause a considerable amount of pain when I struck my wrist with it. The *kakure* had flogged their bodies with such whips.

Even this act of penitence did not assuage their guilt. The humiliation and anxiety of a traitor does not simply evaporate. The relentless gaze of their martyred comrades and the missionaries who had guided them continued to torment them from afar. No matter how diligently they tried, they could not be rid of those accusing eyes. Their prayers are therefore unlike the awkwardly translated Catholic invocations of the present day; rather, they are filled with faltering expressions of grief and phrases imploring forgiveness. These prayers, uttered from the stammering mouths of illiterate *kakure,* all sprang from the midst of their humiliation. "Santa Maria, Mother of God, be merciful to us sinners in the hour of death." "We beseech thee, as we weep and moan in this vale of tears. Intercede for us, and turn eyes filled with mercy upon us."

As I listened to the thrashing of the sea in the darkness, I thought of the *kakure,* finished with their labours in the fields and their fishing upon the waters, muttering these prayers in their rasping voices. They could only pray that the mediation of the Holy Mother would bring forgiveness of their frailties. For to the *kakure*, God was a stern paternal figure, and as a child asks its mother to intercede with its father, the *kakure* prayed for the Virgin Mary to intervene on their behalf. Faith in Mary was particularly strong among the *kakure*, and I concluded that their weakness had also prompted them to worship a figure that was a composite of the Holy Mother and Kannon, the Buddhist Goddess of Mercy.

I could not sleep even after I crawled into bed. As I lay beneath the thin coverlet, I tried to sing the words of the song that Jirō had performed that evening, but I couldn't remember them.

I had a dream. It seemed that my operation was over and I had just been wheeled back to my room; I lay back on the bed like a dead man. A rubber tube connected to an oxygen tank was thrust into my nostril, and transfusion needles from the plasma bottles hung over my bed had been inserted into my right arm and leg. My consciousness should have been blurred, but I recognized the greyish shadow that clutched my hand. It was my mother, and she was alone with me in my hospital room. There were no doctors; not even my wife.

I saw my mother in other places too. As I walked over a bridge at dusk, her face would sometimes appear suddenly in the gathering clouds overhead. Occasionally I would be in a bar, talking with the hostesses; when the conversation broke off and a sense of empty meaninglessness stole across my heart, I would feel my mother's presence beside me. As I bent over my work desk late in the night, I would abruptly sense her standing behind me. She seemed to be peering over my shoulder at the movements of my pen. I had strictly forbidden my children and even my wife to disturb me while I was working, but strangely it did not bother me to have my mother there. I felt no irritation whatsoever.

At such times, the figure of my mother that appeared to me was not the impassioned woman who had played her violin in search of the one perfect note. Nor was it the woman who had groped for her rosary each morning on the first Hankyū-line train, deserted except for the conductor. It was rather a figure of my mother with her hands joined in front of her, watching me from behind with a look of gentle sorrow in her eyes.

I must have built up that image of my mother within myself, the way a translucent pearl is gradually formed inside an oyster shell. For I have no concrete memory of ever seeing my mother look at me with that weary, plaintive expression.

I now know how that image came to be formed. I superimposed on her face that of a statue of "Mater Dolorosa," the Holy Mother of Sorrows, which my mother used to own.

After my mother's death, people came to take away her kimonos and obis and other possessions one after another. They claimed to be sharing out mementoes of my mother, but to my young eyes, my aunts seemed to be going through the drawers of her dresser like shoppers rifling through goods in a department store. Yet they paid no attention to her most valued possessions—the old violin, the well-used prayer-book she had kept for so many years, and the rosary with a string that was ready to break. And among the items my aunts had left behind was that cheap statue of the Holy Mother, the sort sold at every church.

Once my mother was dead, I took those few precious things with me in a box every time I moved from one lodging-house to another. Eventually the strings on the violin snapped and cracks formed in the wood. The cover was torn off her prayer-book. And the statue of Mary was burned in an air raid in the winter of 1945.

The sky was a stunning blue the morning after the air raid. Charred ruins stretched from Yotsuya to Shinjuku, and all around the embers were still smouldering. I crouched down in the remains of my apartment building in Yotsuya and picked through the ashes with a stick, pulling out broken bowls and a dictionary that had only a few unburned pages remaining. Eventually I struck something hard. I reached into the still-warm ashes with my hand and pulled out the broken upper half of that statue. The plaster was badly scorched, and the plain face was even uglier than before. Today, with the passage of time the facial features have grown vaguer. After I was married, my wife once dropped the statue. I repaired it with glue, with the result that the expression on the face is all the more indistinct.

When I went into hospital, I placed the statue in my room. After the first operation failed and I began my second year in hospital, I had reached the end of my rope both financially and emotionally. The doctors had all but given up hope for my recovery, and my income had dissolved to nothing.

At night, beneath the dim lights, I would often stare from my bed at the face of the Holy Mother. For some reason her face seemed sad, and she appeared to be returning my gaze. It was unlike any Western painting or sculpture of the Mother of God that I had ever seen. Its face was cracked from age and from the air raid, and it was missing its nose; where the face had once been, only sorrow remained. When I studied in France, I saw scores of statues and portraits of the "Mater Dolorosa," but this memento of my mother had lost all traces of its origins. Only that sorrow lingered.

At some point I must have blended together the look on my mother's face and the expression on that statue. At times the face of the Holy Mother of Sorrows seemed to resemble my mother's face when she died. I still remember clearly how she looked laid out on top of her quilt, with that shadow of pain etched into her brow.

Only once did I ever tell my wife about my mother appearing to me. The one time I did say something, she gave some sort of reply, but a look of evident displeasure flickered on her face.

There was fog everywhere.

The squawking of crows could be heard in the mist, so we knew that the village was near at hand. With my reduced lung capacity, it was quite a struggle to make it all this way. The mountain path was very steep, but my greatest difficulty was that the boots which Jirō had lent me kept slipping in the sticky clay.

Even so, Mr. Nakamura explained, we were having an easier time of it than in the old days. Back then—and we couldn't see it now because of the fog—there had been just one mountain path to the south, and it had taken half a day to reach the village. The resourceful *kakure* had deliberately chosen such a remote location for their village in order to avoid surveillance by the officials.

There were terraced fields on both sides of the path, and the black silhouettes of trees emerged from the fog. The shrieking of the crows grew louder. I remembered the flock of crows that had circled the summit of the Isle of Rocks on the previous day.

Mr. Nakamura called out to a mother and child working in the fields. The mother removed the towel that covered her face and bowed to him politely.

"Kawahara Kikuichi's house is just down this way, isn't it?" Nakamura asked. "There's a Sensei from Tokyo here who'd like to talk to him."

The woman's child gawked at me curiously until his mother scolded him, at which point he charged off into the field.

It had been Mr. Nakamura's sensible suggestion that we bring along a bottle of *sake* from the village as a gift for Mr. Kawahara. Jirō had carried it for me on our trek, but at this point I took it from him and followed the two men into the village. A radio was playing a popular song. Some of the houses had motorcycles parked in their sheds.

"All the young people want to get out of this place."

"Do they come to town?"

"No, a lot of them go to work in Sasebo or Hirado. I suppose it's hard for them to find work on the island when they're known as children of the *kakure.*"

The crows were still following us along the road. They settled on the thatched roof of a house and cawed. It was as if they were warning the villagers of our arrival.

The house of Kawahara Kikuichi was somewhat larger than the others in the village, with a tiled roof and a giant camphor tree growing at the back. A single look at the house and it was obvious Kikuichi was the "Village Elder," the individual who performed the role of priest in this community.

Leaving me outside, Mr. Nakamura went into the house and negotiated with the family for a few minutes. The child we had seen in the field watched us from a distance, his hands thrust into trousers that had half fallen down. I glanced at him and realized that his bare feet were covered with mud. The crows squawked again.

I turned to Jirō. "It looks as though he doesn't want to meet us."

"Oh, no. With Mr. Nakamura talking to him, everything will be just fine," he reassured me.

Finally an agreement was reached. When I stepped inside the earthen entranceway, a woman was staring at me from the dark interior. I held out the bottle of *sake* and told her it was a small token of my gratitude, but there was no response.

Inside the house it was incredibly dark. The weather was partly to blame, but it was so dark I had the feeling it would be little different on a clear day. And there was a peculiar smell.

Kawahara Kikuichi was a man of about sixty. He never looked directly at me, but always kept his fearful eyes focused on some other spot in the room as he spoke. His replies were truncated, and he gave the impression that he wanted us to leave as soon as possible. Each time the conversation faltered, my eyes shifted to different corners of the room, to the stone mortar in the entranceway, to the straw matting, or to the sheaves of straw. I was searching for the characteristic staff that belonged to the "Village Elder," and for the place where they had concealed their icons.

The Village Elder's staff was something only he was allowed to possess. When he went to perform baptisms, he carried a staff made of oak; to drive evil spirits from a home, he used a silverberry staff. His staff was never made from bamboo. Clearly these staffs were an imitation of the croziers carried by priests in the Christian age.

I searched carefully, but I was unable to locate either a staff or the closet where the icons were hidden away. Eventually I was able to hear the prayers handed down to Kikuichi from his ancestors, but the hesitant expressions of grief and the pleas for forgiveness were like every other *kakure* supplication I had heard.

"We beseech thee, as we weep and moan in this vale of tears." As he intoned the melody, Kikuichi stared into space. "Intercede for us, and turn eyes filled with mercy upon us." Like the song Jirō had crooned the previous evening, this was just a string of clumsy phrases addressed as an appeal to someone.

"As we weep and moan in this vale of tears . . ." I repeated Kikuichi's words, trying to commit the tune to memory.

"We beseech thee . . ."

"We beseech thee."

". . . Turn eyes filled with mercy . . ."

"Turn eyes filled with mercy . . ."

In the back of my mind was an image of the *kakure* returning to their village one night each year after being forced to trample on the *fumie* and pay their respects at the Buddhist altars. Back in their darkened homes, they recited these words of prayer. "Intercede for us, and turn eyes filled with mercy upon us . . ."

The crows shrieked. For a few moments we were all silent, staring out at the thick mist that drifted past the veranda. A wind must have got up, for the milky fog swirled by more quickly than before.

"Could you perhaps show me your . . . your altar icons?" I stammered through my request, but Kikuichi's eyes remained fixed in another direction, and he gave no answer. The term "altar icons" is not Christian jargon, of course, but refers more generally to the Buddhist deities which are worshipped in an inner room of the house. Among the *kakure,* however, the object to which they prayed was concealed in the most inconspicuous part of the house; to deceive the officials, they referred to these images as their "altar icons." Even today, when they have full freedom of worship, they do not like to show these images to nonbelievers. Many of them believe that they defile their hidden icons by displaying them to outsiders.

Mr. Nakamura was somewhat firmer in his request. "He's come all the way from Tokyo. Why don't you show them to him?"

Finally Kikuichi stood up.

We followed him through the entranceway. The eyes of the woman in the darkened room were riveted on our movements.

"Watch your head!" Jirō called out from behind as we entered the inner room. The door was so low we had to bend over in order to go in. The tiny room, darker than the entranceway, was filled with the musty smells of straw and potatoes. Straight ahead of us was a small Buddhist altar decorated with a candle. This was certainly a decoy. Kikuichi's eyes shifted to the left. Two pale blue curtains hung there, though I had not noticed them when we came through the door. Rice cakes and a white bottle of offertory wine had been placed on the altar stand. Kikuichi's wrinkled hand slowly drew aside the curtains. Gradually the sections of an ochre-coloured hanging scroll were revealed to us.

Behind us, Jirō sighed, "It's just a picture."

A drawing of the Holy Mother cradling the Christ child—no, it was a picture of a farm woman holding a nursing baby. The robes worn by the child were a pale indigo, while the mother's kimono was painted a murky yellow. It was clear from the inept brushwork and composition that the picture had been painted many years before by one of the local *kakure.* The farm woman's kimono was open, exposing her breast. Her obi was knotted at the front, adding to the impression that she was dressed in the rustic apparel of a worker in the fields. The face was like that of every woman on the island. It was the face of a woman who gives suckle to her child even as she ploughs the fields and mends the fishing-nets. I was suddenly reminded of the woman earlier who had removed the towel from her face and bowed to Mr. Nakamura.

Jirō had a mocking smile on his face. Mr. Nakamura was pretending to look serious, but I knew that inside he was laughing.

Still, for some time I could not take my eyes off that clumsily drawn face. These people had joined their gnarled hands together and offered up supplications for forgiveness to this portrait of a mother. Within me there welled up the feeling that their intent had been identical to mine. Many long years ago, missionaries had crossed the seas to bring the teachings of God the Father to this land. But when the missionaries had been expelled and the churches demolished, the Japanese *kakure,* over the space of many years, stripped away all those parts of the religion that they could not embrace, and the teachings of God the Father were gradually replaced by a yearning after a Mother—a yearning which lies at the very heart of Japanese religion. I thought of my own mother. She stood again at my side, an ashen-coloured shadow. She was not playing the violin or clutching her rosary now. Her hands were joined in front of her, and she stood gazing at me with a touch of sorrow in her eyes.

The fog had started to dissipate when we left the village, and far in the distance we could see the dark ocean. The wind seemed to have stirred up the sea again. I could not see the Isle of Rocks. The mist was even thicker in the valley. From somewhere in the trees that rose up through the mist, crows cried out. "In this vale of tears, intercede for us; and turn eyes filled with mercy upon us." I hummed the melody of the prayer that I had just learned from Kikuichi. I muttered the supplication that the *kakure* continually intoned.

"How ridiculous! Sensei, it must have been a terrible disappointment to have them show you something so stupid." As we left the village, Jirō apologized to me over and over, as though he were personally responsible for the whole thing. Mr. Nakamura, who had picked up a tree branch along the way to use as a walking-stick, walked ahead of us in silence. His back was stiff. I couldn't imagine what he was thinking.

HEINRICH BÖLL

Candles for the Madonna

My stay here was a brief one; I had an appointment in the late afternoon with the representative of a firm that was toying with the idea of taking over a product which has been causing us something of a headache: candles. We put all our money into the manufacture of tremendous stocks on the assumption that the electricity shortage would continue indefinitely. We have worked very hard, been thrifty and honest, and when I say "we" I mean my wife and myself. We are producers, wholesalers, retailers; we combine every stage in the holy estate of commerce: we are agents, workmen, traveling salesmen, manufacturers.

But we put our money on the wrong horse. There is not much demand for candles these days. Electricity rationing has been abolished, even most basements now have electric light again; and at the very moment when our hard work, our efforts, all our struggles, seemed about to bear fruit—the production of a large quantity of candles—at that precise moment the demand dried up.

Our attempts to do business with those religious enterprises dealing in what are known as devotional supplies came to nothing. These firms had hoarded candles in abundance—better ones than ours, incidentally, the fancy kind, with green, red, blue, and yellow ribbons, embroidered with little golden stars, winding around them—like Aesculapius' snake —and enhancing both their reverent and esthetic appeal; they also come in various lengths and sizes whereas ours are all identical and of simple design: about ten inches long, smooth, yellow, quite plain, their only asset the beauty of simplicity.

We were forced to admit that we had miscalculated; compared with the splendid products displayed by the devotional supply houses, our candles look humble indeed, and nobody buys anything humble-looking. Nor has our willingness to reduce our price resulted in any increase in sales. On the other hand, of course, we lack the money to plan new designs, let alone manufacture them, since the income we derive from the limited sale of the stock we have produced is barely enough to cover our living expenses and steadily mounting costs. I have, for instance, to make longer and longer trips in order to call on genuinely or apparently interested parties, I have to keep on reducing our price, and we know we have no alternative but to unload the substantial stocks still on our hands and find some other means of making a living.

I had come to this town in response to a letter from a wholesaler who had intimated that he would take a considerable quantity off my hands at an acceptable price. I was foolish enough to believe him, came all the way here, and was now calling on this fellow. He had a magnificent apartment, luxurious, spacious, furnished in great style, and the large office where he received me was crammed with samples of all the various products that make money for his type of business. Arranged on long shelves were plaster saints, statuettes of Joseph, Virgin Marys, bleeding Sacred Hearts, mild-eyed, fair-haired penitents whose plaster pedestals bore the name, in a variety of languages and embossed lettering (choice of gold or red): Madeleine, Maddalena, Magdalena, Magdalene; Nativity scenes (complete or sectional), oxen, asses, Infant Jesuses in wax or plaster, shepherds, and angels of all ages: tots, youths, children, graybeards; plaster palm leaves adorned with gold or silver Hallelujahs, holy-water stoups of stainless steel, plaster, copper, pottery: some in good taste, some in bad.

The man himself—a jovial, red-faced fellow—asked me to sit down, affected some initial interest, and offered me a cigar. He wanted to know how we happened to get into this particular branch of manufacturing, and after I had explained that we had inherited nothing from the war but a huge pile of stearin which my wife had salvaged from four blazing trucks in front of our bombed-out house and which no one had since claimed as their property, after I had smoked about a quarter of my cigar, he suddenly said, without any preamble: "I'm sorry I had you come here, but I've changed my mind." Perhaps my sudden loss of color did strike him as odd after all. "Yes," he went on, "I really am sorry about it, but after considering all the angles I've come to the conclusion that your product won't sell. It won't sell! Believe me, I know! Sorry!" He smiled, shrugged his shoulders, and held out his hand. I put down the half-smoked cigar and left.

By this time it was dark, and I was a total stranger in the town. Although, in spite of everything, I was aware of a certain relief, I had the terrible feeling that I was not only poor, deceived, the victim of a misguided idea, but also ridiculous. It would seem that I was unfit for the so-called battle of life, for the career of manufacturer and dealer. Our candles would not sell even for a pittance, they weren't good enough to hold their own in the field of devotionalist competition, and we probably wouldn't even be able to give them away, whereas other, inferior candles were being bought. I would never discover the secret of business success, although, with my wife, I had hit upon the secret of making candles.

I lugged my heavy sample case to the streetcar stop and waited a long time. The darkness was soft and clear, it was summer. Streetlights were on at the crossings, people were strolling about in the evening, it was quiet; I was standing beside a big circular traffic island—fringed by dark empty office buildings—behind me a little park; I heard the sound of running water, and on turning round I saw a great marble woman standing there, with thin jets of water spouting from her rigid breasts into a copper basin; I felt chilly and realized I was tired. At last the streetcar arrived; soft music poured from brightly lit cafés, but the station was in an empty, quiet part of town. All I could glean from the big blackboard there was the departure time of a train which would get me only halfway home and which, if I took it, would cost me a whole night of waiting-room, grime, and a bowl of repulsive soup at the station in a little place with no hotel. I turned away, went outside again, and counted my money by the light of a gas lamp: nine marks, return ticket, and a few pfennigs. Some cars were standing there that looked as if they had been waiting there forever, and little trees, cropped like new recruits. Dear little trees, I thought, nice little trees, obedient little trees. Doctors' white nameplates showed up against a few unlighted houses, and through a café window I looked in on a gathering of empty chairs for whose benefit a writhing violinist was producing sobs that might have moved stones but hardly a human being. At last, in a lane skirting the bulk of a dark church, I came upon a painted green sign: "Rooms." I stepped inside.

Behind me I could hear the streetcar on its return trip to the better lighted, more populated part of town. The hall was empty, and I turned to the right into a little room containing four tables and twelve chairs; to the left, bottles of beer and lemonade stood in metal display stands on a built-in counter. Everything looked clean and plain. Green hessian, divided by narrow strips of brown wood, had been tacked to the walls with rosette-shaped copper nails. The chairs were green too, upholstered in some soft, velvety material. Light-yellow curtains had been drawn closely across the windows, and behind the counter a serving hatch opened into a kitchen. I put down my suitcase, drew a chair toward me, and sat down. I was very tired.

How quiet it was here, even quieter than the station which, strangely enough, was some distance from the business center, a gloomy, cavernous place filled with the muffled sounds of an invisible bustle: bustle behind closed wickets, bustle behind wooden barriers.

I was hungry, too, and I found the utter futility of this journey very depressing. I was glad of the few minutes to myself in this quiet, unpretentious room. I would have liked to smoke but found I had no cigarettes, and now I regretted having abandoned the cigar in the wholesale devotionalist's office. Although I might well be depressed at having gone on yet another wild-goose chase, I was aware of a growing sense of relief that I couldn't quite define or account for, but perhaps in my heart I rejoiced at my final expulsion from the devotional-supply trade.

I had not been idle after the war; I had helped clear away ruins, remove rubble, scrape bricks clean, build walls, haul sand, shift lime, I had submitted applications—many, many applications—thumbed through books, carefully watched over my pile of stearin. On my own, with no help from those who might have given me the benefit of their experience, I had found out how to make candles, beautiful, simple, good-quality candles, tinted a soft yellow that gave them the luster of melting beeswax. I had done everything to get on my feet, as they say: to find some way of earning a living, and although I ought to have been sad—the very futility of my efforts was now filling me with a joy such as I had never known.

I had not been ungenerous, I had given away candles to people living in cramped unlighted holes, and whenever there had been a chance of profiteering I had avoided it. I had gone hungry and devoted myself single-mindedly toward this method of making a living; but, although I might have expected a reward for what one might call my integrity, I almost rejoiced to find myself evidently unworthy of any reward.

The thought also crossed my mind: perhaps we would have done better after all to manufacture shoe polish, as someone had advised us, to mix other ingredients with the basic material, to get hold of some formulas, acquire a stock of cardboard containers, and fill them up.

In the midst of my musings the landlady entered the room, a slight, elderly woman. Her dress was green, the green of the beer and lemonade bottles on the counter. "Good evening," she said pleasantly. I returned her greeting, and she asked: "What can I do for you?"

"I would like a room, if you have one."

"Certainly," she said, "what price had you in mind?"

"The cheapest."

"That would be three marks fifty."

"Fine," I said, relieved. "And perhaps something to eat?"

"Certainly."

"Bread, some cheese and butter, and . . ." I ran my eyes over the bottles on the counter, "perhaps some wine."

"Certainly," she said, "a bottle?"

"No, no! A glass and—how much will that come to?"

She had gone behind the counter and was already pushing back the hook to open the serving hatch, but she paused to ask: "Altogether?"

"Yes, please, altogether."

She reached under the counter, took out pad and pencil, and again it was very quiet while she slowly wrote and added up. Despite the reserve in her manner, her whole presence, as she stood there, radiated a reassuring kindness. And she endeared herself to me still further by apparently making several mistakes in her addition. She slowly wrote down the items, frowned as she added them up, shook her head, crossed them out, rewrote everything, added up again, this time without frowning, and in gray pencil wrote the result at the bottom, finally saying in her soft voice: "Six-twenty—no, six, I beg your pardon."

I smiled. "That's fine. And have you any cigars?"

"Certainly." She reached under the counter again and held out a box. I took two and thanked her. The woman quietly gave the order through to the kitchen and left the room.

Scarcely had she gone when the door opened and in walked a young man, of slight build, unshaven, wearing a light-colored raincoat; behind him was a girl in a brown coat, hatless. The couple approached quietly, almost diffidently, and with a brief "Good evening" turned toward the counter. The boy was carrying the girl's shabby leather holdall, and although he was obviously at pains to appear undaunted and to display the bravado of a man who regularly spends the night with his girl in a hotel, I could see his lower lip trembling and tiny beads of sweat on the stubble of his beard. The couple stood there like customers awaiting their turn in a store. The fact that they were hatless and that the holdall was their only luggage made them look like refugees who had arrived at some transit camp. The girl was beautiful, her skin alive, warm, and slightly flushed, and her heavy brown hair hanging loosely over her shoulders seemed almost too heavy for her slender feet; she nervously moved her black dusty shoes, shifting her weight from one foot to the other more often than was necessary; the young man kept brushing back a few strands of hair as they fell over his forehead, and his small round mouth expressed a painful but at the same time elated determination. I could see they were deliberately avoiding each other's eyes, and they did not speak to one another, while I for my part was glad to be busily occupied with my cigar, to be able to clip it, light it, look critically at the tip, relight it, and start smoking. Every second of waiting must be agony, I knew; for the girl, no matter how unabashed and happy she might look, continued to shift her weight as she tugged at her coat, while the boy continued to pass his hand over his forehead although there were no more strands of hair to brush back. At last the woman reappeared, quietly said "Good evening," and placed the bottle of wine on the counter.

I jumped up at once, saying: "Allow me!" She looked at me in surprise, then set down the glass, handed me the corkscrew, and asked the young man: "What can I do for you?" As I put the cigar between my lips and twisted the corkscrew into the cork, I heard the young man ask: "Can you let us have two rooms?"

"Two?" asked the landlady: just then I pulled out the cork and from the corner of my eye saw the girl flush, while the boy bit hard on his lower lip and, barely opening his mouth, said: "Yes, two."

"Oh, thank you," the landlady said, filling the glass and passing it to me. I went back to my table, began to sip the gentle wine, and could only hope that the inevitable ritual would not be dragged out even further by the arrival of my supper. But the entries in the register, the filling out of forms, and the producing of gray-blue identity cards, all took less time than I had expected; and at one point, when the boy opened the holdall to get out the identity cards, I saw that it contained greasy paper bags, a crumpled hat, some packets of cigarettes, a beret, and a shabby old red wallet.

During all this time the girl tried to look poised and confident; with an air of nonchalance she surveyed the bottles of lemonade, the green of the hessian wall-covering, and the rosette-shaped nails, but the flush never left her cheeks, and when everything was finally settled they took their keys and hurried upstairs without saying good night. A few minutes later my supper was passed through the hatch; the landlady brought me my plate, and when our eyes met she did not smile, as I had thought she would, but looked gravely past me and said: "I hope you enjoy your supper, sir."

"Thank you," I replied. She remained standing beside me.

I slowly began my meal, helping myself to bread, butter, and cheese. She still did not move. "Smile," I said.

And she did smile, but then she sighed, saying: "There's nothing I can do about it."

"Do you wish there were?"

"Oh yes," she said fervently, sitting herself down beside me, "indeed I do. I'd like to do something about a lot of things. But if he asks for two rooms . . . If he had asked for one, now . . ." she paused.

"What then?" I asked.

"What then?" she mimicked angrily. "I would have thrown him out."

"What for?" I said wearily, putting the last piece of bread in my mouth. She said nothing. What for, I thought, what for? Doesn't the world belong to lovers, weren't the nights mild enough, weren't other doors open, dirtier ones perhaps, but doors one could close behind one? I looked into my empty glass and smiled . . .

The landlady had risen, fetched her big book and a pile of forms, and sat down beside me again.

She watched me as I filled everything out. I paused at the column "Occupation," raised my eyes, and looked into her smiling face. "Why do you hesitate?" she asked calmly, "have you no occupation?"

"I don't know."

"You don't know?"

"I don't know whether I am a workman, a salesman, a manufacturer, unemployed, or only an agent . . . but whose agent . . ." whereupon I quickly wrote down "Agent" and gave her back the book. For a moment I considered offering her candles—twenty, if she liked, for a glass of wine, or ten for a cigar. I don't know why I didn't, perhaps I was just too tired, or too lazy, but the next morning I was glad I hadn't.

I relighted my dead cigar and got to my feet. The woman had shut the book, laying the forms between the pages, and was yawning.

"Would you like coffee in the morning?" she asked.

"No, thank you, I have to catch an early train. Good night."

"Good night," she said.

But next morning I slept late. The passage, which I had glimpsed the previous evening—carpeted in dark red—had remained silent throughout the night. The room was quiet too. The unaccustomed wine had made me sleepy but also happy. The window was open, and all I could see against the quiet, deep-blue summer sky was the dark roof of the church opposite; farther to the right I could see the colorful reflection of the town lights, hear the noise of the livelier district. I took my cigar with me as I got into bed so that I could read the newspaper, but fell asleep at once . . .

It was after eight when I woke up. The train I had meant to catch had already left, and I was sorry I had not asked to be woken. I washed, decided to go out for a shave, and went downstairs. The little green room was now light and cheerful, the sun shining in through the thin curtains, and I was surprised to see tables laid for breakfast, with breadcrumbs, empty jam dishes, and coffeepots. I had felt as if I were the only guest in this silent house. I paid my bill to a friendly maid and left.

Outside I hesitated. The cool shadow of the church surrounded me. The lane was narrow and clean; to the right a baker had opened his shop, loaves and rolls shone pale brown and yellow in the glass cases, and farther on jugs of milk stood at a door to which a thin, blue-white trail of milk drops led. The other side of the street was entirely taken up by a high black wall built of great square blocks of stone; through a big arched gateway I saw green lawn and walked in. I was standing in a monastery garden. An old, flat-roofed building, its stone window frames touchingly whitewashed, stood in the middle of a green lawn; stone tombs in the shade of weeping willows. A monk was padding along a flagged path toward the church. In passing, he gave me a nod of greeting, I nodded back, and when he entered the church I followed him, without knowing why.

The church was empty. It was old, devoid of decoration, and when by force of habit I dipped my hand in the stoup and bent my knee toward the altar, I saw that the candles must have just gone out: a thin, black ribbon of smoke was rising from them into the clear air. There was no one in sight; mass seemed to be over for this morning. My eyes involuntarily followed the black figure as it bobbed an awkward genuflection in front of the tabernacle and vanished into a side aisle. I went closer and came to a sudden halt: I found myself looking at a confessional, the young girl of the previous evening was kneeling in a pew in front of it, her face hidden in her hands, while at the edge of the nave, showing no apparent interest, stood the young man, the holdall in one hand, the other hanging slackly by his side, his eyes on the altar . . .

In the midst of this silence I could hear my heart beating, louder, stronger, strangely unquiet, and I could feel the boy looking at me. Our eyes met, he recognized me, and flushed. The girl was still kneeling there, her face in her hands. A thin, faint thread of smoke was still rising from the candles. I sat down in a pew, placed my hat beside me, and put my suitcase on the ground. I felt as if I were waking up for the first time, as if until now I had seen everything with my eyes only, a detached spectator—church, garden, street, girl, man—it had all been like a stage set that I had brushed by as an outsider, but now, looking at the altar, I longed for the young man to go and confess too. I wondered when I had last gone to confession, found it hard to keep track of the years—roughly it would be about seven—but as I went on thinking about it I realized something much worse: I couldn't put my finger on any sin. No matter how honestly I tried, I couldn't think of any sin worth confessing, and this made me very sad. I felt unclean, full of things that needed to be washed away, but nowhere was there actually anything that in coarse, rough, sharp, clear terms could have been called sin. My heart beat louder than ever. Last night I had not envied the young couple, but now I did envy that ardent kneeling figure, still hiding her face in her hands, waiting. The young man stood completely motionless and detached.

I was like a pail of water that has remained exposed to the air for a long time. It looks clean, a casual glance reveals nothing in it: nobody has thrown stones, dirt, or garbage into it, it has been standing in the hallway or basement of a well-kept, respectable house; the bottom appears to be immaculate; all is clear and still, yet, when you dip your hand into the water, there runs through your fingers an intangible repulsive fine dirt that seems to be without shape, without form, almost without dimension. You just know it is there. And on reaching deeper into this immaculate pail, you find at the bottom a thick indisputable layer of this fine disgusting formless muck to which you cannot put a name; a dense, leaden sediment made up of these infinitesimal particles of dirt abstracted from the air of respectability.

I could not pray, I could only hear my heart beating and wait for the girl to go into the confessional. At last she raised her hands, laid her face against them for an instant, stood up, and entered the wooden box.

The young man kept his place. He stood there aloof, having no part in it, unshaven, pale, his face still expressing a mild yet insistent determination. When the girl emerged, he suddenly put down the holdall and stepped into the confessional.

I still could not pray, no voice spoke to me or in me, nothing moved, only my heart was beating, and I could not curb my impatience. I stood up, left my suitcase where it was, and crossed over to the side aisle, where I stood beside a pew. In the front pew the young woman was kneeling before an old stone Madonna standing on a bare, disused altar. The Virgin's face was coarse-featured but smiling, a piece of her nose was missing, the blue paint of her robe had flaked off, and the gold stars on it were now no more than lighter spots; her scepter was broken, and of the Child in her arms only the back of the head and part of the feet were still visible. The center part, the torso, had fallen out, and she was smilingly holding this fragment in her arms. A poor monastic order, evidently, that owned this church.

"Oh, if I could only pray!" I prayed. I felt hard, useless, unclean, unrepentant. I couldn't even produce one sin. The only thing I possessed was my pounding heart and the knowledge that I was unclean . . .

The young man brushing past me from behind roused me from my thoughts, and I stepped into the confessional . . .

By the time I had been dismissed with the sign of the cross, the young couple had left the church. The monk pushed aside the purple curtain of the confessional, opened the little door, and padded slowly past me; once again he genuflected awkwardly before the altar.

I waited until I had seen him disappear, then quickly crossed the nave, also genuflecting, carried my suitcase back to the side aisle, and opened it: there they all lay, tied in bundles by my wife's loving hands, slim, yellow, unadorned, and I looked at the cold, bare stone plinth on which the Madonna stood and regretted for the first time that my suitcase was not heavier. I ripped open the first bundle and struck a match . . .

Warming each candle in the flame of another, I stuck them all firmly onto the cold plinth that quickly allowed the soft wax to harden; on they all went, until the whole surface was covered with restless flickering lights and my suitcase was empty. I left it where it was, seized my hat, genuflected once more, and left: it was as if I were running away.

And now at last, as I walked slowly toward the station, I recalled all my sins, and my heart was lighter than it had been for a long time . . .

J. F. POWERS

The Warm Sand

Once as well liked as any guy in his class, Joe was generally avoided during his last years at the seminary—sometimes referred to as a gadfly, which he didn't mind; sometimes as a pain in the ass, which he did. His unpopularity was flattering in a way—in the light of "If the world hate you, know ye that it hath hated me before you," but that was pushing it in Joe's case. Besides, too many freaks and losers took comfort in Scripture, and Joe didn't see himself as either. He came from a family more than just well-to-do, and, unlike most of his classmates (but like St. Augustine), he had lived some before discovering his vocation to the priesthood. So he couldn't be looked down on, nor could his views be gainsaid on the ground that it was a species of pride for him to cite Doctors of the Church in support of them, though this was often tried by his critics. "Pride?" he'd replied. (He'd *replied* a lot at the seminary.) "I'd cite you guys if you ever said anything worth citing." That was his style.

It wasn't so much his all-around unpopularity as something said to him in the confessional ("We have to watch ourselves. A holier-than-thou attitude toward others doesn't become us in the sight of God") that made Joe decide, about a month before ordination, to show more charity toward others. Maybe there hadn't been time enough for others to notice the change in him, though, for he was still generally avoided.

About a month after ordination, at the class's first little get-together, to which he had to be invited (he did see it like that) and which was held in a private room in a restaurant, Joe watched himself (that is, shut up) and listened to the clerical shoptalk. He enjoyed it, too, though not as much as some of the others at the big table for twelve. Mooney and Rooney gloried in it. But it went on too long, and thinking, Oh-oh, here I go again, Joe said, "W. G. Ward. That name mean anything to you guys? No? Well, Ward, and *not* Newman, was the first convert from the Oxford Movement. He says any priest without personal knowledge of Christ, *which knowledge can only come from contemplation"*—Joe had supplied and stressed that part to make his point better—"ought to seek out some desolate island so as to live alone and do no harm."

"Words," said Cooney, once Joe's best friend but cool to him since Joe had got religion, as Cooney told it. (Joe hated the hillbilly sound of that, as he did Cooney's worldlier-than-thou attitude.) "Hard words, Joe."

"No harder than those of Our Lord to Martha," Joe replied.

"But *you're* not Our Lord!" cried a couple of deep thinkers at the table. Joe ignored them. He quoted from Luke 10, where Martha complains that she has her hands full serving Our Lord and the Disciples and could use some help from Mary, her sister, who sits listening to the conversation, and Our Lord replies, "Mary hath chosen the best part."

"Try telling that to the Chancery," said Rooney, who had earlier been complaining or bragging about having to do all the work in the parish where he was the assistant.

"Contemplation's all very well," said Mooney, whom Joe regarded as none too bright and pretty lucky to have been ordained. "Some of the saints, I know, went in for it. But it's still an extra. We have to make a distinction, Joe, between following the counsels of perfection and doing the job—and a mighty big job it is—we've been ordained to do. How many of us can do both?"

"That so-called distinction is the biggest out in all theology," Joe replied. "Why *not* do both? At least *try.*"

"You're doing both at Holy Faith?" said Rooney.

Cooney cut in, "According to Lefty Beeman" (a problem priest, always on the move; formerly at Holy Faith, he was now an assistant at St. Isidore's with Cooney), "the assistant at Holy Faith does the job, the pastor does the contemplating."

Joe replied, "Well, of course, I haven't been there as long as Beeman was. How long was he there? Six months?" This was not only cruel but wasted, and Joe, regretting it, shut up and listened to the others discuss the situation at Holy Faith.

"Two oddballs in one parish."

"Certainly an odd appointment."

"Crazy."

"Not fair to Joe—as a new man, I mean."

"Not fair to the pastor, you mean."

"Not fair to the *parishioners.*"

"The Archbishop's slipping."

His appointment to Holy Faith, as assistant to Father Van Slaag, the only known contemplative in the diocese (among pastors), was not crazy, Joe believed. No, the Chancery must have heard of his hard times at the seminary, where he'd been the only known contemplative— he didn't really qualify as such, he knew, unless maybe by desire, but he did have that reputation—and the Archbishop must have decided to make it two of a kind at Holy Faith. It was an odd appointment, perhaps, but it appeared odder than it was to those who recalled the efforts of the old Archbishop to strike a balance in parishes by pairing athletes with aesthetes, scholars with dunces, fat kine with lean. The new Archbishop was known to have said that his priests had enough to do without working out on each other; not that it was his policy to accommodate *everybody*—poker players, hi-fi'ers, photographers, astronomers, activists, liturgists—and not that some of his appointments didn't smack of old-fashioned therapy: a lush in the suburbs who'd lost his driver's license could find himself walking the corridors of a five-hundred-bed hospital in the city as a chaplain under the thumb of nuns; a big spender could find himself operating under the buddy or commissar system, with an assistant empowered to act for him and the parish in all money matters over two dollars and fifty cents.

Joe believed that his appointment, in a similar way—not, of course, in the same way—showed special concern on the part of the Archbishop, by whose wisdom and grace both pastor and assistant at Holy Faith were spared that heckling suspicion that is the lot of contemplatives, and even more of would-be contemplatives, in the modern world. With no need to apologize or explain, as each would have had to do with any other priest in the diocese, they could get on with or, in Joe's case, down to the job of working and praying for their personal sanctification and salvation (and their parishioners'). And that was what they were doing, though not everything was perfect at Holy Faith.

There was the problem of the housekeeper, Mrs. Cox, a plump tough-talking TV fan, who called Father Van Slaag Van to his face and Slug to her friends on the phone. (And Joe was pretty sure he was the one she referred to as Shorty.) There was the problem of Mrs. Cox's dog, Boots, a female bull terrier that would go for your ankles unless you carried a weapon. ("She's all right," the housekeeper would say with a hearty laugh. "She just hates men.") Joe had found a cane in the umbrella stand and took it with him whenever he left his bedroom.

There was also the problem of Father Van Slaag. Joe, for his part, had hoped to spend most of his free time in the church, in the presence of the Blessed Sacrament, but Father Van Slaag was already doing this— the man practically lived in the church. Pastor and assistant at first were absent from the rectory for long periods, until Joe asked himself, "Shepherd, what of the sheep?" This question, which could have come from Satan (who would doubtless employ any means to get a priest off his knees and out of a church) or from the Archbishop, was resolved for Joe after he discovered that he couldn't concentrate, let alone contemplate, when Father Van Slaag was in the church, as he was whenever Joe went there. Not wanting to ask when his free time was, or when Father Van Slaag's wasn't, Joe moved an old prie-dieu, which had been serving as a plant stand, into his bedroom. He now carried on from there with his spiritual exercises, and also—not the least of his duties—answered the phone there, more often than not while kneeling at the prie-dieu.

So, though not in the church much, Joe was on his knees a lot. When he considered the state of his knees, however, which were only lightly callused (nothing like those he'd once seen on a visiting Trappist monk in the showers at the seminary—horny gray growths like the chestnuts on the legs of a horse), Joe felt he had a long way to go. The question was whether a diocesan priest—not the really rare one, like Father Van Slaag, but the merely unusual one, like Joe—with his ministry in and to the world, which would rub off on him, could ever go very far; whether in time, after constant, close association with parishioners and coming under their subtle influence, he wouldn't cease to be spiritually, perhaps even mentally, an adult. What was true in other fields of human endeavor at the highest level, in the arts and sciences and sports—namely, that success involves a hell of a lot of slogging—just had to be true, Joe believed, in the field of spirituality: not a crowded field but the trickiest of all to get anywhere in. The notion, so popular nowadays, that the best kind of spirituality just happens, and is the by-product of routine apostolic activity, or, as some of Joe's critics at the seminary had claimed, is actually the same thing—well, Joe hadn't believed it then and didn't now.

"The priest's life," Joe said at the class's next little get-together, to which he'd received what had seemed to him a last-minute invitation, *"any* priest's life, *anybody's* life, in order to be fruitful in this world, to say nothing of the next, has to be rooted in contemplation. This is especially true of *our* life, which otherwise becomes one of sheer activity —the occupational disease of the diocesan clergy."

"Look," Rooney said. "I don't want to listen to that stuff tonight. I'm here to relax. You guys don't know what it's like to run a four-hundred-family parish all by yourself."

"That so?" replied Joe. "Happens to be what I'm doing at Holy Faith."

"Another parish heard from," said Cooney.

"Bob," Mooney said to Rooney, "we all have our crosses to bear."

"I *still* don't want to listen to that stuff tonight," Rooney said. "I had a tough day." So Joe shut up, and the clerical shoptalk, which he'd only cut into because it had gone on too long, continued.

At the very end, when Joe was leaving the restaurant for the parking lot, he was approached by Rooney. "Sorry, Joe," Rooney said. "But I had a tough one today."

"Bob, I know what you mean."

They went out to their cars together.

In the weeks that followed, Joe and Bob saw more of each other than they ever had before, except for a short time at the seminary when Bob had embraced the contemplative life. Joe hoped that Bob was having second thoughts about the active life, that it wasn't only their plight as overworked assistants that had drawn them together again, but in any case he had a friend in Bob. They knew each other's phone number by heart, and frequently met in the course of their duties—Bob pausing at Holy Faith on his way home from downtown, Joe at St. John Bosco's, Bob's parish, after visiting the hospital nearby.

St. John Bosco's, unlike Holy Faith, was a new plant, with paid secretaries, the latest in equipment, and programs and organizations galore, many overlapping. The parish was too much for one man—even for him, Bob said, unless he was there every minute, which he couldn't be. The pastor, Monsignor McConkie, or Mac, as Bob called him, a handsome silver-haired glad-hander, who had long ago joined everything joinable and now acknowledged when he got up in the morning, if he did, that he was in too deep and had a serious drinking problem, expected Bob to "represent" him and the parish at functions that Mac was under both doctor's and confessor's orders to stay away from. The worst ones—worst because there was no end to them—were service-club luncheons at downtown hotels. Bob attended three or four of these a week, and it was usually after one of them, in the middle of the afternoon, in high spirits or low, that he paused at Holy Faith.

Joe, usually in the office at that time of day—he'd moved the old prie-dieu down there—would make a drink for the visitor, as was the practice at St. John Bosco's, and they'd discuss what was uppermost in their minds: Boots, if she'd gone for Bob on the way in; Mrs. Cox, if the TV in the living room was coming through well; or problems of universal concern. One of these was church finance, a subject that Bob had ideas about and that Joe, though he'd scorned it and clerical bookkeeping at the seminary, now felt he should interest himself in. To judge by some correspondence from the Chancery in the files, nobody else at Holy Faith had done so in recent times. What could be said of the take at Holy Faith—not enough—could also be said of organizations: only two, the Holy Name Society (men) and the Christian Mothers (their wives). Reluctantly, Joe would agree that something should be done about Youth or, anyway, about Young People and Young Marrieds—Bob had ideas about all these—but then Joe would renege and say he didn't want to bite off more than he could chew: a veiled reference to the situation at St. John Bosco's.

"Heaven forbid!" Bob said. "Still, we're in the same boat, Joe."

That they were in the same boat (a commonplace in their discussions) and that Bob was having a rougher ride Joe would accept, but he couldn't agree that there was so little to choose between those responsible for their plights—between, if you didn't count the Archbishop, a mystic and a drunk—as to make no difference. One afternoon, Joe told Bob that it was the Father Van Slaags, oddly enough, and not the Monsignor McConkies, who kept the world going, who, by their feats of prayer and abnegation, stayed the hand of God. This, though he didn't like to hear it—non-contemplatives never did—Bob knew to be the accepted and time-honored belief of the Church.

Joe would have made his point even better had he spoken of what he'd seen the night before, when he'd gone to Father Van Slaag's room to complain about Boots and Mrs. Cox's TV, only to change his mind and ask permission to order Sunday-collection envelopes from another supplier, and then to retire to think, as he'd been doing ever since, on what he'd seen through the gaps in the old, almost buttonless cassock that Father Van Slaag wore for a nightshirt—the horny gray growths on the knees, the dogtooth wounds on the ankles. Dear God! What Joe had wondered about ever since coming to Holy Faith was clear to him then: why Father Van Slaag did nothing about Mrs. Cox's dog and TV. He was using them, these crosses, as a means to sanctification and salvation —making life make sense, which it otherwise wouldn't. Out of prudence, and out of reverence for Father Van Slaag, Joe didn't tell Bob or anyone else what he'd seen that night, but thereafter, whenever Bob said that their pastors ought to be put away—Mac in a sanatorium, Van in a cloister or cave—Joe was silent, brooding on those ankles and knees in awe and humility. He had decided that Father Van Slaag was—and not just in the sense that the word applied to anybody in the state of grace but in the sense that it applied to the big-time mystics and martyrs—a saint.

Before that night in Father Van Slaag's room, Joe had tried to do the job he'd been ordained to do for God and humanity while also trying, for the sake of the former, to preserve himself to a degree from the latter, but afterward there was a change in him. Without exactly going ape, Joe let down the barrier and no longer distinguished as he had before, sharply, between the religious and the social demands of parishioners. Mrs. Cox noticed it. "What?" she would say. "Stepping out again?"

In this change in him there was a certain despair, a giving up on himself and the contemplative life. Why not? When he tried to look down as God must and saw one man fending off Boots with a cane, the other allowing himself to be savaged by her, amortizing the world's great debt of sin a little, deferring foreclosure—really, there was no comparison. In that kind of company, Joe just didn't figure. Still, you never knew where you were in the spiritual life; that was the hell of it— only God knew. Joe's hope had to be that he was, without knowing it, a sleeper. He thought of Cardinal Merry del Val, who, as Pius X's secretary of state, was another overworked assistant to a saint, and perhaps one himself; among his personal effects, after his death, had been discovered (a shock to his friends in high places and low, these instruments of penance) two barbed-wire undershirts and a scourge with dried blood on it. But that sort of thing, though still nice to know—edifying—was discouraging if dwelt on, intimidating, like Father Van Slaag's ankles and knees. Joe took more comfort in Scripture—in "Whosoever shall seek to save his life, shall lose it," in "Greater love than this no man hath, that a man lay down his life for his friends," though this, too, was pushing it in his case. The truth was, *he* hadn't sacrificed his spiritual life—it had been done for him, by his appointment to Holy Faith. All he'd done since then, and might deserve credit for, was to stop grudging the time spent in doing the routine work of the parish, the time he might have spent in prayer. The old prie-dieu, which he'd been carrying back up to his bedroom one morning when the office phone rang, was still where he'd left it then, on the stair landing where he'd first found it, and since Mrs. Cox had come along before he could get back to it, it was serving as a plant stand again. He didn't mind. Though praying a lot less these days, he prayed harder when he did (as recommended by Merry del Val), and though working harder and seeing more people, he had more appetite for them. The truth was, he'd always had a weakness for people, a weakness suppressed at the seminary but now indulged and transformed into a strength, a virtue.

He was good with people when he wished to be, as he did now. He sparkled in maternity wards ("Bring us another round of orange juice, Sister, and this time put something in it"); sparkled at parish meetings, of which there were more since he'd decided to come to grips with Youth, Young People, and Young Marrieds ("What are we waiting for? I'm here"); sparkled at home ("My compliments to the chef, Mrs. Cox"). Occasionally, he even sat with Mrs. Cox in the evening if there was a game of some kind on TV; at first he had to get her to switch channels and to instruct her, but now he had to do neither, and it was gratifying to see her interest in sports quicken and to know it was genuine (with so many women it wasn't)—to come in from a meeting and find her and Boots watching the Twins. With Boots, however, Joe was still persona non grata, and still went about the house with his cane, which he left on the back porch when he stepped out and picked up when he returned.

But the best times for Joe were those times when he could be of real use to people as a priest—those times of trial, tragedy, and ordinary death—into which he entered deeper than he had before. "After years of trying to walk on the water, you know," he told Bob, who was increasingly impatient with parishioners (and Mac), "it's good to come ashore and feel the warm sand between my toes."

This was not to say that Joe couldn't get enough of people. He could. And when he did, after a tough day, or when he just craved faster company, he went to play poker with Cooney and the gang at St. Isidore's, a hard-drinking rectory, and the next morning it wasn't easy for him to get going. (He did not believe in Beeman's solution: "Weak drinks, more of 'em—that way you get more liquids into your system.") All in all, though, he felt better about himself both as a priest and as a person, as others appeared to these days—certainly Mrs. Cox, and even Cooney, who was becoming his best friend again.

"Joe," Cooney said one night at St. Isidore's, "know who you are?"

"Who?"

"Lemme put it another way. Know who Van is?"

"Who?"

"Mary. You're Martha, Joe."

Only now and then, late at night before he got to sleep, or early in the morning before he got going, did Joe look back and regret the change in himself.

A tough day. During breakfast, Joe had simply said, "Somebody ought to poison that bitch," meaning Boots, and now Mrs. Cox wouldn't talk to him. Later that morning, while trying to sparkle in a maternity ward, he'd simply said, "So *that's* the little bastard," and had been asked to leave by its mother. That afternoon, he had a visit from a young lady in real estate whom he'd just about enticed into fleeing the world and joining the Carmelites, and learned that she'd received a big promotion and therefore would be staying in the world after all. Early that evening, two converts in the making, Tex and Candy, who'd been taking instructions with a view to marrying Margie and Mike, failed to show, and it developed after a couple of phone calls that they'd eloped together. While Joe was working this out for Margie and Mike in the office, on hold in the living room he had an old parishioner who was upset over a nine-dollar error in his account—under Joe's new system, actually Bob's, receipts were mailed out to contributors at the end of the fiscal year—and who, though Joe tried everything, even offering to reimburse the old devil on the spot, wouldn't go away until he'd seen the pastor.

"He's in the church," Joe said, and fled.

Later, Joe went over to St. Isidore's for poker, and it turned out to be a tough night, too. He was there to relax, but the others wouldn't let him. Bob, who had just come from driving Mac to the sanatorium (and felt a little sad about it, though it was all for the best), kept after Joe to talk to Van about checking in to a cloister. Beeman, not for the first time, advised Joe to just look Boots in the eye, which was what he'd always done at Holy Faith. "And don't let her see you're afraid of her," he said, and suggested (though he admitted he had only heard about this, hadn't tried it himself), "Chuck her lightly under the jaw. Try it." When Joe mentioned the nine-dollar bookkeeping error, Beeman advised him in future just to say, "We all make mistakes. That's why they put erasers on lead pencils," which was what he always did in such a case. "Try it," he said. When Joe mentioned the young lady who'd received a big promotion and let him down, Bob said, "Hell, you can't blame her," and then had the nerve to say, alluding to his two weeks as a contemplative, "In my case, after trying to walk on the water, it was good to reach dry land and feel the warm sand under my feet," as if these words were entirely his own. Joe felt better after he heard Cooney's comment, "Bob, you never went out without your water wings," but a moment later he applied it to himself, with remorse. And Cooney, perhaps sensing this, tried to do his "Know who you are?" business with Joe again, but Joe foiled him by answering right away, "Martha." Then Cooney's pastor, one of the few really good poker players in the diocese and m.c. of its weekly TV program, said to Joe, "Found y'self, baby," and asked him if he'd ever considered how much he owed the Arch for sending him to Father Van Slaag at Holy Faith. Joe said he had, but unfortunately didn't leave it at that.

"Just one thing wrong with Van," he said. "Not doing his job." Joe had never said this, or anything like it, before, and immediately regretted it. Only the truth, yes, and they all knew it, but from him a betrayal.

From that point on, Joe, who hadn't taken a pot, won steadily. Later, much later, after a lot of standing around, though Joe himself was sitting down, and a lot of talk about cars and driving, Joe left St. Isidore's with Bob, he thought, and the next thing he knew, not counting a bad dream—"Mrs. Boots, come and get Cox!"—he was in bed and it was morning. He couldn't remember how the night had ended, and didn't want to, but had the presence of mind not to phone the police after he looked out the window and saw his car was missing from its usual place in the driveway. He took a hot bath, and in the course of it, soaping himself, he discovered and examined the marks on his right ankle—superficial wounds, five in number. They made him think but otherwise didn't hurt. He painted them with antiseptic, dressed, and went downstairs, armed only with a ruler, and got going again.

JOHN McGAHERN

The Recruiting Officer

Two cars outside the low concrete wall of Arigna School, small and blue-slated between the coal mountains; rust of iron on the rocks of the trout stream that ran past the playground; the chant of children coming through the open windows into the rain-cleaned air: it was this lured me back into the schoolroom of this day—to watch my manager, Canon Reilly, thrash the boy Walshe; to wait for the Recruiting Officer to come —but a deeper reason than the quiet picture of the school between mountains in bringing me back, can only be finally placed on something deep in my own nature, a total paralysis of the will, and a feeling that any one thing in this life is almost as worth doing as any other.

I had got out of the Christian Brothers, I no longer wore the black clothes and white half-collar, and was no longer surrounded by the rules of the order in its monastery; but then after the first freedom I was afraid, it was that I was alone.

I had come to visit one of my married sisters, when I saw the quiet school. I said I too would live out my life in the obscurity of these small places; if I was lucky I'd find a young girl. To grow old with her among a people seemed ambition enough, there might even be children and fields and garden.

I got a school immediately, without trouble; the newly trained teachers wanted places in the university towns, not in these backwaters.

Now I am growing old in the school where I began. I have not married. I lodge in a pub in Carrick-on-Shannon, I travel in and out the seven miles on a bike to escape the pupils and their parents once the school is shut, to escape from always having to play an expected role. It is rumoured that I drink too much.

With mostly indifference I stand at the window and watch Canon Reilly shake a confession out of the boy Walshe much as a dog shakes life out of a rat; and having nothing to do but watch I think of the sea. We went to the sea in summer, a black straggle in front of Novicemaster O'Grady, in threes, less risk of buggery in threes than pairs, the boards of the bridge across to the Bull hollow under the tread of our black sandals, and below the tide washing against the timber posts. Far out on the Wall we stripped, guarding our eyes on the rocks facing south across the bay to the Pidgeon House, and when O'Grady blew the whistle we made signs of the cross on ourselves with the salt water and jumped in. He blew it again when it was time for us to get out, we towelled and dressed on the rocks, guarding our eyes, glad no sand could get between our toes, and in threes trooped home ahead of O'Grady past the wired-down idiotic palm trees along the front.

The bell for night prayers went at nine-thirty, the two rows of pews stretching to the altar, a row along each wall and the bare lino-covered space between empty of all furniture, and we knelt in the long rows in order of our rank, the higher the rank the closer to the altar. On Friday nights we knelt in the empty space between the pews and said: My very dear Brothers, I accuse myself of all the faults I have committed since my last accusation, I broke the rule of silence twice, three times I failed to guard my eyes. After a certain rank and age the guarding of the eyes wasn't mentioned, you were supposed to be past all that by then, but I never reached that stage, I got myself booted out before I became impervious to a low view of passing girls, especially on windy days.

The sea and the bell, nothing seems ever ended, it is such nonsenses I'd like written on my gravestone in the hope they'd cause confusion.

"You admit it now after you saw you wouldn't brazen your way out of it," Reilly shouts at the boy, he holds him by the arm in the empty space between the table and the long benches where the classes sit in rows, in this the schoolroom of the day.

"Now. Out with what you spent the money on."

"Lemonade," the low answer comes, the white-faced boy starting to blubber.

"Lemonade, yes, lemonade, that's how you let the cat out of the bag. The Walshes don't have shillings to squander in the shops on lemonade every day of the week."

Still gripping the boy by the arm he turns to the rows of faces in the benches.

"What sins did Walshe commit—mind I say *sins*, not one sin—but I don't know how to call it—this foul act?"

I watch the hands shoot up with more attention than I'd given to the dreary inquisition of the boy, I was under examination now.

"The sin of stealing, Canon."

"Good, but mind I said sins. It is most important in an examination of conscience before confession to know all the sins of your soul. One foul act can entail several sins."

"Lies, Canon."

"Good, but I'm looking for the most grievous sin of all."

He turned from the blank faces to look at me: why do they not know?

"Where was the poorbox when it was broken open?" I ask, having to force the question out, even after the years of inspectors I've never got used to teaching in another's presence, the humiliation and the sense of emptiness in turning oneself into a performing robot in a semblance of teaching.

"In the church, sir."

"An offence against a holy person, place, or thing—what is that sin called?"

"Sacrilege," the hands at once go up.

"Good, but if you know something properly you shouldn't need all that spoonfeeding," the implied criticism of me he addresses to the children.

"Stealing, lies, and blackest of all—sacrilege," he turns again to the boy in his grip.

"If I hand you over to the police do you know where that will lead, Walshe? To the reformatory. Would you like to go to the reformatory, Walshe?"

"No, Canon."

"You have two choices then. You can either take your medicine from me here in front of the class or you can come to the barracks. Which'll you take?"

"You, Canon," he tries to appease with an appearance of total abjection and misery.

"It's going to be no picnic then. You'll have to be taught once and for all in your life that the church of God is sacred," he raises his voice close to declamation, momentarily releases his grip on the arm, takes a length of electric wire from his pocket; the boy whimpers as quietly the priest folds it in two before taking a firm grip on the arm again.

"It's going to hurt, Walshe. But if you're ever again tempted to steal from the church you'll have something to remember!"

In a half-circle the beating moves, the boy trying to sink to the floor to escape the whistle and thud of the wire wrapping round his bare legs but held by the arm, the boy's screaming and the heavy breathing of the priest filling the silence of the faces watching from the long benches in frightened fascination. When he finally lets go the arm the boy sinks in a heap on the floor, the moaning changing to an hysterical sobbing.

"Get up and go to your place and I hope that's the last lesson you'll have to be ever taught," he puts the length of wire back in his pocket, and takes out a blue cloth to wipe his forehead.

The boy cowers as he rises, arms automatically protecting the torn legs, moves in a beaten crawl to his place, plunges his face in rage and shame in the folds of his arms and continues hysterically sobbing.

"Open your geographies and get on with your study of the Shannon," I say as the heads turn to Walshe. There's the flap of the books being opened, they find the page, stealing a quick furtive look towards the boy as they bend their heads. In the sobbing silence the clock ticks.

"An example had to be made to nip that blackguardism in the bud," he turns to me at the window.

"I suppose."

"How do you mean *suppose?*" the eyes are dangerous.

"I suppose it was necessary to do."

"It *was* necessary," he emphasizes and after a pause, "What I'd like to see is religious instruction to counteract such influences after Second Mass every Sunday. Mr. McMurrough always took it."

"It's too far for me to come from the town to take."

"I can't see any justification for you living in the town. I can't see why you can't live in the parish. The Miss Bambricks at the post office have mentioned to me that they'd be glad to put you up."

The Miss Bambricks were two church-mad old maids who grew flowers for the altar and laundered the linen.

Old McMurrough, whom I had replaced, now lay in the Sligo madhouse reciting poetry and church doctrine, had taken catechism in the church each Sunday, while the Canon waited at the gate to bear any truant who tried to escape with the main congregation back in triumph by the ear to the class in the side-chapel.

"But I am happy where I am," I said.

"And there are many in the parish who think a public house in town is no lodgings for a person who has charge of youth."

"I conduct myself there."

"I'd sincerely hope so, but, if I may say so, it's not very co-operative."

"I am sorry but I do not want to change," I answer doggedly. With bent heads the class follows each word with furtive attention, but he changes in frustration at last, "The Christian Brother will come after lunch today."

"I'll take the other children outside while he speaks to the boys."

"They're getting it very tough to get vocations. Even tougher still to keep those they do get. They're betwixt and between, neither priests nor laymen," he volunteers but I don't want discussion.

"They may be lucky."

"The backward rural areas are their great standby. Even if they don't stay the course they'll get an education which they'd not get otherwise."

"That's how I got mine."

The hurt from my own mouth was not as great as if it had come from his.

"Well, it was some use then."

"Yes. It was some use."

I watch him on his way, at the door he shouts a last warning to the sniffling Walshe, "I hope that'll be one lesson your life will never forget and you can count yourself lucky that there was no police."

There'd be no repercussions from the beating except Walshe'd probably get beaten again when the news travelled home, and in a few days if asked who'd scored his legs, he'd answer that he fell in briars.

I watch the black suit shiny from car leather climb the last steps to the road gate, pausing once to inspect a crack in the concrete, and I turned to wipe the blackboard, afraid of my own hatred.

"Now I'll see what you've learned about the Shannon."

Papers rustle in the benches, there's a quick expectant buzz. Outside, the three stone walls of the playground run down to the lake, the centre wall broken by the concrete lavatory, above it the rapid sparkle of pinpoint flashes of sunlight on the wings of the blackdust swarm of flies, and on the sill in a jam jar a fistful of primroses some child has gathered from the May banks. In the stream of sunlight across the blackboard the chalkdust floats, millions of white grains, breathed in and out all day, found at night in the turnups of trousers, all the aridity of this empty trade.

"You, Murphy, tell me where the Shannon rises?"

A blank face answers in a pretence of puzzled concentration, and why should he know, his father's fields and cattle will see him through.

"Please, sir."

The room is full of hands.

"Tell Murphy where the Shannon rises, Handley," a policeman's son who'll have to put his trust in his average wits.

"Shannon Pot, sir, in the Cuilceach Mountains."

"Can you tell the class now, Murphy, where it rises?"

"Shannon Pot, sir, in the Cuilceach Mountains," a look of triumph shows on his well-fed face as he haltingly repeats it.

"Where does it flow, Mary?"

"Southwards into Lough Allen close to the town of Drumshambo," the quick answer comes.

"What factory have they there?"

"Breffni Blossom jams."

"Anybody's father send apples there?"

Three hands.

"Prior? Tell about the sending of the apples."

"We pick them, sir. Put them in a heap, same as potatoes, but on the ground, we cover them with straw."

"Why do you cover them with straw?"

"Frost, sir."

A low knock comes on the door that leads to the infant classroom and my one assistant, Mrs. Maguire, appears. She is near retirement: the slack flesh fills the ample spaces of the loose black dress, but the face in contrast is curiously hard, as if all the years of wrestling with children had hardened it into intransigent assurance.

"When Mrs. Maguire says something Mrs. Maguire means what she says," the third-person reference punctuates everything she says. Now a look of anxious concern shows in the unblinking eyes.

"What happened with the Canon?"

"He thrashed Walshe for breaking into one of the poorboxes."

I didn't want her to stay, though I too had often used the glow of fabricated concern to hurry or escape the slow minutes of the school-day.

"Terrible. Awful," she echoes a dull safety, hers and mine.

"We'll talk about it at lunch then."

"The world, the world," she ponders as she withdraws to her own room.

I look at the clock, the crawl of the minutes, never the happiness of imagining it two o'clock and looking up and finding it half past three.

"Will you be an absorbed teacher where your work will be like a game or a clockwatcher?" Jordan, the Education Lecturer, had asked after a lecture, it was his custom after a lecture to select one student to walk with him through the corridor with its shine of wax and the white marble busts of the saints and philosophers on their pedestals along the walls.

"I hope I'll be absorbed, sir."

"I hope so too for your sake. I can imagine few worse hells than a teacher who is a clockwatcher, driven to distraction by the children, while the day hangs about him like lead."

I could answer him now, I was a clockwatcher, and the day mostly hung like lead, each morning a dislocation of your life in order to entice or bend their opposing wills to yours, and the day a concentration on this hollow grapple, but it seems good as anything else and it's easier to stay than move.

"We'll leave the apples for a time and go on with the Shannon."

The class drags on until the iron gate on the road sounds. A woman comes down the concrete steps.

A mother comes to complain, I think and instinctively start to marshal the reassuring clichés, "The child is sensitive, and when it loses the sensitivity will surprise us all, to force it now can only cause damage, you have nothing to worry about."

"That was my trouble so at that age, I was too sensitive, I was never understood," she'd reply.

"Thank you for coming to see me."

"I feel less worried now."

In the beginning, everybody was sensitive, and never understood, but hides hardened.

This time, no mother, a Miss Martin: she lived with her brother across the empty waste of wheat-coloured sedge and stunted birch of the Gloria bog. She made toys from used matchsticks in the winter nights.

"I wonder if I could take young Horan from his lessons for a few minutes, sir. It's the ringworm."

"Luke, see Miss Martin in the porch." The boy goes quietly out to the porch, already charmingly stolid in the acceptance of his power, Luke, magical fifth in a line of male children unbroken by girls; and while he wailed under the water of his baptism at the stone font in Cootehall church a worm was placed in his hand, either the priest didn't see or was content to ignore it, but the Horans rejoiced, their fifth infant boy would grow up with the power of healing ringworm.

On Tuesdays and on Fridays, days of the sorrowful mysteries, he touched the sores thrice in the name of the Father and Son and Holy Ghost, and the invisible worm widening the raw coin on the skin dies, power of magic and religion killing the slow worm patiently circling.

"Did you wash your hands, Luke?"

"Yes, sir. I used the soap."

"Show them to me."

"All right. You can get on with your work."

The last to come before lunch was the tinker, with pony and cart, the brass shining on the harness, to clean out the lavatory, and as I give him the key we make polite professional remarks about the flies and heat.

"Ah, but not to worry, sir, I'll bury it deep," he touches his cap. Soon, soon, they'll come and flush him and me into the twentieth century whatever the good that will do, and I grow ashamed of the violence of the thought, and as if to atone, over lunch, give Mrs. Maguire a quiet account of the poorbox.

After lunch he comes, dressed all in black, with a black briefcase, the half-collar of the Christian Brother on the throat instead of the priest's full collar, a big white-haired man, who seemed made more to follow ploughing horses than to stand in classrooms. The large hand lifts the briefcase on the table.

"My name is Brother Mahon and Canon Reilly kindly gave me permission to speak to the senior boys about a vocation to the Irish Christian Brothers." I wonder if he knows I too had been once as he is now; if he looks at me as a rotten apple in the barrel, but if he does he says nothing, all glory to the power of the Lie or Silence that makes people easy in the void, all on our arses except the helping hand they give us on our way.

"I told Canon Reilly I'd take the other children out to the playground while you spoke."

"Lucky to have such a fine manager as the Canon, takes a great interest in schools."

"Couldn't ask for a better manager," I answer, the brick supports the brick above it, I'm a rogue and you're another. "I'll just take them outside now."

"All except the boys of the sixth class take your English book and follow me outside," and again, because I feel watched, the voice is not my own, a ventriloquist's dummy that might at any minute fall apart.

The Brother motions the scattered boys closer to the table, "It'll only be just a man to man chat," as I take the others out, to sit against the white wall of the school in the sun, facing the lake, where the tinker is putting the green sods back above the buried shit, the flies thick above the cart and grazing pony.

Through the open window the low voice drifts out into the silence of the children against the wall in the sun, and I smile as I listen, if one could wait long enough everything was repeated. I wonder who'll rise to the gleaming spoon and find the sharpened hooks as I did once.

"I want you to imagine a very different lake shore to your own little lake below your school.

"Hot sands," his words drift out. "Palm trees, glittering sea, tired after fishing all the night and washing their nets, tall dark man comes through the palms down to the water.

"We have laboured all the night and have taken nothing, the fishermen answer. The two boats were so full of fish that they began to sink, after they put out at his word, fall on their knees on the sand, and the tall man for it was Jesus lifted them up and said to them follow me, from henceforth you will catch men.

"In this schoolroom two thousand years later I bring you the same message. Follow me and catch men. Follow me into the Irish Christian Brothers, where as teachers you will lead the little children He so loved to Christ.

"For death comes as a thief in the night, the longest life is but a day, and when you go before the Judgement Seat can you without trembling say to Jesus I refused the call even the tired fishermen answered, and what if He refuses you as you refused Him."

He sends them out into the porch, and brings them back one by one to interview them alone, while the tinker hands me back the keys, "I've buried it deep, sir. There'll be no flies," and the rise and fall of voices comes from Mrs. Maguire's infant prison house *Eena, meena, mina moo, capall, asal agus bo.*

Name, age, your father's farm? he asks and more to silence my own memory than the low chatter of the children I force, "Come on now, get on with your reading," but after they grow silent to covertly read my real mood the chatter grows loud again.

"You have listened to all that I've said?" I'd been asked once too.

"Yes, Brother," I'd answered.

"Do you think you could spend your life as a Christian Brother?"

"I'm not sure, Brother."

"Do you think your parents would have any objection?"

"I don't know, Brother."

"What do you say we go and have a little talk with them after I've seen the rest of the boys?"

It was finished then, my mother's face had lighted when he drove me home, "It'd be an honour to have a Christian Brother in the family." "He'll get a free education too, the best there is," and that August I was in the train with the single ticket, fear of the unknown rooms and people. My brother inherited the bare acres in my place, and married, and with the same strength as she had driven me away he put her in a back room with the old furniture of her marriage while his new wife reigned amid the new furniture of the best rooms; and now each summer I take her to her usual small hotel at the sea, and I walk by her side on the sand saying, "Yes and yes and yes," to her complaints about my brother and his wife until she tires herself into relief and changes "Do you think should I go to the baths after lunch?" "Go to the baths, it'll do your arthritis good."

"I think I'll go then."

I want to ask her why she wanted the acres for my brother, why she pushed me away, but I don't ask, I walk by her side on the sand, and echo her life with "Yes and yes and yes," for it is all a wheel.

A light tap comes from the classroom window, a gesture of spread hands that he is finished, and I take the children in. Two of the boys have been set apart, with their schoolbags.

"I'm driving John and Jim to their houses, we'll talk over everything with their parents."

"I hope it'll be all right."

"We'll see that everything is made clear. Thank you for your help."

After the shaking of hands I turn to the board but I do not want to teach.

"Open your English books and copy page forty-one in your best handwriting."

I stand at the window while the nibs scrape. Certainly nothing I've ever done resembles so closely the shape of my life as my leaving of the Holy Brothers; having neither the resolution to stay on or the courage to leave, the year before Final Vows I took to bed and refused to get up.

"The doctor says you're in perfect health. That there's nothing the matter with you," old Cogger, the boss, had tried to reason. "So why can't you get up when we are even short-staffed in the school?"

"I can't get up."

"What's wrong with you that you can't get up?"

"Nothing."

"If you don't get up I have no option but to report you to General Headquarters."

I did not get up, he had no option, and the result was an order for my dismissal, but as quietly as possible so as not to scandalize my brothers in J. C. or the good people of the town. Old Cogger showed me the letter. I was to get a suit of clothes, underwear, railway ticket, and one pound. It revived me immediately. I told him the underwear I had would do and he raised the one pound to five.

The next hurdle was how to get my fit in clothes in a small town without causing scandal. Old Cogger dithered till the day before I had to leave, but at nightfall brought home two likely fits. I picked one, and packed it, and off we set by bus for Limerick, to all appearances a young Christian Brother and an old on some ordinary business to town, but old Cogger would come back alone. We did not speak on the way.

Behind a locked door and drawn curtains I changed in the guest-room of the house in Limerick. I've wondered what happened to the black uniform I left behind, whether they gave it to another C.B. or burned it as they burn the clothes of the dead. Cogger showed me to the door as I left for the train but I can't remember if he wished me luck or shook hands or just shut the door on my back. I had a hat too, yes a brown hat and a blue suit, but I didn't realize how bloody awful they looked until I met my sisters on O'Connell Bridge. They coloured with shame, afraid to be seen walking with me they rushed me into a taxi and didn't speak until they had me safely inside the front door of the flat, when one doubled up on the sofa unable to stop laughing, and the other swore at me, "In the name of Jasus what possessed the Christians to sail you out into the world in a getup the like of that or you to appear in it." Though what I remember most was the shock of *sir* when the waiter said "Thank you, sir," as I paid him for the cup of tea I had on the train.

Even if the memories are bitter they still quicken the passing of time. It is the sly coughing of the children that tell me the hands have passed three.

"All right. Put your books away and stand up."

In a fury the books are put away and they are waiting for me on their feet.

"Bless yourselves."

They bless themselves and chant their gratitude for the day.

"Don't rush the door, it's just as quick to go quietly."

I hear their hoops of joy go down the road, and I linger over the locking up. I am always happy at this hour, it's as if the chains of the day were worth wearing to feel them drop away. I feel born again as I start to pedal towards the town. How, how, though, can a man be born again when he is old? Can he enter a second time his mother's bag of tricks? I laugh at last.

Was it not said by *Water* and the *Holy Spirit?*

Several infusions of whiskey at the Bridge Bar, contemplation of the Shannon through its windows: it rises in the Shannon Pot, it flows to the sea, there are stranger pike along its banks than in its waters, will keep this breath alive until the morning's dislocation.

WALKER PERCY

The Promiscuous Self

Why is it that One's Self often not only does not Prefer Sex with one's Chosen Mate, Chosen for His or Her Attractiveness and Suitability, even when the Mate is a Person well known to one, knowing of one, loved by one, with a Life, Time, and Family in common, but rather prefers Sex with a New Person, even a Total Stranger, or even Vicariously through Pornography

A recent survey in a large city reported that 95 percent of all video tapes purchased for home consumption were *Insatiable,* a pornographic film starring Marilyn Chambers.

Of all sexual encounters on soap opera, only 6 percent occur between husband and wife.

In some cities of the United States, which now has the highest divorce rate in the world, the incidence of divorce now approaches 60 percent of married couples.

A recent survey showed that the frequency of sexual intercourse in married couples declined 90 percent after three years of marriage.

"A female sexologist reported . . ." that a favorite fantasy of American women, second only to oral sex, was having sex with two strange men at once.

According to the president of the North American Swing Club Association, only 3 percent of married couples who are swingers get divorces, as compared with over 50 percent of non-swinging couples.

In large American cities, lunch-break liaisons between business men and women have become commonplace.

Sexual activity and pregnancy in teenagers have increased dramatically in the last twenty years, in both those who have received sex education in schools and those who have not. In some cities, more babies are born to single women than to married women.

A radio psychotherapist reported that nowadays many young people who disdain marriage, preferring "relationships" and "commitments," speak of entering into simultaneous relationships with a second or third person as a growth experience.

In San Francisco's Buena Vista Park, to the outrage of local middle-class residents, homosexuals cruise and upon encountering a sexual prospect, always a stranger, exchange a word or a sign and disappear into the bushes. In a series of interviews, Buena Vista homosexuals admitted to sexual encounters with an average of more than 500 strangers.

A survey by a popular magazine reported that the incidence of homosexuality in the United States had surpassed that of the Weimar Republic and is approaching that of England.

Question: Do Americans, as well as other Westerners, prefer sexual variety, both heterosexual and homosexual, because

(a) The sexual revolution has occurred, which is nothing else but the overthrow of the unnatural repressions and taboos of 1,900 years of Christianity and the exploration of the free and healthy practices of a sexually liberated society.

(b) Humans are biologically as promiscuous as chimpanzees. It is only the cultural constraints of society, probably imposed by the economic necessities of an agricultural society, which required a monogamous union and children as a reliable labor source.

(c) No, man is by nature monogamous, as ethnologists have demonstrated in most cultures. It is Western society which is disintegrating, to a degree remarkably similar to the decline of the Roman Empire in the fifth century, when similar practices were reported.

(d) No, Western man is promiscuous because promiscuous sexuality is the obverse or flip side of Christianity and is in fact specified by Christianity as its opposite. Thus, pornography is something new in the world, having no parallel in ancient, so-called pagan cultures. Accordingly, there is little if any difference between present-day promiscuity and that of, say, the Victorian era. The so-called sexual revolution is

nothing but the legitimizing of the secret behavior of the Victorians and its extension to women.

(e) Western man is promiscuous because something unprecedented has happened. As a consequence of the scientific and technological revolution, there has occurred a displacement of the real as a consequence of which genital sexuality has come to be seen as the substratum of all human relationships, of friendship, love, and the rest. This displacement has come to pass as a consequence of a lay misperception of the physicist's quest for establishing a molecular or energic basis for all interactions and of what is perceived as Freud's identification of genital sexuality as the ground of all human relationships.

A letter to Dear Abby:

> I am a twenty-three-year-old liberated woman who has been on the pill for two years. It's getting pretty expensive and I think my boyfriend should share half the cost, but I don't know him well enough to discuss money with him.*

(f) The Self since the time of Descartes has been stranded, split off from everything else in the Cosmos, a mind which professes to understand bodies and galaxies but is by the very act of understanding marooned in the Cosmos, with which it has no connection. It therefore needs to exercise every option in order to reassure itself that it is not a ghost but is rather a self among other selves. One such option is a sexual encounter. Another is war. The pleasure of a sexual encounter derives not only from physical gratification but also from the demonstration to oneself that, despite one's own ghostliness, one is, for the moment at least, a sexual being. Amazing! Indeed, the most amazing of all the creatures of the Cosmos: a ghost with an erection! Yet not really amazing, for only if the abstracted ghost has an erection can it, like Jove spying Europa on the beach, enter the human condition.

(g) It's not that complicated. It's simply that people nowadays have too much money and time to spend and don't know what to do with themselves and so will try anything out of boredom.

(h) Why go further than the orthodox Judaeo-Christian belief that monogamous marriage was ordained by God for man's happiness, that the devil goes about like a roaring lion seeking whom he may devour, and that as a consequence modern man has lost his way, has not the

* Abigail Van Buren, *The Best of Dear Abby* (New York: Andrews and McMeel, 1981), p. 242.

faintest notion who he is or what he is doing, and nothing short of catastrophe will bring him to his senses. At the height of a hurricane, husbands come to themselves and can even embrace their wives. During hurricane Camille, one Biloxi couple, taking refuge in a tree house, reported that, during the passage of the eye, they had intercourse for the first time in years.

(i) No, the explanation is biological. Man is undergoing a mutation in sexual behavior which will in the end, like the tooth of the saber-toothed tiger, render him extinct. Since most of the emerging varieties of sexual expression—homosexuality, anal and oral sex—do not reproduce the species and therefore have no survival value, the species will become extinct.

(j) None of the above. It has always been so. That is to say, the sexual behavior of humans has not changed. Therefore, there is nothing to explain.

(CHECK ONE OR MORE)

Thought Experiment

THE LAST DONAHUE SHOW

The Donahue Show is in progress on what appears at first to be an ordinary weekday morning.

The theme of this morning's show is Donahue's favorite, sex, the extraordinary variety of sexual behavior—"sexual preference," as Donahue would call it—in the country and the embattled attitudes toward it. Although Donahue has been accused of appealing to prurient interest, with a sharp eye cocked on the ratings, he defends himself by saying that he presents these controversial matters in "a mature and tasteful manner"—which he often does. It should also be noted in Donahue's defense that the high ratings of these sex-talk shows are nothing more nor less than an index of the public's intense interest in such matters.

The guests today are:

Bill, a homosexual and habitué of Buena Vista Park in San Francisco

Allen, a heterosexual businessman, married, and a connoisseur of the lunch-hour liaison

Penny, a pregnant fourteen-year-old

Dr. Joyce Friday, a well-known talk-show sex therapist, or in media jargon: a psych jockey

BILL'S STORY: Yes, I'm gay, and yes, I cruise Buena Vista. Yes, I've probably had over five hundred encounters with lovers, though I didn't keep count. So what? Whose business is it? I'm gainfully employed by a savings-and-loan company, am a trustworthy employee, and do an honest day's work. My recreation is Buena Vista Park and the strangers I meet there. I don't molest children, rape women, snatch purses. I contribute to United Way. Such encounters that I do have are by mutual consent and therefore nobody's business—except my steady live-in friend's. Naturally he's upset, but that's our problem.

DONAHUE (*striding up and down, mike in hand, boyishly inarticulate*): C'mon, Bill. What about the kids who might see you? You know what I mean. I mean— (*Opens his free hand to the audience, soliciting their understanding*)

BILL: Kids don't see me. Nobody sees me.

DONAHUE (*coming close, on the attack but good-naturedly, spoofing himself as prosecutor*): Say, Bill. I've always been curious. Is there some sort of signal? I mean, how do you and the other guy know—help me out—

BILL: Eye contact, or we show a bit of handkerchief here. (*Demonstrates*)

STUDIO AUDIENCE: (*Laughter*)

DONAHUE (*shrugging [Don't blame me, folks], pushes up nose-bridge of glasses, swings mike over to Dr. J.F. without looking at her*): How about it, Doc?

DR. J.F. (*in her not-mincing-words voice*): I think Bill's behavior is immature and depersonalizing. (*Applause from audience*) I think he ought to return to his steady live-in friend and work out a mature, creative relationship. You might be interested to know that studies have shown that stable gay couples are more creative than straights. (*Applause again, but more tentative*)

DONAHUE (*eyes slightly rolled back, swings mike to Bill*): How about it, Bill?

BILL: Yeah, right. But I still cruise Buena Vista.

DONAHUE (*pensive, head to one side, strides backward, forward, then over to Allen*): How about you, Allen?

ALLEN'S STORY: I'm a good person, I think. I work hard, am happily married, love my wife and family, also support United Way, served in the army. I drink very little, don't do drugs, have never been to a porn movie. My idea of R & R—maybe I got it in the army—is to meet an attractive woman. What a delight it is, to see a handsome mature woman, maybe in the secretarial pool, maybe in a bar, restaurant, anywhere, exchange eye contact, speak to her in a nice way, respect her as a person, invite her to join me for lunch (no sexual harassment in the office—I hate that!), have a drink, two drinks, enjoy a nice meal, talk about matters of common interest—then simply ask her—by now, both of you know whether you like each other. What a joy to go with her up in the elevator of the downtown Holiday Inn, both of you silent, relaxed, smiling, anticipating— The door of the room closes behind you. You look at her, take her hand. There's champagne already there. You stand at the window with her, touch glasses, talk—there's nothing vulgar. No closed-circuit TV. Do you know what we did last time? We turned on *La Bohème* on the FM. She loves Puccini.

DONAHUE: C'mon, Allen. What are ya handing me? What d'ya mean you're happily married? You mean *you're* happy.

ALLEN: No, no. Vera's happy, too.

AUDIENCE (*mostly women, groaning*): Nooooooo.

DONAHUE: Okay-okay, ladies, hold it a second. What do you mean, Vera's happy? I mean, how do you manage—help me out, I'm about to get in trouble—hold the letters, folks—

ALLEN: Well, actually, Vera has a low sex drive. We've always been quite inactive, even at the beginning—

AUDIENCE (*groans, jumbled protests*): Nooooo.

DONAHUE (*backing away, holding up placating free hand, backing around to Dr. J.F.*): It's all yours, Doc.

DR. J.F.: Studies have shown that open marriages can be growth experiences for both partners. However—(*groans from audience*)—However: it seems to me that Vera may be getting the short end here. I mean, I don't know Vera's side of it. But could I ask you this? Have you and Vera thought about reenergizing your sex life?

ALLEN: Well, ah—

DR. J.F.: Studies have shown, for example, that more stale marriages have been revived by oral sex than any other technique—

DONAHUE: Now, Doc—

DR. J.F.: Other studies have shown that mutual masturbation—

DONAHUE (*eyes rolled back*): We're running long, folks, we'll be right back after this—don't go away. Oh boy. *(Lets mike slide to the hilt through his hand, closes eyes, as camera cuts away to a Maxithins commercial)*

DONAHUE: We're back. Thank the good Lord for good sponsors. *(Turns to Penny, a thin, inattentive, moping teenager, even possibly a preteen):* Penny?

PENNY *(chewing something):* Yeah?

DONAHUE *(solicitous, quite effectively tender):* What's with you, sweetheart?

PENNY: Well, I liked this boy a lot and he told me there was one way I could prove it—

DONAHUE: Wait a minute, Penny. Now this, your being here, is okay with your parents, right? I mean, let's establish that.

PENNY: Oh, sure. They're right over there—you can ask them. *(Camera pans over audience, settling on a couple with mild, pleasant faces. It is evident that on the whole they are not displeased with being on TV)*

DONAHUE: Okay. So you mean you didn't know about taking precautions—

DR. J.F. *(breaking in):* Now, that's what I mean, Phil.

DONAHUE: What's that, Doc?

DR. J.F.: About the crying need for sex education in our schools. Now if this child—

PENNY: Oh, I had all that stuff at Ben Franklin.

DONAHUE: You mean you knew about the pill and the other, ah—

PENNY: I had been on the pill for a year.

DONAHUE *(scratching head):* I don't get it. Oh, you mean you slipped up, got careless?

PENNY: No, I did it on purpose.

DONAHUE: Did what on purpose? You mean—

PENNY: I mean I wanted to get pregnant.

DONAHUE: Why was that, Penny?

PENNY: My best friend was pregnant.

AUDIENCE: *(Groans, laughter)*

DR. J.F.: You see, Phil, that's just what I mean. This girl is no more equipped with parenting skills than a child. She is a child. I hope she realizes she still has viable options.

DONAHUE: How about it, Penny?

PENNY: No, I want to have my baby.

DONAHUE: Why?

PENNY: I think babies are neat.

DONAHUE: Oh boy.

DR. J.F.: Studies have shown that unwanted babies suffer 85 percent more child abuse and 150 percent more neuroses later in life.

DONAHUE *(striding):* Okay, now what have we got here? Wait. What's going on?

There is an interruption. Confusion at the rear of the studio. Heads turn. Three strangers, dressed outlandishly, stride down the aisle.

DONAHUE *(smacks his forehead):* What's this? What's this? Holy smoke!

Already the audience is smiling, reassured both by Donahue's comic consternation and by the exoticness of the visitors. Clearly, the audience thinks, they are part of the act.

The three strangers are indeed outlandish.

One is a tall, thin, bearded man dressed like a sixteenth-century reformer. Indeed, he could be John Calvin, in his black cloak, black cap with short bill, and snug earflaps.

The second wears the full-dress uniform of a Confederate officer. Though he is a colonel, he is quite young, surely no more than twenty-five. Clean-shaven and extremely handsome, he looks for all the world like Colonel John Pelham, Jeb Stuart's legendary artillerist. Renowned both for his gallantry in battle and for his chivalry toward women, the beau ideal of the South, he engaged in sixty artillery duels, won them all, lost not a single piece. With a single Napoleon, he held off three of Burnside's divisions in front of Fredericksburg before being ordered by Stuart to retreat.

The third is at once the most ordinary-looking and yet the strangest of all. His dress is both modern and out-of-date. In his light-colored double-breasted suit and bow tie, his two-tone shoes of the sort known in the 1940s as "perforated wing-tips," his neat above-the-ears haircut, he looks a bit like the clean old man in the Beatles movie *A Hard Day's Night,* a bit like Lowell Thomas or perhaps Harry Truman. It is as if he were a visitor from the Cosmos, from a planet ten or so light-years distant, who had formed his notion of earthlings from belated transmissions of 1950 TV, from watching the Ed Sullivan Show, old Chester

Morris movies, and Morey Amsterdam. Or, to judge from his speaking voice, he could have been an inveterate listener during the Golden Age of radio and modeled his speech on that of Harry Von Zell.

DONAHUE *(backpedaling, smacking his head again):* Holy smoke! Who are these guys? *(Beseeching the audience with a slow comic pan around)*

The audience laughs, not believing for a moment that these latecomers are not one of Donahue's surprises. And yet—

DONAHUE *(snapping his fingers):* I got it. Wait'll I get that guy. It's Steve Allen, right? Refugees from the Steve Allen Show, *Great Conversations?* Famous historical figures? You know, folks, they do that show in the studio down the hall. Wait'll I get that guy.

General laughter. Everybody remembers it's been done before, an old show-biz trick, like Carson barging in on Rickles during the C.P.O. Sharkey taping.

DONAHUE: Okay already. Okay, who we got here? This is Moses? General Robert E. Lee? And who is this guy? Harry Truman? Okay, fellas, let's hear it. *(Donahue, an attractive fellow, is moving about as gracefully as a dancer)*

THE STRANGER *(speaks first, in his standard radio-announcer's voice, which is not as flat as the Chicagoans who say, Hyev a hyeppy New Year):* I don't know what these two are doing here, but I came to give you a message. We've been listening to this show.

DONAHUE *(winking at the audience):* And where were you listening to us?

STRANGER: In the green room.

DONAHUE: Where else? Okay.Then what do you think? Let's hear it first from the reverend here. What did you say your name was, Reverend?

STRANGER: John Calvin.

DONAHUE: Right. Who else? Okay, we got to break here for these messages. Don't go 'way, folks. We're coming right back and sort this out, I promise.

Cut to Miss Clairol, Land O Lakes margarine, Summer's Eve, and Alpo commercials.

But when the show returns, John Calvin, who does not understand commercial breaks, has jumped the gun and is in mid-sentence.

CALVIN *(speaking in a thick French accent, not unlike Charles Boyer):* —of his redemptive sacrifice? What I have heard is licentious talk about deeds which are an abomination before God, meriting eternal damnation unless they repent and throw themselves on God's mercy. Which they are predestined to do or not to do, so why bother to discuss it?

DONAHUE *(gravely):* That's pretty heavy, Reverend.

CALVIN: Heavy? Yes, it's heavy.

DONAHUE *(mulling, scratching):* Now wait a minute, Reverend. Let's check this out. You're entitled to your religious beliefs. But what if others disagree with you in all good faith? And aside from *that (prosecutory again, using mike like forefinger)* what's wrong with two consenting adults expressing their sexual preference in the privacy of their bedroom or, ah, under a bush?

CALVIN: Sexual preference? *(Puzzled, he turns for help to the Confederate officer and the Cosmic stranger. They shrug)*

DONAHUE *(holding mike to the officer):* How about you, sir? Your name is—

CONFEDERATE OFFICER: Colonel John Pelham, C.S.A., commander of the horse artillery under General Stuart.

PENNY: He's cute.

AUDIENCE: *(Laughter)*

DONAHUE: You heard it all in the green room, Colonel. What 'dya think?

COLONEL PELHAM *(in a soft Alabama accent):* What do I think of what, sir?

DONAHUE: Of what you heard in the green room.

PELHAM: Of the way these folks act and talk? Well, I don't think much of it, sir.

DONAHUE: How do you mean, Colonel?

PELHAM: That's not the way people should talk or act. Where I come from, we'd call them white trash. That's no way to talk if you're a man or a woman. A gentleman knows how to treat women. He knows because he knows himself, who he is, what his obligations are. And he discharges them. But after all, you won the war, so if that's the way you want to act, that's your affair. At least, we can be sure of one thing.

DONAHUE: What's that, Colonel?

PELHAM: We're not sorry we fought.

DONAHUE: I see. Then you agree with the reverend, I mean Reverend Calvin here.

PELHAM: Well, I respect his religious beliefs. But I never thought much about religion one way or the other. In fact, I don't think religion has much to do with whether a man does right. A West Point man is an officer and a gentleman, religion or no religion. I have nothing against religion. In fact, when we studied medieval history at West Point, I remember admiring Richard Coeur de Lion and his recapturing Acre and the holy places. I remember thinking: I would have fought for him, just as I fought for Lee and the South.

Applause from the audience. Calvin puts them off, but this handsome officer reminds them of Rhett Butler–Clark Gable, or rather Ashley Wilkes–Leslie Howard.

DONAHUE *(drifting off, frowning; something is amiss but he can't put his finger on it. What is Steve Allen up to? He shakes his head, blinks)*: You said it, Colonel. Okay. Where were we? *(Turning to Cosmic stranger)* We're running a little long. Can you make it brief, Harry— Mr. President, or whoever you are? Oh boy.

THE COSMIC STRANGER *(stands stiffly, hands at his sides, and begins speaking briskly, very much in the style of the late Raymond Gram Swing)*: I will be brief. I have taken this human form through a holographic technique unknown to you in order to make myself understood to you.

Hear this. I have a message. Whether you heed it or not is your affair.

I have nothing to say to you about God or the Confederacy, whatever that is—I assume it is not the G2V Confederacy in this arm of the galaxy—though I could speak about God, but it is too late for you, and I am not here to do that.

We are not interested in the varieties of your sexual behavior, except as a symptom of a more important disorder.

It is this disorder which concerns us and which we do not fully understand.

As a consequence of this disorder, you are a potential threat to all civilizations in the G2V region of the galaxy. Throughout G2V you are known variously and jokingly as the Ds or the DDs or the DLs, that is, the ding-a-lings or the death-dealers or the death-lovers. Of all the species here and in all of G2V, you are the only one which is by nature sentimental, murderous, self-hating, and self-destructive.

You are two superpowers here. The other is hopeless, has already succumbed, and is a death society. It is a living death and an agent for the propagation of death.

You are scarcely better—there is a glimmer of hope for you—but that is of no interest to me.

If the two of you destroy each other, as appears likely, it is of no consequence to us. To tell you the truth, G2V will breathe a sigh of relief.

The danger is that you may not destroy each other and that your present crude technology may constitute a threat to G2V in the future.

I am here to tell you three things: what is going to happen, what I am going to do, and what you can do.

Here's what will happen. Within the next twenty-four hours, your last war will begin. There will occur a twenty-megaton airburst one mile above the University of Chicago, the very site where your first chain reaction was produced. Every American city and town will be hit. You will lose plus-minus 160 million immediately, plus-minus 50 million later.

Here's what I am going to do. I have been commissioned to collect a specimen of DD and return with it so that we can study it toward the end of determining the nature of your disorder. Accordingly, I propose to take this young person referred to as Penny—for two reasons. One, she is perhaps still young enough not to have become hopeless. Two, she is pregnant and so we will have a chance to rear a DD in an environment free of your noxious influence. Then perhaps we can determine whether your disorder is a result of some peculiar earth environmental factor or whether you are a malignant sport, a genetic accident, the consequence of what you would have called, quite accurately, in an earlier time an MD—*mutatio diabolica,* a diabolical mutation.

Finally, here's what you can do. It is of no consequence to us whether you do it or not, because you will no longer be a threat to anyone. This is only a small gesture of goodwill to a remnant of you who may survive and who may have the chance to start all over—though you will probably repeat the same mistake. We have been students of your climatology for years. I have here a current read-out and prediction of the prevailing wind directions and fallout patterns for the next two weeks. It so happens that the place nearest you which will escape all effects of both blast and fallout is the community of Lost Cove, Tennessee. We do not anticipate a stampede to Tennessee. Our projection is that very few of you here and you out there in radio land will attach credibility to this message. But the few of you who do may wish to use this information. There is a cave there, corn, grits, collard greens, and smoked sausage in abundance.

That is the end of my message. Penny—

DONAHUE: We're long! We're long! Heavy! Steve, I'll get you for this. Oh boy. Don't forget, folks, tomorrow we got surrogate partners and a Kinsey panel—come back—you can't win 'em all—'bye! Grits. I dunno.

AUDIENCE: *(Applause)*

Cut to station break, Secure Care 65 commercial, Alpo, Carefree Panty Shields, and Mentholatum, then *The Price Is Right.*

Question: If you heard this Donahue Show, would you head for Lost Cove, Tennessee?

(a) Yes
(b) No

(CHECK ONE)

WALTER M. MILLER, JR.

Crucifixus Etiam

Manue Nanti joined the project to make some dough. Five dollars an hour was good pay, even in A.D. 2134 and there was no way to spend it while on the job. Everything would be furnished: housing, chow, clothing, toiletries, medicine, cigarettes, even a daily ration of one-hundred-eighty-proof beverage alcohol, locally distilled from fermented Martian mosses as fuel for the project's vehicles. He figured that if he avoided crap games, he could finish his five-year contract with fifty thousand dollars in the bank, return to Earth, and retire at the age of twenty-four. Manue wanted to travel, to see the far corners of the world, the strange cultures, the simple people, the small towns, deserts, mountains, jungles —for until he came to Mars, he had never been farther than a hundred miles from Cerro de Pasco, his birthplace in Peru.

A great wistfulness came over him in the cold Martian night when the frost haze broke, revealing the black, gleam-stung sky, and the blue-green Earth-star of his birth. *El mundo de mi carne, de mi alma,* he thought—yet, he had seen so little of it that many of its places would be more alien to him than the homogenously ugly vistas of Mars. These he longed to see: the volcanoes of the South Pacific, the monstrous mountains of Tibet, the concrete cyclops of New York, the radioactive craters of Russia, the artificial islands in the China Sea, the Black Forest, the Ganges, the Grand Canyon—but most of all, the works of human art: the pyramids, the Gothic cathedrals of Europe, *Notre Dame du Chartres,* Saint Peter's, the tile-work wonders of Anacapri. But the dream was still a long labor from realization.

Manue was a big youth, heavy-boned and built for labor, clever in a simple mechanical way, and with a wistful good humor that helped him take a lot of guff from whiskey-breathed foremen and sharp-eyed engineers who made ten dollars an hour and figured ways for making more, legitimately or otherwise.

He had been on Mars only a month, and it hurt. Each time he swung the heavy pick into the red-brown sod, his face winced with pain. The plastic aerator valves, surgically stitched in his chest, pulled and twisted and seemed to tear with each lurch of his body. The mechanical oxygenator served as a lung, sucking blood through an artificially grafted network of veins and plastic tubing, frothing it with air from a chemical generator, and returning it to his circulatory system. Breathing was unnecessary, except to provide wind for talking, but Manue breathed in desperate gulps of the 4.0 psi Martian air; for he had seen the wasted, atrophied chests of the men who had served four or five years, and he knew that when they returned to Earth—if ever—they would still need the auxiliary oxygenator equipment.

"If you don't stop breathing," the surgeon told him, "you'll be all right. When you go to bed at night, turn the oxy down low—so low you feel like panting. There's a critical point that's just right for sleeping. If you get it too low, you'll wake up screaming, and you'll get claustrophobia. If you get it too high, your reflex mechanisms will go to pot and you won't breathe; your lungs'll dry up after a time. Watch it."

Manue watched it carefully, although the oldsters laughed at him—in their dry wheezing chuckles. Some of them could scarcely speak more than two or three words at a shallow breath.

"Breathe deep, boy," they told him. "Enjoy it while you can. You'll forget how pretty soon. Unless you're an engineer."

The engineers had it soft, he learned. They slept in a pressurized barrack where the air was ten psi and twenty-five percent oxygen, where they turned their oxies off and slept in peace. Even their oxies were self-regulating, controlling the output according to the carbon dioxide content of the input blood. But the Commission could afford no such luxuries for the labor gangs. The payload of a cargo rocket from Earth was only about two percent of the ship's total mass, and nothing superfluous could be carried. The ships brought the bare essentials, basic industrial equipment, big reactors, generators, engines, heavy tools.

Small tools, building materials, foods, non-nuclear fuels—these things had to be made on Mars. There was an open pit mine in the belly of the Syrtis Major where a "lake" of nearly pure iron-rust was scooped into a smelter, and processed into various grades of steel for building purposes, tools, and machinery. A quarry in the Flathead Mountains dug up large quantities of cement rock, burned it, and crushed it to make concrete.

It was rumored that Mars was even preparing to grow her own labor force. An old-timer told him that the Commission had brought five hundred married couples to a new underground city in the Mare Erythraeum, supposedly as personnel for a local commission headquarters, but according to the old-timer, they were to be paid a bonus of three thousand dollars for every child born on the red planet. But Manue knew that the old "troffies" had a way of inventing such stories, and he reserved a certain amount of skepticism.

As for his own share in the Project, he knew—and needed to know— very little. The encampment was at the north end of the Mare Cimmerium, surrounded by the bleak brown and green landscape of rock and giant lichens, stretching toward sharply defined horizons except for one mountain range in the distance, and hung over by a blue sky so dark that the Earth-star occasionally became dimly visible during the dim daytime. The encampment consisted of a dozen double-walled stone huts, windowless, and roofed with flat slabs of rock covered over by a tarry resin boiled out of the cactus-like spineplants. The camp was ugly, lonely, and dominated by the gaunt skeleton of a drill rig set up in its midst.

Manue joined the excavating crew in the job of digging a yard-wide, six-foot-deep foundation trench in a hundred-yard square around the drill rig, which day and night was biting deeper through the crust of Mars in a dry cut that necessitated frequent stoppages for changing rotary bits. He learned that the geologists had predicted a subterranean pocket of tritium oxide ice at sixteen thousand feet, and that it was for this that they were drilling. The foundation he was helping to dig would be for a control station of some sort.

He worked too hard to be very curious. Mars was a nightmare, a grim, womanless, frigid, disinterestedly evil world. His digging partner was a sloe-eyed Tibetan nicknamed "Gee" who spoke the Omnalingua clumsily at best. He followed two paces behind Manue with a shovel, scooping up the broken ground, and humming a monotonous chant in his own tongue. Manue seldom heard his own language, and missed it; one of the engineers, a haughty Chilean, spoke the modern Spanish, but

not to such as Manue Nanti. Most of the other laborers used either
Basic English or the Omnalingua. He spoke both, but longed to hear the
tongue of his people. Even when he tried to talk to Gee, the cultural
gulf was so wide that satisfying communication was nearly impossible.
Peruvian jokes were unfunny to Tibetan ears, although Gee bent double
with gales of laughter when Manue nearly crushed his own foot with a
clumsy stroke of the pick.

He found no close companions. His foreman was a narrow-eyed,
orange-browed Low German named Vögeli, usually half-drunk, and
intent upon keeping his lung-power by bellowing at his crew. A meaty,
florid man, he stalked slowly along the lip of the excavation, pausing to
stare coldly down at each pair of laborers who, if they dared to look up,
caught a guttural tongue-lashing for the moment's pause. When he had
words for a digger, he called a halt by kicking a small avalanche of dirt
back into the trench about the man's feet.

Manue learned about Vögeli's disposition before the end of his first
month. The aerator tubes had become nearly unbearable; the skin, in
trying to grow fast to the plastic, was beginning to form a tight little
neck where the tubes entered his flesh, and the skin stretched and
burned and stung with each movement of his trunk. Suddenly he felt
sick. He staggered dizzily against the side of the trench, dropped the
pick, and swayed heavily, bracing himself against collapse. Shock and
nausea rocked him, while Gee stared at him and giggled foolishly.

"Hoy!" Vögeli bellowed from across the pit. "Get back on that pick!
Hoy, there! Get with it—"

Manue moved dizzily to recover the tool, saw patches of black swimming before him, sank weakly back to pant in shallow gasps. The nag-
ging sting of the valves was a portable hell that he carried with him
always. He fought an impulse to jerk them out of his flesh; if a valve
came loose, he would bleed to death in a few minutes.

Vögeli came stamping along the heap of fresh earth and lumbered up
to stand over the sagging Manue in the trench. He glared down at him
for a moment, then nudged the back of his neck with a heavy boot.
"Get to work!"

Manue looked up and moved his lips silently. His forehead glinted
with moisture in the faint sun, although the temperature was far below
freezing.

"Grab that pick and get started."

"Can't," Manue gasped. "Hoses—hurt."

Vögeli grumbled a curse and vaulted down into the trench beside him. "Unzip that jacket," he ordered.

Weakly, Manue fumbled to obey, but the foreman knocked his hand aside and jerked the zipper down. Roughly he unbuttoned the Peruvian's shirt, laying open the bare brown chest to the icy cold.

"No!—not the hoses, please!"

Vögeli took one of the thin tubes in his blunt fingers and leaned close to peer at the puffy, calloused nodule of irritated skin that formed around it where it entered the flesh. He touched the nodule lightly, causing the digger to whimper.

"No, please!"

"Stop sniveling!"

Vögeli laid his thumbs against the nodule and exerted a sudden pressure. There was a slight popping sound as the skin slid back a fraction of an inch along the tube. Manue yelped and closed his eyes.

"Shut up! I know what I'm doing." He repeated the process with the other tube. Then he seized both tubes in his hands and wiggled them slightly in and out, as if to ensure a proper resetting of the skin. The digger cried weakly and slumped in a dead faint.

When he awoke, he was in bed in the barracks, and a medic was painting the sore spots with a bright yellow solution that chilled his skin.

"Woke up, huh?" the medic grunted cheerfully. "How you feel?"

"Malo!" he hissed.

"Stay in bed for the day, son. Keep your oxy up high. Make you feel better."

The medic went away, but Vögeli lingered, smiling at him grimly from the doorway. "Don't try goofing off tomorrow too."

Manue hated the closed door with silent eyes, and listened intently until Vögeli's footsteps left the building. Then, following the medic's instructions, he turned his oxy to maximum, even though the faster flow of blood made the chest valves ache. The sickness fled, to be replaced with a weary afterglow. Drowsiness came over him, and he slept.

Sleep was a dread black-robed phantom on Mars. Mars pressed the same incubus upon all newcomers to her soil: a nightmare of falling, falling, falling into bottomless space. It was the faint gravity, they said, that caused it. The body felt buoyed up, and the subconscious mind recalled down-going elevators, and diving airplanes, and a fall from a high cliff. It suggested these things in dreams, or if the dreamer's oxy were set too low, it conjured up a nightmare of sinking slowly deeper and deeper in cold, black water that filled the victim's throat. Newcomers were segregated in a separate barracks so that their nightly screams would not disturb the old-timers who had finally adjusted to Martian conditions.

But now, for the first time since his arrival, Manue slept soundly, airily, and felt borne up by beams of bright light.

When he awoke again, he lay clammy in the horrifying knowledge that he had not been breathing! It was so comfortable not to breathe. His chest stopped hurting because of the stillness of his rib cage. He felt refreshed and alive. Peaceful sleep.

Suddenly he was breathing again in harsh gasps, and cursing himself for the lapse, and praying amid quiet tears as he visualized the wasted chest of a troffie.

"Heh heh!" wheezed an oldster who had come in to readjust the furnace in the rookie barracks. "You'll get to be a Martian pretty soon, boy. I been here seven years. Look at *me.*"

Manue heard the gasping voice and shuddered; there was no need to look.

"You just as well not fight it. It'll get you. Give in, make it easy on yourself. Go crazy if you don't."

"Stop it! Let me alone!"

"Sure. Just one thing. You wanta go home, you think. I went home. Came back. You will too. They all do, 'cept engineers. Know why?"

"Shut up!" Manue pulled himself erect on the cot and hissed anger at the old-timer, who was neither old nor young, but only withered by Mars. His head suggested that he might be around thirty-five, but his body was weak and old.

The veteran grinned. "Sorry," he wheezed. "I'll keep my mouth shut." He hesitated, then extended his hand. "I'm Sam Donnell, mech-repairs."

Manue still glowered at him. Donnell shrugged and dropped his hand.

"Just trying to be friends," he muttered and walked away.

The digger started to call after him but only closed his mouth again, tightly. Friends? He needed friends, but not a troffie. He couldn't even bear to look at them, for fear he might be looking into the mirror of his own future.

Manue climbed out of his bunk and donned his fleeceskins. Night had fallen, and the temperature was already twenty below. A soft sift of icedust obscured the stars. He stared about in the darkness. The mess hall was closed, but a light burned in the canteen and another in the foremen's club, where the men were playing cards and drinking. He went to get his alcohol ration, gulped it mixed with a little water, and trudged back to the barracks alone.

The Tibetan was in bed, staring blankly at the ceiling. Manue sat down and gazed at his flat, empty face.

"Why did you come here, Gee?"

"Come where?"

"To Mars."

Gee grinned, revealing large black-streaked teeth. "Make money. Good money on Mars."

"Everybody make money, huh?"

"Sure."

"Where's the money come from?"

Gee rolled his face toward the Peruvian and frowned. "You crazy? Money come from Earth, where all money comes from."

"And what does Earth get back from Mars?"

Gee looked puzzled for a moment, then gathered anger because he found no answer. He grunted a monosyllable in his native tongue, then rolled over and went to sleep.

Manue was not normally given to worrying about such things, but now he found himself asking, "What am I doing here?"—and then, "What is *anybody* doing here?"

The Mars Project had started eighty or ninety years ago, and its end goal was to make Mars habitable for colonists without Earth support, without oxies and insulated suits and the various gadgets a man now had to use to keep himself alive on the fourth planet. But thus far, Earth had planted without reaping. The sky was a bottomless well into which Earth poured her tools, dollars, manpower, and engineering skill. And there appeared to be no hope for the near future.

Manue felt suddenly trapped. He could not return to Earth before the end of his contract. He was trading five years of virtual enslavement for a sum of money which would buy a limited amount of freedom. But what if he lost his lungs, became a servant of the small aerator for the rest of his days? Worst of all: whose ends was he serving? The contractors were getting rich—on government contracts. Some of the engineers and foremen were getting rich—by various forms of embezzlement of government funds. But what were the people back on Earth getting for their money?

Nothing.

He lay awake for a long time, thinking about it. Then he resolved to ask someone tomorrow, someone smarter than himself.

But he found the question brushed aside. He summoned enough nerve to ask Vögeli, but the foreman told him harshly to keep working and quit wondering. He asked the structural engineer who supervised the building, but the man only laughed and said: "What do you care? You're making good money."

They were running concrete now, laying the long strips of Martian steel in the bottom of the trench and dumping in great slobbering wheelbarrowfuls of gray-green mix. The drillers were continuing their tedious dry cut deep into the red world's crust. Twice a day they brought up a yard-long cylindrical sample of the rock and gave it to a geologist who weighed it, roasted it, weighed it again, and tested a sample of the condensed steam—if any—for tritium content. Daily, he chalked up the results on a blackboard in front of the engineering hut, and the technical staff crowded around for a look. Manue always glanced at the figures but failed to understand.

Life became an endless routine of pain, fear, hard work, anger. There were few diversions. Sometimes a crew of entertainers came out from the Mare Erythraeum, but the labor gang could not all crowd in the pressurized staff-barracks where the shows were presented, and when Manue managed to catch a glimpse of one of the girls walking across the clearing, she was bundled in fleeceskins and hooded by a parka.

Itinerant rabbis, clergymen, and priests of the world's major faiths came occasionally to the camp: Buddhist, Muslim, and the Christian sects. Padre Antonio Selni made monthly visits to hear confessions and offer Mass. Most of the gang attended all services as a diversion from routine, as an escape from nostalgia. Somehow it gave Manue a strange feeling in the pit of his stomach to see the Sacrifice of the Mass, two thousand years old, being offered in the same ritual under the strange dark sky of Mars—with a section of the new foundation serving as an altar upon which the priest set crucifix, candles, relic stone, missal, chalice, paten, ciborium, cruets, et cetera. In filling the wine cruet before the service, Manue saw him spill a little of the red-clear fluid upon the brown soil—wine, Earth-wine from sunny Sicilian vineyards, trampled from the grapes by the bare stamping feet of children. Wine, the rich red blood of Earth, soaking slowly into the crust of another planet.

Bowing low at the consecration, the unhappy Peruvian thought of the prayer a rabbi had sung the week before: "Blessed be the Lord our God, King of the Universe, Who makest bread to spring forth out of the Earth."

Earth chalice, Earth blood, Earth God, Earth worshipers—with plastic tubes in their chests and a great sickness in their hearts.

He went away saddened. There was no faith here. Faith needed familiar surroundings, the props of culture. Here there were only swinging picks and rumbling machinery and sloshing concrete and the clatter of tools and the wheezing of troffies. Why? For five dollars an hour and keep?

Manue, raised in a back-country society that was almost a folk culture, felt deep thirst for a goal. His father had been a stonemason, and he had labored lovingly to help build the new cathedral, to build houses and mansions and commercial buildings, and his blood was mingled in their mortar. He had built for the love of his community and the love of the people and their customs, and their gods. He knew his own ends, and the ends of those around him. But what sense was there in this endless scratching at the face of Mars? Did they think they could make it into a second Earth, with pine forests and lakes and snow-capped mountains and small country villages? Man was not that strong. No, if he were laboring for any cause at all, it was to build a world so un-Earthlike that he could not love it.

The foundation was finished. There was very little more to be done until the drillers struck pay. Manue sat around the camp and worked at breathing. It was becoming a conscious effort now, and if he stopped thinking about it for a few minutes, he found himself inspiring shallow, meaningless little sips of air that scarcely moved his diaphragm. He kept the aerator as low as possible, to make himself breathe great gasps that hurt his chest, but it made him dizzy, and he had to increase the oxygenation lest he faint.

Sam Donnell, the troffie mech-repairman, caught him about to slump dizzily from his perch atop a heap of rocks, pushed him erect, and turned his oxy back to normal. It was late afternoon, and the drillers were about to change shifts. Manue sat shaking his head for a moment, then gazed at Donnell gratefully.

"That's dangerous, kid," the troffie wheezed. "Guys can go psycho doing that. Which you rather have: sick lungs or sick mind?"

"Neither."

"I know, but—"

"I don't want to talk about it."

Donnell stared at him with a faint smile. Then he shrugged and sat down on the rock heap to watch the drilling.

"Oughta be hitting the tritium ice in a couple of days," he said pleasantly. "Then we'll see a big blow."

Manue moistened his lips nervously. The troffies always made him feel uneasy. He stared aside.

"Big blow?"

"Lotta pressure down there, they say. Something about the way Mars got formed. Dust cloud hypothesis."

Manue shook his head. "I don't understand."

"I don't either. But I've heard them talk. Couple of billion years ago, Mars was supposed to be a moon of Jupiter. Picked up a lot of ice crystals over a rocky core. Then it broke loose and picked up a rocky crust—from another belt of the dust cloud. The pockets of tritium ice catch a few neutrons from uranium ore—down under. Some of the tritium goes into helium. Frees oxygen. Gases form pressure. Big blow."

"What are they going to do with the ice?"

The troffie shrugged. "The engineers might know."

Manue snorted and spat. "They know how to make money."

"Heh! Sure, everybody's gettin' rich."

The Peruvian stared at him speculatively for a moment.

"Señor Donnell, I—"

"Sam'll do."

"I wonder if anybody knows why . . . well . . . why we're really here."

Donnell glanced up to grin, then waggled his head. He fell thoughtful for a moment, and leaned forward to write in the earth. When he finished, he read it aloud.

"A plow plus a horse plus land equals the necessities of life." He glanced up at Manue. "A.D. Fifteen Hundred."

The Peruvian frowned his bewilderment. Donnell rubbed out what he had written and wrote again.

"A factory plus steam turbines plus raw materials equals necessities plus luxuries. A.D. Nineteen Hundred."

He rubbed it out and repeated the scribbling. "All those things plus nuclear power and computer controls equal a surplus of everything. A.D. Twenty-one Hundred."

"So?"

"So, it's either cut production or find an outlet. Mars is an outlet for surplus energies, manpower, money. Mars Project keeps money turning over, keeps everything turning over. Economist told me that. Said if the Project folded, surplus would pile up—big depression on Earth."

The Peruvian shook his head and sighed. It didn't sound right somehow. It sounded like an explanation somebody figured out after the whole thing started. It wasn't the kind of goal he wanted.

Two days later, the drill hit ice, and the "big blow" was only a fizzle. There was talk around the camp that the whole operation had been a waste of time. The hole spewed a frosty breath for several hours, and the drill crews crowded around to stick their faces in it and breathe great gulps of the helium oxygen mixture. But then the blow subsided, and the hole leaked only a wisp of steam.

Technicians came and lowered sonar "cameras" down to the ice. They spent a week taking internal soundings and plotting the extent of the ice dome on their charts. They brought up samples of ice and tested them. The engineers worked late into the Martian nights.

Then it was finished. The engineers came out of their huddles and called to the foremen of the labor gangs. They led the foremen around the site, pointing here, pointing there, sketching with chalk on the foundation, explaining in solemn voices. Soon the foremen were bellowing at their crews.

"Let's get the derrick down!"

"Start that mixer going!"

"Get that steel over here!"

"Unroll that dip wire!"

"Get a move on! Shovel that fill!"

Muscles tightened and strained, machinery clamored and rang. Voices grumbled and shouted. The operation was starting again. Without knowing why, Manue shoveled fill and stretched dip wire and poured concrete for a big floor slab to be run across the entire hundred-yard square, broken only by the big pipe casing that stuck up out of the ground in the center and leaked a thin trail of steam.

The drill crew moved their rig half a mile across the plain to a point specified by the geologists and began sinking another hole. A groan went up from structural boys: "Not *another* one of these things!"

But the supervisory staff said, "No, don't worry about it."

There was much speculation about the purpose of the whole operation, and the men resented the quiet secrecy connected with the project. There could be no excuse for secrecy, they felt, in time of peace. There was a certain arbitrariness about it, a hint that the Commission thought of its employees as children, or enemies, or servants. But the supervisory staff shrugged off all questions with: "You know there's tritium ice down there. You know it's what we've been looking for. Why? Well— what's the difference? There are lots of uses for it. Maybe we'll use it for one thing, maybe for something else. Who knows?"

Such a reply might have been satisfactory for an iron mine or an oil well or a stone quarry, but tritium suggested hydrogen fusion. And no transportation facilities were being installed to haul the stuff away—no pipelines or railroad tracks or glider ports.

Manue quit thinking about it. Slowly he came to adopt a grim cynicism toward the tediousness, the back-breaking labor of his daily work; he lived from day to day like an animal, dreaming only of a return to Earth when his contract was up. But the dream was painful because it was distant, as contrasted with the immediacies of Mars: the threat of atrophy, coupled with the discomforts of continued breathing, the nightmares, the barrenness of the landscape, the intense cold, the harshness of men's tempers, the hardship of labor, and the lack of a cause.

A warm, sunny Earth was still over four years distant, and tomorrow would be another back-breaking, throat-parching, heart-tormenting, chest-hurting day. Where was there even a little pleasure in it? It was so easy, at least, to leave the oxy turned up at night, and get a pleasant restful sleep. Sleep was the only recourse from harshness, and fear robbed sleep of its quiet sensuality—unless a man just surrendered and quit worrying about his lungs.

Manue decided that it would be safe to give himself two completely restful nights a week.

Concrete was run over the great square and troweled to a rough finish. A glider train from the Mare Erythraeum brought in several huge crates of machinery, cut-stone masonry for building a wall, a shipful of new personnel, and a real rarity: lumber, cut from the first Earth trees to be grown on Mars.

A building began going up with the concrete square for foundation and floor. Structures could be flimsier on Mars; because of the light gravity, compression stresses were smaller. Hence, the work progressed rapidly, and as the flat-roofed structure was completed, the technicians began uncrating new machinery and moving it into the building. Manue noticed that several of the units were computers. There was also a small steam-turbine generator driven by an atomic-fired boiler.

Months passed. The building grew into an integrated mass of power and control systems. Instead of using the well for pumping, the technicians were apparently going to lower something into it. A bomb-shaped cylinder was slung vertically over the hole. The men guided it into the mouth of the pipe casing, then let it down slowly from a massive cable. The cylinder's butt was a multi-contact socket like the female receptacle for a hundred-pin electron tube. Hours passed while the cylinder slipped slowly down beneath the hide of Mars. When it was done, the men hauled out the cable and began lowering stiff sections of pre-wired conduit, fitted with a receptacle at one end and a male plug at the other, so that as the sections fell into place, a continuous bundle of control cables was built up from "bomb" to surface.

Several weeks were spent in connecting circuits, setting up the computers, and making careful tests. The drillers had finished the second well hole, half a mile from the first, and Manue noticed that while the testing was going on, the engineers sometimes stood atop the building and stared anxiously toward the steel skeleton in the distance. Once while the tests were being conducted, the second hole began squirting a jet of steam high in the thin air, and a frantic voice bellowed from the rooftop.

"Cut it! Shut it off! Sound the danger whistle!"

The jet of steam began to shriek a low-pitched whine across the Martian desert. It blended with the rising and falling *OOOOawwww* of the danger siren. But gradually it subsided as the men in the control station shut down the machinery. All hands came up cursing from their hiding places, and the engineers stalked out to the new hole carrying Geiger counters. They came back wearing pleased grins.

The work was nearly finished. The men began crating up the excavating machinery and the drill rig and the tools. The control-building devices were entirely automatic, and the camp would be deserted when the station began operation. The men were disgruntled. They had spent a year of hard labor on what they had thought to be a tritium well, but now that it was done, there were no facilities for pumping the stuff or hauling it away. In fact, they had pumped various solutions *into* the ground through the second hole, and the control station shaft was fitted with pipes that led from lead-lined tanks down into the earth.

Manue had stopped trying to keep his oxy properly adjusted at night. Turned up to a comfortable level, it was like a drug, ensuring comfortable sleep—and like addict or alcoholic, he could no longer endure living without it. Sleep was too precious, his only comfort. Every morning he awoke with a still, motionless chest, felt frightening remorse, sat up gasping, choking, sucking at the thin air with whining, rattling lungs that had been idle too long. Sometimes he coughed violently, and bled a little. And then for a night or two he would correctly adjust the oxy, only to wake up screaming and suffocating. He felt hope sliding grimly away.

He sought out Sam Donnell, explained the situation, and begged the troffie for helpful advice. But the mech-repairman neither helped nor consoled nor joked about it. He only bit his lip, muttered something noncommittal, and found an excuse to hurry away. It was then that Manue knew his hope was gone. Tissue was withering, tubercles forming, tubes growing closed. He knelt abjectly beside his cot, hung his face in his hands, and cursed softly, for there was no other way to pray an unanswerable prayer.

A glider train came in from the north to haul away the disassembled tools. The men lounged around the barracks or wandered across the Martian desert, gathering strange bits of rock and fossils, searching idly for a glint of metal or crystal in the wan sunshine of early fall. The lichens were growing brown and yellow, and the landscape took on the hues of Earth's autumn, if not the forms.

There was a sense of expectancy around the camp. It could be felt in the nervous laughter, and the easy voices, talking suddenly of Earth and old friends and the smell of food in a farm kitchen, and old half-forgotten tastes for which men hungered: ham searing in the skillet, a cup of frothing cider from a fermenting crock, iced melon with honey and a bit of lemon, onion gravy on homemade bread. But someone always remarked, "What's the matter with you guys? We ain't going home. Not by a long shot. We're going to another place just like this."

And the group would break up and wander away, eyes tired, eyes haunted with nostalgia.

"What're we waiting for?" men shouted at the supervisory staff. "Get some transportation in here. Let's get rolling."

Men watched the skies for glider trains or jet transports, but the skies remained empty, and the staff remained close-mouthed. Then a dust column appeared on the horizon to the north, and a day later a convoy of tractor-trucks pulled into camp.

"Start loading aboard, men!" was the crisp command.

Surly voices: "You mean we don't go by air? We gotta ride those kidney bouncers? It'll take a week to get to Mare Ery! Our contract says—"

"Load aboard! We're not going to Mare Ery yet!"

Grumbling, they loaded their baggage and their weary bodies into the trucks, and the trucks thundered and clattered across the desert, rolling toward the mountains.

The convoy rolled for three days toward the mountains, stopping at night to make camp, and driving on at sunrise. When they reached the first slopes of the foothills, the convoy stopped again. The deserted encampment lay a hundred and fifty miles behind. The going had been slow over the roadless desert.

"Everybody out!" barked the messenger from the lead truck. "Bail out! Assemble at the foot of the hill."

Voices were growling among themselves as the men moved in small groups from the trucks and collected in a milling tide in a shallow basin, overlooked by a low cliff and a hill. Manue saw the staff climb out of a cab and slowly work their way up the cliff. They carried a portable public address system.

"Gonna get a preaching," somebody snarled.

"Sit down, please!" barked the loudspeaker. "You men sit down there! Quiet—quiet, please!"

The gathering fell into a sulky silence. Will Kinley stood looking out over them, his eyes nervous, his hand holding the mike close to his mouth so that they could hear his weak troffie voice.

"If you men have questions," he said, "I'll answer them now. Do you want to know what you've been doing during the past year?"

An affirmative rumble arose from the group.

"You've been helping to give Mars a breathable atmosphere." He glanced briefly at his watch, then looked back at his audience. "In fifty minutes, a controlled chain reaction will start in the tritium ice. The computers will time it and try to control it. Helium and oxygen will come blasting up out of the second hole."

A rumble of disbelief arose from his audience. Someone shouted: "How can you get air to blanket a planet from one hole?"

"You can't," Kinley replied crisply. "A dozen others are going in, just like that one. We plan three hundred, and we've already located the ice pockets. Three hundred wells, working for eight centuries, can get the job done."

"Eight centuries! What good—"

"Wait!" Kinley barked. "In the meantime, we'll build pressurized cities close to the wells. If everything pans out, we'll get a lot of colonists here, and gradually condition them to live in a seven or eight psi atmosphere—which is about the best we can hope to get. Colonists from the Andes and the Himalayas—they wouldn't need much conditioning."

"What about us?"

There was a long plaintive silence. Kinley's eyes scanned the group sadly, and wandered toward the Martian horizon, gold and brown in the late afternoon. "Nothing—about us," he muttered quietly.

"Why did we come out here?"

"Because there's danger of the reaction getting out of hand. We can't tell anyone about it, or we'd start a panic." He looked at the group sadly. "I'm telling you now, because there's nothing you could do. In thirty minutes—"

There were angry murmurs in the crowd. "You mean there may be an explosion?"

"There *will* be a limited explosion. And there's very little danger of anything more. The worst danger is in having ugly rumors start in the cities. Some fool with a slipstick would hear about it and calculate what would happen to Mars if five cubic miles of tritium ice detonated in one split second. It would probably start a riot. That's why we've kept it a secret."

The buzz of voices was like a disturbed beehive. Manue Nanti sat in the midst of it, saying nothing, wearing a dazed and weary face, thoughts jumbled, soul drained of feeling.

Why should men lose their lungs that, after eight centuries of tomorrows, other men might breathe the air of Mars as the air of Earth?

Other men around him echoed his thoughts in jealous mutterings. They had been helping to make a world in which they would never live.

An enraged scream arose near where Manue sat. "They're going to blow us up! They're going to blow up Mars."

"Don't be a fool!" Kinley snapped.

"Fools they call us! We *are* fools! For ever coming here! We got sucked in! Look at *me!*" A pale, dark-haired man came wildly to his feet and tapped his chest. "Look! I'm losing my lungs! We're all losing our lungs! Now they take a chance on killing everybody."

"Including ourselves," Kinley called coldly.

"We oughta take him apart. We oughta kill everyone who knew about it—and Kinley's a good place to start!"

The rumble of voices rose higher, calling both agreement and dissent. Some of Kinley's staff were looking nervously toward the trucks. They were unarmed.

"You men sit down!" Kinley barked.

Rebellious eyes glared at the supervisor. Several men who had come to their feet dropped to their haunches again. Kinley glowered at the pale upriser who called for his scalp.

"Sit down, Handell!"

Handell turned his back on the supervisor and called out to the others: "Don't be a bunch of cowards! Don't let him bully you!"

"You men sitting around Handell. Pull him down."

There was no response. The men, including Manue, stared up at the wild-eyed Handell gloomily but made no move to quiet him. A pair of burly foremen started through the gathering from its outskirts.

"Stop!" Kinley ordered. "Turpin, Schultz—get back. Let the men handle this themselves."

Half a dozen others had joined the rebellious Handell. They were speaking in low tense tones among themselves.

"For the last time, men! Sit down!"

The group turned and started grimly toward the cliff. Without reasoning why, Manue slid to his feet quietly as Handell came near him. "Come on, fellow, let's get him," the leader muttered.

The Peruvian's fist chopped a short stroke to Handell's jaw, and the dull *thuk* echoed across the clearing. The man crumpled, and Manue crouched over him like a hissing panther. "Get back!" he snapped at the others. "Or I'll jerk his hoses out."

One of the others cursed him.

"Want to fight, fellow?" the Peruvian wheezed. "I can jerk several hoses out before you drop me!"

They shuffled nervously for a moment.

"The guy's crazy!" one complained in a high voice.

"Get back or he'll kill Handell!"

They sidled away, moved aimlessly in the crowd, then sat down to escape attention. Manue sat beside the fallen man and gazed at the thinly smiling Kinley.

"Thank you, son. There's a fool in every crowd." He looked at his watch again. "Just a few minutes, men. Then you'll feel the Earth-tremor, and the explosion, and the wind. You can be proud of that wind, men. It's new air for Mars, and you made it."

"But we can't breathe it!" hissed a troffie.

Kinley was silent for a long time, as if listening to the distance. "What man ever made his own salvation?" he murmured.

They packed up the public address amplifier and came down the hill to sit in the cab of a truck, waiting.

It came as an orange glow in the south, and the glow was quickly shrouded by an expanding white cloud. Then, minutes later, the ground pulsed beneath them, quivered and shook. The quake subsided but remained as a hint of vibration. Then, after a long time, they heard the dull-throated roar thundering across the Martian desert. The roar continued steadily, grumbling and growling as it would do for several hundred years.

There was only a hushed murmur of awed voices from the crowd. When the wind came, some of them stood up and moved quietly back to the trucks, for now they could go back to a city for reassignment. There were other tasks to accomplish before their contracts were done.

But Manue Nanti still sat on the ground, his head sunk low, desperately trying to gasp a little of the wind he had made, the wind out of the ground, the wind of the future. But his lungs were clogged, and he could not drink of the racing wind. His big calloused hand clutched slowly at the ground, and he choked a brief sound like a sob.

A shadow fell over him. It was Kinley, come to offer his thanks for the quelling of Handell. But he said nothing for a moment as he watched Manue's desperate Gethsemane.

"Some sow, others reap," he said.

"Why?" the Peruvian choked.

The supervisor shrugged. "What's the difference? But if you can't be both, which would you rather be?"

Nanti looked up into the wind. He imagined a city to the south, a city built on tear-soaked ground, filled with people who had no ends beyond their culture, no goal but within their own society. It was a good sensible question: Which would he rather be—sower or reaper?

Pride brought him slowly to his feet, and he eyed Kinley questioningly. The supervisor touched his shoulder.

"Go on to the trucks."

Nanti nodded and shuffled away. He had wanted something to work for, hadn't he? Something more than the reasons Donnell had given. Well, he could smell a reason, even if he couldn't breathe it.

Eight hundred years was a long time, but then—long time, big reason. The air smelled good, even with its clouds of boiling dust.

He knew now what Mars was—not a ten-thousand-a-year job, not a garbage can for surplus production. But an eight-century passion of human faith in the destiny of the race of Man. He paused short of the truck. He had wanted to travel, to see the sights of Earth, the handiwork of Nature and of history, the glorious places of his planet.

He stooped and scooped up a handful of the red-brown soil, letting it sift slowly between his fingers. Here was Mars—his planet now. No more of Earth, not for Manue Nanti. He adjusted his aerator more comfortably and climbed into the waiting truck.

JOHN L'HEUREUX

The Comedian

Corinne hasn't planned to have a baby. She is thirty-eight and happy and she wants to get on with it. She is a stand-up comedian with a husband, her second, and with no thought of a child, and what she wants out of life now is a lot of laughs. To give them, and especially to get them. And here she is, by accident, pregnant.

The doctor sees her chagrin and is surprised, because he thinks of her as a competent and sturdy woman. But that's how things are these days and so he suggests an abortion. Corinne says she'll let him know; she has to do some thinking. A baby.

"That's great," Russ says. "If you want it, I mean. I want it. I mean, I want it if you do. It's up to you, though. You know what I mean?"

And so they decide that, of course, they will have the baby, of course they want the baby, the baby is just exactly what they need.

In the bathroom mirror that night, Russ looks through his eyes into his cranium for a long time. Finally he sees his mind. As he watches, it knots like a fist. And he continues to watch, glad, as that fist beats the new baby flat and thin, a dead slick silverfish.

Mother. Mother and baby. A little baby. A big baby. Bouncing babies. At once Corinne sees twenty babies, twenty pink basketball babies, bouncing down the court and then up into the air and—whoosh—they swish neatly through the net. Babies.

Baby is its own excuse for being. Or is it? Well, Corinne was a Catholic right up until the end of her first marriage, so she thinks maybe it is. One thing is sure: the only subject you can't make a good joke about is abortion.

Yes, they will have the baby. Yes, she will be the Mother. Yes.

But the next morning, while Russ is at work, Corinne turns off the television and sits on the edge of the couch. She squeezes her thighs together, tight; she contracts her stomach; she arches her back. This is no joke. This is the real thing. By an act of the will, she is going to expel this baby, this invader, this insidious little murderer. She pushes and pushes and nothing happens. She pushes again, hard. And once more she pushes. Finally she gives up and lies back against the sofa, resting.

After a while she puts her hand on her belly, and as she does so, she is astonished to hear singing.

It is the baby. It has a soft reedy voice and it sings slightly off-key. Corinne listens to the words: "Some of these days, you'll miss me, honey . . ."

Corinne faints then, and it is quite some time before she wakes up.

When she wakes, she opens her eyes only a slit and looks carefully from left to right. She sits on the couch, vigilant, listening, but she hears nothing. After a while she says three Hail Marys and an Act of Contrition, and then, confused and a little embarrassed, she does the laundry.

She does not tell Russ about this.

Well, it's a time of strain, Corinne tells herself, even though in California there isn't supposed to be any strain. Just surfing and tans and divorce and a lot of interfacing. No strain and no babies.

Corinne thinks for a second about interfacing babies, but forces the thought from her mind and goes back to thinking about her act. Sometimes she does a very funny set on interfacing, but only if the audience is middle-aged. The younger ones don't seem to know that interfacing is laughable. Come to think of it, *nobody* laughs much in California. Everybody smiles, but who laughs?

Laughs: that's something she can use. She does Garbo's laugh: "I am so hap-py." What was that movie? "I am so hap-py." She does the Garbo laugh again. Not bad. Who else laughs? Joe E. Brown. The Wicked Witch of the West. Who was she? Somebody Hamilton. Will anybody remember these people? Ruth Buzzi? Goldie Hawn? Yes, that great giggle. Of course, the best giggle is Burt Reynolds's. High and fey. Why does he do that? Is he sending up his own image?

Corinne is thinking of images, Burt Reynolds's and Tom Selleck's, when she hears singing: "Cal-i-for-nia, here I come, Right back where I started from . . ." Corinne stops pacing and stands in the doorway to the kitchen—as if I'm waiting for the earthquake, she thinks. But there is no earthquake; there is only the thin sweet voice, singing.

Corinne leans against the doorframe and listens. She closes her eyes. At once it is Easter, and she is a child again at Sacred Heart Grammar School, and the thirty-five members of the children's choir, earnest and angelic, look out at her from where they stand, massed about the altar. They wear red cassocks and white surplices, starched, and they seem to have descended from heaven for this one occasion. Their voices are pure, high, untouched by adolescence or by pain; and, with a conviction born of absolute innocence, they sing to God and to Corinne, "Cal-i-for-nia, here I come."

Corinne leans against the doorframe and listens truly now. Imagination aside, drama aside—she listens. It is a single voice she hears, thin and reedy. So, she did not imagine it the first time. It is true. The baby sings.

That night, when Russ comes home, he takes his shower, and they settle in with their first martini and everything is cozy.

Corinne asks him about his day, and he tells her. It was a lousy day. Russ started his own construction company a year ago just as the bottom fell out of the building business, and now there are no jobs to speak of. Just renovation stuff. Clean-up after fires. Sometimes Victorian restorations down in the gay district. But that's about it. So whatever comes his way is bound to be lousy. Corinne knows this, but she asks how his day was anyhow, and he tells her. This is Russ's second marriage, though, so he knows not to go too far with a lousy day. Who needs it?

"But I've got you, babe," he says, and pulls her toward him, and kisses her.

"We've got each other," Corinne says, and kisses him back. "And the baby," she says.

He holds her close then, so that she can't see his face. She makes big eyes like an actor in a bad comedy—she doesn't know why; she just always sees the absurd in everything. After a while they pull away, smiling, secret, and sip their martinis.

"Do you know something?" she says. "Can I tell you something?"

"What?" he says. "Tell me."

"You won't laugh?"

"No," he says, laughing. "I'm sorry. No, I won't laugh."

"Okay," she says. "Here goes."

There is a long silence, and then he says, "Well?"

"It sings."

"It sings?"

"The baby. The fetus. It sings."

Russ is stalled, but only for a second. Then he says, "Plain chant? Or rock and roll?" He begins to laugh, and he laughs so hard that he chokes and sloshes martini onto the couch. "You're wonderful," he says. "You're really a funny, funny girl. Woman." He laughs some more. "Is that for your act? I love it."

"I'm serious," she says. "I mean it."

"Well, it's great," he says. "They'll love it."

Corinne puts her hand on her stomach and thinks she has never been so alone in her life. She looks at Russ, with his big square jaw and all those white teeth and his green eyes so trusting and innocent, and she realizes for one second how corrupt she is, how lost, how deserving of a baby who sings; and then she pulls herself together because real life has to go on.

"Let's eat out," she says. "Spaghetti. It's cheap." She kisses him gently on his left eyelid, on his right. She gazes into his eyes and smiles, so that he will not guess she is thinking: Who is this man? Who am I?

Corinne has a job, Fridays and Saturdays for the next three weeks— at the Ironworks. It's not The Comedy Shop, but it's a legitimate gig, and the money is good. Moreover, it will give her something to think about besides whether or not she should go through with the abortion. She and Russ have put that on hold.

She is well into her third month, but she isn't showing yet, so she figures she can handle the three weekends easily. She wishes, in a way, that she were showing. As it is, she only looks . . . She searches for the word, but not for long. The word is *fat*. She looks fat.

She could do fat-girl jokes, but she hates jokes that put down women. And she hates jokes that are blue. Jokes that ridicule husbands. Jokes that ridicule the joker's looks. Jokes about nationalities. Jokes that play into audience prejudice. Jokes about the terrible small town you came from. Jokes about how poor you were, how ugly, how unpopular. Phyllis Diller jokes. Joan Rivers jokes. Jokes about small boobs, wrinkles, sexual inadequacy. Why is she in this business? she wonders. She hates jokes.

She thinks she hears herself praying: Please, please.

What should she do at the Ironworks? What should she do about the baby? What should she do?

The baby is the only one who's decided what to do. The baby sings. Its voice is filling out nicely and it has enlarged its repertoire considerably. It sings a lot of classical melodies Corinne thinks she remembers from somewhere, churchy stuff, but it also favors golden oldies from the forties and fifties, with a few real old-timers thrown in when they seem appropriate. Once, right at the beginning, for instance, after Corinne and Russ had quarreled, Corinne locked herself in the bathroom to sulk and after a while was surprised, and then grateful, to hear the baby crooning, "Oh, my man, I love him so." It struck Corinne a day or so later that this could be a baby that would sell out for *any* one-liner . . . if indeed she decided to have the baby . . . and so she was relieved when the baby turned to more classical pieces.

The baby sings only now and then, and it sings better at some times than at others, but Corinne is convinced it sings best on weekend evenings when she is preparing for her gig. Before she leaves home, Corinne always has a long hot soak in the tub. She lies in the suds with her little orange bath pillow at her head and, as she runs through the night's possibilities, preparing ad libs, heckler put-downs, segues, the baby sings to her.

There is some connection, she is sure, between her work and the baby's singing, but she can't guess what it is. It doesn't matter. She loves this: just she and the baby, together, in song.

Thank you, thank you, she prays.

The Ironworks gig goes extremely well. It is a young crowd, mostly, and so Corinne sticks to her young jokes: life in California, diets, dating, school. The audience laughs, and Russ says she is better than ever, but at the end of the three weeks the manager tells her, "You got it, honey. You got all the moves. You really make them laugh, you know? But they laugh from here only"—he taps his head—"not from the gut. You gotta get gut. You know? Like feeling."

So now the gig is over and Corinne lies in her tub trying to think of gut. She's gotta get gut, she's gotta get feeling. Has she ever *felt*? Well, she feels for Russ; she loves him. She felt for Alan, that bastard; well, maybe he wasn't so bad; maybe he just wasn't ready for marriage, any more than she was. Maybe it's California; maybe nobody *can* feel in California.

Enough about feeling, already. Deliberately, she puts feeling out of her mind and calls up babies instead. A happy baby, she thinks, and at once the bathroom is crowded with laughing babies, each one roaring and carrying on like Ed McMahon. A fat baby, and she sees a Shelley Winters baby, an Elizabeth Taylor baby, an Orson Welles baby. An active baby: a mile of trampolines and babies doing quadruple somersaults, backflips, high dives. A healthy baby: babies lifting weights, swimming the Channel. Babies.

But abortion is the issue, not babies. Should she have it, or not?

At once she sees a bloody mess, a crushed-looking thing, half animal, half human. Its hands open and close. She gasps. "No," she says aloud, and shakes her head to get rid of the awful picture. "No," and she covers her face.

Gradually she realizes that she has been listening to humming, and now the humming turns to song—"It ain't necessarily so," sung in a good clear mezzo.

Her eyes hurt and she has a headache. In fact, her eyes hurt all the time.

Corinne has finally convinced Russ that she hears the baby singing. Actually, he is convinced that Corinne is halfway around the bend with worry, and he is surprised, when he thinks about it, to find that he loves her anyway, crazy or not. He tells her that as much as he hates the idea, maybe she ought to think about having an abortion.

"I've actually gotten to like the singing," she says.

"Corinne," he says.

"It's the things I see that scare me to death."

"What things? What do you see?"

At once she sees a little crimson baby. It has been squashed into a mason jar. The tiny eyes almost disappear into the puffed cheeks, the cheeks into the neck, the neck into the torso. It is a pickled baby, ancient, preserved.

"Tell me," he says.

"Nothing," she says. "It's just that my eyes hurt."

It's getting late for an abortion, the doctor says, but she can still have one safely.

He's known her for twenty years, all through the first marriage and now through this one, and he's puzzled that a funny and sensible girl like Corinne should be having such a tough time with pregnancy. He had recommended abortion right from the start, because she didn't seem to want the baby and because she was almost forty, but he hadn't really expected her to take him up on it. Looking at her now, though, it is clear to him that she'll never make it. She'll be wacko—if not during the pregnancy, then sure as hell afterward.

So what does she think? What does Russ think?

Well, first, she explains in her new, sort of wandering way, there's something else she wants to ask about; not really important, she supposes, but just something, well, kind of different she probably should mention. It's the old problem of the baby . . . well, um, singing.

"Singing?"

"Singing?" he asks again.

"And humming," Corinne says.

They sit in silence for a minute, the doctor trying to decide whether or not this is a joke. She's got this great poker face. She really is a good comic. So after a while he laughs, and then when she laughs, he knows he's done the right thing. But what a crazy sense of humor!

"You're terrific," he says. "Anything else? How's Russ? How was the Ironworks job?"

"My eyes hurt," she says. "I have headaches."

And so they discuss her vision for a while, and stand-up comedy, and she makes him laugh. And that's that.

At the door he says to her, "Have an abortion, Corinne. Now, before it's too late."

They have just made love and now Russ puts off the light and they lie together in the dark, his hand on her belly.

"Listen," he says. "I want to say something. I've been thinking about what the doctor said, about an abortion. I hate it, I hate the whole idea, but you know, we've got to think of you. And I think this baby is too much for you, I think maybe that's why you've been having those headaches and stuff. Don't you think?"

Corinne puts her hand on his hand and says nothing. After a long while Russ speaks again, into the darkness.

"I've been a lousy father. Two sons I never see. Beth took them back when they were, what, four and two, I guess. Back east. I never see them. The stepfather's good to them, though; he's a good father. I thought maybe I'd have another chance at it, do it right this time, like the marriage. Besides, the business isn't always going to be this bad, you know; I'll get jobs; I'll get money. We could afford it, you know? A son. A daughter. It would be nice. But what I mean is, we've got to take other things into consideration, we've got to consider your health. You're not strong enough, I guess. I always think of you as strong, because you do those gigs and you're funny and all, but, I mean, you're almost forty, and the doctor thinks that maybe an abortion is the way to go, and what do I know? I don't know. The singing. The headaches. I don't know."

Russ looks into the dark, seeing nothing.

"I worry about you, you want to know the truth? I do. Corinne?"

Corinne lies beside him, listening to him, refusing to listen to the baby, who all this time has been singing. Russ is as alone as she is, even more alone. She is dumbfounded. She is speechless with love. If he were a whirlpool, she thinks, she would fling herself into it. If he were . . . but he is who he is, and she loves only him, and she makes her decision.

"Corinne?" There is fear in his voice now.

"You think I'm losing my mind," she says.

Silence.

"Yes."

More silence.

"Well, I'm not. Headaches are a normal part of lots of pregnancies, the doctor said, and the singing doesn't mean anything at all. He explained what was really going on, why I thought I heard it sing. You see," Corinne says, improvising freely now, making it all up, for him, her gift to him, "you see, when you get somebody as high-strung as me and you add pregnancy right at the time I'm about to make it big as a stand-up, then the pressures get to be so much that sometimes the imagination can take over, the doctor said, and when you tune in to the normal sounds of your body, you hear them really loud, as if they were amplified by a three-thousand-watt PA system, and it can sound like singing. See?"

Russ says nothing.

"So you see, it all makes sense, really. You don't have to worry about me."

"Come on," Russ says. "Do you mean to tell me you never heard the baby singing?"

"Well, I heard it, sort of. You know? It was really all in my mind. I mean, the *sound* was in my body physiologically, but my hearing it as *singing* was just . . ."

"Just your imagination."

Corinne does not answer.

"Well?"

"Right," she says, making the total gift. "It was just my imagination."

And the baby—who has not stopped singing all this time, love songs mostly—stops singing now, and does not sing again until the day scheduled for the abortion.

The baby has not sung in three weeks. It is Corinne's fifth month now, and at last they have been able to do an amniocentesis. The news is bad. One of the baby's chromosomes does not match up to anything in hers, anything in Russ's. What this means, they tell her, is that the baby is not normal. It will be deformed in some way; in what way, they have no idea.

Corinne and Russ decide on abortion.

They talk very little about their decision now that they have made it. In fact, they talk very little about anything. Corinne's face grows daily more haggard, and Corinne avoids Russ's eyes. She is silent much of the time, thinking. The baby is silent all the time.

The abortion will be by hypertonic saline injection, a simple procedure, complicated only by the fact that Corinne has waited so long. She has been given a booklet to read and she has listened to a tape, and so she knows about the injection of the saline solution, she knows about the contractions that will begin slowly and then get more and more frequent, and she knows about the dangers of infection and excessive bleeding.

She knows moreover that it will be a formed fetus she will expel.

Russ has come with her to the hospital and is outside in the waiting room. Corinne thinks of him, of how she loves him, of how their lives will be better, safer, without this baby who sings. This deformed baby. Who sings. If only she could hear the singing once more, just once.

Corinne lies on the table with her legs in the thigh rests, and one of the nurses drapes the examining sheet over and around her. The other nurse, or someone—Corinne is getting confused; her eyesight seems fuzzy—takes her pulse and her blood pressure. She feels someone washing her, the careful hands, the warm fluid. So, it is beginning.

Corinne closes her eyes and tries to make her mind a blank. Dark, she thinks. Dark. She squeezes her eyes tight against the light, she wants to remain in this cool darkness forever, she wants to cease being. And then, amazingly, the dark does close in on her. Though she opens her eyes, she sees nothing. She can remain this way forever if she wills it. The dark is cool to the touch, and it is comforting somehow; it invites her in. She can lean into it, give herself up to it, and be safe, alone, forever.

She tries to sit up. She will enter this dark. She will do it. Please, please, she hears herself say. And then all at once she thinks of Russ and the baby, and instead of surrendering to the dark, she pushes it away.

With one sweep of her hand she pushes the sheet from her and flings it to the floor. She pulls her legs from the thigh rests and manages to sit up, blinded still, but fighting.

"Here now," a nurse says, caught off guard, unsure what to do. "Hold on now. It's all right. It's fine."

"Easy now. Easy," the doctor says, thinking Yes, here it is, what else is new.

Together the nurses and the doctor make an effort to stop her, but they are too late, because by this time Corinne has fought free of any restraints. She is off the examining couch and, naked, huddles in the corner of the small room.

"No," she shouts. "I want the baby. I want the baby." And later, when she has stopped shouting, when she has stopped crying, still she clutches her knees to her chest and whispers over and over, "I want the baby."

So there is no abortion after all.

By the time she is discharged, Corinne's vision has returned, dimly. Moreover, though she tells nobody, she has heard humming, and once or twice a whole line of music. The baby has begun to sing again.

Corinne has more offers than she wants: the hungry i, the Purple Onion, the Comedy Shop. Suddenly everybody decides it's time to take a look at her, but she is in no shape to be looked at, so she signs for two weeks at My Uncle's Bureau and lets it go at that.

She is only marginally pretty now, she is six months pregnant, and she is carrying a deformed child. Furthermore, she can see very little, and what she does see, she often sees double.

Her humor, therefore, is spare and grim, but audiences love it. She begins slow: "When I was a girl, I always wanted to look like Elizabeth Taylor," she says, and glances down at her swollen belly. Two beats. "And now I do." They laugh with her, and applaud. Now she can quicken the pace, sharpen the humor. They follow her; they are completely captivated.

She has found some new way of holding her body—tipping her head, thrusting out her belly—and instead of putting off her audience, or embarrassing them, it charms them. The laughter is *with* her, the applause *for* her. She could do anything out there and get away with it. And she knows it. They simply love her.

In her dressing room after the show she tells herself that somehow, magically, she's learned to work from the heart instead of just from the head. She's got gut. She's got feeling. But she knows it's something more than that.

By the end of the two weeks she is convinced that the successful new element in her act is the baby. This deformed baby, this abnormal baby she has tried to kill. And what interests her most is that she no longer cares about success as a stand-up.

Corinne falls asleep that night to the sound of the baby's crooning. She is trying to pray, Please, please, but with Russ's snoring and the baby's lullaby, they all get mixed up together in her mind—God, Russ, the baby—and she forgets to whom she is praying or why. She sleeps.

The baby sings all the time now. It starts first thing in the morning with a nice soft piece by Telemann or Brahms; there are assorted lullabyes at bedtime; and throughout the day it is bop, opera, ragtime, blues, a little rock and roll, big-band stuff—the baby never tires.

Corinne tells no one about this, not even Russ.

She and Russ talk about almost everything now: their love for each other, their hopes for the baby, their plans. They have lots of plans. Russ has assured Corinne that whatever happens, he's ready for it. Corinne is his whole life, and no matter how badly the baby is deformed, they'll manage. They'll do the right thing. They'll survive.

They talk about almost everything, but they do not talk about the baby's singing.

For Corinne the singing is secret, mysterious. It contains some revelation, of course, but she does not want to know what that revelation might be.

The singing is somehow tied up with her work; but more than that, with her life. It is part of her fate. It is inescapable. And she is perfectly content to wait.

Corinne has been in labor for three hours, and the baby has been singing the whole time. The doctor has administered a mild anesthetic and a nurse remains at bedside, but the birth does not seem imminent, and so for Corinne it is a period of pain and waiting. And for the baby, singing.

"These lights are so strong," Corinne says, or thinks she says. "The lights are blinding."

The nurse looks at her for a moment and then goes back to the letter she is writing.

"Please," Corinne says, "thank you."

She is unconscious, she supposes; she is imagining the lights. Or perhaps the lights are indeed bright and she sees them as they really are *because* she is unconscious. Or perhaps her sight has come back, as strong as it used to be. Whatever the case, she doesn't want to think about it now. Besides, for some reason or other, even though the lights are blinding, they are not blinding her. They do not even bother her. It is as if light is her natural element.

"Thank you," she says. To someone.

The singing is wonderful, a cappella things Corinne recognizes as Brahms, Mozart, Bach. The baby's voice can assume any dimension it wants now, swelling from a single thin note to choir volume; it can take on the tone and resonance of musical instruments, violin, viola, flute; it can become all sounds; it enchants.

The contractions are more frequent; even unconscious, Corinne can tell that. Good. Soon the waiting will be over and she will have her wonderful baby, her perfect baby. But at once she realizes hers will not be a perfect baby; it will be deformed. "Please," she says, "please," as if prayer can keep Russ from being told—as he will be soon after the birth —that his baby has been born dumb. Russ, who has never understood comedians.

But now the singing has begun to swell in volume. It is as if the baby has become a full choir, with many voices, with great strength.

The baby will be fine, however it is, she thinks. She thinks of Russ, worried half to death. She is no longer worried. She accepts what will be.

The contractions are very frequent now and the light is much brighter. She knows the doctor has come into the room, because she hears his voice. There is another nurse too. And soon there will be the baby.

The light is so bright that she can see none of them. She can see into the light, it is true; she can see the soft fleecy nimbus flowing beyond the light, but she can see nothing in the room.

The singing. The singing and the light. It is Palestrina she hears, in polyphony, each voice lambent. The light envelops her, catches her up from this table where the doctor bends over her and where already can be seen the shimmering yellow hair of the baby. The light lifts her, and the singing lifts her, and she says, "Yes," she says, "thank you."

She accepts what will be. She accepts what is.

The room is filled with singing and with light, and the singing is transformed into light, more light, more lucency, and still she says, "Yes," until she cannot bear it, and she reaches up and tears the light aside. And sees.

Part IV
RESIGNATION

GRAHAM GREENE

A Visit to Morin

Le Diable au Ciel—there it was on a shelf in the Colmar bookshop causing a memory to reach out to me from the past of twenty years ago. One didn't often, in the 1950s, see Pierre Morin's novels on display, and yet here were two copies of his once famous book, and looking along the rows of paper bindings I discovered others, as though there existed in Alsace a secret *cave,* like those hidden cellars where wines were once preserved from the enemy for the days when peace would return.

I had admired Pierre Morin when I was a boy, but I had almost forgotten him. He was even then an older writer on the point of abandonment by his public, but the language class in an English public school is always a long way behind the Paris fashions. We happened at Collingworth to have a Roman Catholic master who belonged to the generation which Morin had pleased or offended. He had offended the orthodox Catholics in his own country and pleased the liberal Catholics abroad; he had pleased, too, the Protestants who believed in God with the same intensity that he seemed to show, and he used to find enthusiastic readers among non-Christians who, when once they had accepted imaginatively his premises, perhaps detected in his work the freedom of speculation which put his fellow Catholics on their guard. How fresh and exciting his work had appeared to my schoolmaster's generation; and to me, brought up in a lower form on *Les Misérables* and the poems of Lamartine, he was a revolutionary writer. But it is the fate of revolutionaries that the world accepts them. The excitement has gone from Morin's pages. Only the orthodox read him now, when the whole world seems prepared to believe in a god, except strangely enough—but I will not anticipate the point of my small anecdote which may yet provide a footnote to the literary history of Morin's day. When I publish it no harm can be done. Morin will be dead in the flesh as well as being dead as a writer, and he has left, so far as I am aware, no descendants and no disciples.

I yet recall with pleasure those French classes presided over by a Mr. Strangeways from Chile; his swarthy complexion was said by his enemies to indicate Spanish blood (it was the period of the Spanish Civil War when anything Spanish and Roman was regarded as Fascist) and by his friends, of whom I was one, a dash of Indian. In dull fact his father was an engineer from Wolverhampton and his mother came from Louisiana and was only Latin after three removes. At these senior classes we no longer studied syntax—at which Mr. Strangeways was in any case weak. Mr. Strangeways read aloud to us and we read aloud to him, but after five minutes we would launch into literary criticism, pulling to pieces with youthful daring—Mr. Strangeways like so many schoolmasters remained always youthful—the great established names and building up with exaggerated appreciation those who had not yet "arrived." Of course Morin had arrived years before, but of that we were unaware in our brick prison five hundred miles from the Seine—he hadn't reached the school textbooks; he hadn't yet been mummified by Messrs. Hachette et Cie. Where we didn't understand his meaning, there were no editor's notes to kill speculation.

"Can he really believe that?" I remember exclaiming to Mr. Strangeways when a character in *Le Diable au Ciel* made some dark and horrifying statement on the Atonement or the Redemption, and I remember Mr. Strangeways' blunt reply, flapping the sleeves of his short black gown, "But I believe it too, Dunlop." He did not leave it at that or allow himself to get involved in a theological debate, which might have imperilled his post in my Protestant school. He went on to indicate that we were unconcerned with what the author believed. The author had chosen as his viewpoint the character of an orthodox Catholic—all his thoughts therefore must be affected, as they would be in life, by his orthodoxy. Morin's technique forbade him to play a part in the story himself; even to show irony would be to cheat, though perhaps we might detect something of Morin's view from the fact that the orthodoxy of Durobier was extended to the furthest possible limits, so that at the close of the book we had the impression of a man stranded on a long strip of sand from which there was no possibility of advance, and to retreat towards the shore would be to surrender. "Is this true or is it not true?" His whole creed was concerned in the answer.

"You mean," I asked Mr. Strangeways, "that perhaps Morin does not believe?"

"I mean nothing of the kind. No one has seriously questioned his Catholicism, only his prudence. Anyway that's not true criticism. A novel is made up of words and characters. Are the words well chosen and do the characters live? All the rest belongs to literary gossip. You are not in this class to learn how to be gossip writers."

And yet in those days I would have liked to know. Sometimes Mr. Strangeways, recognizing my interest in Morin, would lend me Roman Catholic literary periodicals which contained notices of the novelist's work that often offended his principle of leaving the author's views out of account. I found Morin was sometimes accused of Jansenism—whatever that might be: others called him an Augustinian—a name which meant as little to me—and in the better printed and bulkier reviews I thought I detected a note of grievance. He believed all the right things, they could find no specific fault, and yet . . . it was as though some of his characters accepted a dogma so wholeheartedly that they drew out its implications to the verge of absurdity, while others examined a dogma as though they were constitutional lawyers determined on confining it to a kind of legal minimum. Durobier, I am sure, would have staked his life on a literal Assumption: at some point in history, somewhere in the latter years of the first century A.D., the body of the Virgin had floated skywards, leaving an empty tomb. On the other hand there was a character called Sagrin, in one of the minor novels, perhaps *Le Bien Pensant,* who believed that the holy body had rotted in the grave like other bodies. The strange thing was that both views seemed to possess irritating qualities to Catholic reviewers, and yet both proved to be equally in accordance with the dogmatic pronouncement when it came. One could assert therefore that they were orthodox; yet the orthodox critics seemed to scent heresy like a rat dead somewhere under the boards, at a spot they could not locate.

These, of course, were ancient criticisms, fished out of Mr. Strangeways' cupboard full of old French magazines dating back to his long-lost sojourn in Paris some time during the late twenties, when he had attended lectures at the Sorbonne and drunk beer at the Dôme. The word "paradox" was frequently used with an air of disapproval. Perhaps after all the orthodox were proved right, for I certainly was to discover just how far Morin carried in his own life the sense of paradox.

2

I am not one of those who revisit their old school, or what a disappointment I would have proved to Mr. Strangeways, who must by now be on the point of retirement. I think he had pictured me in the future as a distinguished writer for the weeklies on the subject of French literature—perhaps even as the author of a scholarly biography of Corneille. In fact, after an undistinguished war record, I obtained a post, with the help of influential connections, in a firm of wine merchants. My French syntax, so neglected by Mr. Strangeways, had been improved by the war and proved useful to the firm, and I suppose I had a certain literary flair which enabled me to improve on the rather old-fashioned style of the catalogues. The directors had been content for too long with the jargon of the Wine Society—"An unimportant but highly sympathetic wine for light occasions among friends." I introduced a more realistic note and substituted knowledge for knowingness. "This wine comes from a small vineyard on the western slopes of the Mont Soleil range. The soil in this region has Jurassic elements, as the vineyard is on the edge of the great Jurassic fissure which extends across Europe from the Urals, and this encourages the cultivation of a small, strong, dark grape with a high sugar-content, less vulnerable than more famous wines to the chances of weather." Of course it was the same "unimportant" wine, but my description gave the host material for his vanity.

Business had brought me to Colmar—we had found it necessary to change our agent there—and as I am a single man and find the lonely Christmases of London sad and regretful, I had chosen to combine my visit with the Christmas holiday. One does not feel alone abroad; I imagined drinking my way through the festival itself in some *Bierhaus* decorated with holly, myself invisible behind the fumes of cigars. A German Christmas is Christmas *par excellence:* singing, sentiment, gluttony.

I said to the shop assistant, "You seem to have a good supply of M. Morin's books."

"He is very popular," she said.

"I got the impression that in Paris he is no longer much read."

"We are Catholics here," she said with a note of reproof. "Besides, he lives near Colmar, and we are very proud he chose to settle in our neighborhood."

"How long has he been here?"

"He came immediately after the war. We consider him almost one of us. We have all his books in German also—you will see them over there. Some of us feel he is even finer in German than in French. German," she said, scrutinizing me with contempt as I picked up a French edition of *Le Diable au Ciel,* "has a better vocabulary for the profundities."

I told her I had admired M. Morin's novels since my school days. She softened towards me then, and I left the shop with M. Morin's address —a village fifteen miles from Colmar. I was uncertain all the same whether I would call on him. What really had I to say to him to excuse the vulgarity of my curiosity? Writing is the most private of all the arts, and yet few of us hesitate to invade the writer's home. We have all heard of that one caller from Porlock, but hundreds of callers every day are ringing doorbells, lifting receivers, thrusting themselves into the secret room where a writer works and lives.

I doubt whether I should have ventured to ring M. Morin's bell, but I caught sight of him two days later at the Midnight Mass in a village outside Colmar; it was not the village where I had been told he lived, and I wondered why he had come such a distance alone. Midnight Mass is a service which even a non-believer like myself finds inexplicably moving. Perhaps there is some memory of childhood which makes the journey through the darkness, the lighted windows and the frosty night, the slow gathering of silent strangers from the four quarters of the countryside moving and significant. There was a crib to the left of the door as I came in—the plaster baby sprawled in the plaster lap, and the cows, the sheep, and the shepherd cast long shadows in the candlelight. Among the kneeling women was an old man whose face I seemed to remember: a round head like a peasant's, the skin wrinkled like a stale apple, with the hair gone from the crown. He knelt, bowed his head, and rose again. There had just been time, I suppose, for a formal prayer, but it must have been a short one. His chin was stubbled white like the field outside, and there was so little about him to suggest a member of the French Academy that I might have taken him for the peasant he appeared to be, in his suit of respectable and shiny black and his black tie like a bootlace, if I had not been attracted by the eyes. The eyes gave him away: they seemed to know too much and to have seen further than the season and the fields. Of a very clear pale blue, they continually

shifted focus, looking close and looking away, observant, sad and curious like those of a man caught in some great catastrophe which it is his
duty to record, but which he cannot bear to contemplate for any length
of time. It was not, of course, during his short prayer before the crib
that I had time to watch Morin so closely; but when the congregation
was shuffling up towards the altar for Communion, Morin and I found
ourselves alone among the empty chairs. It was then I recognized him
—perhaps from memories of old photographs in Mr. Strangeways' reviews, I do not know; yet I was convinced of his identity, and I wondered what it was that kept this old distinguished Catholic from going
up with the others, at this Mass of all Masses in the year, to receive the
Sacrament. Had he perhaps inadvertently broken his fast, or was he a
man who suffered from scruples and did he believe that he had been
guilty of some act of uncharity or greed? There could not be many
serious temptations, I thought, for a man who must be approaching his
eightieth year. And yet I would not have believed him to be scrupulous;
it was from his own novels I had learnt of the existence of this malady
of the religious, and I would never have supposed the creator of
Durobier to have suffered from the same disease as his character. However, a novelist may sometimes write most objectively of his own fail-
ings.

We sat there alone at the back of the church. The air was as cold and
still as a frozen tree and the candles burned straight on the altar and
God, so they believed, passed along the altar rail. This was the birth of
Christianity: outside in the dark was old savage Judea, but in here the
world was only a few minutes old. It was the Year One again, and I felt
the old sentimental longing to believe as those, I suppose, believed who
came back one by one from the rail, with lips set like closed doors
around the dissolving wafer and with crossed hands. If I had said to one
of them, "Teach me why you believe," what would the answer have
been? I thought perhaps I knew, for once in the war—driven by fear
and disgust at the sight of the dead—I had spoken to a Catholic chaplain in just that way. He didn't belong to my unit, he was a busy man—
it isn't the job of a chaplain in the line to instruct or convert and he was
not to blame that he could convey nothing of his faith to an outsider
like myself. He lent me two books—one a penny catechism with its
catalogue of preposterous questions and answers, smug and explana-
tory: mystery like a butterfly killed by cyanide, stiffened and laid out
with pins and paper-strips; the other a sober enough study of Gospel

dates. I lost them both in a few days, with three bottles of whiskey, my jeep, and the corporal whose name I had not had time to learn before he was killed, while I was peeing in the green canal close by. I don't suppose I'd have kept the books much longer anyway. They were not the kind of help I needed, nor was the chaplain the man to give it me. I remember asking him if he had read Morin's novels. "I haven't time to waste with him," he said abruptly.

"They were the first books," I said, "to interest me in your faith."

"You'd have done much better to read Chesterton," he said.

So it was odd to find myself there at the back of the church with Morin himself. He was the first to leave and I followed him out. I was glad to go, for the sentimental attraction of a Midnight Mass was lost in the long ennui of the Communions.

"M. Morin," I said in that low voice we assume in a church or hospital.

He looked quickly, and I thought defensively, up.

I said, "Forgive my speaking to you like this, M. Morin, but your books have given me such great pleasure." Had the man from Porlock employed the same banal phrases?

"You are English?" he asked.

"Yes."

He spoke to me then in English. "You write yourself? Forgive my asking, but I do not know your name."

"Dunlop. But I don't write. I buy and sell wine."

"A profession more worthy of respect," M. Morin said. "If you would care to drive with me—I live only ten kilometres from here—I think I could show you a wine you may not have encountered."

"Surely it's rather late, M. Morin. And I have a driver . . ."

"Send him home. After Midnight Mass I find it difficult to sleep. You would be doing me a kindness." When I hesitated he said, "As for tomorrow, that is just any day of the year, and I don't like visitors."

I tried to make a joke of it. "You mean it's my only chance?" and he replied "Yes" with seriousness. The doors of the church swung open and the congregation came slowly out into the frosty glitter, pecking at the holy-water stoup with their forefingers, chatting cheerfully again as the mystery receded, greeting neighbours. A wailing child marked the lateness of the hour like a clock. M. Morin strode away and I followed him.

3

M. Morin drove with clumsy violence, wrenching at his gears, scraping the right-hand hedgerows as though the car were a new invention and he a courageous pioneer in its use. "So you have read some of my books?" he asked.

"A great many, when I was a schoolboy . . ."

"You mean they are fit only for children?"

"I mean nothing of the sort."

"What can a child find in them?"

"I was sixteen when I began to read them. That's not a child."

"Oh well, now they are only read by the old—and the pious. Are you pious, Mr. Dunlop?"

"I'm not a Catholic."

"I'm glad to hear that. Then I shan't offend you."

"Once I thought of becoming one."

"Second thoughts are best."

"I think it was your books that made me curious."

"I will not take responsibility," he said. "I am not a theologian." We bumped over a little branch railway track without altering speed and swerved right through a gateway much in need of repair. A light hanging in a porch shone on an open door.

"Don't you lock up," I asked him, "in these parts?"

He said, "Ten years ago—times were bad then—a hungry man was frozen to death near here on Christmas morning. He could find no one to open a door: there was a blizzard, but they were all at church. Come in," he said angrily from the porch; "are you looking round, making notes of how I live? Have you deceived me? Are you a journalist?"

If I had had my own car with me I would have driven away. "M. Morin," I said, "there are different kinds of hunger. You seem only to cater for one kind." He went ahead of me into a small study—a desk, a table, two comfortable chairs, and some bookshelves oddly bare—I could see no sign of his own books. There was a bottle of brandy on the table, ready perhaps for the stranger and the blizzard that would never again come together in this place.

"Sit down," he said, "sit down. You must forgive me if I was discourteous. I am unused to company. I will go and find the wine I spoke of.

Make yourself at home." I had never seen a man less at home himself. It was as if he were camping in a house that belonged to another.

While he was away, I looked more closely at his bookshelves. He had not rebound any of his paperbacks and his shelves had the appearance of bankrupt stock: small tears and dust and the discoloration of sunlight. There was a great deal of theology, some poetry, very few novels. He came back with the wine and a plate of salami. When he had tasted the wine himself, he poured me a glass. "It will do," he said.

"It's excellent. Remarkable."

"A small vineyard twenty miles away. I will give you the address before you go. For me, on a night like this, I prefer brandy." So perhaps it was really for himself and not for the stranger, I thought, that the bottle stood ready.

"It's certainly cold."

"It was not the weather I meant."

"I have been looking at your library. You read a lot of theology."

"Not now."

"I wonder if you would recommend . . ." But I had even less success with him than with the chaplain.

"No. Not if you want to believe. If you are foolish enough to want that you must avoid theology."

"I don't understand."

He said, "A man can accept anything to do with God until scholars begin to go into the details and the implications. A man can accept the Trinity, but the arguments that follow . . ." He gave a gesture of rejection. "I would never try to determine some point in differential calculus with a two-times-two table. You end by disbelieving the calculus." He poured out two more glasses and drank his as though it were vodka. "I used to believe in Revelation, but I never believed in the capacity of the human mind."

"You used to believe?"

"Yes, Mr. Dunlop—was that the name?—*used.* If you are one of those who come seeking belief, go away. You won't find it here."

"But from your books . . ."

"You will find none of them," he said, "on my shelves."

"I noticed you have some theology."

"Even disbelief," he said, with his eye on the brandy bottle, "needs bolstering somehow." I noticed that the brandy very quickly affected him, not only his readiness to communicate with me, but even the physical appearance of his eyeballs. It was as if the little blood-cells had been waiting under the white membrane to burst at once like buds with the third glass. He said, "Can you find anything more inadequate than the scholastic arguments for the existence of God?"

"I'm afraid I don't know them."

"The arguments from an agent, from a cause?"

"No."

"They tell you that in all change there are two elements, that which is changed and that which changes it. Each agent of change is itself determined by some higher agent. Can this go on *ad infinitum?* Oh no, they say, that would not give the finality that thought demands. But does thought demand it? Why shouldn't the chain go on forever? Man has invented the idea of infinity. In any case how trivial any argument based on what human thought demands must be. The thoughts of you and me and Monsieur Dupont. I would prefer the thoughts of an ape. Its instincts are less corrupted. Show me a gorilla praying and I might believe again."

"But surely there are other arguments?"

"Four. Each more inadequate than the other. It needs a child to say to these theologians, Why? Why not? Why not an infinite series of causes? Why should the existence of a good and a better imply the existence of a best? This is playing with words. We invent the words and make arguments from them. The better is not a fact: it is only a word and a human judgment."

"You are arguing," I said, "against someone who can't answer you back. You see, M. Morin, I don't believe either. I'm curious, that's all."

"Ah," he said, "you've said that before—curious. Curiosity is a great trap. They used to come here in their dozens to see me. I used to get letters saying how I had converted them by this book or that. Long after I ceased to believe myself I was a carrier of belief, as a man can be a carrier of disease without being sick. Women especially." He added with disgust, "I had only to sleep with a woman to make a convert." He turned his red eyes towards me and really seemed to require an answer when he said, "What sort of Rasputin life was that?" The brandy by now had really taken a hold; I wondered how many years he had been waiting for some stranger without faith to whom he could speak with frankness.

"Did you never tell this to a priest? I always imagined in your faith . . ."

"There were always too many priests," he said, "around me. The priests swarmed like flies. Near me and any woman I knew. First I was an exhibit for their faith. I was useful to them, a sign that even an intelligent man could believe. That was the period of the Dominicans, who liked the literary atmosphere and good wine. Then afterwards when the books stopped, and they smelt something—gamey—in my religion, it was the turn of the Jesuits, who never despair of what they call a man's soul."

"And why did the books stop?"

"Who knows? Did you never write verses for some girl when you were a boy?"

"Of course."

"But you didn't marry the girl, did you? The unprofessional poet writes of his feelings and when the poem is finished he finds his love dead on the page. Perhaps I wrote away my belief as the young man writes away his love. Only it took longer—twenty years and fifteen books." He held up the wine. "Another glass?"

"I would rather have some of your brandy." Unlike the wine it was a crude and common mark, and I thought again, For a beggar's sake or his own? I said, "All the same you go to Mass."

"I go to Midnight Mass on Christmas Eve," he said. "The worst of Catholics goes then—even those who do not go at Easter. It is the Mass of our childhood. And of mercy. What would they think if I were not there? I don't want to give scandal. You must realize I wouldn't speak to any one of my neighbours as I have spoken to you. I am their Catholic author, you see. Their Academician. I never wanted to help anyone to believe, but God knows I wouldn't take a hand in robbing them . . ."

"I was surprised at one thing when I saw you there, M. Morin."

"Yes?"

I said rashly, "You and I were the only ones who didn't take Communion."

"That is why I don't go to the church in my own village. That too would be noticed and cause scandal."

"Yes, I can see that." I stumbled heavily on (perhaps the brandy had affected me too). "Forgive me, M. Morin, but I wondered at your age what kept you from Communion. Of course now I know the reason."

"Do you?" Morin said. "Young man, I doubt it." He looked at me across his glass with impersonal enmity. He said, "You don't understand a thing I have been saying to you. What a story you would make of this if you were a journalist, and yet there wouldn't be a word of truth . . ."

I said stiffly, "I thought you made it perfectly clear that you had lost your faith."

"Do you think that would keep anyone from the confessional? You are a long way from understanding the Church or the human mind, Mr. Dunlop. Why, it is one of the most common confessions of all for a priest to hear—almost as common as adultery. 'Father, I have lost my faith.' The priest, you may be sure, makes it himself often enough at the altar before he receives the Host."

I said—I was angry in return now—"Then what keeps you away? Pride? One of your Rasputin women?"

"As you so rightly thought," he said, "women are no longer a problem at my age." He looked at his watch. "Two-thirty. Perhaps I ought to drive you back."

"No," I said, "I don't want to part from you like this. It's the drink that makes us irritable. Your books are still important to me. I know I am ignorant. I am not a Catholic and never shall be, but in the old days your books made me understand that at least it might be possible to believe. You never suddenly closed the door in my face as you are doing now. Nor did your characters, Durobier, Sagrin." I indicated the brandy bottle. "I told you just now—people are not only hungry and thirsty in that way. Because you've lost *your* faith . . ."

He interrupted me ferociously. "I never told you that."

"Then what have you been talking about all this time?"

"I told you I had lost my belief. That's quite a different thing. But how are you to understand?"

"You don't give me a chance."

He was obviously striving to be patient. He said, "I will put it this way. If a doctor prescribed you a drug and told you to take it every day for the rest of your life and you stopped obeying him and drank no more, and your health decayed, would you not have faith in your doctor all the more?"

"Perhaps. But I still don't understand you."

"For twenty years," Morin said, "I excommunicated myself voluntarily. I never went to Confession. I loved a woman too much to pretend to myself that I would ever leave her. You know the condition of absolution? A firm purpose of amendment. I had no such purpose. Five years ago my mistress died and my sex died with her."

"Then why couldn't you go back?"

"I was afraid. I am still afraid."

"Of what the priest would say?"

"What a strange idea you have of the Church. No, not of what the priest would say. He would say nothing. I dare say there is no greater gift you can give a priest in the confessional, Mr. Dunlop, than to return to it after many years. He feels of use again. But can't you understand? I can tell myself now that my lack of belief is a final proof that the Church is right and the faith is true. I had cut myself off for twenty years from grace and my belief withered as the priests said it would. I don't believe in God and His Son and His angels and His saints, but I know the reason why I don't believe and the reason is—the Church is true and what she taught me is true. For twenty years I have been without the sacraments and I can see the effect. The wafer must be more than wafer."

"But if you went back . . ."

"If I went back and belief did not return? That is what I fear, Mr. Dunlop. As long as I keep away from the sacraments, my lack of belief is an argument for the Church. But if I returned and they failed me, then I would really be a man without faith, who had better hide himself quickly in the grave so as not to discourage others." He laughed uneasily. "Paradoxical, Mr. Dunlop?"

"That is what they said of your books."

"I know."

"Your characters carried their ideas to extreme lengths. So your critics said."

"And you think I do too?"

"Yes, M. Morin."

His eyes wouldn't meet mine. He grimaced beyond me. "At least I am not a carrier of disease any longer. You have escaped infection." He added, "Time for bed, Mr. Dunlop. Time for bed. The young need more sleep."

"I am not as young as that."

"To me you seem very young."

He drove me back to my hotel and we hardly spoke. I was thinking of the strange faith which held him even now after he had ceased to believe. I had felt very little curiosity since that moment of the war when I had spoken to the chaplain, but now I began to wonder again. M. Morin considered he had ceased to be a carrier, and I couldn't help hoping that he was right. He had forgotten to give me the address of the vineyard, but I had forgotten to ask him for it when I said good night.

MORLEY CALLAGHAN

Absolution

For years Jennie Hughes had been a steady customer at Jeremiah Mallory's bar. She was a woman about forty-five years old, the wife of a lawyer who had abandoned her ten years ago, but who still sent her a little money to pay for her room and liquor. At one time she had been active and shapely; now she was rather slow and stout and her cheeks were criss-crossed with fine transparent veins. When she had first come to the neighbourhood people called her Mrs. Hughes, but now everybody just called her Jennie.

In the bar she used to sit by herself with an air of great gentility at a table opposite the bar, when she didn't have enough money to pay for a bottle to take home. Her gentility was perhaps most obvious when she was not quite sober, and if anybody in her street disturbed her at such a time, she was apt to yell and scream at the top of her voice. Neighbours, who at one time had felt sorry for her, were now anxious to have her move away. Jennie's landlady, Mrs. Turner, had been trying for two months to get rid of her, but Mrs. Turner had been unfortunate enough to try to argue the question when Jennie was tipsy.

One night Jennie was wondering if Jerry Mallory would give her any more whiskey on credit. For two weeks she hadn't paid him. She had been drinking mildly in the afternoon and now felt it necessary to have a bottle for Sunday. There were only about two fingers in the bottle left standing on the bureau. She began to put on her hat and look at herself in the mirror. Though she was aware that styles changed, she didn't seem to be able to keep up with them; now she was wearing a short skirt when everybody else was wearing their dresses long, and two years ago she had worn a long dress when other women were wearing skimpy short skirts. She was looking at herself with approval when she heard somebody coming up the stairs. Turning, and staring at the door, for she expected her landlady, Mrs. Turner, to appear, she thrust her chin out angrily. "Come in," she called out when there was a knock on the door.

A huge man over six feet came in, a great big serious-looking priest with thin gray hair, a large red face, and a tiny nose. "Good evening, Mrs. Hughes," he said politely without smiling.

"Good evening, father," Jennie said. She had never seen the man before and she began to feel uneasy. She was actually beginning to feel nervous and ashamed of herself for some reason as she looked guiltily at the bottle on the bureau. She said suddenly, and shrewdly: "Did somebody send you here, father?"

"Now never mind that," the priest said sternly. "It's enough that I'm here and you can thank God that I came." He was an old, serious, unsentimental priest who was not at all impressed by the fawning smile and the little bow she made for him. Shaking his head to show his disgust with her, he said flatly: "Mrs. Hughes, there's nothing more degrading in this world than a tipsy woman. A drunken man, Lord knows, is bad enough, but a drunken woman is somehow lower than a beast in the field."

Jennie's pride was hurt, and she said angrily, without inviting him to sit down: "Who sent you here? Who sent you here to butt into my business? Tell me that."

"Now listen to me, Mrs. Hughes. It's time someone brought you to your senses."

"You don't know me. I don't know you," Jennie said abruptly.

"I know all about you. I know that you ought to be looking after your two children instead of having them in orphanages. But I'm not going to argue with you. I want to give you a very solemn warning. If you don't change your life you'll go straight to hell."

"You leave me alone, do you hear? Go on away," Jennie said.

"And I'll tell you this," he said, bending close to her and lifting his finger. "If you were to die at this moment and I were asked to give you absolution I doubt if my conscience would permit me to do it. Now for God's sake, woman, straighten up. Go to church. Go this night to confession and ask God to forgive you. Promise me you'll go to confession. At one time you must have been a decent Catholic woman. Promise me."

"You can't force me to do anything I don't want to do. I know. It was that Mrs. Turner that sent you here. I'll fix her. And don't you butt in either," Jennie said.

The big priest looked at her coolly, nodded his head with a kind of final and savage warning, and went out without saying another word.

As a defiant gesture Jennie drained the last inch of whiskey from the bottle and muttered: "Trying to drive me to confession, eh?" But she felt she was too much of a sporting lady to waste time sympathizing with herself. Making up her mind to abuse Mrs. Turner as soon as she saw her, she decided to go over to Jeremiah Mallory's bar at once.

That extra drink of whiskey had made Jennie tipsy, and as she remembered that the old priest had said she would go to hell when she died, she felt like crying. The priest, who had looked at her as if he had wanted to shake her, had half-pleased her by saying so bluntly that at one time she must have been a very good woman. With a serious expression on her face she walked along the lighted street, a stout woman in a short skirt leaning forward a bit, her wide velvet hat too far back on her head. Groping in her listless memory, she tried to remember the faces of her two children, a boy and a girl, but she hardly seemed to know them. The priest had aroused in her an uneasy longing for a time she was hardly able to remember, a time when she had dressed well, gone to church, and gone to confession, too, when she was a much younger woman.

Approaching the bar, whose drawn blinds concealed the light inside, she wondered what she might say to Mallory to persuade him she intended to pay at the end of the month. The door-keeper who let her in nodded familiarly without speaking and she went through to the lighted bar-room. No one paid any attention to her. Men and women were standing at the bar, sitting at the tables by the door, or at the small tables opposite the bar. Jennie sat down by herself at an empty table from where she could see Jerry himself, clean-shaven and neat in his blue suit, standing behind the bar, smiling affably at everybody and sometimes helping the busy young man, Henry, to pass out the drinks.

Finally Henry, looking competent with his sleeves rolled up and his bow-tie, came over to Jennie and said: "Hello, Jennie, what'll it be tonight?" He spoke as if he didn't believe there would be anything for Jennie.

"I'd like a little gin, to take out with me," she said soothingly. "Only about a quart. And tell Jerry I'll fix it up with him next week. How are you, Henry?" She hoped he could see how nicely she was smiling.

"I don't know, Jennie," he said doubtfully.

"Look here, you know I'll pay at the end of the month," she said gently.

"It's like this," Henry said pleasantly. "I'd do it. You know that. But the boss won't let me."

"Then let me speak to Jerry," she said brusquely.

In a moment Henry returned and said: "Jerry's awfully busy right now, Jennie. Maybe some other time . . ."

"I'll sit here and wait," Jennie said firmly, folding her arms. "I'll sit right here till doomsday and wait."

"All right. But he's awfully busy. He may not come."

Jennie waited and felt alone at her table, in a little alcove, and nobody paid any attention to her. She felt tired. Many thoughts and images drifted through her head. As she crossed her legs at the ankles and put her head back against the wall, she felt drowsy and dizzy. "I oughtn't to have taken that last drink before coming here," she thought. She tried to keep awake by muttering: "That old priest couldn't scare me, bless him," but she went on having the most disconnected thoughts about Eastertime and choir music. Soon she fell sound asleep, breathing steadily.

She began to breathe so heavily that customers at the bar, turning, snickered. Looking over at her, Jerry Mallory frowned irritably. She was an old, though difficult, customer, so he went over to her with a business-like air and shook her shoulder lightly. She stirred, waking. It had been very strong in her thoughts that the old priest had wanted her to go to confession and now, only half-awake, she mumbled uneasily: "Bless me, father, for I have sinned."

"Hey, Jennie, where do you think you are? Bless you, bless you, old girl," he said, starting to laugh.

"Eh, eh? Oh, it's you, Jerry. I forgot where I was."

She was wide awake now, and so sober that he thought she might have been deliberately kidding him. He laughed loudly. "You're a card, Jennie!" he said. "You're a grand old gal. And I'll get you a little gin for old times' sake."

He turned and said to the three men at the bar who were nearest to him: "Did you hear what Jennie just pulled on me?"

Jennie's face was hot and ashamed. Breathing irregularly, she stood up, in her skirt that was too short, with her black velvet hat too far back on her head. The men started to laugh mildly. Then they started to laugh louder and louder. The sound of their laughter at first made Jennie angry, with something of a fine woman's disgust and anger, and then, with humility, she felt herself reaching out gropingly toward a faintly remembered dignity. Erect, she walked out.

JOSEPHINE JACOBSEN

Jack Frost

Mrs. Travis was drinking a sturdy cup of tea. She sat in the wicker rocker on her back porch, in a circle of sun, after picking Mrs. James her flowers. Exhausted, she felt a little tired, and she rested with satisfaction. Mrs. James's motley bouquet sat by her knee, in one of the flower tins.

Mrs. Travis wore a blue cotton dress with a man's suitcoat over it, and around that a tie, knotted for a belt. Her legs were bare, but her small feet had on them a pair of child's galoshes, the sort that have spring buckles. Since several springs were missing, she wore the galoshes open, and sometimes they impeded her.

Half of her back porch, the left-hand side, was clear, and held her wicker rocker with its patches of sprung stiff strands; but the other half was more fruitful, a great pile of possessions which she needed, or had needed, or in certain possible circumstances might come to need: a tin foot-tub containing rope, twine, and a nest of tin containers from the insides of flower baskets; a hatchet; a galosh for the right foot; garden tools; a rubber mat; a beekeeper's helmet for the black-fly season. Near by, a short length of hose; chunks of wood. The eye flagged before the count.

There was a small winding path, like the witch's in a fairy tale, between cosmos so tall they brushed the shoulders. To its right almost immediately, vegetables grew: the feathery tops of carrots, dusty beet-greens, a few handsome mottled zucchini, the long runners of beans. Last year there had still been tomatoes, but the staking-up and coaxing had become too much; she said to herself instead that such finicking had come to bore her. To the left of the cosmos, below a small slope of scratchy lawn, was the garden proper—on this mellow September afternoon a fine chaos of unchosen color, the Mexican shades of zinnias, the paper-cutout heads of dahlias, a few grownover roses, more cosmos, the final spikes of some fine gladioli, phlox running heavily back to magenta, and closer to the cooling ground, the pink and purple of asters. There were even a few pansies, wildly persisting in a tangle of grass and weeds.

Until a few years ago her younger brother Henry had driven over two hundred miles, up from Connecticut, to help her plant both gardens, but Henry had died at eighty-two. Mrs. Travis herself did not actually know how old she was. She believed herself to be ninety-three; but having several years ago gone suddenly to check the fact of the matter in the faint gray handwriting of her foxed Bible, a cup of strong tea in her hand, she had sloshed the tea as she peered, and then on the puffed, run surface, she could no longer read the final digit. 3? 7? 1883? Just possibly, 1887? For a moment she felt youth pressing on her; if it were, if it possibly were 1887, several years had lifted themselves off. There they were, still to come with all the variety of their days. Turn those to hours, those to minutes, and it was a gigantic fresh extension. But she thought the figure was a 3. It was the last time she looked in the back of the Bible.

Tacked onto the porch wall was a large calendar; each day past was circled in red. Only three such showed; she would circle September 4th when she closed the door for the night.

Now before she could swallow the last of her tea, here came Mrs. James's yellow sweater, borne on a bicycle along the dirt road outside the hedge. Dismounted, Mrs. James wheeled the bicycle up the path and leaned it against the porch post. She was sweaty with effort over the baked ridges of the road, and, half a century younger than her hostess, she radiated summer-visitor energy and cheer.

"Oh Mrs. Travis!" she cried. "You've got them all ready! Aren't they lovely!" She was disappointed, since she had hoped to choose the picking; but she and her summer friends regarded Mrs. Travis's activity as much like that of Dr. Johnson's dog walking on its hind legs.

Mrs. Travis looked with satisfaction at the jumble of phlox, gladioli, dahlias, and zinnias which, with all the slow, slow bending and straightening, had cost her an hour.

"Oh, it's so *warm,*" said Mrs. James with pleasure, sitting down on the step at Mrs. Travis's feet.

Mrs. Travis had so few occasions to speak that it always seemed to take her a minute to call up her voice, which arrived faint with distance. "Yes," she said, almost inaudibly. "It's a very good day."

"Oh look!" said Mrs. James, pleased. "Look how well the rose begonia's doing!" She had given it to Mrs. Travis early in the summer, it was one of her own bulbs from California, and she could see its full gorgeousness now, blooming erratically beside the path, hanging its huge rosy bloom by the gap-toothed rake and a tiny pile of debris, twigs, dead grass, a few leaves.

Mrs. Travis did not answer, but Mrs. James saw it was because she was looking at the begonia's gross beauty with a powerful smugness. They sat companionably for a moment. Mrs. James seemed to Mrs. Travis like one of the finches, or yellow-headed sparrows, which frequented her for the warmest weeks. Exactly as she thought so, Mrs. James said, suddenly sad, "Do you know the birds are all going, *already?*"

"No, not all," said Mrs. Travis soothingly. "The chickadees won't go." But Mrs. Travis did not really care; it was the flowers she created out of nothing.

"I hate to see them go so soon," said Mrs. James, stubbornly sad.

"But you'll be going too," said Mrs. Travis, faintly and comfortingly. Mrs. James, lifting her chin, looked at Mrs. Travis. "Are you going to stay here all winter, *again?*" she asked.

Mrs. Travis looked at her with stupefaction. Then she said, "Yes." She was afraid Mrs. James was going to repeat what she had said for the past two autumns, about Mrs. Travis moving into the village for the winter; here she was, no phone, no close neighbors; nothing but snow, and ice, and wind, and the grocery boy with his little bag, and the mailman's Pontiac passing without stopping. But Mrs. James said only, "Look, here comes Father O'Rourke."

There was the clap of a car door, and Father O'Rourke appeared between the cosmos, surprisingly wearing his dog collar, his black coat slung over his white shoulder. Mrs. James stood up, pleased that Mrs. Travis had a visitor. "I've got to get these flowers back," she said. Now came the embarrassing moment. "How—er, they're so lovely; what . . . ?"

"That's three dollars for the pailful," said Mrs. Travis with satisfaction. Mrs. James, whose grandmother, as a little girl, had known Mrs. Travis in Boston, continued to feel, no matter what she paid, that the flowers had come as a gift from Mrs. Travis's conservatory. She laid three dollars inconspicuously on the table by the oil lamp, and Mrs. Travis watched her and Father O'Rourke saying hello, and good-bye for the winter, to each other in the hot slanting sun.

As Mrs. James wheeled her bicycle away, Father O'Rourke replaced her on the step. He did not offer to shake hands, having noticed that such gestures seemed to distract Mrs. Travis, as some sort of clumsy recollected maneuver. He had just come from making the final plans for the Watkins wedding, and, fresh from all that youth and detail, he looked at Mrs. Travis, whose pale small blue eyes looked back at him, kindly, but from a long distance. The purpose of Father O'Rourke's visit embarrassed him; he was afraid of Mrs. Travis's iron will.

"What a lot of flowers you've still got," began Father O'Rourke, obliquely.

Mrs. Travis looked out over the ragged rainbow on the slope. The sun, at its western angle, was still a good bit above the smaller of the big dark mountains behind which it would go. "Oh yes," she said, "they'll be here for a long time. A couple of weeks, probably." He saw that she meant just that.

"Well," he said, "you know, Mrs. Travis, after five years here, I've found we just don't know. Things may go on almost to October; and then, again, a night in late August will do it."

Mrs. Travis did not reply to this, and Father O'Rourke plunged. "I saw Mrs. Metcalfe at the post office this morning," he said, looking placatingly at Mrs. Travis's profile. "Did you know that she's finished making that big sitting-room off her south porch into that little apartment she's going to rent out?"

Mrs. Travis, who had had enough of this for one day, indeed for one lifetime, turned her head and looked him straight in his hazel eye.

"I'm not going anywhere," she said, surprisingly loudly, adding, from some past constraint, "Father O'Rourke."

A final sense of the futility of his effort struck him silent. They sat quietly for a few seconds. What on earth am I trying to do? he thought suddenly. Why *should* she move? Well, so many reasons; he wondered if they were all worthless. He knew that before he was born, Mrs. Travis had enlisted in the army of eccentric hermits, isolates, writing their own terms into some curious treaty. But she was so much older than anyone

else that the details became more and more obscure; also, more roman-
ticized. There was even doubt as to a dim and distant husband. A fallen
or faithless lover appeared, along with factual but tinted tales of early
privilege. But the Miss Havisham motif he tended to discount; it was so
widely beloved.

All he knew for certain was that, with Mrs. Travis, he was in the
presence of an authenticity of elimination which caused him a curiously
mingled horror and envy. At times he thought that her attention,
fiercely concentrated, brought out, like a brilliant detail from an immense canvas, a quality of some nonverbal and passionate comprehen-
sion. At other times he saw a tremendously old woman, all nuances of
the world, her past, and the earth's present, ignored or forgotten; brittle
and single, everything rejected but her own tiny circle of motion.

With a fairly complex mind, Father O'Rourke combined a rather
simple set of hopes, not many of which were realized. One of these was
to enter Mrs. Travis's detail, as some sort of connection with a comfort,
or even a lack of finality. The bond between them, actually, was a belief
in the physical, a conviction of the open-ended mystery of matter. But
since Mrs. Travis had never been a Catholic, that particular avenue
wasn't open to him. Her passion was in this scraggy garden, but he
distinguished that it was coldly unsentimental, unlike that of most lady
gardeners he knew. He was not sure just how Mrs. Travis did feel about
her flowers. He considered that, in homily and metaphor, the garden
thing—Eden to Gethsemane—had been overdone; nevertheless, in connection with Mrs. Travis, he always thought of it. He had, on a previous
visit last month, brought up some flower passages from the Bible; but
the only interest she had shown was by a question as to which type of
lily the lilies of the field had been. She had at least five kinds, lifting
their slick and sappy stalks above confusion. But when he had said they
were most like anemones, she had lost interest, having forgotten, after
fifty years in the New Hampshire mountains, what anemones looked
like.

"I have to go back to the Watkinses again tomorrow," said Father
O'Rourke. He knew he should have been back at the rectory half an
hour ago. Here he sat, mesmerized somehow by the invisible movement
of the sun across the step, by the almost total stillness. It was cooling
rapidly, too. He picked up his coat and hunched his arms into it. "Can I
bring you anything, then?"

"No," she said. She was sorry to see him go. She turned her head to look fully at him. "Do you want any flowers?" she asked.

He hesitated, thinking of Mrs. Metcalfe's pious arrangement, three pink gladioli in a thin-stemmed glass on each side of the altar. "Well," he said, "how about some zinnias for my desk? I'll pick them tomorrow," he added hastily, as he saw her eyes cloud, rallying for action. On the step he lingered, smiling at her. Oppressed. "Well," he said idiotically, "don't let Jack Frost get your flowers."

She watched him attentively down the path. Just as his starter churned, the sun left the porch and, looking up to the mountain, Mrs. Travis saw that it had gone for the day.

She went in at once, forgetting her rake, lying in the garden, her empty teacup and the three dollars on the table, but carrying a short chunk of wood under each arm. She took at least one each time she went into the house. She never turned on the furnace before October, but there was a small chunk stove in the corner, by the lamp table, and it warmed the room in a matter of minutes. She decided to have supper right now. She had a chop; and there was still some lettuce. She had picked a fine head this morning, it was right in the colander, earth still clinging to its bottom.

By eight o'clock it had got very cold, outside. But the room was warm. Mrs. Travis went to sleep in her chair. Sleep often took her now with a ferocious touch, so that everything just disappeared, and when she woke up, she found that hours had passed. On a warm night in July she had slept in her chair all night long, waking up, disoriented, to a watery dawn.

Now she not only slept, she dreamed. An unpleasant dream, something extremely unusual. She was in a dark huge city lit by thin lamps, and she was afraid. She was afraid of a person, who might be coming toward her, or coming up behind her. And yet, more than a person—though she knew it was a man in a cap. She must get into a house before he found her. Or before he found someone else. A strange-looking girl went by her, hurrying, very pale, with a big artificial rose in her hair. She turned suddenly into an opening on the dreamer's right; it was the darkest of alleys and the dreamer hurried faster than ever. Ahead of her, in the fog, she could see the dimly lit sign of an inn, but as she hurried faster, a terrible scream, high and short, came out of the alley. It woke Mrs. Travis, her hands locked hard on the arms of the chair.

She sat quite still, looking around the familiar room. Then memory handed her one of the clear messages that now so seldom arrived. The Lodger. That was just it. She had suddenly, after all these years, had a dream about Jack the Ripper, as she had had several times when she first read of his foggy city streets a very long time ago. But why this dream should have escaped from the past to molest her, she could not think.

The little fire in the stove was out, but the stove itself still ticked and settled with heat. The wall clock said two minutes to eight. Stiff from sleep, Mrs. Travis reached over and turned the dial of the small discolored radio under the table lamp, and immediately a loud masculine voice said, ". . . front, all the way from the Great Lakes, throughout northern New England, and into Canada. Frost warnings have been issued for the mountain areas of Vermont and New Hampshire. Tomorrow the unseasonable cold will continue, for a chilly Labor Day; but by Wednesday . . ." Appalled, Mrs. Travis switched off the evil messenger.

Frost. It was not that it was so strange; it was so sudden. She could still feel the heat of the sun, on the porch, on her hands and her ankles. Two weeks, she had thought.

As she sat, staring for a moment straight ahead, a brand-new fury started up, deep inside her. Two weeks. It was an eternity of summer. The long nights, the brutal chill, the endless hardness of the earth, they were reasonable enough, in their time. In their time. But this was her time, and they were about to invade it. She began to tremble with anger. She thought of her seeds, and how dry and hard they had been; of her deathlike bulbs, slipping old skin, with everything locked inside them, and she, her body, had turned them into that summer of color and softness and good smells that was out there in the dark garden.

She turned her head, right, and left, looking for an exit for her rage. Then suddenly she sat forward in her chair. An idea had come to her with great force and clarity. It grew in the room, like an enormous plant covered with buds. Mrs. Travis knew exactly what she was going to do. Her intention was not protective, but defiant; her sense was of battle, punitive battle.

She stood up carefully, and went and got the flashlight from the shelf over the woodbox. She went to the porch door and opened it, and then closed it hastily behind her, protecting the room's warmth. There was no sound or light in any direction, but there was a diffused brightness behind the mountain's darker bulk. She tipped over the pail that had held Mrs. James's flowers, so that the leafy water poured down the sloping porch. Then she began fitting the tin flower-holders into it. She could not get them all in, and she took her pail into the house and came back for the last three. She arranged the pail and the tins on the kitchen floor, and then she attached a short length of hose to the cold-water spigot, dropped the other end in the pail, and turned on the water. She filled the big tins the same way, and then lifted the small ones into the sink, removing the hose, and filled them. Turning with satisfaction to look through the doorway at the clock, she was disconcerted to see that it said five minutes after nine. She stared at it, skeptical but uncertain. It could *stop;* but surely it couldn't skip *ahead.* Perhaps she had mistaken the earlier time. She began to move more rapidly; though she was so excited, all her faculties had come so strongly into one intention, that it seemed to her that she was already moving at a furious pace.

She went over to the kitchen door and took off its hook a felt hat and an ancient overcoat of Henry's. She put the hat on her head, got carefully into the overcoat and stuffed her flashlight into the pocket. She took down from the top of the refrigerator a cracked papier-mâché tray Mrs. James had sent her several Christmases ago; its design of old coins had almost disappeared. At an open drawer she hesitated over a pair of shears. Lately she had found them hard to open and close, and after standing there for half a minute, she took a thick-handled knife instead. She went to look at the empty sitting room and then moved back through the kitchen faster than seemed possible.

Out on the porch, a square of light came through the window, and looking up, she could make out a cloud over the mountain, its edges stained with brightness.

She lit her flashlight, and went cautiously down the step and along the path, carrying her tray under her arm. Faces of cosmos, purple and pink, loomed at her as she went, but even in her tremendous excitement, she knew she couldn't bring in everything, and she went on, the tops of her galoshes making a little flapping noise in the silence. She turned carefully down the slight slope, and here were the zinnias, towered over by the branchy dahlias. She laid her tray on the ground.

But now, breathing more rapidly, she saw that she was in trouble. To cut with her knife, she had to hold the flower's stem, and she had to hold her flashlight to see it, and she had two hands. Fiercely she looked about for an idea; and at just that moment, a clear thin light streamed over the edge of the cloud and lit her. The moon was full. She might have known; that was when a black frost always came.

Mrs. Travis made an inarticulate sound of fierce pleasure and dropped the flashlight into the tray. Then she began to cut the flowers, working as fast as she could, giving little pants of satisfaction as the shapes heaped themselves up below her. Inch by inch she moved along the ragged rows, pushing, with a galoshed toe, the tray along the ground before her. She cut all the gladioli, even the ones which were still mostly flaccid green tips; she cut all the dahlias, even the buds, and every zinnia. She felt light and warm, and drunk with resistant power. Finally the tray was so full that blooms began to tip over and fall into the cold grass.

Very cautiously indeed she got the tray up, but she could not hold it level and manipulate the flashlight. It made no difference. The moon, enormous and fully round, had laid light all over the garden; the house's shadow was black, as though a pale sun were shining.

Teetering a little to hold the tray level, Mrs. Travis went up the path, carefully up the step. She set the tray on the table, knocking over her dirty teacup and saucer, and each broke cleanly in two pieces. She stepped over them, opened the door on warmth, and went back for her load.

First she filled the pail; then every tin. There was a handful of zinnias left, and a pile of phlox. Threatened, Mrs. Travis looked about the kitchen, but saw nothing helpful. She could feel her cheeks burning in the room's summer, and with a little noise of triumph, she went through the door to the bedroom and came back with the big china chamberpot. It had a fine network of fractured veins, and on it was a burst of painted magenta foliage. When she had filled it under the tap it was too heavy to lift down, so she stuffed in the flowers and left it there. A small chartreuse-colored spider began to run up and down the sink's edge.

Then, just as she was turning to look at all she had done, like a cry from an alley, like a blow between the shoulders, to her mind's eye came the rose begonia. She could positively see in the air before her its ruffled heavy head, the coral flush of its crowded petals; from its side sprang the bud, color splitting the sheath. The bulb had thrust it up, and there it was, out there.

Though she felt as though she were drunk, she also felt shrewd. Think of the low ones you can't stoop to tonight, she thought, the nasturtiums, the pansies, the bachelor's buttons, the ragged robins. But it made no difference. She knew that unless she took the rose begonia, she had lost everything. She looked at the clock; it was half past ten. She could be back in ten minutes; and she decided that then she would sit right down by the stove and sleep there, deliberately, and not move into the cold bed and take off bit by bit so many clothes.

There were four sticks of wood by the stove, and under the lid the embers were bright. She put in three sticks; then she went empty-handed to the porch. It was very cold and absolutely still. The moon was even brighter; it was almost halfway up the sky. She found a terra-cotta flowerpot on the porch corner, and she rooted in the footbath until she found her trowel. Then she went, as fast as she could go, down the path to the halfway point, where she came upon the rose begonia, paled by the chill of the light. As she bent over, her head roared; so she kneeled, and drove the blunt trowel-edge into the earth.

When the roots came up in a great ball of earth she pressed them into the pot, stuffing more clods of fibrous earth around them. Then she started to get up. But with the pot in one hand and the trowel in the other, it was impossible.

She dropped the trowel. She did not even think that she could get it tomorrow. Suddenly she was cold to her very teeth. She thought just of the room, the hot, colored, waiting room. Holding the pot in her left hand, pushing with her right, she got herself upright; but it made her dizzy, and as she lurched a little to the side the rake's teeth brought her down in a heavy fall. The flower shot from her hand and disappeared into the shadows and a bright strong pain blasted her. It was her ankle; and she lay with her face close to the cold dirt, feeling the waves of pain hit her.

Mrs. Travis raised her head, to see how far away the porch was. It was perhaps ten or eleven yards. Another country. Things seemed dimmer, too, and wrenching her head sideways and up, she saw that the huge moon had shrunk; it sat high and small, right at the top of the sky.

Mrs. Travis lowered her head gently and began to crawl, pushing with her hands and the knee of her good leg. She went along, inch by inch, foot by foot; she had no fear, since there was an absolute shield between one second and the next.

The porch was so shadowed now that she nearly missed it, the step struck her advancing hand. It took her three tries, but she got up over it, and went on, inch by inch, toward the door. A sliver of china bit her hand. Bright light came through the keyhole. She reached up and easily turned the doorknob, then like a crab she was across the sill.

She could not, she found, turn; but she pushed out with her left foot, and miraculously the door clicked shut just behind her. She felt no pain at all, but there was something forming under her ribs.

In the room's heat, the foliage of the marigolds gave out a spicy smell, stronger than the fragrance of the phlox. A dozen shapes and colors blazed before her eyes, and a great tearing breath came up inside her like an explosion. Mrs. Travis lifted her head, and the whole wave of summer, advancing obedient and glorious, in a crest of color and warmth and fragrance broke right over her.

Profiles of the Authors

HEINRICH BÖLL was born on December 21, 1917, into a Catholic family of leftist and pacifist sympathies in Cologne, Germany. Anti-Nazi feelings were strong in his family, but he was conscripted into the German Army and served from 1939 to 1945, when he was captured by the Americans. His first collection of stories, *The Train Was On Time,* appeared in 1949, and his first novel, *And Where Were You, Adam?,* in 1951. Before his death in 1985, Böll published scores of stories and a dozen novels as well as plays and essays. Although he refused to declare himself a Catholic on government tax forms, he always maintained his allegiance to the church and explored religious questions in his writing. Böll won the Nobel Prize for Literature in 1972.

MORLEY CALLAGHAN was born on September 22, 1903, in Toronto. In the eighty-three years since then he has become Canada's premier man of letters writing in English, prolific both as a short story writer and as a novelist. His novels include *Such Is My Beloved* (1934), *A Many Coloured Coat* (1960), and *Close to the Sun Again* (1977). Ironically, he is perhaps best known in the United States as the author of a memoir of Hemingway and Fitzgerald, *That Summer in Paris* (1963). Writing in 1965, Edmund Wilson described Callaghan as "today, perhaps the most unjustly neglected novelist in the English-speaking world." He has received several prestigious Canadian awards for literature.

ELIZABETH CULLINAN was born on June 7, 1933, in New York City. She received her education at Marymount College. In addition to her two novels, *House of Gold* (1970) and *A Change of Scene* (1982), Cullinan has published two collections of short stories: *The Time of Adam* (1971) and *Yellow Roses* (1977). Most of the stories appeared originally in *The New Yorker,* to which she continues to contribute. Commenting on her intelligence and craftsmanship as well as on her precise attention to domestic detail, Joyce Carol Oates remarked, "It takes immense skill, after all, to deal with trivia and escape becoming trivial."

ANDRE DUBUS was born in Lake Charles, Louisiana, on August 11, 1936. After serving in the Marines, which he left as a captain in 1964, he took an M.F.A.

degree in writing at the University of Iowa in 1966 and subsequently taught at Bradford College in Massachusetts. His first novel, *The Lieutenant,* appeared in 1967, and since that time he has published four collections of stories: *Separate Flights* (1975), *Adultery and Other Choices* (1977), *Finding a Girl in America* (1980), and *The Times Are Never So Bad* (1983), from which "A Father's Story" is taken. His second novel, *Voices from the Moon,* appeared in 1984. Critics have commented both on the spareness of Dubus's prose ("a rigorous paring-back, a concern for what is implied rather than what is stated") and on the luminous effects of his commitment to realism ("the equivalent of Hopper landscapes, anywhere in small town America").

STUART DYBEK was born on April 10, 1942, in Chicago, where he attended Loyola University, earning a bachelor's degree in 1964 and a master's in 1967. He received his M.F.A. degree in writing from the University of Iowa in 1973. Dybek has published a collection of poems, *Brass Knuckles* (1979), and a collection of short stories, *Childhood and Other Neighborhoods* (1980). His remarks about the connection between these two books apply as well to the short story in this anthology, which appeared first in *Antaeus* and was chosen as co-winner of first prize in *Prize Stories 1985: The O. Henry Awards:* "My first two books, though written in different genres, attempt to evoke the same world. Both the poems and stories combine naturalism with the fantastic; both are urban, set in Chicago." Dybek teaches at Western Michigan University in Kalamazoo.

SHUSAKU ENDO was born in Tokyo on March 27, 1923. He graduated with a degree in French literature from Keio University and then studied for several years in Lyon. Endo's many novels have received both popular acclaim and numerous literary awards in his native Japan. More recently, he has received international attention as his works have been translated into more than a dozen languages. In 1970 he received the Santo Silvestri award from Pope Paul VI. Reviewing *Silence,* Endo's best-known novel, Anthony Thwaite touched on a central theme of his work: "What interests Mr. Endo—to the point of obsession—are the concerns of both the sacred and the secular realms: moral choice, moral responsibility."

MARY GORDON was born on Long Island, New York, on December 8, 1949. She did her undergraduate work at Barnard College, receiving a B.A. in 1971. She subsequently took a master's degree in writing from the University of Syracuse in 1973. She is the author of three novels, *Final Payments* (1978), *The Company of Women* (1981), and *Men and Angels* (1985), each of which has been in varying degrees both a critical and a commercial success. She has been called "her generation's preeminent novelist of Roman Catholic mores and manners" by Francine du Plessix Gray. She has also published essays and stories in various journals and magazines; a collection of the stories is in preparation.

GRAHAM GREENE was born in Berkhamsted, England, on October 2, 1904. He studied at Balliol College, Oxford, and received his B.A. degree in 1925. In the ensuing six decades, he has worked as a journalist, a film critic, a literary editor, and a director of a publishing house. But his principal work has been that of a novelist, short story writer, and playwright, to all of which forms he has contributed generously. Among his awards have been the Hawthornden Prize for *The Power and the Glory* (1940), and the James Tait Black Memorial Prize for *The Heart of the Matter* (1948); most recently he was named to the exclusive Order of Merit by Queen Elizabeth II. Many readers and critics consider him to be the greatest living writer in English.

JOSEPHINE JACOBSEN was born in Cobourg, Ontario, on August 19, 1908. Her schooling was largely by private tutors in Baltimore, where she still makes her home. She has published several collections of poetry, including *For the Unlost* (1946), *The Shade Seller* (1974), and *The Chinese Insomniacs* (1981). She served as the poetry consultant at the Library of Congress from 1971 to 1973 and remains a consultant in American letters. Her short stories have appeared in both *The Best American Short Stories* and *O. Henry Prize Stories* annual anthologies, and have been collected in *A Walk with Raschid* (1978); a second collection is in preparation.

JOHN L'HEUREUX was born on October 26, 1934, in South Hadley, Massachusetts. He attended Holy Cross College, whence he entered the Society of Jesus in 1954, remaining until 1971. He has been a contributing editor to *The Atlantic* and a visiting professor at Tufts and Harvard. He is currently Lane Professor in the Humanities at Stanford University. His published writings include collections of poetry: *Quick as Dandelions* (1964), *Rubrics for a Revolution* (1967), *One Eye and a Measuring Rod* (1968), *No Place for Hiding* (1971); two novels: *Tight White Collar* (1972), *The Clang Birds* (1972); and two collections of short stories, *Family Affairs* (1974) and *Desires* (1981).

BERNARD MACLAVERTY was born in Northern Ireland in 1942. He has published two collections of short stories, *Secrets and Other Stories* (1977) and *A Time to Dance* (1982), and two novels, *Lamb* (1980) and *Cal* (1983). In a general comment on his writing, which certainly applies to "The Beginnings of a Sin" in this collection, Deirdre Donahue has remarked, "The theme of knowledge blasting innocence runs throughout MacLaverty's work."

FRANÇOIS MAURIAC was born on October 11, 1885, in Bordeaux, France. He received his degree from the University of Bordeaux and began his writing career as a journalist in 1908, an occupation he returned to intermittently throughout his life, especially during the Second World War as his contribution to the Resistance. He is best known, however, as a novelist, with a special skill in delineating psychological and religious motivation. These novels include *Thérèse Desqueyroux* (1927), *Viper's Tangle* (1932), *A Woman of the Pharisees* (1941), *The Lamb* (1954). Like Graham Greene, he preferred to describe himself not as "a Catholic novelist," but as a novelist who is a Catholic. He received the Nobel Prize for Literature in 1952.

JOHN McGAHERN was born in Dublin on November 12, 1934, but raised in County Roscommon in the west of Ireland. He studied at St. Patrick's Training College in Drumcondra, and at University College, Dublin. He subsequently taught at a boys' school for seven years until his first novel, *The Barracks,* was published in 1964. He has since published three more novels: *The Dark* (1965), *The Leavetaking* (1974), and *The Pornographer* (1979); as well as two collections of short stories: *Nightlines* (1970) and *Getting Through* (1978). He was the first prose writer to receive the A.E. Memorial Award, and he was also granted the Arts Council Macauley Fellowship, both for *The Barracks.*

WALTER M. MILLER, JR. was born in New Smyrna Beach, Florida, on January 23, 1923. He studied first at the University of Tennessee and later, after the Second World War, completed his studies at the University of Texas. He had already established himself as a significant contributor to the science fiction field when he published his first novel, *A Canticle for Liebowitz,* in 1960. That novel, which has remained in print ever since, brought him a much wider audience. He has since published several other collections of short fiction, most easily available now in a paperback entitled *The Best of Walter M. Miller, Jr.* (1980), from which "Crucifixus Etiam" is taken.

FLANNERY O'CONNOR was born on March 25, 1925, in Savannah, Georgia. In 1947 she took her M.F.A. degree in writing from the University of Iowa. Before her death in 1964, she completed two novels, *Wise Blood* (1952) and *The Violent Bear It Away* (1960); and two collections of short stories, *A Good Man Is Hard to Find* (1955) and *Everything That Rises Must Converge* (1965). Her *Complete Stories* appeared posthumously in 1971 and contains several previously unpublished stories taken from her Iowa M.F.A. thesis, *The Geranium.* This collection won the National Book Award for fiction in 1972. When asked to comment on her extreme situations and unusual characters, Flannery O'Connor replied with characteristic bluntness, "To the hard of hearing you shout, and for the almost-blind you draw large and startling figures."

BREECE D'J PANCAKE is by far the youngest author included in this volume. He was born in Milton, West Virginia, in 1952, and he died, an apparent suicide, while a student in the graduate writing program at the University of Virginia, shortly before his twenty-seventh birthday in 1979. His total oeuvre consists of one collection of short stories, published posthumously in 1983. It was greeted with mixed but mainly positive reviews, including a front-page one in the New York *Times Book Review* by Joyce Carol Oates, who summed up the appeal of the stories in the following way: "So thoroughly does he know and sympathize with the people of his doomed region that one comes away immersed in their desperate yet tragically kindred fates."

WALKER PERCY was born in Birmingham, Alabama, on May 28, 1916. He majored in chemistry at the University of North Carolina, taking his degree in 1937, and went on from there to complete an M.D. degree at Columbia University in 1941. His psychiatric studies were interrupted when he developed pulmonary tuberculosis, while interning at Bellevue Hospital in New York. During his two-year recuperation, he read widely in philosophical work and turned his attention from medicine to writing. His first novel, *The Moviegoer* (1961), received the National Book Award for fiction. He subsequently published four other novels: *The Last Gentleman* (1966), *Love in the Ruins* (1971), *Lancelot* (1977), and *The Second Coming* (1980). His continuing interest in philosophy and linguistics is evident in his collection of essays, *The Message in the Bottle* (1975), and in the more recent *Lost in the Cosmos* (1983), from which the selection in this anthology is taken.

J. F. POWERS was born on July 8, 1917, in Jacksonville, Illinois. He attended Northwestern University and has taught creative writing at several universities, most recently at St. John's University, Collegeville, Minnesota. He is an elected member of the National Institute of Arts and Letters. His short story collections include *Prince of Darkness and Other Stories* (1947), *The Presence of Grace* (1956), and *Look How the Fish Live* (1975). His one novel, *Morte d'Urban,* which won the National Book Award for fiction, appeared in 1962. He continues to publish stories, often with a clerical setting, in various journals, including *The New Yorker,* from which "The Warm Sand" is taken. One critic has seen as his principal theme "the problem of how to put the Christian tradition of smiling contempt for the world into action in the grim, restricted society of organized modern America."

IGNAZIO SILONE was born in Pescina, Italy, on May 1, 1900, a significant date given his lifelong commitment to socialist ideals. During the 1920s he was an active member of the Communist Party in Italy, which sent him to Russia and then to Spain; despite his break with the Communist Party in 1930, he continued his fight against fascism in Italy and later, during the Second World War, as a resistance worker in Switzerland. His novels, which clearly reflect his political commitments, include: *Fontamara* (1930), *Bread and Wine* (1936), *The Seed Beneath the Snow* (1941), and *The Fox and the Camellias* (1961). Both his novels and his stories have a strong autobiographical flavor, dealing as they do with the struggle to maintain both a religious and a political faith in the face of their institutional distortions.

MURIEL SPARK was born in Edinburgh on February 1, 1918. She is the author of some two dozen novels and collections of short stories, for which she has won numerous literary awards, including the James Tait Black Memorial Prize for *The Mandelbaum Gate* (1966), and an honorary membership in the American Academy of Arts and Letters. She began her writing career as a free-lance journalist, and later became editor of the *Poetry Review*. She became a Catholic in 1954, inspired in part by the writings of Cardinal Newman. Her novels include: *Memento Mori* (1959), *The Prime of Miss Jean Brodie* (1961), *The Abbess of Crewe* (1974), and *Loitering with Intent* (1981).

TOBIAS WOLFF was born in Birmingham, Alabama, on June 19, 1945. From 1964 to 1968 he served in the U.S. Army Special Forces, including time in Vietnam. He subsequently studied at the universities of Oxford and Stanford and currently teaches in the English Department at Syracuse University. His first collection of short stories, *In the Garden of the North American Martyrs,* was published in 1981 to considerable acclaim, and his novel, *The Barracks Thief,* won the P.E.N./Faulkner Award for Fiction in 1985. His most recent book, a second collection of short stories, was published in 1985, with the title *Back in the World.* Three of his stories have received O. Henry short story prizes, and he has also been the recipient of Guggenheim and National Endowment for the Arts fellowships. In describing the common characteristics of authors he anthologized in *Matters of Fact and Fiction* (1983), Wolff had these self-revealing things to say: "They speak to us, without flippancy, about things that matter. They write about what happens between men and women, parents and children. They write about fear of death, fear of life, the feelings that bring people together and force them apart, the cost of intimacy . . . They are, every one of them, interested in what it means to be human."